Praise for the Perspective Series

"Give Amanda Giasson and Julie B. Campbell a chance and they'll draw you into a world of intrigue…It's a place where beauty and horror live side by side."
- Susan Doolan
Special Arts & Life Reporter to the Barrie Examiner

*"Amanda Giasson and Julie B. Campbell have crafted the **perfect combination of strength and vulnerability** in Megan Wynters and Irys Godeleva, the **female dynamic duo** that resides within the fantastical world of Qarradune. We are whisked away with our delightful female protagonists where there are twists and turns and nothing is as it seems in this **mesmerizing tale of chivalry, bravery, and honor**."*
- John Darryl Winston
Author of the IA Series (www.johndarrylwinston.com)

*"I **instantly fell in love** with the writing and the characters in Love at First Plight. Right from the start, the **plot draws you in** and I appreciated the great deal of care that went into writing this novel - the expertly crafted sentences and subtle details made for a very satisfying reading experience."*
- Kat Stiles
Author of the *Connected* series (www.katstiles.com)

*"Julie B. Campbell and Amanda Giasson easily bring you into the world of Megan and Irys, and **once you are in their world you never want to leave**. From the first page, to that last moment you are left wanting more."*
- Diane Hodgson
Elementary Teacher

*"J. Campbell and A. Giasson do a brilliant job of weaving their two writing styles together to create well developed characters and a **captivating storyline** that had my daughter and I struggling to share the book! We are **eagerly awaiting the next novel** in the series!"*
- J. Tauskela
Avid Reader

*"Diving into a debut book proved exciting and extremely rewarding – especially when the book ends up **blowing away my expectations** and surprisingly, it left me hanging."*
- Sandy Pestill
Nautica Book Club coordinator

Megan & Irys' Stories Continue

Read all the books in the Perspective Series

Love at First Plight

Second Wind

Third Time's a Charmer

So On and So Fourth

~

It's Early Days (short story)

Thayn Varda: An Early Journal (novella)

So On and So Fourth

Book 4 of the Perspective Series

Amanda Giasson
&
Julie B. Campbell

Qarradune Books
Ontario, Canada

Copyediting by John Campbell and Donna Campbell

ISBN: 9798736502301

First Printing: 2021

www.PerspectiveBookSeries.com

Love the Perspective Book Series?

Check out the official website at
http://www.PerspectiveBookSeries.com

Follow us on social media:

Facebook (@PerspectiveBooks)
http://facebook.com/perspectivebooks

Instagram (@PerspectiveBooks)
https://www.instagram.com/perspectivebooks/

Twitter (@QarraduneBooks)
https://twitter.com/QarraduneBooks

YouTube (Perspective Books)
https://www.youtube.com/channel/UC9Sx6EXyP_oQ5pVQFxdk_Dg

Chapter 1

Irys

I woke with a gasp, sitting straight up.

Great Goddess, what is happening to me in my sleep?

Looking around, I desperately searched my surroundings for anything familiar. It took a moment before my mind could catch up with my eyes. I had no idea where I was or how I would ever find my way home again. I was in an abandoned building after having escaped Kavylak's Capital City and military compound, travelling with a defected Warrior, former-Lieutenant Acksilivcs Fhir.

Acksil was seated on the floor next to me. He reached out a gloved hand and rested it reassuringly on my arm.

"It's alright. You're safe. You were sleeping," he said.

I shook my head to clear the fog as I rested one of my hands on his. "It was another nightmare. That's all," I agreed, more in an effort to convince myself of that fact than to inform him of anything new.

"Was it Xandon?"

"Yes." I nodded. I couldn't remember the nightmare, but I was certain of it, nonetheless. This specific disturbing feeling was becoming all-too familiar.

"Your hair has changed again." His tone didn't convey any of the concern he must have been feeling.

I frowned. I was already scarred with an iridescent white streak in my deep purple hair. The thought of more of it was less than appealing to me.

"Is it much worse than it was?" I asked in the hope that the difference was only a minor one.

"You have another streak of the white." He ran his fingers along a section near the front of my hairline, so I'd know where it travelled through my braided hair.

My frown deepened as I touched my fingers to the lock of hair that Acksil had indicated was changed. It felt the same. It seemed strange to me that the white strands didn't feel any different than my purple ones. I'd expected the texture to have altered as well.

"What's happening to me?" I asked Acksil, knowing that he couldn't have any more answers than he had already shared but still hoping he might suddenly remember something he hadn't previously mentioned.

"I don't know, Irys. I've never seen this happen to anyone before. My best guess would be that Xandon is attempting to change you as he did me and the rest of the Warriors. But he never altered us like that. And I don't understand why he would want to make you a Warrior. You haven't shown any particular exceptional skill, that is, a unique ability that makes you different from normal people."

"Did this happen to you before you became a Warrior? Did he affect you in your dreams to turn you into what you are today?" I asked as all manner of terrifying scenarios flooded my imagination.

"No. At least, I wasn't altered as I slept. I can't say for certain if he ever did this to any of the other Warriors, but it was not how it was for me. I've also never seen the type of physical change happening to your hair. When I became a Warrior, my skill was enhanced, but physically I was unchanged."

Reaching out, I took his hand, taking security from the warmth I could feel through the black leather of his glove. It wasn't a romantic gesture. It felt nothing like it did to hold Sir Dynan Fhirell's hand. Dynan's touch was a gentle comforting caress. With Acksil, I had a desperate need to cling to something that wouldn't threaten me. It was as though my very survival depended on this contact.

What could Xandon want from me? I can't be a Warrior. I don't have any of their magic skills. Why would changing my hair colour be beneficial to him?

His fingers closed around mine, and I was grateful to him for the gentle firmness of his grasp.

"We will figure this out, Irys. I'm confident that the farther we get from him, the less he will be able to reach you."

I chose to believe the confidence in his tone. Certainly, there wasn't any way for him to know that distance was the key to extracting Xandon from my mind, but if Acksil wanted to comfort me, I was willing to accept the reassurance.

I looked around the fire-lit room framed in darkness. The sun wasn't up yet. I hadn't any idea how long I'd been asleep before the nightmare had arrived. Hours? Minutes? Exhaustion wanted to draw my eyes closed, but fear kept them wide open.

Bowing my head, I allowed my gaze to travel over my black leather-like leggings and my nearly knee-high suede boots which had a soft, quiet sole. Over the leggings, my long black tunic was hardly what I would call modest, but I'd come to understand the practicality of it and why Acksil had selected it for me. Still, it was my black hooded cloak that appealed to me the most as it effectively covered the rest of my travelling outfit.

"What time is it?" I asked, wondering how long it would be before morning came and we would be moving, doubting that I would be able to sleep again. "Did I sleep long?"

"You slept for a few hours. It's nearly dawn," he replied. "It's been quiet. We'll leave at first light. Our journey will be long enough that if we come across some horses, we'll take them." My face must have shown my distress as he immediately amended his statement. "We won't take them from good people. They'd likely belong to Raiders."

If I'd looked concerned before, his additional explanation certainly didn't help things. It didn't seem at all wise to me to steal horses from Raiders. The Tarvak Raiders were militant thieves and highwaymen that preyed on travellers making their way through remote parts of the world, particularly those parts that were in turmoil after war or invasion. If it wasn't for the Paladins, I'd have had no doubt that Gbat Rher would also struggle with Raiders.

"If we don't find horses, will we need to travel for many days on foot?"

"It will be a three- or four-day journey, depending on the number of obstacles we face along the way."

The thought of walking for that long made my feet begin to ache, but it also fired my determination.

I can do this. Great Goddess, I will not fail everyone who is worried about my disappearance. Acksil's efforts won't have been made in vain. Please shine your Light on our path, so we will arrive safely.

"Have you ever ridden astride, Irys? Will you need to ride with me?" he asked, breaking me from my thoughts.

"I haven't ever ridden astride on my own, but if there is a saddle, I'm sure I will manage. I'm a strong rider. I will adapt," I said with a confidence I wasn't sure I felt. "If we find only one horse, I will ride with you. I trust you."

"I'm glad you do, Irys. It will be more important in the coming days than it has been until now. I'm taking you to meet good people, but they will not be happy to see me. They view me as a traitor."

"You're a Warrior. I can't imagine many people outside the Kavylak military would welcome your presence."

"It's more than that," he said with depth to his tone. "You remember that I told you we're headed to see Storr Dimog, leader of the Dsumot Rebels? A long time ago, before I was a Warrior, he was my teacher and took me in when I was going through a dark time. I'd been a part of the rebellion for a while, but I betrayed them, these people who were my family, for the enemy we had been fighting together."

I remembered. *How could I forget?* We were headed toward a group that hated Kavylak and Syliza alike. It certainly didn't assuage any of my concerns to know that this group also had a very specific reason to dislike Acksil beyond the obvious.

"I can understand how they might feel that way. That wasn't very gracious of you, Acksil," I scolded before I could think. I regretted the words as soon as I'd spoken them. The strain of our situation was cutting holes in the fabric of my filter.

He merely shook his head. "It wasn't," he agreed. After a breath, a small smirk tugged at his lips. The light and shadow of the firelight on his rich dark skin only added to the naughtiness of the expression. My scolding, it seemed, was amusing to him.

"What could have made you leave such kind people in order to join your enemy?" I asked, since it appeared that the subject didn't seem to cause him pain.

"Because they could no longer give me what I wanted. What I needed. I needed to be better, and Storr wanted to set me on a path that wasn't of my choosing."

"When you face Mr. Dimog, do you plan to apologize? What will you tell him? Do you think he will believe you?"

With the way he immediately shook his head, it was clear that there was no doubt in his mind. "I don't plan to apologize. I wouldn't waste our time trying to explain my actions. He won't trust me. When I face him, I plan to tell him that he needs to help you. Through you, I might be able to rebuild some of the trust I have broken."

"I will do what I must to convince him that you are trustworthy today, even if you were not once upon a time. If I manage to gain his trust, then I will be sure to tell him why I have come to trust you."

"Whatever might happen or whatever they might do to me, Irys, they are not a threat to you. Don't plead my case. Let them help you."

"No," I replied firmly, crossing my arms. I wasn't about to allow him to risk his life for me only to walk into a situation that would place him in further danger. How could I live with myself if I committed such a selfish act? How could I ever expect the Goddess to forgive me? "That's not how this will happen. I'm not going to leave you if the Rebels threaten you. I'm not going to plead my own case and abandon yours. You have saved my life three times, twice at great risk to your own. I intend to stand up for you or to run with you. This is not open for debate. We have made this escape together."

At first, he watched me with a furrowed brow, but his expression softened, replaced by amusement. "Yes ma'am," he said as though he were speaking to a superior officer.

Nodding, I returned my arms to my sides, the fire inside me eased. Without my consent, a smile broke on my lips. I had, after all, just made a Warrior alter his strategy and say "yes ma'am" to me.

We allowed this peaceful moment to surround us for a quiet pause before more serious thoughts were permitted to return.

"If the Warriors should find us, I will do everything in my power to make sure you get away. Do not turn back for me. This isn't open for debate either, Irys. Promise me this." It wasn't a recommendation. It wasn't even a plea. It was a demand. He required this of me.

"I will do what I feel is right. I will do what I feel must be done. I will act smartly. That is what I will promise you." It was the only oath I knew I could keep. Still, I knew it wouldn't be enough for him.

"No," he said with a shake of his head. "If the Warriors have me, you must leave. When it comes to them, you won't win. Neither of us will. I knew of this risk when I made the decision to get us out of Capital City. There are no second chances for you in Kavylak. If you try to help me, you will be within Xandon's reach again. You will never escape. This is it for you, Irys. Now, promise me."

I understood what he was saying. My mind crawled over his words, trying to discover an alternative. I wanted to find a way to promise to do my best without agreeing to abandon him. There was nothing I could say. I had to do what he'd asked of me.

"I understand," I replied tentatively, but then added with conviction, "If I feel the only thing I can do is to run on my own, I will. I promise to make the decision I know is right, Acksil. I will not sacrifice us both if there is hope for me to escape by myself. But if I feel certain that I will be able to help both of us, I will use that chance."

"Don't let what I have done be for nothing."

"It cannot be for nothing. It has already been for something. Even having come this far has meant the world to me, Acksil."

He stared at me deeply, raising his hand as though he was about to touch my face, but he changed his mind. His hand hung in the air for a moment, until he set it back down again.

"Has Sir Fhirell asked to court you?"

I was taken off guard. As my eyes fixed on his, the sound of Sir Fhirell's name echoed in my ears. The syllables wrapped their arms around my soul in a longing embrace. I wondered at the thread to Acksil's thoughts that must have brought him to ask this question. It was posed as though he already knew the answer.

"Yes. Not yet formally. He intended to ask for Lord Godeleva's permission to court me once we'd returned to Lorammel," I replied. Despite my honesty and the soft tone of my voice as I addressed him, I felt as though I were being unkind.

Acksil's face was emotionless and unreadable. "Take care with him, Irys. He isn't who he seems to be."

I wondered if it could have been jealousy that caused him to say such a thing. His face revealed no anger. Until now, I wouldn't have thought of Acksil as a petty man. Still, I refused to believe him. I could not.

"Sir Fhirell is a good man," I said firmly. "I trust him. He has proven himself to me."

Though he opened his mouth to respond, he shut it quickly at the sound of boots walking through the rubble outside the building.

"I told you I could smell smoke," said a man's voice.

My eyes were wide, staring through the darkness as though I'd be able to see through the stone wall if I tried hard enough. I glanced at Acksil and grabbed my bag, scrambling behind a mound of furniture parts and broken stones from a partially collapsed wall. I tucked myself behind it, trying to be as small and invisible as I could.

Acksil doused the flames of our fire with water, and I strained my ears to listen for the men past the hissing of the steam. In a blink, he was next to me, crouching close to the floor.

"Whatever happens, stay here and be quiet," he whispered into my ear, making me shiver.

I nodded, not seeing any point in arguing or asking questions. Instead, I pulled up my hood to make sure I was as hidden as possible. Though I'd expected Acksil to hide with me, he gave my shoulder a squeeze and slid along the darkness of the wall. I couldn't figure out where he was going and felt far more exposed without him there with me.

Before I could do so much as crane my neck to try to discover his strategy, footsteps approached, and I was forced to freeze in place.

"There's no fire here," said a woman's voice.

"There was. Smell the smoke in here," replied the man.

I couldn't see either of them through the darkness, aside from a pale outline of the man. He was large and appeared to move comfortably through the obscurity. I knew he wasn't someone I wanted to meet.

"No one's…" the woman started to say, but she stopped abruptly as sounds of a struggle took over.

"Hey!" shouted the man.

The struggle continued. There wasn't any doubt in my mind that Acksil must have made his move. Had there been even one lit torch in the room, I would have been able to see what was happening. As it was, I could hear grunts and exclamations as well as scuffing and finally the sound of a large man hitting the floor. I kept my hand over my own mouth the entire time, just in case my throat felt the need to try to scream.

"Irys," Acksil whispered, approaching.

I removed my hand from my mouth, flexing my fingers, which had gone stiff from tension.

"I'm still here," I whispered in response.

"We should move on now. There are probably more Raiders around."

Approaching him, I looked toward where the man had fallen and was surprised to see another figure – whom I could only assume was the woman - lying there as well.

"Those are Raiders?" I asked foolishly.

"Yes. No local folk live here anymore, and Rebels don't look like that."

"Do you think they have horses?" I made the sign of the Goddess with my fingers, hoping the two Raiders were merely unconscious.

"Let's find out." His grin was wide and just barely visible through the darkness of the room. He scooped up my bag, bringing the strap across his body before offering me his hand.

Looking at the hand, I didn't immediately take it. Before we were to head out, something needed to change. I couldn't remain fully dependent on him any longer. It was time to learn to pull my own weight - or at least as much of it as I could.

"I need something to defend myself," I informed him. "I know I'm not a fighter, but I have nothing to use to keep myself safe. Had there been three Raiders, one of them might have found me. I'd have been better off armed."

The look Acksil gave me was serious, but it didn't take long before he nodded, the silhouettes of his many short rope-like hair braids swinging with the gesture. Without questioning my request, he crouched and withdrew a dagger from his boot. "Here." He offered it to me, handle first.

I hadn't expected him to give me a weapon this easily. It felt as though my hands were unprepared to accept the offering. After a brief hesitation, I took the dagger, likely appearing as though I was being handed a serpent.

It wasn't an impressive weapon, but it was functional enough. For some reason, when he'd withdrawn the dagger from his boot, I'd expected it to be ornamented in some way. A decorative handle or a blade with multiple metals. The smooth, plain surface revealed that this was nothing like the type of dagger a man would have given a woman in any of the adventure stories I'd read.

"Only defend yourself if you need to, Irys. Otherwise, just stay hidden. I can take on more than two Raiders," he said, breaking me from my brief reverie.

I nodded, sliding the sheathed dagger into the opening of my own boot. "I likely won't use it. I don't want to have to use it. I don't really know how. It makes me feel better to know I have it if I need to try."

"I can understand that."

Smiling, I reached out and took the hand he'd offered me earlier. "Thank you. I'm ready to go now."

Together, we quietly left the building. I held onto him while stepping precisely where he guided me. I could make out the biggest obstacles in our path, but he was far more skilled at spotting tripping hazards along the way.

Outside, we kept as close to the buildings as we could. It was clear that Acksil expected us to run into more Raiders, and I was determined not to be the cause of our being found. After a short while, Acksil brought us to a sudden stop and pressed his back against the nearest building. I did the same without needing to be told to do so.

"More Raiders," he whispered so quietly that he was nearly just mouthing the words.

I tilted my head down to allow my black hood to cover as much of my face as possible. Occasionally, I gave a slight peek out from under it. We were very fortunate that I managed not to jump as three more Raiders passed us. They didn't notice us. It dawned on me that all the Raiders we'd seen so far were on foot. There wasn't any sign of horses.

The group of Raiders stopped a short distance from us. We weren't in their direct sight line, but they were still close enough that we could hear them when they spoke.

"Do you really think more Rebels are stupid enough to come through here?" asked one man.

"Delmorden certainly thinks so, and he wasn't wrong the last time," replied another. "The Vutol paid well for the last Rebel we brought them. It's worth it to see if we can grab another."

If there was a single word that could make me further dread capture from these Raiders, it was "Vutol". The Vutol was a loathsome organization to say the least. It was something I tried not to think about.

It upset me even to believe it could exist. Its vile members had chapters all over the world, buying, selling, and trafficking slaves for every wretched taste and disgusting purpose. Attractive or exotic-looking people of all ages were captured, collared, and sold into horrifying secret collections or for underground pleasure houses. The Vutol wasn't legal in a single country in the world and yet it managed to thrive in the shadows.

"Did you hear that Rixta caught a Sefaline?" asked the first man, who sounded amused. My free hand involuntarily reached toward the hilt of my dagger. Images of Fhurrk and the love he shared with his mate turned my blood from icy at the sound of the word "Vutol" to a nearly immediate boil.

"Yeah. It was just a little brat. That animal will bring Rixta quite a lot of coin when she finds the right buyer."

My anger rose further. They had captured a Sefaline child and intended to make a sale.

Great Goddess, please don't forget that child in this hour of desperate need. Shine your Light upon that child. Please, Great Goddess, don't allow these followers of Chaos to succeed in their evils.

The Raiders started to walk again, and it wasn't long before we couldn't hear them anymore.

"Let's move," Acksil whispered, giving my hand a gentle tug.

I nodded and kept up with him as we edged our way along the buildings, remaining out of sight. Light was beginning to creep over the horizon. Every handful of minutes made it easier to see where we were going. While I appreciated the added confidence in my steps, I knew it wouldn't be long before we would be quite visible unless we kept to alleyways between buildings. That could slow us down substantially.

"There," Acksil indicated ahead of us. "Horses."

Thank you, Great Goddess. You always know just when to share your gifts.

Three horses were tethered near a low-burning campfire. Unfortunately, their three riders were seated nearby. From that distance, I could tell neither if they were Raiders or Rebels, nor if they were awake. I desperately wanted one of those horses. If those were Raiders, I wouldn't feel the slightest guilt for stealing one. It likely had been stolen in the first place.

"Are they sleeping?" I asked Acksil.

"I don't know," he replied.

"Then I will go and speak with them while you take one of their horses. Be careful with me when you pick me up as you ride by," I instructed him, only to receive a look from him that suggested he felt I'd slipped into madness.

"Irys, I'm not going to let you walk up to Raiders and talk to them," he said in a flat whisper.

"I'm not going to get too close. I'll stay well away from them. I'll simply stand so that their backs will be to you as you take one of the horses," I tried to sound certain in my whispered voice. "Can you think of a better way to take one of those horses?"

"I can do it without you needing to..." Acksil was interrupted before he could finish his statement.

"Hey, you!" called someone from behind us, causing us both to turn sharply. Before us stood a Raider, and he was approaching fast.

"Run and take one of those horses now?" I asked Acksil in a rapid, frightened voice, backing away from the Raider.

"Yes! Go!" He let go of my hand.

Chapter 2

Megan

"*WAAAAAHHNNNNG!*"
    An ear-splitting noise tore me from sleep. My eyes sprang
open to darkness, and I gasped.

What in the world is happening? Are we under attack?

"Oh holy Chaos," Aésha muttered beside me, sounding annoyed.
"I remember why I stopped sleeping in these places." She pulled a
pillow over her head, grumbling.

Okay. She doesn't seem worried.

I allowed my racing heart to calm once I realized we weren't in
imminent danger.

"What's happening?" I whispered.

"It's just the morning alarm, Baby." Aésha's muffled voice spoke
from under the pillow.

"Oh. Wow. Really?"

Worst. Wake-up alarm. Ever.

Knowing that this would be my first day of work, I slowly dragged
myself to a sitting position, rubbed at my eyes, and tried to blink away
the sleep that clouded my vision. The action did little to improve what
I could see. My tiny apartment was simply too dark.

Is it even dawn yet?

I heard Aésha shift and felt her arms slide around my middle. She
gently pulled me back down to lie beside her.

"Aww, I'd love to stay here with you, Aésha, but I have to get up
and get to work before I'm thrown in jail or worse." I had no idea what

the penalty would be for skipping work, but I knew it was something I didn't want to find out.

Aésha kissed the back of my shoulder. "Mez got you the day off," she whispered sleepily. "Well, technically I did, but he told me to."

That surprised me. "What? Really? Um, thanks."

She nodded against me. "Shh! More sleeping."

She didn't need to tell me twice, and I wasn't about to question a day off. I snuggled in with her and sleep quickly reclaimed me.

*   *   *   *   *

I felt Aésha gently slide away from me. Opening groggy eyes, I saw her standing and pulling on a shirt and pants over the tank top and underwear she'd worn to bed. I didn't know how much time had passed since the alarming-hour, but the sun's morning light was now seeping through the small, curtained window, casting a dim warm glow in the room.

"Leaving so soon?" I croaked.

She nodded, turning to flash her enchanting smile at me. "Mez didn't get the day off for me, Baby."

"That wasn't very nice of him."

She shook her head, playing along. "I'm going to punish him later." She winked.

"Ooh, lucky him." I chuckled.

She laughed and leaned down, drawing her face close to mine as if she were going to kiss me. For a moment, I thought she was as her lips came close to mine. I lay there frozen with uncertainty and anticipation.

At the last second, I shut my eyes, ready for anything, and felt her soft lips press against the skin directly next to my mouth.

Opening my eyes, I looked at her with surprise, not just because of what she'd done, but also because I'd realized I was disappointed that she hadn't actually kissed me. Aésha was seriously starting to make me wonder if I was bi.

She only grinned back, clearly proud of herself for having rattled me as she had intended with the maneuver.

"You're bad," I told her in a teasing, chastising tone.

"Oh no, Baby. I'm very, very good," she said with a wicked smirk, pulling on her boots.

I laughed and chucked a pillow at her, which she batted away with ease.

"Will I see you later?" I asked.

"You never can tell." Her smirk grew into a beautiful, alluring smile. "But I'd like that. Maybe you can sleep in my quarters this time instead," she suggested.

"Sounds good. I bet your bed is a lot better than this one."

"It is. It has me in it."

I chortled. She really did have a line for everything.

"Until then," she said and opened the door. She turned and blew me a kiss before leaving. A quiet *"click"* sound a few seconds later told me that she'd locked the door from the outside. I'd never met anyone who could manipulate locks like she could.

I sighed and rolled over on my side, cocooning myself in the blanket. If I had the day off, I had every intention of being as lazy as possible.

* * * * *

The noise of cupboards being loudly shut in the kitchen I shared with Asimara woke me. I winced a little when I opened my eyes to the bright natural light that was now pouring in through the thread-bare curtains.

Yawning, I stretched and pushed myself up, letting the blanket tumble into my lap. I half debated going back to bed but knew that it had to be approaching midday by this point and decided that it would be more interesting to see what my neighbour was up to. I was especially curious, since the last time I'd seen her, she was being rather affectionate with the other Charmer, Arik Atrix.

While it certainly wasn't strange seeing a person being all goo-goo eyed at Arik or Aésha, it was strange in Asimara's case, because when I had overheard her with Arik, she hadn't sounded smitten with him. She had sounded genuinely in love with him, and he with her. In fact, they'd even said "love you" to each other before parting.

Due to their ever-playful and ever-flirtatious personalities, it was odd imagining a Charmer being truly in love with anyone, never mind someone as down to Earth—er Qarradune as Asimara.

Wait a minute...am I imagining things or did Aésha tell me last night that she, a Charmer, is married?

I abruptly shook my head at the thought. I wasn't feeling brave enough yet to think about last night, because it would mean I'd have to think about what had happened with Thayn. Thinking about that was the last thing I wanted to do right now.

Getting up and looking down at myself, I remembered that I'd been too distraught over what had happened with Thayn to change my clothes before I'd crawled into bed with Aésha. I was still wearing the track pants and tank top I'd worn yesterday.

Oh well. Whatever. This makes life easier.

Grabbing the matching jacket from the floor, where I had abandoned it last night, I slipped my arms into it and opened the kitchen door.

"Hi, Asimara," I greeted her in a gravelly voice.

She jumped in surprise. "Oh! Goodness! I didn't know you were home. I'm sorry I was noisy," she apologized, tossing a dish rag into the sink.

"That's alright. You weren't being all that noisy." I opened a cupboard, taking a clean glass, and filled it with water. "I just wanted to say 'hi'." I smiled at her, before taking a drink to moisten my dry throat and shake off the sleepy-voice-raspies.

"Hi." She managed to smile back, but I could see that it was an effort for her. Clearly, something was wrong. She wasn't the same bubbly person I'd met a day ago.

"Are you alright?"

"Oh yeah," she said with a small wave of her hand as if it were no big deal. "Just had a disagreement with a friend."

I nodded in response, took another small sip of water, and couldn't help but wonder if the friend to whom she was referring was Arik. I didn't dare ask though, because I had no intention of revealing I'd eavesdropped on her private conversation with him yesterday.

"Hey, is today your day off?" she asked.

"Yup."

"Want to go into the city? I could use a bit of a change of scenery."

"Sure...I mean, if I'm allowed to do that."

She nodded without hesitation. "We'll pick up our passes."

I grinned. "Then, yeah. Count me in!"

She smiled, genuinely this time, looking brighter. "In that case, I'll stop beating up the kitchen, and we can have lunch out there if that's alright with you."

"Sounds good to me. I'll get ready."

She nodded. "I'll change, too, and meet you here when we're both ready." Asimara turned, exiting the kitchen, and walked into her quarters.

Taking my glass of water with me, I headed back into my apartment, and beelined for the bathroom.

Finishing the water, I left the glass at the sink, washed up, cleaned my teeth, and ran a brush through my hair. I decided to just leave it down but secured a just-in-case hair tie around my wrist on the off chance it was windy.

Feeling a little revitalized, I opened my wardrobe to change into fresh clothes and frowned at my options. Truth be told, all I wanted was to throw on a pair of jeans and a T-shirt, but I knew I'd have no such luck. Instead, what greeted me was my freshly washed signature Kavylak "Denizen" attire of nondescript black pants and short- or long-sleeved black shirt. This had pretty much been the extent of my wardrobe after I'd been taken from Syliza. I had no intention of wearing those clothes again for as long as I could help it.

My next option had to be my work uniform, because it looked identical to the uniforms I had seen yesterday in the main building. It hung in all its stiff glory and was a dark moody grey, like the colour of clouds threatening rain.

Yuck! Oh well. Look on the bright side, Megan. At least it's not the ugly brown one.

Beside the uniform hung my final and only real selections: two long skirts and two V-neck blouses, one short- and one long-sleeved.

Deciding on the black, shin-length, A-line pleated skirt and a teal, long-sleeved blouse, I quickly changed into my new outfit and was pleasantly surprised at how soft and supple the fabric was. It fit in all the right places without clinging to me, leading me to believe that Aésha hadn't just given me any old thing she could find. This was quality clothing.

I picked up one of the black, almond-toe pumps I intended to wear, to look at the sole to see if – like the athletic shoes she'd given me – there was a kiss mark.

Yup!

The bright pink kiss mark had been placed on the arch. I grinned, wondering again if this was a designer's trademark or if Aésha had added it herself. Whatever the case, it made me happy because it made me think of her.

The pumps were easy to slip into, had a comfortable two-inch block heel, and fit me like a glove. With everything Aésha had given me fitting so well, I was starting to wonder if she had measured me in my sleep.

Discovering an empty cloth bag in the closet, I decided I'd use it for storing my dirty laundry. Before tossing in my track suit, I took Rral's ring and Irys' handkerchief from the pants' pocket and placed them in my nightstand drawer. Now that I had no intention of leaving Kavylak, I knew I'd be returning to this apartment and didn't feel the usual urgency I'd had to keep them with me at all times.

Making sure I had my identity tags around my neck, I placed my apartment key into my skirt pocket, and returned to the kitchen, finding Asimara waiting for me. Her long brown hair was in a ponytail, and she had changed into the blue jean-like pants I had seen her in the first time I'd met her. She was also sporting brown boots, a white T-shirt, and a weathered brown leather jacket that looked like it had been her favourite for years. Over one of her shoulders hung a simple brown handbag with a long strap.

I was immediately envious of her outfit.

"You really need to tell me where you got your pants. I used to have pants similar to those, and I miss them."

She looked down at her pants and then back at me. "I didn't get them here. I got them in the town near where my parents live, where I grew up. People in the city don't wear this kind of thing," she informed me and then laughed. "These are my sulking pants."

I chuckled, and she shook her head at her own silliness. "Alright, they're my all-the-time pants, but I pretend I wear them as comfort clothes."

"Well, I happen to like your sulking-all-the-time pants."

She had no idea how much.

"I sulk a lot!" She laughed and added, "Next time I head home, I'll pick you up a pair. If they're not quite the right fit, I'm sure you can find a seamstress in town to fix them."

"Really?" I smiled brightly at her. "Thanks!"

"Sure," she said easily. "Ready?"

I nodded, feeling good. I liked Asimara a lot. Like Amorette, I had a solid feeling about her. I trusted that she would be a great friend.

Asimara headed out of the kitchen and through her own quarters. I followed her out, knowing Aésha had locked my door when she'd left. Asimara locked her door behind us.

"We just need to get our passes from the office and then we can leave," she told me as we walked toward the main building.

I nodded, glancing about the grounds as we made our way to the enormous structure. Many of the buildings were still in various degrees of ruin from the battle with Syliza. Soldiers and other uniformed people were busy working on cleanup and reconstruction, while other members of Kavylak's army were busy performing drills and exercises. I didn't catch sight of a Warrior or anyone else I recognized before we made it to our destination.

As we entered the main building, a pit of uneasiness formed in my stomach at the memory of sneaking in with Mez to see Thayn. I bit my lip, forcing down the overwhelming feeling of sadness that threatened to take hold of me for the second time today.

Stop thinking about Thayn, Megan. It's over. You ended it. You told him to leave you behind. You wanted him to. You made your choice. You want to go home. Let it go. Let him go.

Asimara led us to the second floor, and we entered an office where we got our passes from a woman who acted more like a robot than a person. I noticed she was clothed in the identical grey uniform I would soon be wearing. I hoped her robo-personality wasn't a side effect of her outfit.

Thankfully, obtaining passes to leave the compound was not as difficult as I'd thought it would be. For a day pass, all I needed was my name, the ID number on my tags, and my residential building number. The worst part about getting the pass was being in that stuffy, rigid office and talking to the half-dead clerk.

"Are you hungry right away?" Asimara asked when we left the office with our yellow paper card passes.

"Sure, I haven't had anything to eat today."

She nodded, and we descended the stairs. On the last set of stairs that would take us to the main level, I saw Arik Atrix making his way up toward us. I watched him and stole a quick glance at Asimara, wondering if they were going to share some secret look.

They didn't. Asimara looked at him in the way every woman - including me - looked at Arik, like we were in the presence of some deep-blue-haired Adonis, and we couldn't resist giving him our attention. Beyond that, her expression was unreadable.

It was Arik who really surprised me, though. His expression was one of intense focus, and he didn't even look up as he passed us. It was like we weren't there. This was really strange, because, like Aésha, every time I'd been anywhere near Arik, he'd purposely drawn me in with his dazzling blue eyes, knowing I'd be smitten after a single look. Still, it was even weirder that he didn't look at Asimara.

Dude! You said you loved her yesterday. I heard you! Oh no! What if they had a falling out? What if they broke up? Is this why Asimara was so upset earlier?

Although I didn't know the reason, I knew that, based on our lack of encounter with Arik, he must have had something pretty heavy on his mind and that he had to have somehow been the cause of Asimara's sour mood. I hated that I felt I couldn't ask her about it. I wanted to be a good friend to her, but there was no way I could breeze into that conversation without revealing that I had big-fat eavesdropped. I kept my mouth shut, deciding to let her be the first to speak. We walked out of the building in silence.

Approaching the gate, I nervously glanced at my yellow card of city freedom, wondering if getting through the guards at the gate would be as simple as obtaining the pass.

"First time off the base?" Asimara asked, breaking the ice.

"Yup. First time."

"I'm not a fan of the city, but it's way better than the base." She laughed.

"Good. I'm looking forward to it."

Asimara nodded and stepped up to the gate guards, holding out her pass. A guard looked at her pass, nodded to her, and let her through. I watched what she did and copied her, holding out my pass to let a guard inspect it. He did, then looked at me, nodded, and I walked past him and out the gate toward Asimara, who was waiting for me.

Tucking the pass back into my skirt pocket and sticking close to Asimara, we walked into the buzzing city. Unlike the orderly military base and the busy harbour I had walked through upon first arriving in Kavylak, with its potent-smelling factories and refineries, the hustle and bustle of the inner city greeted me with an array of interesting aromas, sights, and sounds. I found it fascinating, instantly overwhelming to my senses, and oddly comforting all at the same time.

There were a million things to see, no matter where I looked. All around us were brick buildings of different shapes and sizes that ranged in various shades of red, brown, tan, and grey, containing all sorts of shops, businesses, restaurants, and cafés. The city was also teeming with people.

People. Were. Everywhere.

They moved in every direction. Some were walking in the streets like Asimara and me, others were on patios eating, drinking, or selling things, while others were riding horses, driving wagons, or pulling rickshaws. There were no traffic lanes either, which made the whole situation even more wild. People went where they fit. I'd never seen anything like it.

"I was thinking of something good and filling," Asimara said, drawing my stunned gaze to her. "Nothing light and fluffy. Sound good?"

"I'm game for anything," I told her, because I was hungry and because I had already made the decision that I'd go wherever she chose and eat whatever she wanted to eat.

Asimara nodded and suddenly veered to the right, walking with new purpose. I followed closely, knowing she clearly had a destination in mind.

"I used to get lost every time I left the base," she spoke up over the city's noise and laughed.

"I can believe it! I was just thinking about how glad I am to be with you and not on my own. I'd have no idea where to go. It's so overwhelming!"

She flashed me a knowing grin before heading down a smaller street until we popped out onto another busy one. "Outside or inside?" she asked.

"Outside," I decided. In spite of the overall industrial stink in the air, it was a warm, sunny, and pleasant day.

She nodded and headed over to a restaurant patio that had a little metal fence around it. She opened the gate, holding it open for me, and then walked over to an empty table. "This one?"

"Sure," I agreed, and we each took a seat on one of the four dark brown metal chairs that surrounded the matching table.

Upon seeing us, a waitress strolled over and placed menus down. "I'll come back with your coffees," she informed us and left without another word or glance in our direction.

Wow. Okay. I guess you get coffee here whether you like it or not.

I picked up the paper menu and looked over my options. Oddly, I knew by the font of the writing that the words I was looking at were in the Kavylak language. I still found it so crazy that I could read, write, and understand the different languages of Qarradune without having any idea of why or how that was even possible. It all looked and sounded like English to me, with each language having its own unique accent when spoken and unique script when written. The whole thing was just as bizarre to me as it sounded.

I recognized some of the words, like sausage and bacon, but others like "toograt" were a total mystery to me. Since I'd been on Qarradune, I had found that some of the foods were the same or nearly similar to those on Earth, while others were wildly different. This was why I guessed that there were sometimes no direct translations if something was colloquial or beyond my personal English-language knowledge.

Not really knowing what to choose, I looked up over my menu at Asimara. "What are you going to have? Because I think I'm just going to have that, too."

"You're going to have whatever I have?" Asimara chuckled with amusement.

"Yeah. Well, as long as you're going to have more than toast." I laughed.

"What if I have horrible taste?" She looked almost wicked.

"Then it's my own fault." I grinned.

She laughed and studied the menu, purposely wearing an expression that said she was either going to pick something that was awesome or disgusting.

I looked back at the menu as she decided, and it was then that I first noticed each menu item was attached to a price. Feeling myself go cold with instant shock and shame, it occurred to me that I had no money to pay for this food. Since being on Qarradune, food had always been provided for me. I had never been given money. I had always depended on the charity of others, and I stupidly hadn't realized that until this moment. My face grew hot with embarrassment.

"Um, Asimara," I said meekly. "I just realized that I don't have any money on me."

She looked up from her menu and stared at me in shock for a moment before cracking up. "I guess I'm taking you to lunch," she said. "You get the next one, though, you cheap neighbour!"

I flushed further, feeling like a total dope, but laughed at her reaction, grateful that she didn't freak out and that she was such a great friend.

"I'm sorry. I definitely will," I promised.

She smiled good naturedly and then looked back at the menu. "So, it looks like we're both having toast and water," she joked.

"And coffee," I tacked on with a snort.

"And coffee," she agreed, setting down the menu just as the waitress returned with our coffees. The waitress placed the steaming mugs in front of us and nothing else. No sugar, no cream, no milk, no nada.

O-kay. Guess I drink my coffee black now.

"Ready to order?" the waitress inquired with strained patience as if this was the third time she'd come back to our table to ask.

"We'll both have the Woodsman's Lunch," Asimara answered.

Woah! That sounds like some lunch.

The waitress lit up at her words, looking us over with newfound respect. "Hungry women," she said approvingly, taking the menus. "Won't be long," she added, heading off.

"The Woodsman's Lunch?" I queried, raising a brow at Asimara.

She smiled broadly, looking proud of herself, and nodded. "Yup."

I really, really, like you Asimara.

Beaming at her, I picked up my coffee and sipped it, surprised to find that the flavour was full-bodied and smooth. It wasn't sour or bitter as I had expected it to be without cream or sugar.

"So, is Mez Basarovka secretly your boyfriend?"

Taken off guard by her question, I nearly sprayed the coffee I had yet to swallow, in her face. I forced myself to gulp the hot liquid, which burned uncomfortably on its way down.

"Nope," I croaked and cleared my throat, resting the coffee down on the table. "Like I told you yesterday, we're just good friends. We won't be more than that. I'm not really looking for a relationship," I leveled with her. "Plus, he's way out of my league, anyway."

Seriously, a guy like Mez would not be romantically interested in a world-class screw up like me, no matter what we'd been through. Every time he was around me, bad things happened to him. You know, like him getting whomped by bricks or being horse-whipped and strung up in a tree to die…

Asimara laughed. "He is not. And what if a relationship just happens even though you're not looking for it? I mean, can you really be good friends with a man like Basarovka?"

"Sure. Some relationships do just happen," I agreed, "And I'm not going to pretend like I don't find him attractive. He's got a lot of amazing qualities, and he's been very good to me. But I do think I can be just friends with him." I picked up my coffee again to give it another sip before deciding to casually ask, "What about you? Have you been dating Lieutenant Atrix for long?"

She instantly laughed. Not the reaction I was expecting.

"Oh, I'm not dating Lieutenant Atrix. Nobody dates him," she said as if I was being silly for asking. Her response was so smooth and casual that had I not overheard them yesterday, I would have believed her.

"No? He's just a friend, then?" I pressed.

She shrugged. "I suppose. We do things together on occasion." She picked up her coffee and took a long sip of it.

"Oh yeah? What sort of things?" I smiled playfully.

She opened her mouth to answer but a loud siren rang out from the base before she got the chance. I tensed all over, recognizing the sound. It was the same one I had heard the night Syliza had come to the base to rescue Thayn and me.

Asimara's eyes widened. She immediately put down her coffee and rose from her seat. People in the streets scattered and began moving quickly in various directions.

Abandoning my own coffee, I stood, looking at Asimara like a frightened deer in headlights. "What's going on?"

"We have to get back to the base," was all she said before she picked up a table knife and held its handle out to me. "Take it," she instructed. I did, and she reached down to pull out a dagger that had been concealed in her left boot.

Without another word or explanation, she grabbed my free hand and pulled me after her, out into the chaos of the street.

Chapter 3

Irys

I scrambled forward, grabbing my cloak in my arms, so it wouldn't wrap itself around my legs.

"Stop!" shouted the Raider again. "Idiots! Wake up!" he yelled to his three companions around the campfire, who were apparently Raiders, too, and who had indeed been sleeping, until they heard the shouts, causing them to snap to action.

Running as hard as I could, I refused to look behind me. My legs were burning from moving more quickly than I'd ever made them. They stung nearly as much as my lungs, which I forced to fill and refill with air. I didn't want to know if there was a Raider immediately behind me. I needed to believe that I would reach those horses.

By the grace of the Goddess, I did. Nothing but divine intervention could have explained how I'd been able to rip the reins from the broken-down fence to which the horses had been haphazardly tied. I hefted myself up onto the saddle of the startled-looking creature.

I turned the horse, ready to bolt and was startled to see that Acksil was just reaching his own animal, deftly untying it and leaping into its saddle with excitement-fuelled ease.

Fussing, I couldn't manage to find the second stirrup of the saddle with the toe of my boot. My movements were too desperate, kicking aimlessly for the loop. Out of the corner of my eye, I saw Acksil turn to leave, and I gave up on the second stirrup, leaving my foot to dangle and hanging on with my knees.

Taking off, I galloped the horse as quickly as it could run, hanging on for dear life, unfamiliar with the feeling of riding astride, particularly with only one foot in the stirrup.

Acksil wasn't far behind me. That said, it was then that I noticed he wasn't alone. A Raider had managed to mount his own horse and was grabbing at Acksil with a large, muscled arm. The Raider was as confident a rider as I had ever seen, leaning sideways in his saddle without holding on to it. The reins were bundled in one hand as he swiped at Acksil with the other.

To my surprise, as focused as Acksil was, he appeared quite calm. He swayed out of the way of the Raider's hand as though he was already aware of the choreography of the movements. Finally, he slashed at the Raider with a dagger, and I quickly looked away. By the time I turned to check on Acksil again, the Raider was nowhere to be seen.

My heart felt as though it would pound right out of my chest. I could feel its thundering jolting my body in time with my horse's gait. I could see thicker trees approaching and hoped they would bring me out of this abandoned town and not simply into a treed park. Either way, the cover was welcome. I slowed the horse as I started weaving between trunks, allowing Acksil to catch up with me.

"It's alright now," he said as we both slowed further. "We're not being followed anymore. I took care of it."

"May we stop for a moment?" My legs were trembling with the exertion of staying on the horse at that speed with only one stirrup.

"Yes," he nodded, and we brought our mounts to a rest.

As soon as we weren't moving anymore, I managed to fit my toe into the second stirrup. With both feet in place, some of the ache released from my muscles. With as much dignity as I could muster, I massaged my thigh muscles, adjusted my cloak, and tucked a loose lock of hair out of the way.

"Thank you," I said, pleased with how composed I sounded despite how unsettled I felt. "We may proceed when you're ready."

I couldn't decide whether the glance he gave me was of amusement or admiration. Perhaps it was both. He nodded, but before we could do anything at all, a large shadow dropped from the tree above him, knocking him in the head and dragging him off his horse.

A sharp shriek involuntarily escaped my throat as I watched my dear Warrior fall. Instinct threw my hand down to my boot and drew the dagger he had given me. I hoped it looked as though I knew what I was doing with it.

I wanted nothing more than to leap down off my horse and find out if he was badly injured but was too afraid of making myself any more vulnerable than I already was. Still, I debated it. Had I truly any advantage up here that I would not have had on the ground? I could not delude myself into thinking that if I were to try to escape on horseback, I would have any chance of success if that shadow-person wanted to stop me.

Any inclination to move rapidly fled at the sound of a deep growl. The shadow person wasn't alone. I knew that sound. It was not of an animal. It was far too specific. Too deliberate and measured. It was Sefaline.

"I wouldn't use that if you don't want harm to come to you," said a thickly accented voice, speaking the Common Tongue as it rumbled with the growl. I was right. There was no escape. A Sefaline man stepped out from behind a nearby tree, his eyes gleaming in the dim light.

"I don't want to use it," I replied honestly. "I want to help my friend and ride safely away from here with him."

"Your friend is our enemy," he replied bluntly and with distaste.

His enemy? Have these people recognized Acksil as a Warrior or is he their enemy from before that? From his days as a Rebel?

"He was my enemy once, too," I informed the Sefaline. "He has saved my life. He saved me from the Warriors. How could I but call him a friend?"

"Just because someone saves your life, this does not make them a friend. Get down from your horse."

"No," I replied boldly. "I'm afraid you'll take it. I need it. We're not trying to cause trouble. We are merely travelling to our destination."

"You are travelling with a traitor," he said, clearly unmoved. "Get off your horse. I will not ask you again."

"He may be a traitor to you, but he is my guard. We're not here to harm you. I promise."

The shadow person who had been bent over Acksil stood and faced us. To my shock, it was a woman, dressed entirely in black leather-like pants not dissimilar to my own leggings, though without the modesty of a cloak. Her outfit was completed by a fitted but high-necked and long-sleeved shirt made from that same unique fabric. Black gloves covered her hands.

Her long, sleek black hair was drawn into a tight braid that fell down her back. Her overall look reminded me of Lieutenant Jadusyr Odurog, the Warrior originally from Sorcheena. I briefly wondered if she was originally from the destroyed nation, as well.

"Take her off the horse and bind her. Neither of them can be trusted," she said sternly.

"No! Please! I'll get down," I begged, kicking my foot out of a stirrup so I would be able to dismount. I tucked my dagger away and tossed my cloak to one side, hoping it covered my awkward movements. I wasn't used to dismounting from having ridden astride. I was accustomed to having the assistance of a mounting block and a gentleman's hand. It felt as though I was dropping from a giant of a horse, and I stumbled to one knee when I landed. My legs were weak and wobbly, but I drew myself to standing, holding my reins tightly in one hand. I was terrified and felt like a coward.

The Sefaline's eyes never left me. Though his expression hadn't changed, I could feel the weight of his judgment pressing down on my shoulders.

He was dressed in a sleeveless brown leather shirt that provided only slightly more coverage than a vest. This made it easy to see the Sefaline markings that covered the golden skin of his arms, neck, and upper chest. These were quite unlike Lieutenant Fhurrk's. While the Warrior's markings were intricate and came to sharp points, this Sefaline's markings consisted primarily of deep brown spots that evolved into smooth swirls.

I could see now what Lieutenant Fhurrk had meant when he said that each clan had its own distinct patterns. It was clear that this man was in no way related to my Warrior acquaintance.

The pattern was also visible on the tops of his bare feet, which I noticed had widely spread toes which curled just slightly downward and had thick, sharp claw-like nails I could only assume made it as easy to run across the ground as it did to climb a tree.

The Sefaline's hair was a striking deep orange, leaning toward a fiery red. The majority of his well-groomed hair was loose and flowed in different lengths down his back, but certain locks near the front were tied in sections along their length. I assumed that this style was as much for the practical reason of keeping his hair out of his face as it was for aesthetic purposes. Interestingly, he was also very tall, whereas Lieutenant Fhurrk wasn't much taller than me.

Turning my head from him, my gaze fell on the shadow woman. She stripped Acksil of his weapons and roughly pushed him onto his front with her foot before tying his wrists and ankles behind him. I brushed the Sefaline's judgment away, squaring my shoulders once again.

"Are you Rebels?" I demanded more than asked. "Part of the rebellion against Kavylak, that is?"

Though I spoke in a firm tone and volume, the shadow woman behaved as though she hadn't heard me.

"I'll keep an eye on him. Put him on the horse," she told the Sefaline.

I looked to the Sefaline in case he might react or respond any more than the shadow had, but he didn't. Obediently, he picked up Acksil and laid him over his horse. It was not a gentle maneuver and would not be a comfortable way for Acksil to ride.

"Why is a Sylizan travelling with a Warrior," asked the shadow before I could make any move to interfere with the Sefaline's handling of Acksil.

I considered lying to her. My mind whirled with stories I might tell her. Several may have been convincing provided they were delivered well enough. In the end, I chose not to fool myself or her. I was a terrible liar. Only the truth would suffice. Acksil's life was already in danger. I would not place him at any greater risk by being caught in a lie.

"I travel with him because I was a prisoner of the Kavylak Military, and he chose to help me to escape. We were travelling to meet some people he knows, who might be able to bring me home."

She stared at me for a long moment before exchanging a glance with the Sefaline.

"What people?" she asked me as the Sefaline finished securing Acksil to the horse and took its reins, preparing to lead it. He held his hand out for mine, and after a hesitation, I handed them over, recognizing that he would have them in the end, whether I relinquished them or not.

"Friends he once had," I said, not entirely knowing the answer. "People he once knew and whose trust he once had. People he knows are good and to whom he knows he owes a great deal but to whom he wants to repay his debt." That wasn't exactly the truth, but I hoped it wouldn't hurt to place Acksil in a slightly better light than the true story. Perhaps when Acksil were to see his old friends, he might feel that way.

"By what name do you know this Warrior?" asked the shadow in an unfriendly, no-nonsense way.

"Lieutenant Acksilives Fhir."

She nodded to me and then to the Sefaline. "Let's head back," she said to him. "You, come with us or go your own way," she said to me.

"Where are we going?" I asked. I wasn't posing the question to help me to decide whether or not I would go along as well. I wouldn't leave Acksil alone with them. Still, this seemed to be the best time to find out where they would bring my former-Warrior friend.

"We're returning to Dsumot where your 'friend' will be judged."

Dsumot! "Dsumot! We are trying to get to Dsumot. Are you one of the Rebels, Miss...uh..." I realized that I was about to call her "Shadow" but that she must have a real name, of course.

"Kaiwa," she informed me in a bitter introduction. "This is Rrokth. Yes, we are Rebels."

I couldn't help but smile. "Are you going anywhere near Storr Dimog's home in Dsumot?"

After a short pause, she gave a single solid nod.

"That's just where we are heading." I smiled tentatively.

Rrokth gave a growl that evolved into speech. "He should be killed, and she should be left behind, Kaiwa."

"Please don't," I pleaded.

"That's your solution to everything, Rrokth," said a third voice dismissively, making me start. "And yours, too, Kaiwa, for that matter."

I turned toward the voice to see a man walking toward us, leading two horses. His accent was different from both Kaiwa's and Rrokth's, and his appearance was unlike that of anyone I'd ever met. At first glance, he looked to have blue skin. *Blue!* Taking another look, I allowed my rational mind to process what I was seeing.

This man was entirely bald. *No, not bald, hairless.* He didn't have eyebrows, either. What had initially appeared to be blue skin was actually a countless number of interwoven tattoos. He was dressed in brown and yellow robes that were, in combination with his tattooing, unmistakably those of a Lhador monk.

"That was Rrokth's suggestion, not mine," Kaiwa disagreed with the monk. "I happen to disagree with Rrokth in this particular case. But he has a point, Rakej. Fhir isn't just some man. Who knows the real story between him and this Sylizan? There's never only one Warrior. There are always more."

"If there is more than one Warrior, then they are already in the area," the monk Rakej stated calmly, comfortably. "Killing him won't help our cause. We may as well find out what is going on. This isn't their style. They don't just wander along the borders of foreign countries with random Sylizan women. Something's happening here. We're a part of it now. We may as well figure it out." He nodded toward Acksil's unconscious body. "You know Storr will want to see him."

Though Kaiwa looked displeased, she nodded. "Lida and Sicer will, too. They're not going to be happy about this. Lida, most of all."

"They won't." Again, Rakej's agreement was completely congenial as though the subject matter was an easy one. "But they will agree with me. Plus, it will give Lida the chance to deal with him." A grin grew on his lips. At first, it was amused, but it rapidly became sly.

"That's the only reason I didn't kill him on sight," Kaiwa appeared to agree. "If anyone deserves the chance to do it, it's her. I would not take that from her." Her stern face seemed to solidify. "Let's go."

Go? "May I ride my horse, please?" I asked, hoping the offer to allow me to travel with them was still standing.

"No," Kaiwa replied decidedly. "You will be bound and tied to that horse like your 'friend'."

I frowned, debating in my mind whether arguing with Kaiwa would help to make things better or ensure that things would get worse.

"If I am free to stay or go, why must you bind me?" I asked, deciding that it was worth my while to try to stand up for myself. If I was to avoid being a victim, I needed to stop behaving like one.

"Because I don't trust you," Kaiwa replied simply.

"I'm going to the same place as you, and I want to speak with Mr. Dimog. Why would I try anything to harm you? I'm outnumbered, we both know you're a better fighter than I am, and you have my friend. It's safer for me if this group remains intact. The more of us there are the better if we should come across Raiders." I hoped she would listen to my explanation and not simply disagree out of spite.

"Why do you want to speak with Dimog?" Kaiwa demanded. Rrokth and Rakej went on preparing to move out.

"I'm not entirely sure," I confessed. "Acksil believes he is our best hope at finding a safe way for me to go home. He said he wasn't expecting a happy welcome after having done something dishonest but that he believes Mr. Dimog will be interested in helping me. That's how I understood it, at least."

"Mmm." Her expression continued to be stern and indecipherable. "What is your name?"

I wished Acksil was awake. I wanted to look to him for guidance. I wanted to know if I should tell her my real name or make something up. There wasn't any way for me to know if being recognized could benefit me or harm me. Would a Rebel all the way in Dsumot recognize the Godeleva name? If so, what opinion would a Dsumot Rebel have of the Godelevas?

I made my choice.

Chapter 4

Megan

"Asimara, what's going on?" I asked in alarm and jumped at the sudden sound of multiple doors and window shutters slamming shut.

She shook her head. "I don't know, but we're under attack," she replied in a no-nonsense voice, pulling me after her as we joined the sea of people in the street. "Stay with me. I won't let anything happen to you, alright?"

"I'll stay close," I promised, clutching the knife in my hand.

The streets were jammed with people, horses, and carts. As we squeezed our way through the crowd, I became increasingly tense.

A horse suddenly reared in front of us, and a cart tipped over. I gasped. People screamed and began to run in every direction. Asimara pulled me backward by my arm with a bruising vice-grip and started to run away from the crowd. Not resisting, I ran with her, trusting that she was my best way to safety.

More screams erupted on a nearby street and seconds later an explosion rang out. My body shuddered, and the windows on the street rattled from the intensity of the blast. I forced myself to stay with Asimara, even though all I wanted was to run and hide until this madness was over.

Asimara seemed unfazed by the noises and the absolute bedlam around us. I guessed it must have been because of her army training that she was able to keep such a level head. She brought us back toward the first large main street I'd seen on our way into the city. Except this time, instead of citizens going about their regular business, the place had become a war zone with people fighting both bare-handed and with knives.

"Rebels," Asimara said.

A shiver ran down my spine at the word. My first encounter with the Rebels hadn't been a pleasant one, and I wasn't keen to have a second. I really didn't want to get captured by them again.

Frantically trying to get my bearings, I spotted the gates to the military building. To my distress, they were closed, and there were tons of people between us and them. I glanced at Asimara. She was intensely focused, likely assessing our best options.

Suddenly, the distinct sound of heavy footfalls rushing at us from behind cut through the tumult of shouts and screams. I whirled around in their direction, clutching my knife, instinctively knowing someone was charging toward us. Asimara was already way ahead of me. She stepped between me and the charging man - whom I assumed was a Rebel - brandishing her dagger.

"Don't even bother," she said in a dangerous tone that made it more than obvious she wouldn't hesitate to use her weapon.

The man halted in his tracks, sized her up in a single look, and then backed off and away from us, smartly deciding that she wasn't bluffing.

"Do you see anywhere to go?" she asked me. "Or somewhere to hide?"

"No." I wished I had a better answer for her.

A rock flew past us, narrowly missing our heads. We both gasped in surprise, and Asimara took my arm again and started toward the base, moving us deeper into the crowd.

"Is there some back entrance into the base?" I asked, as we slowly shoved our way through the throng of people that was shoving back.

"No. At least not one I know about."

Darn! I would have thought this place would have had a dozen secret entrances.

Asimara pulled me out of the crowd and over to the front of a building with a sheltered doorway. She pushed me against the door and stood in front of me like a sentinel, ready for anything.

"Why is this happening? Why are the Rebels attacking like this?" I asked desperately.

· "I don't know. I don't know which rebels they are. I've never seen anything like this," she said.

She doesn't know which rebels they are? There's more than one kind of rebel? Geeze! How many enemies did Kavylak have?

All of them, Megan. The answer is all of them.

Why did I choose to stay here, again?

A streak of familiar, shining silver hair caught my eye, and I recognized its owner immediately.

"It's Mez!" I exclaimed to Asimara, pointing to where he was currently making his way forward through the mob, toward the military base.

Asimara's eyes widened. "Mez Basarovka!" she shouted, louder than I'd ever heard anyone holler.

"Mez!" I yelled, joining in with Asimara and waved my arms frantically over my head in the hopes of better capturing his attention. We kept up our celebrity-fan-shrieking tactic until we were sure he had definitely seen us.

It worked. He looked in our direction, altered his original course, and made his way toward us. Both Asimara and I stopped shouting and stared, gobsmacked, as the crowd around him parted and cleared a path, allowing him to walk an unobstructed line in our direction. His mind-manipulation Warrior skill never ceased to amaze and unnerve me.

"What are you doing out here?" Mez asked me upon reaching us, before turning the same questioning gaze to Asimara. "Come with me," he added, not bothering to wait for us to answer. He snagged my free hand, holding it firmly as he led us back into the crowd.

Asimara still clung to my arm with bruising force. People moved out of our path as they had previously done for Mez. It was like we were surrounded by an invisible forcefield.

Too weird.

Once we reached the gate, the guards nodded to Mez and opened it just wide enough to let us pass and then immediately slammed them shut.

"Thank you, Lieutenant Basarovka," Asimara said gratefully.

"You're welcome." He nodded to her, looking a little paler and slightly weary around the eyes. I recognized that look. It was how he had appeared after the Warriors had come to rescue Amorette, Fiffine, and I from the Rebels. Using his skill to such a degree had taken a toll on him. He looked like someone who was trying to push through a migraine.

Asimara nodded and walked with us toward the main building but stopped short when she saw a group of soldiers marching in our direction. They were being led by Major Relah Tovash. She was the tall, tough-as-nails, yet big-blue-eyed blond woman I had met a few days ago, when I'd first arrived on the base with Thayn.

Major Tovash had given me my identity tags and told me what my job would be. She was both terrifying and awesome, the type of person who made a first impression you'd never forget. Her face and name were permanently etched into my brain.

"That's my unit," Asimara said to us. "I'd better grab my stuff and head back out with them." She looked at me. "You're alright, Megan?"

"Yes," I said.

"I'll help her," Mez assured her.

"Thank you for helping me out there, Asimara, and for getting me back here safe."

She patted my arm lightly with a wry smile. "We'll have fun again another time."

"We will," I agreed, returning her smile. She nodded and ran off without wasting another moment. I watched her, feeling annoyed that our time had been cut short and worried about her return into that chaotic mess.

"Do you urgently need anything from your place?" Mez asked. "If not, it would be better to come inside CCMB1 until the soldiers are done marching."

"I don't think I need anything. Um, what is CCMB1?" I asked, hoping he wasn't taking me to some underground bunker like he had when Syliza had attacked the base.

"Capital City Military Building One," he said and nodded in the direction of the large main building on the base toward which we were briskly walking.

Interesting. I didn't realize the building had a name or designation. This is probably good to know.

"Can I bring you to see anyone?"

"Hmm. Maybe Amorette, if she's home?" I suggested, keeping pace with his fast stride.

"That's easy to check. She and Amarogq are my neighbours."

"Yes. I noticed that when I went on a little tour with Amorette yesterday. Hey, um, Mez? Why are the Rebels…" My question died on my lips. Standing immediately between us and the building door was a very, very, pale - almost deathly pale - woman.

If I hadn't seen her blink, I would have had a hard time believing she was alive. The black leather armour she wore from her neck to her toes was in such sharp contrast to the ghastly pallor of her face and hands, that her skin looked nearly blue and bloodless. Her deathly pale appearance was only emphasised further by her white hair that shone almost iridescent in the sunlight.

The hair on the back of my neck stood on end at the sight of her. Every instinct in my body told me that something was very unnatural and wrong with her. Whoever she was and whatever she was, she wasn't human.

Her icy gaze slid from Mez and froze on me.

"Elindria," she spoke in a tone as frigid as her stare, "I am your servant. Prepare to die."

Who the heck is Elindria, and what the heck is happening?

Before either one of us could speak, the woman raised her arms, and Mez and I were suddenly imprisoned in a small four-walled cell of ice that extended a few feet above our heads.

What the...?

"Mez! Mez, what's going on?" I asked frantically, feeling my panic hit new heights as my brain desperately tried to make sense of this crazy situation, and my eyes desperately searched for a way out of the cramped ice prison.

Was she some crazy Warrior I'd never met before?

"I don't know," Mez responded intensely, dropping my hand to push against the ice. He then took a dagger from his belt and started hacking at it.

Remembering I still had my own knife, I joined him in the hacking effort, only to realize as quickly as he did that the effort was futile. The ice that surrounded us was thick, and we were barely chipping it.

"We won't be here long," Mez said with his usual calm confidence. "There are too many Warriors nearby."

"Who is that woman? Did she make this ice? Is she a Warrior?" I could hear my voice growing more shrill with each word.

Mez may be calm and mostly unfazed by this situation, but I'm not Mez. I'm very, very fazed.

He paused his ice-hacking to look at me. "No, she's not a Warrior. I've never seen her before. Why did she call you Elindria?"

"I don't know. I don't know who that is. I've never..." I trailed off, realizing the name "Elindria" wasn't entirely foreign to me. I had heard the name before, but I was too terrified to recall from where.

"Are you alright?" Mez asked, obviously seeing I'd zoned out in my attempt to remember the name.

"No. I mean, physically, yes, but no."

He nodded, accepting my explanation, and was about to say something when a huge burst of orange-coloured light struck our ice prison and was followed by a maniacal cackle.

I'd recognize that cackle anywhere. Galnar.

Mez immediately stepped back and pulled me with him until our backs were both solidly pressed against the freezing ice wall.

A figure in black approached and peered into the ice, looking directly at us with orange-red fire eyes.

Yup. Galnar. Okay, I can admit it. In this one particular instance, I'm really glad to see him...I hope.

He lifted his arms above his head, and before my astonished eyes, I watched as his entire body was engulfed in flames.

I shrieked, convinced I'd just seen a man burned alive. My shriek quickly silenced into an open-mouthed "O" of terror when his deranged laughter returned. I watched as he purposely laid his flaming palms on the ice wall. Within a matter of seconds, the ice in front of Mez and me began to sweat.

Mez moved, placing his body in front of me as if to create a barrier between Galnar and me.

"He knows when to stop, right?" I asked, terrified. I knew that, based on previous encounters with our "rescuer", being reasonable wasn't exactly his strong suit.

"Oh, he knows when," Mez said, not elaborating further. He didn't need to. By positioning himself in front of me, I knew that Mez wasn't entirely confident that his captain would stop before he barbequed us in the ice-melting process.

I gasped as the coldest water I'd ever felt rained down on our heads. Galnar's constant fire power was overwhelming the frozen structure. I drew right up against Mez as the walls began to melt, clutching tightly to the leather of his black uniform jacket, instinctively wanting to shield myself from the cold and wet. Mez brought his arms around me, and I shut my eyes, burying my face into his chest. The freezing water poured down with greater intensity, soaking my hair and clothes.

Eventually, I began to detect an intense, burning heat. The moment my nose picked up the smell of cooking leather, I heard Mez call out: "We can take it from here, Galnar, thanks."

The heat stopped. I dared to peek around Mez and saw Galnar. His head and shoulders were now visible over the wall he'd melted. His body was no longer on fire, but his eyes were still ablaze. His gaze locked on mine, and the most disturbing grin I'd ever seen split across his face. I stared in horror and disbelief. He looked entirely mad, unnatural, and demonic, like something born from hell. I couldn't tell if he intended to fry us or if he was going to skip off on his merry way to torch something else.

Then, as quickly as his grin had appeared, it slid off his face. The flames in his eyes diminished. Within seconds, the whites of his scleras returned, and his irises faded from a bright ember-orange, to an angry coal-red, to their usual smoldering ash-grey.

To my astonishment, a hint of what looked like concern crossed his face when he turned his attention to Mez.

"You're not injured?" he asked in a calculated and controlled voice, a total contrast from the nutcase he'd been only moments ago.

"No, sir," Mez responded, still holding me.

Galnar nodded, looked at me for a solid second, and then back at Mez. "And Wynters?"

"She is uninjured, sir."

Galnar nodded, turned, and broke into a run.

"God, sometimes I wish I was a fainter," I muttered to myself, watching transfixed as Galnar's body ignited in a cascade of flames before he tore out of sight.

"I'm glad you're not. It'd be a real nuisance to get you out of this thing if you were unconscious," Mez said, drawing my attention back to him, my freezing temperature, and trembling body.

I realized that I was still clutching to the front of his uniform with a death grip. Looking up at him, I saw that he was wearing a small, friendly smile and was just as soaked as me. If the deep shade of purple-blue his lips were turning was any indication, I guessed he was probably as cold as I was, too.

"I'll climb out first, then help you out. We'll head right in, and you can get warm."

I nodded in agreement, teeth chattering, and released him, hugging my arms tightly around myself.

He didn't waste any time and placed his hands-on top of the shortest part of the slick, melting ice wall. Pushing himself up and out of the opening, he awkwardly slid down the other side, but still managed to make the maneuver look cool by landing a smooth somersault from which he rose to stand again.

I would have clapped under other circumstances. At the moment, frigid water was steadily raining down on me, and I couldn't remember feeling more miserable.

Mez walked back up to the ice wall and reached over toward me. "Put your hands on my shoulders," he instructed.

I did. After placing his hands directly under my arms, he lifted me enough that I could raise my legs over the wall. He backed up until I was clear of the ice, and I could put my feet on the ground.

"Thank you," I chattered.

He nodded and released me. "Let's go in so you can get warm."

I agreed. The thought of getting warm was the only motivation that drove me forward. I hoped that when I saw Amorette, she would have a towel and some dry clothes I could borrow until I could return to fetch my things from my apartment.

Mez and I walked toward the building doors, which proved to be quite the challenge as my legs had numbed a great deal and each step took a surprising amount of effort.

As we slowly made our way toward our destination, we avoided patches of ice and puddles along our way. Some of the grass and dirt was also peppered with scorch marks, indicating that the ice woman and Galnar must have been battling.

"Do you think she's gone?" I asked Mez. "Whoever that was?"

"I don't know, but she won't get inside. The building is full of soldiers and Warriors. You'll be safe," he assured me.

"Um, was it just me or did she look like she was, like, a little dead to you?" That was definitely one of the oddest things I had asked to date.

"Pale, yes. Dead? She was a little too active for that," Mez observed.

"Yeah, I guess."

He did have a point, but seriously, that woman's complexion was *not* just pale. I'd seen pale: Mez was pale; Irys was very pale; Xandon was really pale; and Galnar was really, really pale. That woman was corpse coloured.

Mez opened the door for me, and we entered. The warm, climate-controlled temperature of the building wasn't the comfort I'd hoped it to be. Instead, it just made my cold, soaked body feel instantly clammy. Even worse, I became all too aware of my drenched hair plastered to the sides of my face, the blouse that clung uncomfortably to my torso, and my dripping, water-weighted skirt that now hung too low on my hips.

So much for looking half-way decent. I was starting to wonder if Mez was ever going to see me look nice or if I was forever destined to be a disaster every time I was around him. Never mind that, I was beginning to wonder if there would ever be a time that being in my presence wouldn't cause Mez to be in mortal danger.

There's no way he'll ever want to get a coffee with me now...

I frowned at the thought and officially began questioning whether I'd made the wrong decision regarding Thayn.

Should I have left with him? Was staying in Kavylak a mistake?

"Hi, Mez!" a cheerful male voice said. I looked back to the owner of the voice and couldn't help but be surprised by what I saw, in spite of everything I'd already witnessed today. The man, who was now walking in stride with us, was just as soaked as we were and had large, feathered wings protruding from his back. His wings were the same colour as his long jet-black hair and Warrior uniform. "She got you, too?" He observed, more than asked, in a soft, musical voice.

"Are you an angel?" I blurted, unable to take my eyes from the picture-perfect young man and his glistening wings.

"No, I'm just a Zari." He said with a shake of his head, giggling in a super-cute and infectious way.

I couldn't help but giggle in return at his reaction, despite the fact that I really wasn't in a giggly sort of mood.

Maybe his giggle is literally infectious. Oh man! That's not his Warrior skill, is it?

"Zari? I'm sorry, I don't know what that is…" I trailed off, as a memory of Irys took over my thoughts. He had wings. She'd told me about a winged people when we were dressed for the Masque, because her costume had been based on them. At the time I'd thought she'd been pulling my leg, but clearly, she wasn't.

Mental note, Megan: when Irys tells you something - no matter how nutty it might sound - trust that she's telling you the truth.

Now, what was it that she called these people, again? Eransays, Ernasies-er something…

Musical giggling interrupted my mental tirade.

"Zari is my name," the Warrior introduced himself. "Well, it's Lieutenant Tedzarid Banarica, but Zari is a lot easier to remember." He flashed me a bright smile that was so warm and genuine, I couldn't resist mirroring it.

"I'm Megan."

"Hi Megan," he said cheerily.

"It's really great to meet you, Zari, but I imagine you want to dry off and get warm as much as I do." I certainly couldn't speak for him and Mez, but I was freezing, and the thrill of meeting someone with wings was wearing off quickly.

"Yes," he said with a giggle, and I couldn't help but giggle back. "Bye!" He smiled to both Mez and me before heading past us and jogging up the stairs.

I watched him go as I continued walking with Mez. "Is he an Eransy-uh-person?"

Wow. Nice, Megan.

"Eransian. Yes," he confirmed. "Though his wings are black. Usually, Eransians have white wings and hair. I think his turned black so he would look tougher," he joked with a chuckle.

I had to laugh, too. I didn't think there was anything Zari could do to make himself look tough. Even if he could, one little giggle would be all it would take to soften his efforts. That said, I'm glad Mez told me that the average Eransian had white wings. That would explain why Irys had a white Masque costume and not a black one.

"Zari's shadow, however. Now that looks tough," Mez added as we walked up the stairs.

"His shadow?" I immediately shook my head, holding up my hand. "Never mind. Don't tell me."

He grinned and respected my request, not elaborating further.

I was glad for it. At the moment, I really didn't want to know what Zari's shadow was. I got the feeling that it must have something to do with his unique Warrior skill, and I'd already met my crazy quota today. I didn't think my brain could handle one more paranormal Qarradune fact.

We reached the fourth floor and stopped in front of Amarogq's door. After a quick glance to Mez, who gave a simple nod, I raised my fist and knocked.

"Amorette? Are you there? It's Megan."

Chapter 5

Irys

"Irys," I replied firmly to Kaiwa's request for my name. Everyone here had given me a first name. I hoped it would not be strange if I introduced myself in the same way.

Though it felt unfamiliar to me not to share my family name, Kaiwa appeared to be satisfied with my introduction. She mounted Acksil's horse ahead of him and nodded to Rrokth, who, not without displeasure, handed me my reins. I mounted the horse before minds could be changed. Rrokth and Rakej mounted their horses as well, and we walked them for a while until reaching what appeared to be a tiny camp. Right away, I could see two people were already there, a man and a woman.

The man stood to face us as we approached. Dressed in brown and green leather-like material, he looked prepared for anything from sleeping outdoors to fighting with a blade. He had rich brown skin and dark brown hair that made me wonder if he was born a Northerner. That said, it was difficult to pay attention to anything about him at all aside from the fact that he had only one eye. While one sharp blue eye was focused on me, where the other would have been, there was a large gash that had healed into a scar that permanently sealed the other eye shut.

"You found more horses," he started to say until his eye fell on me and then on Acksil.

The woman stood at that point, too, looking braced for anything. The other Rebels dismounted, so I did the same. I didn't want to appear defiant.

"More than horses," Kaiwa said with sarcastic dryness. "We also brought a Sylizan and an old ally but new enemy."

The woman approached us. She looked like she may have been from Dsumot or Edilnir, as far as I could tell. She had long brown hair, brown eyes, and skin far paler than her companion's. She was dressed similarly to him in her brown clothes of the same leather-like material. I would have to ask Acksil about this fabric as I had never seen anything like it before my own leggings, but it was clearly very popular among the Rebels.

The expression on the woman's face was casual enough, nearly cocky, as she stepped up to Acksil, but the colour drained from her face once she recognized him.

"Lida," Rrokth said protectively, wrapping the reins of his horse around a large low tree branch before walking up to her and placing a hand on her shoulder in a paternal way.

"It's him," she said to Rrokth, resting her hand over his. Her voice was quiet, but I was close enough to hear her clearly.

"If you want him beaten or killed, no one will stop you," Kaiwa informed Lida. I had no doubt that she was serious.

Lida gave a small nod to Kaiwa but didn't move from where she was. "Where was he? This woman was with him? Is she valuable?"

"We found them riding, most likely on the run from Raiders. There were a few in the town. I knocked him out and she, Irys, claims to be his friend. She says he saved her life when she was a prisoner in Kavylak. She claims he was taking her to see Storr," Kaiwa supplied.

I was standing perfectly still as they conversed. It seemed that the less I drew attention to myself, the better I would fare. Unfortunately, my plans were taken off their intended course when both women looked at me. It was clear they were waiting for me to speak.

"Yes. He did save my life. I was a prisoner of the Kavylak Military. We have been on the run from them. We stayed in a building in the town overnight because it was too dark to travel."

The one-eyed man stepped closer to me. I resisted the inclination of my muscles to tense.

"You were running from Raiders, too? Are you injured in any way?" he asked.

"I was not injured. Thank you for your concern. Acksil kept me safe," I said appreciatively.

"I'm Sicer Dimog. Storr Dimog, the man you are seeking, is my father."

I gave him a quick curtsy. It felt strange doing so in pants, and I used my cloak as a bit of a skirt, but I wanted to show this man my respect.

"It is an honour to meet you, Mr. Dimog," I said with a tentative smile.

"Did Kavylak take you directly from Syliza? How did you manage to become their prisoner?" he asked. His voice was calm and conversational.

"This was the second time they had taken me. I was enslaved the first time, taken from my home in Lorammel, and imprisoned the second time, taken accidentally from a home in Gbat Rher," I said, allowing my tone to convey that the complete explanation involved quite the lengthy story.

The Rebels exchanged looks, appearing quite curious but confused by my words.

"Do you know why you are the Kavylak Military's target?" Mr. Dimog asked.

I shook my head. "No. Not exactly. I have come to suspect that it has something to do with Xandon, but I cannot fathom what." I decided to take a risk and offer this man some trust. He was the son of the very man Acksil and I were headed to see. If I wanted this group to extend even a shred of trust to me, I would need to show that I was willing to offer them mine. The mention of Xandon's name brought a new intensity to the group.

"Do you have reason to believe that Xandon may be sending other Warriors or Kavylak soldiers after you?" Mr. Dimog asked.

"Yes, I believe so," I confessed. "But we have a substantial head start. They cannot be anywhere near here yet."

"Why did Fhir help you escape?"

I looked him directly in the eye. I hoped he would see my sincerity this way. "He may have been a Warrior, but he is a good man. This was the third time he had saved my life. Twice, he placed his own life at risk in order to do so. This time, most greatly. He knew it was right to help me, so he did."

As Mr. Dimog considered my words, Lida spoke up, never leaving Acksil's side.

"Has he fallen in love with you?" Her eyes narrowed as she spoke.

"Oh no, no. He barely knows me," I said, unbalanced by her. "At least not in the sense that he could ever..." I completed the thought with a shake to my head.

Of course not! Why would she think such a thing? Could a man not do what he knew in his heart was right by saving a woman, without holding that woman in his heart? What a discomforting thought!

I could feel the eyes of the entire group watching me and was drawn from my musings.

Lida appeared skeptical. She reached out and stroked her fingers down the side of Acksil's face. It looked as though she was trying to convince herself of something. The poor former Warrior remained unconscious. I was becoming increasingly concerned for him.

"The man you know as the Warrior Acksilivcs Fhir was once one of us, a Dsumot Rebel we knew as Nydo Acksilivcs," Mr. Dimog explained, surprising me that Acksil was once known as anything other than the name he had given me. "He fought by our side, and Lida was his best friend. We trusted him, and he betrayed us all, abandoning our cause and joining the very enemy we were fighting in order to protect our people and our country. He left us to become one of those who warred against us."

"I understand why you do not trust him," I replied with sincerity. "I can only swear to you that I do not believe his intentions toward your group are malicious. He has left the Warriors. He defected in order to rescue me. You are the people he was confident would help us. Despite all he did to you, he trusts you."

"We will take him back to my father and will let Fhir speak his case," said Mr. Dimog decidedly. "Then we will determine what is to be done with him and with you."

I couldn't have asked for more from him. I did understand his unwillingness to trust Acksil or to simply believe me.

"If I may make one more request," I asked hesitantly. "Please don't tie me up while we ride to meet your father. We share the same destination. I won't try to run off."

At that, to my great surprise, Mr. Dimog chuckled. "I imagine that was Kaiwa's threat. You won't be tied, Irys. Unless you decide to make yourself a threat or a nuisance, there's no reason for that."

"Thank you, Mr. Dimog."

"Nydo rides with me," Lida interrupted.

This drew a look from Rrokth. I wasn't sure how to interpret it. Mr. Dimog's expression, on the other hand, seemed more understanding and accepting. With a quick nod, he agreed with her choice, not that she appeared open to negotiating.

"I will ride with Irys," Rrokth then said.

Every member of the group reacted differently to the Sefaline's pronouncement. From Lida's surprise to Rakej's amusement, everyone had a different opinion on the matter. In my case, what started as shock graduated to an equally unexpected feeling of comfort. If I was to be required to ride with someone, my preference would most certainly have been to ride with Acksil. That being out of the question, the strength, natural instincts, and blatant honesty of a Sefaline was more appealing than any of these other Rebels.

"We don't have enough horses," Mr. Dimog explained to me. He must have caught my initial reaction. "You don't need to ride with Rrokth, but you will need to ride with one of us."

"I will ride with Rrokth," I said, giving my new riding companion a respectful nod. "I also want to keep my things with me," I stipulated.

Rrokth nodded without any apparent objections to my condition. "I ride near Lida. This will keep you close to the traitor."

The corner of my mouth twitched. That was very considerate of him. "Thank you."

At that, Acksil began to stir. Relief and fear simultaneously washed over me.

"Irys," he said groggily, shifting uncomfortably in what had to be quite the painful position, still draped over the back of a horse.

I took a step toward him, but Lida marched up to him before I could cross the distance between us. Roughly, she gripped his jaw and turned his face to force him to look at hers.

"Guess again," Lida said darkly.

Despite the fact that he was looking at her nearly upside down, and he was only just regaining consciousness, he recognized her immediately. "Lida?"

Everything about her exuded disgust. "Don't struggle, and I won't kill you before we reach our destination."

"Where is the woman I was travelling with? Irys. Do you have her? Is she safe?" Nothing about Acksil's voice suggested that Lida's threats concerned him.

"She's fine. Stay still," Lida said as though the words were a great inconvenience to her.

"I'm here," I called out to him, since it was evident that Lida had no intention of telling him that I was nearly next to him, simply out of his line of sight. "I'm coming too. I'm not hurt."

Acksil turned his head in my direction, trying to see me. "These are good people, Irys. Everything's going to be alright now." He shifted against his restraints. I wished Lida would have allowed him to ride normally now that he was conscious. Why was it that all the tenderness she had appeared to have for him before he regained consciousness had vanished now that he was awake?

"They are," I agreed, moving a few steps closer so he could see me. "They're taking us where we want to go."

Looking up at Rrokth, I nodded to him to indicate I was ready to leave when he was. I had no intention of making this trip a moment longer for Acksil than it needed to be. Rrokth stepped over to his horse and mounted deftly. From there, he turned toward me and reached a strong arm down to me. I took it, and he pulled me up, so I could ride behind him.

"You have that Sefaline scent," I noted as I settled in behind him. "I hadn't noticed before." It was certainly an odd thing to say under normal circumstances, but Fhurrk seemed to take great pride in this particular attribute. My hope was that this was a common trait among Sefaline and that Rrokth would feel similarly.

"You have known other Sefaline?" he asked with curiosity, heading off with the group as Kaiwa gave him the nod to do so. I brought my arms loosely around him, feeling the distinctive warmth of his people.

"A couple," I replied, counting them in my head. "Three, I suppose, but I believe one was only half Sefaline."

"How did you meet so many Sefaline? Raiders?"

"I met them while I was a Kavylak prisoner. I met the Sefaline Warrior and his mate, then briefly crossed paths with another young Sefaline woman who was there with another Warrior."

Rrokth made a sharp snarling sound at the mention of Lieutenant Fhurrk. His scent picked up and became much spicier and harder on the nose. "That abomination and those with him are not *true* Sefaline."

"I didn't realize..." I corrected nervously. "I apologize. I thought they were. Thank you for correcting me."

This seemed to calm him quickly enough. His scent returned to normal, and the tension in his muscles eased. "You are not Sefaline. You would not have known."

Smiling appreciatively, I confessed, "I'm far too ignorant about such things. I'm grateful that you're willing to share with me. I won't make that mistake again." I certainly wouldn't. It felt integral to keep this man's positive sentiments toward me. Still, whether he acknowledged Lieutenant Fhurrk or not, I was willing to count on some similarities in their responses. To test one of my theories, I started to hum as we rode.

As I couldn't see his face, it was difficult to tell what effect this might have been having on him. Still, I couldn't detect any more tension in him, so I decided that I was correct in assuming he would enjoy music.

Glancing over at Acksil, I winced as he bounced along with every step the horse took. His eyes were closed. I imagined this was to help him focus on distractions from his discomfort.

Quite suddenly, Rrokth held up his hand, and we all slowed to a stop.

"What is it?" Mr. Dimog asked just above a whisper. The riders all came close together to be able to hear what was being said.

"Raiders," Rrokth replied just as quietly.

Oh Goddess, not again...

I wished Acksil were untied. He was more than likely by far the best fighter in our group.

"You will be safe, Irys. Whatever happens, remain on this horse," Rrokth instructed me.

"I will," I agreed, having had every intention to do as I was told.

"I can help," Acksil spoke up. "You know I can, Lida."

"We don't need your help," Lida said without bothering to look at Acksil.

"Do we need his help?" Rakej asked Rrokth.

"No," Rrokth and Mr. Dimog replied in unison.

"He is a prisoner and is more of a threat to us than the Raiders," Mr. Dimog added.

Lida glanced smugly at me before turning her attention back to the situation.

I wondered why we were waiting here instead of trying to make our escape but assumed the Rebels had experienced encounters with the Raiders often enough that they knew the best strategy for dealing with them.

The Raiders were closer than I had realized. Four of them appeared, riding slowly and very confidently as they allowed their eyes to travel over us. They were looking for anything of value that they could take.

The Rebels looked unshaken, standing their ground without drawing a weapon. Every instinct I had told me to get off the horse and run.

"Well, aren't you a strange band of travellers," observed the one woman among the Raiders. She was dressed in a worn brown leather jacket and trousers with heavy boots on her feet. Her long black hair was unkempt with old braids knotted into it. Her tanned skin was further darkened by an overall dirtiness.

Her three large-muscled, leather clad companions slowly circled us as she continued to speak. "Have anything to trade? I'm feeling generous today. If you have something good, I might take it from you and leave you with your lives in exchange...well, most of you."

Chapter 6

Megan

Amorette answered the door a few moments after I knocked and didn't hide her surprise to see Mez and me but smiled all the same.

"Hello...did you need a towel?" she asked. One eyebrow slowly raised as she took in our very wet and shivery appearances as well as the puddle of water our dripping clothes were leaving in the doorway.

I laughed awkwardly. "Yes, um, if you don't mind."

"Not for me, thank you." Mez shook his head. "I like how I look this way, and a wet uniform is, well, it's awful, but a towel won't help." He grinned. "I'm just delivering her to your towels," he told Amorette. "I'm needed elsewhere."

Amorette and I laughed in unison at Mez' response. His sense of humor was seriously weird sometimes, but at least it was a good weird.

"I'll find you later." Mez turned to me, and I nodded to him.

"Should I stay in the building until I see you again?" I confirmed more than asked.

"That would be best. I'll be in the building, too. Likely in my office or my quarters in case you need me. If I'm not there, I can be found. Just ask someone."

"Okay." I smiled at him.

"I'll take good care of her," Amorette piped in as if she were my reliable babysitter.

"Thanks, Amorette." Mez chuckled.

He released my hand, and although I knew it was only in my imagination, I felt even colder without the warmth of his hand in mine. We looked at each other for a brief moment before he left. As I watched him squeak down the hall in his wet boots, I felt the warmth I'd thought I'd lost flood my chest, realizing that Mez truly did care about me. Once again, he'd been there to help me through yet another one of the scariest moments of my life.

I entered Amarogq and Amorette's apartment, and she jogged off to fetch me a towel.

"That's water on you, right?" She held a towel out to me. "You don't need a shower before you sit on my furniture?" she half joked.

"Just water, really, really cold water." I took the towel and immediately wrapped it around myself, caring more about locking in some heat than getting dry for the time being. "Some crazy woman attacked us and imprisoned us in ice, which melted all over us when Galnar did his...fire skill...thing."

It was ludicrous to think about what happened, but it sounded even crazier when I retold it to Amorette. I was half expecting her to roll her eyes and laugh as if I were kidding.

She didn't. Her expression became instantly serious, and she frowned. "Oh my Goddess! Was anyone hurt?"

"I don't know. I mean, Mez and I weren't, but I know she had intended to hurt us."

"I wonder what she was after."

I shrugged in response, because I didn't know what answer to give her.

"Do you want a change of clothes?" Amorette offered.

"Yes, please. If you have something you can lend me, I would be eternally grateful. I'm not supposed to go back to my apartment right now. The Rebels are in the city, and Mez thinks it would be better if I stayed in the main building, uh, CCMB1, for the time being."

Amorette nodded. "I heard the alarm. I didn't know it was the Rebels." She shuddered a little, likely remembering our past encounter with the Rebels, before shaking it off and flashing me a smile.

She left the room, and I took in my surroundings for the first time. From where I stood near the front door, I saw a small sitting area with a couch and two chairs. A dark wood coffee table was positioned in the middle of the seating arrangement, under which lay a tasteful, oval area rug in earthy colours. On the far wall was a medium-sized curtained rectangular window, which currently had heavy metal shutters drawn down over it. I guessed the shutters were a safety precaution in response to the Rebel alarm. To the left of the sitting room was a small galley kitchen and to the right were two rooms. The room closest to me must have been the bathroom because this was where Amorette had fetched the towel she'd given me, leading me to surmise that the other room to which she'd disappeared must have been the bedroom.

"These should fit," Amorette announced upon her return, handing me the folded clothing she had in her arms.

"Thanks, Amorette. I'll change quickly."

"Take your time." She nodded her head toward the room I had correctly assumed was the bathroom. "I'll put on some coffee while you're in there."

"I would love coffee! Thanks! You're amazing." She was my personal hero.

"I know," she joked with a chuckle, shaking her long raven hair in amusement as she headed to the kitchen.

I entered the bathroom to change and get dry. Turning on the light and shutting the door behind me, I was immediately jealous. This was nothing like the closet-sized bathroom in my quarters. While still not the amazingness that was my guest bathroom at the Godeleva Estate, it was still three times the size of my current one and had a full-sized vanity and toilet as well as a bathtub and shower stall. I could easily use any one of these features without knocking the walls with my knees or elbows.

Placing the fresh clothes on the counter next to the sink, I peeled off my wet garments as quickly as I could and dried off. Wrapping my hair in a towel, I changed into my new attire. Amorette had lent me stylish pants and a blouse, similar to what she was wearing, only my pants were a deep brown to her navy and my blouse was a grassy green compared to her pastel pink.

I wrung out my wet outfit as best I could in the bathtub and then decided to leave it there, so it wouldn't soak Amorette's floor. Removing the towel from my hair, which was now mostly damp, I let it fall freely in a tangled mess around my back and shoulders, deciding it would dry faster if I didn't strap it down.

I used the towel to give my pumps a wipe. Deciding to leave them off for the time being, I hooked my fingers into the curve of the heels and exited the bathroom in bare feet, feeling a million times better.

"Do you mind if I leave my wet clothes and the towel in the bathtub for now?" I asked Amorette, setting my pumps down on the mat near the front door.

"Sure!" Amorette said easily from where she was sitting on the couch. She beckoned for me to join her, and I did.

"I don't know how you take your coffee. Help yourself," she said, gesturing to the tray on the coffee table in front of her. It contained a metal carafe, two mugs with freshly poured, steaming black coffee, a bowl with sugar cubes and tongs, a matching creamer, and a small jar of what looked like cinnamon. To my utter delight, the tray also held a few finger sandwiches and cookies.

"Thanks!" I added two sugar cubes and cream to one of the coffee mugs and took a generous sip. It was hot, but it didn't burn. It was heaven. I also helped myself to a couple of sandwiches and a cookie, and wolfed them down. The Rebels had ruined my Woodsman's Lunch, and I was really hungry.

"Were you out with Mez when the attack happened?"

"No, with my neighbour, Asimara. Thankfully, she's a soldier, and she kept us safe until we ran into Mez."

"Oh." Amorette sounded almost disappointed to learn I hadn't been with Mez. "I wonder if he was in town visiting his old house again."

I looked at Amorette blankly. "His house?"

What in the world is she talking about?

Amorette nodded, adding a bit of cinnamon to her coffee and sipping it before continuing. "I've seen him go by this house lots of times in town. I just assumed it was where he used to live before he moved here. I thought he might have told you about it."

"Mez has a house in the city?"

Seriously? Why would he choose to live in this place?

"I don't know if it's still his. I'm just assuming it was once. When he looks at it, he gets that expression Warriors get when they think about their former lives."

My eyebrows rose. "I had no idea he had a house." I shrugged and ate another cookie. "Maybe that's where he lived with his wife."

She frowned deeply and nodded. "It's what I'd guess," she agreed, sounding sad.

I mirrored her frown. "Do you know what happened to them?" I asked quietly. "I mean, I know she died, but I guess it was bad?"

Amorette studied me for a moment, clearly curious as to what I might already have known about Mez' past.

"I know bits and pieces," she confessed. "I'm not supposed to, but Amarogq loves me more than Mez." A small smirk graced her lips but faded faster than it had appeared, and her frown returned. "I shouldn't really have joked about that," she chided herself.

I gave her a brief nod in understanding.

Amorette rested her coffee cup down on the tray. "How much do you know?"

"I know that his wife's name was Glenara, and that it took him a long time to convince her to go out with him. When he talked about her, I got the feeling that he loved her very much."

She smiled a little when I mentioned that it took Mez a long time to get Glenara to date him, giving me the impression that she hadn't known that before.

"I think it was true love, if you don't mind that expression," Amorette said. "They weren't married very long before he was taken to become a Warrior. The way I understand it is that he refused to leave his life with her, so the decision was made for him. He's never gone out with any other woman since then, as far as anyone I know has heard. I think he's still stuck in grief for her."

I was horrified. "Oh my gosh! That's awful! They forced him into becoming a Warrior? After ruining his life?"

She nodded. "It's the case for a lot of them. Some sign up. Some are chosen and make a deal. Some are forced if they won't agree."

I was astonished. It would never have occurred to me that Mez or any of the others hadn't made the decision to become a Warrior. They all seemed so sure of themselves. So confident. So proud of who they were.

"Wow. I had no idea." I dared a glance at Amorette. "Was Amarogq forced?" Considering his past with Ash Dancer, I had a bad feeling he might have been forced, too.

"Amarogq won't talk about what he went through. I know he has a deal. I know he didn't volunteer," Amorette told me. "I don't know what his life was like before, though. He always says his life started when he became a Warrior. He's a new person now. Who he was before was another man who died."

My stomach churned at her words. The coffee I'd drunk and the food I'd eaten no longer brought me comfort and was threatening to come back up.

She doesn't know anything about his life before. She doesn't know about Star Archer or Dawn Seer or Ash Dancer or the children. Even Amarogq doesn't know about the children. His *children...*

"Amarogq really loves you," I blurted in a desperate attempt to stop myself from thinking about Ash Dancer and the kids. "I think it's true love with you guys, too. I saw it when he rescued you from the Rebels."

Amorette's face lit up with a warm smile. "He does. I love him, too."

"I hope to be lucky like that one day," I said, coaxing myself to take another sip of coffee while forcing my brain to stop thinking about Thayn and what could have been between us if things had been different.

"I think you're going to be the one to melt that wall of ice around Mez," Amorette declared, nearly causing me to spray coffee out of my nose.

"I don't think so." I laughed, once the shock wore off. "I think I'm more likely to make that ice wall stronger. Every time he's around me, his life ends up in jeopardy somehow."

"Oh, I'm sure that will wear off eventually," she said with an all-knowing chuckle.

"I'm glad you think so." I smirked and then sighed. "In all seriousness, I do hope he finds a good person to love. He's a great guy, and he's got a good heart. He should have happiness in his life."

"He has found a good person to love. He just hasn't realized it yet. Or maybe he has realized it, and he just hasn't told you." She sipped her coffee again looking pleased with her assessment.

I rolled my eyes and shook my head at her. I knew Mez liked me as a friend. Maybe he'd taken a little extra interest in me because he probably felt like he owed me for saving his life. But romance wasn't in the cards for us. For one, as I'd already told Asimara, he was way out of my league, and two, I was committed to finding my way back to Earth. Even Mez knew that.

Amorette only grinned at my reaction, but it quickly fell off her face when she glanced at the wall. "Oh Goddess! Is that the time? I need to take some food over to Remms. Want to come with me?"

I followed Amorette's gaze to the wall and saw what I finally realized – for the first time in my nearly four weeks of living on Qarradune – was a clock. The bizarre round device looked nothing like the clocks on Earth. Instead of numbers it had symbols I didn't understand, and instead of hour, minute, and second hands, a viscous green liquid slowly dripped into a labyrinth of channels, gradually filling the ant-farm-like pathways until it reached the various equally spaced symbols along the way.

That is the craziest looking clock I've ever seen.

Truth be told, it wasn't the first time I'd seen the contraption. I'd encountered it before on the Kavylak ships and in Mez' office but had never given it a second thought. I'd always assumed it was some sort of freaky pro-Kavylak Military art. I mean, seriously, why would I have ever thought *that* was a clock.

"Uh, sure. I wouldn't mind seeing Remms again to find out how he's doing." I was glad for the invite. I did want to see Remms again. I had only met him briefly, but in the short time we spent together, I liked him immensely.

"Great! I'm sure he'll appreciate the company. He can't get out right now, so he's likely pretty lonely."

I nodded, remembering that when I'd first met Remms, he'd told me that when he used his skill to heal others, it took a lot out of him. Since Mez looked like he was totally healed from his People-of-the-North-tree-hanging-back-whipping-nightmare experience, and I assumed Keavren was, too, I could only imagine how weak Remms must have been feeling.

Amorette and I finished our coffees and set them on the tray.

"All set?"

"Let's go," I replied, standing and heading over to my shoes. Thankfully, they were mostly dry when I slid my feet into them.

After taking the coffee tray to the kitchen, Amorette returned with an opaque, covered container and opened the front door. I followed her out, waiting for her as she locked it behind us.

It was a short trip to Remms' quarters as he lived only a few doors down. Amorette knocked. We waited a minute, but there was no response. Amorette knocked a second time and then turned the knob, opening the door enough so that she could pop her head inside.

"Remms?" she called quietly.

"I'm here," returned his faint reply.

Taking that as her cue, she pushed the door open the rest of the way and entered, beckoning me to follow.

I stepped into Remms' apartment and was shocked by its lavish appearance. At first glance, it seemed to be the identical layout to Amarogq and Amorette's apartment. However, unlike their apartment – which had a very homey and welcoming feel - Remms' looked like it was staged and ready to sell on Kavylak's real estate market.

From the vibrant trellis-pattern area rug to the sleek modern coffee table to the matching contemporary sofa and chairs – even right down to the shiny teal throw pillows and complementary wall art – there was no doubt in my mind that every single item and piece of furniture in that room had been carefully selected and deliberately arranged to create the perfect look, without taking up unnecessary room.

It was all very chic and high-end home décor stuff.

Okay. Wow! I guess being a Warrior pays well.

"Want to go in and see him while I put this in the kitchen? I'll only be a moment."

"Sure," I replied to Amorette, happy to stop my gawking. She smiled and pointed me in the direction of his bedroom, and I approached the open door, giving it a light warning knock before entering.

"Hey, Remms. It's Megan. Mind if I come in?" I spotted him sitting in a large deep-red chair in the corner of his room. He had a soft and fuzzy elegant dark grey blanket drawn up around himself.

He gave me a little wave with his fingertips. "Hi, Megan," he said, sounding pleasantly surprised to see me. That said, beyond his little wave, he didn't make a move to rise to greet me. I doubted that he would have had the energy if he'd wanted to.

I was surprised by his appearance. Remms had dark circles under his eyes, looked sickly, and was far thinner than he had been when I'd last seen him. In fact, he was so thin that the bones of his face and hands were much too defined. He wasn't just thinner. He was verging on alarmingly gaunt.

Not wanting to stare and make him think that I was judging his appearance, I forced my eyes to sweep across the bedroom, which was, not surprisingly, just as fashionable as his living room. My envious eyes trailed over his grand king-size bed, sucking in all its splendor and promise of a good night's rest, until they spotted, staring back at me, a small black cat with a sparkly teal rhinestoned collar.

I would know those bright blue, curiosity-filled eyes anywhere.

"Pounce?"

Chapter 7

Irys

"Thank you for your generosity," Rakej spoke up in a tone that suggested that he felt the Raider woman was indeed being kind-hearted with her offer. "I have two full meals' worth of food and a religious text that I would gladly share with you for your mercy." From the look of the bald Lhador monk who was seated on a horse with only small packs, I believed that this was likely everything he was carrying.

The Raider woman gave Rakej a stone-faced look before breaking into loud laughter. "I'm looking for something a little more valuable than that," she said and allowed her eyes to glide over to Rrokth. I resisted the urge to hang onto him as though I would be able to stop her from taking him away.

"You have not come across a group with great material wealth. We value our meals and the wellness of our bodies and spirits. We have no coin or jewellery," Rakej explained calmly as though the Raider had not suggested that we could trade Rrokth for our lives.

"We're not trading a Sefaline or anyone else, for that matter," Kaiwa stepped in, clearly taking a more direct route than the monk. "Either try your best to kill us or get out of our way."

I decided that should we encounter Raiders again, I hoped Kaiwa would not be the person to speak for us.

"I really do think that's best," Lida said, clearly disagreeing with my perspective on negotiation strategy. "None of us are interested in wasting any more time here."

Rakej shrugged. "The lunch I would have traded was a very good one."

The Raider looked entirely unimpressed with having been met with sarcasm. "And who is this you have all tied up?" she asked, looking newly amused at the sight of Acksil lying over the back of Lida's horse. "He looks handsome enough. If you aren't willing to part with the Sefaline, I'll settle for a strong slave."

"He is not for sale," I said, impressed with the danger I could hear in my own voice. I wasn't about to give Lida the opportunity to make any repulsive decisions.

Lida, for her part, looked at me as though I'd said something ridiculous. Rakej raised the place where his right eyebrow would have been if he'd had one. I couldn't tell if he was impressed or if he thought I was as foolish as Lida did.

"Oh? And why is that, Princess? Is he already your slave?" The Raider woman most certainly found me amusing. Apparently, she hadn't thought I sounded nearly as dangerous as I had.

"He is mine," I replied firmly but vaguely. I didn't condone slavery, but if that was what it took for me to take control over Acksil's situation, then I would allow this Raider to assume what she might.

"Then perhaps I'll take you both," she said decidedly, her grin widening. Nodding to her companions, she instructed, "Take the sharp-tongued princess and the tied one. My father will like the look of her face, and I like the look of his."

Great Goddess, what have I done?

Rrokth must have been able to tell that I was trembling as I continued holding onto him. I had every reason to believe that the Raiders intended to take both Acksil and me away, particularly as the men drew their large, ugly weapons and approached us. I wasn't sure how far the Rebels were willing to go to keep us safe.

Without any warning, Kaiwa sprang from her horse, drawing her sword mid-air and landing on one of the Raiders. She drove her blade directly through his chest, and it reappeared from his back, coated in a crimson glaze. With an additional push, she shoved him off his horse, withdrawing her sword as though slipping it through silk and not the body of a large man. At the same time that she was ready to take on another Raider, I was battling with a faintness that caused my head to spin.

At precisely that moment, everyone but Rrokth burst into action. Rrokth's eyes were on the entire scene, flicking from one person to the next. It was clear that he had taken it upon himself to guard me. I knew he would move if one of his companions needed his assistance, but until then, I was being kept safe.

The Raiders were very strong and well armed. They were capable fighters, but the Rebels were skilled and quick, particularly Kaiwa. She moved as though not bound by the same restrictions as the rest of us. Her feet were light, and her balance was flawless.

From her position on the dead Raider's horse, she crouched a little and vaulted onto her next target. It was clear that he, like me, had underestimated Kaiwa's abilities, never having imagined that she could jump that far and with such ease. While still in the air, she shifted positions so that her sword was ready to glide across his throat as she landed on him. He was dealt the fatal blow at precisely the same moment he realized that she was coming his way. I suppressed a gag.

Lida seemed determined to take part and rode her horse - with Acksil still lying across its back – toward the remaining male Raider. She'd seen her opportunity. That man was watching Kaiwa, expecting her to take a third leap, toward him this time. He neither realized that Lida was approaching him nor that Rakej was right behind her.

I kept my eyes on Acksil. He'd been watching me but turned his gaze forward when Lida decided to attack. He didn't look afraid.

Lida rode skillfully, drawing her short sword. She brought the sword down and it connected sharply against the Raider's jagged blade. He grinned at her, showing his filthy teeth. He was going to kill her. She'd made her move and failed and now he would overpower her. He believed it and so did I.

Lida's expression of disgust and rage never changed. The Raider drew back his sword, and I shut my eyes, holding my breath to stifle a scream. After a moment, I opened my eyes again. I'd heard nothing. I'd expected to hear her scream. I'd expected the sound of her body falling to the ground. Instead, the Raider seemed frozen, his blade held aloft, and a look of shock on his face.

What happened?

Kaiwa wasn't there. Rakej had held back. Lida's sword was clean. I glanced at Acksil, but he was still lying on the horse as he had been. Then, I spotted it. Lida moved her hand from the man's middle. I hadn't even realized that it had been there. In his gut, the hilt of a dagger protruded. She'd somehow stabbed him with a second blade, while he'd been focused on the first.

All three male Raiders were subdued, two were most certainly dead. Only the woman remained. For a solid moment, I felt the Rebels' victory with them. That is, until the only living male Raider brought down his raised weapon hand. Roaring in pain, he clubbed Lida in the back with the hilt of his sword. She fell forward against her mount's neck, and I gasped. Even injured, I imagined that the Raider could place a great deal of force behind his swing.

Lida pushed herself up, properly seated in the saddle again, facing him proudly. Rakej rode immediately up to her, raising his foot and using it to give the Raider a sharp shove off his horse.

I turned my attention to the woman Raider to avoid watching the man as he took his last breaths. She turned and rode off on her horse, galloping as hard as she could. The Rebels didn't chase her.

Rrokth gave a growl at the sight of her departure. I could only assume that he disapproved of her choice to abandon her cause.

By the time I turned back to the Raider this time, Rakej was on the ground with him and had sent the man's soul to its next destination. I was grateful to have missed the event itself. There had already been far too much death, and I'd seen far too much of it.

The Rebels didn't seem to struggle with it as I had. Kaiwa and Mr. Dimog quickly dismounted and started looting the dead Raiders' supplies, taking anything of value off the bodies and their horses. I held more tightly to Rrokth, relieved to be able to breathe in his scent to distract my senses from the metallic smell of blood that was filling the air.

"There are enough horses for you to have your own," Mr. Dimog said, walking toward Rrokth and me.

"Thank you," I replied, unsure as to whether or not riding alone was a good idea when I'd felt so much safer riding with Rrokth.

"You can continue riding with me. You are protected with me. We will change horses before this one tires," Rrokth said, looking over his shoulder at me.

"That's very kind of you. I'd like that," I replied, hoping my appreciation was adequately conveyed in my voice.

"If you can ride on your own, Irys, you should. We will need to make better time and leave that Raider's territory before she thinks about returning," Mr. Dimog said.

Thank you for the reminder, Great Goddess. I must stand on my own feet.

"I don't want to delay us. I will ride on my own," I agreed, looking to Rrokth. "Thank you again."

Out of the corner of my eye, I could see Lida rotating her shoulder on the side the Raider had struck her.

"Are you alright?" Acksil asked, watching her.

"Shut up," she snipped at him and looked over at Mr. Dimog. "Did they have anything other than horses to take?

"A bit of money. Not much else," Mr. Dimog replied.

"The woman must have been carrying anything of value they'd had," said Lida.

Rrokth dismounted our horse and held his arms up to help me down. I was grateful to take his assistance.

"You have a nice voice," he said bluntly as my feet met the ground.

I smiled up at him. "Thank you. I'm glad you enjoyed my little humming."

We walked together toward a horse that had belonged to one of the deceased Raiders. Taking his assistance again, I mounted the new horse, trying to tell myself that the saddle was warm from the horse and not from its previous rider.

"Will you please ride close to me while we travel?" I asked him, hoping to enjoy some of the comfort from his protection while I travelled on my own horse. "I will hum to you when I can if you'd like," I added with a cute smile.

"I will," was all he said before mounting his horse once again. Shortly after, he walked his horse up next to mine.

Taking a moment to glance at Acksil again, I met his eyes and caught Lida stealing a look at him as well. As far as I could tell, he was unaware of her.

"You doing alright, Irys?" he asked, his voice strained and bouncing to the rhythm of the horse's gait. How much longer could they continue treating him this way? How much longer could he continue hiding the pain he must have been feeling?

"Yes. Thank you. I'm alright," I assured him. I then decided that if the Rebels weren't going to do something about Acksil's pain, I would. I was finished waiting.

Looking over to Rrokth, who was riding directly next to me, I addressed him. "We would move faster if he were seated upright and tied to his own horse, instead of weighing down Lida's mount." I kept my voice even and my words direct in the same way he usually addressed me.

"Yes," he responded. "We would." He directed the second part of his response toward Lida.

She scowled but slowed her horse to a stop. Rrokth did the same, and I followed suit. Huffing, Lida dismounted and walked around her horse, first untying Acksil from the horse, then untying his feet from each other. She grabbed hold of his belt and gave him a swift yank, pulling him down to the ground. Under other circumstances, I'm sure Acksil would have landed on his feet. However, after having been laid over the horse since he regained consciousness, he was surely not at his best. He tipped to the ground, twisting to the side to land on his shoulder instead of his face as his hands were still tied behind him.

"Get up," she said unfeelingly.

He did, without a word or even an expression of complaint.

"I'm going to untie your hands. If you try anything, I'll kill you," she informed him.

"I understand," he replied, holding her gaze.

Untying his hands, she nodded to the extra horse that had been trailing her own. "Get on your horse," she commanded and handed him the reins.

Obediently, he mounted his horse. Once he had, she proceeded to tie his ankles to his stirrups. He didn't attempt to stop her.

"If you do anything that looks like you are trying to cut, untie, or otherwise escape your bindings, I will kill you. I don't care if you're just trying to scratch your leg. If your hands move anywhere near those ropes, you will die," she informed him.

"I understand," he said again as he had before.

Lida returned to her horse and mounted it again.

Acksil looked far better now that he was sitting up and riding normally. He gave me a nod which bolstered me. I hadn't done much, but I'd done that. I'd stopped waiting for things to happen and opened my mouth to make a difference; and it had.

I nodded to him in return and as soon as the others started to ride, I did as well. They rode hard this time, and I kept up, adapting well to riding astride and feeling proud of my progress. Throughout it all, Rrokth stayed close to me, riding beside me when he could and only just ahead of me when he could not.

We rode and rode until my thighs burned, then ached, then screamed. I bit my lip, then my cheek, then clenched my teeth. Tears filled my eyes, then the wind dried them. Then, as I wondered how I could continue to bear it and prayed until I could think of no other way to beg the Great Goddess for strength, Mr. Dimog spoke up.

"We'll rest up here," he said.

The Rebels all dismounted and went about arranging things to allow us to rest up for a while. Rakej took his horse and Lida's toward a nearby stream to water them. Lida approached Acksil and began untying him.

"If you try anything, I'll kill you," she said to him.

"Yes, Lida. I know." Despite Acksil's obedience until now, it was clear that he was becoming frustrated with the threat.

She narrowed her eyes at him but finished untying him. "Get off and water your horse before you take anything for yourself."

Turning his head, he fixed a look on her for a long moment before dismounting and taking the reins. Instead of walking directly to the stream where Rakej had gone, he guided his horse to me.

"How are you holding up, Irys?" he asked.

Unwilling to speak to him from up on my horse, I brought both my legs to one side of my saddle and lowered myself ungracefully to the ground. After all the riding, I was surprised that my legs were able to hold me and that I didn't immediately drop to the ground. I clung to the stirrup for support until I felt I could balance on my own.

"I'm managing," I said with a quirky smile. I certainly didn't have the right to complain if he didn't do it first. "I'm glad you were permitted to ride normally. This would have been an impossible distance as you were." Taking the reins, I slowly walked my horse toward the stream, hoping he would walk with me and prevent Lida from getting frustrated with him for taking too long to obey her instructions.

Rrokth watched every move we made, so I gave him a nod and a smile to tell him I was safe and happy. Still, I knew that if Acksil were to make a move Rrokth didn't like, the Sefaline would be right there to protect me.

"That's all thanks to you. I owe you one, Dollface," he said with a playful wink.

"We're even," I replied with a grin.

When we reached the stream, the horses drank long. I stroked my horse's neck and shoulder.

"We still have quite a bit of travel left," Acksil pointed out.

I nodded, accepting that I would need to be able to continue riding far more than we already had. Withdrawing a handkerchief, I held it under the water in the stream, wrung it out, and dabbed my face with it. I was desperate to feel clean again. At the very least, I needed to wash as much of the road and horse from my face as I could.

"I don't know if I've ever felt this tired," I confessed with a smile to him. "I'm not sure how I will remain awake for the rest of our journey."

"You'll have to sleep some time. You can't avoid it. When you sleep, I'll keep watch over you. If you seem to be having a nightmare, I'll wake you."

I was relieved to know he understood my concern. I wasn't worried about being able to sleep. I was worried about being unable to resist sleeping and falling into one of my toxic nightmares, only to wake changed.

"I'm afraid I'll fall asleep on my horse."

"You can trust Rrokth. Sefaline don't play games with honesty."

"I do trust him. He has been very kind to me."

"You are talking about me," said Rrokth, stepping up to us. "What are you saying?"

"We were agreeing that you can be trusted to be honest," I informed him, feeling proud that this was the truth. "We were saying that if I were to be afraid of falling asleep and falling from my horse, I would be safe riding with you."

"You would be safe riding with me," Rrokth agreed. "Do you need sleep? If you do, you should ride with me when we go."

"I don't want to sleep," I confessed. "I have nightmares."

"What sort of nightmares?" I hadn't realized that Kaiwa was near, but she'd clearly heard everything we were saying. I wondered if she had been in one of the nearby trees before revealing her presence.

I considered how much of the truth I should reveal. I glanced over at Acksil, debating whether I should tell these people about our suspicions about Xandon. Would they even believe me? I suspected they would deem me a madwoman.

"I have nightmares about my captors in Kavylak," I said, deciding that a truth was appropriate, but a partial one was best.

Kaiwa studied me, narrowing her eyes as though she were trying to figure something out.

"We all have nightmares from time to time," she said but spoke slowly as she asked, "What aren't you saying?"

She could tell I was withholding the details. I felt guilty, though I didn't know why.

"I have them nearly every time I sleep. They're turning my hair white," I explained, indicating the streaks in my hair. I took a breath to build my courage. Letting it out, I breathed the words I dreaded. "I have nightmares of Xandon. I believe he is causing them."

At the sound of Xandon's name, all the Rebels I could see turned their heads to look at me. It seemed I'd spoken considerably louder than I'd thought. They looked from me to Acksil and back to me again. My cheeks burned with a deep blush.

"It's true," Acksil said, addressing everyone, not just Kaiwa. "It's why I helped her escape. I'm trying to get her as far away from Xandon as possible."

Kaiwa looked unimpressed. "I find it difficult to believe that you would want to betray Xandon. Or is betrayal simply your nature, Nydo?"

"I find it hard to believe you would do anything for anyone but yourself," Lida added, arms crossed.

"I know I haven't done anything to earn your trust or respect, but I'm being honest with you. Xandon is not who I thought he was. He is dangerous, and not just to Irys," he told her. I believed him, but doubted Lida did.

"We could have told you that, even back then. You're more of a fool than I thought you were. Here I thought you were just selfish," she said in a voice laced with disdain.

Mr. Dimog took this opportunity to step in. "Will he come after her? After you?" He seemed far more open to believing Acksil than Lida was.

"I believe he will, yes," Acksil nodded to Mr. Dimog. "I've bought us a few days, but if we don't continue to move, he will find us."

"Please don't let him catch up to us, Mr. Dimog," I begged, hoping to remind these Rebels that while they may consider Acksil to be a traitor, he wasn't the only person at risk.

Mr. Dimog frowned. "I have no intention of doing that, Irys. We would be in as much danger as you if Xandon's people were to reach us."

"Thank you." I was flooded with relief.

"Will he send Warriors?" Mr. Dimog directed his question to Acksil.

"Yes. He will likely send his trackers, like Fhurrk, Ioq'wa, or Terredge."

I knew this would upset Rrokth, and his low snarl confirmed it. Kaiwa reached out and gave his arm a supportive squeeze. That seemed to be enough to soothe him. I wished that there was something that could soothe my own gnawing fear. I recognized only Lieutenant Fhurrk's name, but I knew that if the others were Warriors, their skills were not to be taken lightly. It upset me to think that Lieutenant Fhurrk and I might have to face each other again, but as enemies. It terrified me to think that he might be only one of several powerful enemies that I would be facing. The danger was greater than I'd thought.

"Who is Terredge?" Mr. Dimog asked, clearly familiar with the other two Warriors with tracking skills.

"He's a Warrior we should all hope is not deployed on a mission to find me."

Mr. Dimog looked unimpressed with Acksil's reply.

"Why is he worse than the Sefaline Abomination?" demanded Lida. "Or than the one with the wolves, for that matter?"

"He's our assassin, and he never misses. We'll never see him coming. We won't have any warning." By the expression on Acksil's face, it was clear that he wasn't exaggerating.

Lida scoffed. "Rrokth will know he's coming. He can't hide from Rrokth's sense of smell. Why would they send an assassin, anyway? Are they trying to kill you and this woman?"

Acksil shook his head. "Rrokth won't have any more warning than the rest of us. Terredge is virtually invisible in nature. Not just to the eyes. In every way." He took a breath before releasing it. "They would send the assassin for me and likely anyone he didn't recognize but who appeared to be helping me. He would tranquilize Irys and bring her back to Capital City."

"Then we need to travel quickly," Rakej spoke up.

"Agreed," Mr. Dimog said as Kaiwa nodded to Rakej. "We rest and then we move."

I nodded, despite the fact that I didn't want to rest. I didn't want to risk falling asleep. Thoroughly rinsing my handkerchief in the water, I turned to Acksil.

"Could you use a quick face wash?" I offered the handkerchief.

"Thanks, Irys," He took it from me and left me feeling warmed as his hand brushed mine.

I thought of Dynan and how he held my hand in front of the fire in that abandoned Gbat Rher farmhouse. It baffled me that I could remember that moment so clearly and feel the sensation on my hand, even as he was on the far side of the world from me.

Great Goddess, how long will it be before I see him again? Please, return me to him. Let my heart be at ease. Allow us to begin our courtship so we may start a life together. There is only Chaos here. I don't belong in this place. Please, take me along your path and return me safely to my home. Please, protect these good people and keep their homes, too.

My fingers flicked the familiar sign of the Goddess as Acksil washed his face and rinsed out my handkerchief. I took it from him as he held it out to me. Instead of folding it, I tied it around the handle of my bag to give it a chance to dry.

We walked back toward the group. Their small fire was being extinguished, but I took a seat to stay out of the way and rest up a little before our next ride. I remained as far from the group as I politely could. It wasn't long before I could feel my eyelids drooping. I needed sleep. I wouldn't last long without it.

"I think I should ride with Rrokth, so he can wake me if I drift off. I don't want to sleep long enough to send any advantages if that's how this works," I said decidedly to Acksil. If Xandon was somehow communicating with my mind through my sleep, I would do my best to avoid actively providing him with directions to where we were.

"Yes," he replied, holding my gaze.

My eyes remained with his for an extended moment, though I hadn't been staring at him intentionally. As a result, I was startled when Lida abruptly walked up to him.

"Get on your horse so I can tie you. If you do anything…" the rest of her standard threat was implied.

Acksil allowed his eyes to linger on mine for a moment longer before shifting his attention to Lida and nodding his willingness to be tied on the horse.

Rising, I approached Rrokth. "May I?" I softly asked him, indicating his horse with a small tilt to my head.

"Yes." His reply was simple and punctuated with a nod. Without ceremony, he mounted his horse and reached down to help me up behind him. "Hold on to me. I will know if you sleep since your hold will slacken."

At one time, I would have felt scandalized by such an instruction. That time had long passed. Now, I was only grateful and gave him a smile to reflect that.

I leaned forward against him, holding on with my arms around his waist. He was warm and felt strong and stable, a balm in this state of confusion and fear.

"You are very cold," he informed me, rousing me a little.

"Next to you, I am," I agreed.

"No. Colder than those who are not Sefaline. You must not be well." His statement was matter-of-fact. There was no doubt in his mind.

"I think the coldness came with my changing hair colour. They seem to be related."

"There is a healing man where we are going. He should look at you."

"Thank you. That is a comfort."

"Hold on now. We ride."

At that, he turned his horse and the group moved out with us among them.

Chapter 8

Megan

I rushed up to the bed and scooped up my kitten, cuddling her to me. "Oh, Pounce! You're alright! I was so worried. I missed you so much!" Tears threatened to fall as I kissed her fluffy kitten cheek before holding her out in front of me to inspect her. She looked completely healthy, not a black or white fur out of place. The only difference was the new fancy collar she wore. Attached to it was a round silver tag with matching rhinestone. On the tag was the name: "Killer".

Pounce's piercing gaze observed me with a mixture of interest and boredom. Evidently, all the "I was so worried and missed you so much!" vibes were one-sided.

"Oh…"

Remms startled me when he spoke. I was so happy to have found Pounce and to know she was safe that I'd forgotten he was there. I turned to face him and hugged Pounce close again. She settled into my arms as she used to and purred as I stroked her fur.

"You think this is your missing cat?" Remms' voice was laced with concern. "How long did you say your cat was missing?"

"Since the night of the battle with Syliza. I dropped her during the fight."

Remms didn't question me further. I could tell from his devastated expression as he watched me with Pounce that he had accepted the awful truth that was now dawning on me in its full heart-crushing force. I had lost my kitten, and he had unknowingly purchased her. She was my "Pounce", but she was also his "Killer". We both loved her, but we couldn't both keep her.

"I guess...well...thank you for loaning her to me," Remms said, looking horribly sad. "She's really great, Megan."

"She is...and she was a very lucky girl that you found her."

Remms nodded and did his best to blink back tears, using the cuff of his burgundy satin pajama top to dab at his eyes.

I tried to swallow, wanting to say something that would really express how grateful I was that he'd rescued her, but could accomplish neither. I felt just awful. This was not how I imagined my reunion with Pounce would be. I should have felt only overjoyed that I had found my kitten and not like I was ripping her away from someone who seemed to love her as much as I did.

This sucks! Why can't I catch a break? First, I had to say goodbye to Thayn, then I nearly got killed by some psycho ice-queen, and now this? I don't want to give up Pounce, but if I take her from Remms, I'll feel like a monster!

Frowning, I looked at Pounce, who stared back with her big, round blue eyes. I was reminded of other big, round blue eyes I'd seen recently: Major Tovash. An idea struck me.

"You know, Remms," I began, "I'll be starting work tomorrow, and I'll be gone all day long. If you're just going to be here resting up, I'd really appreciate it and feel better if you'd keep her company. That way, I don't have to leave her by herself for hours."

He looked at me, surprised by my offer. Tears fell from his eyes, and he nodded. His lips curved upward. "Yes. I'd really like that."

I smiled.

Hah! Take that, evil Qarradune! Trying to get me down! Positive power! Pew-pew-pew!

"Great! Actually, would you mind if she stayed with you now until I'm done work tomorrow? I need to stay out of my apartment for the time being because of the whole Rebel situation."

"Sure," he said eagerly.

I kissed Pounce's head and drew back, startled by the smooth rounded lump that connected with my lips.

Oh my gosh! She does have horns!

I ran my fingers over her head and discovered that there were indeed two horns just growing in on the top of her skull. I wondered how big they'd get. I gave her one last stroke before holding her out to Remms, who eagerly took her, holding her close. Pounce, for her part, immediately rubbed her cheek against Remms' face, purring up a storm, further proving to me that I'd made the right choice.

"Thank you," he said to me with relief.

"Thank *you*. I really am so glad you found her, Remms. Now that I know she's been with you for almost the whole time, it's a load off my conscience. I want you to know that you can spend time with her whenever you want. She clearly loves you."

"I guess I'll call her Pounce from now on," he said with a crooked smile. "Maybe Killer could be her secret middle name."

"Pounce Killer Wynters-Neajet. It has a certain charm to it," I joked with a chuckle as if we had joint-custody of a kitten. Remms laughed, gazing adoringly at Pounce.

Amorette cleared her throat behind us to announce her presence. "I put some soup in your kitchen for you Remms. You just have to heat it when you want it." From the "awwwwww" expression on her face, she'd obviously been listening in the doorway to our conversation for quite some time. I didn't mind. She was a good friend for not interrupting us sooner.

"Thank you, Amorette," Remms said with appreciation before looking slightly wary. "It doesn't have any of Amarogq's dried meat in it does it?"

"No!" Amorette declared with a grin. "I like you, Remms. I'd never do that to you!" Remms jokingly wiped his forehead with the back of his hand in a "*phew*" motion.

I had to laugh as I remembered the first time I'd tried the dried meat to which Amorette and Remms were referring. Amarogq had given me some of it to try on the ship that had first sailed me to Kavylak. He'd talked about how Amorette, whom I hadn't yet met, hated it. Personally, I didn't think it was that off-putting, although I still stood by the opinion I had formed then: it would never be my favourite snack.

"Will it take you long to get back on your feet, Remms?" I asked.

"A few days. I can't cook, though, so nice people help me out." He smiled at Amorette and then yawned, while Pounce made herself comfortable, curling into a ball on his chest.

Amorette stepped up to Remms and kissed his forehead, giving his hair a gentle stroke. "We'll let you get some rest, Remms."

"I will," he promised, his eyes looking heavier by the second. "Pounce will take good care of me." He smiled sleepily at me.

I nodded with a grin and pointed a finger at the kitten. "Be good. No ripping his nice stuff like you did to Auntie Aésha's nice curtains." Pounce looked at my finger, cross-eyed, then yawned.

Remms giggled. "She said 'yes'."

Chuckling, I gave her horned head a final stroke and looked to Amorette, who nodded that she was ready to go.

"See you soon, Remms," Amorette said.

"Bye Amorette. I'll see you tomorrow, Megan."

"See you then."

Remms adjusted a little in his chair and cuddled in with Pounce and his blanket. I was sure the two of them were sound asleep by the time the door to his apartment latched shut behind us.

"Did you just loan him your cat?" Amorette asked as we walked back toward her apartment.

"Yeah. I couldn't take her from him. It'd be cruel," I admitted. "He's attached to her, and she clearly loves him. I'll be working tomorrow, so it only makes sense."

"You are just too nice." Amorette sounded pleased and impressed, and it made me feel better. It was hard to have Pounce back and then leave her behind. I missed her, and she was all I had that truly felt like mine on Qarradune. She had helped me get through the trauma of Rral's death, a very hard time in my life.

"He's certainly taking good care of her," she added. "Her new collar has more gemstones in it than anything Amarogq has bought me recently." She laughed playfully.

"Her new collar has more gemstones than anything I've ever owned! I'm going to have to tell Mez he really cheaped out on her original collar." Just like Amorette, I was being facetious. The collar Mez had surprised me with, which was his way of revealing to me that he was the one who'd secretly gifted her to me, was so thoughtful, so caring, so perfect...so Mez. It saddened me that, unlike Pounce, her original collar was likely lost.

"Speaking of that 'cheap' Mez, did you want to see if he's home or in his office?"

"Yes. I guess I should find him to see if he's learned anything new. Hopefully something's been figured out, so we can decide what to do with me."

"I'll walk with you there if you want. If he's not around, you can always stay with me or explore more of the building."

"Thanks, Amorette. I'll probably hang with you as long as I won't mess up your day."

"Not at all." She shook her head, stopping at Mez' door. She knocked and nothing happened, so we continued on our Mez-searching journey, heading toward his office.

"Does Amarogq work all day?" I asked Amorette as we made the climb to the fifth floor. "Does he have normal hours, or does he kinda work all over the place?"

"It depends on whether or not he's away on a mission."

That made sense. "So, what do you guys do for fun, when you don't have to work?"

She shrugged. "We head into the city sometimes. There's an Officer's Club for anyone who is or is with an officer, and there's a restaurant on the roof where we like to spend time, too."

I was slightly underwhelmed by her answer. I mean, I know we're not on Earth or in Canada where you can head out shopping, to the theater, café, amusement park, museum, or whatever, but none of those things she mentioned sounded like much fun. Okay, I might have thought differently about going into the city before my second Rebel encounter, but now...

Stop being so judgy, Megan. You asked.

"So, what do you do in the city? Are there any fun activities?"

Maybe there's more to it.

"I like shopping." She grinned. "We'll eat out or just walk around. It's got a few nice areas in it when you get away from the factories and the dockyards."

And the attacking Rebels...Megan! No judgments!

"Are there museums or theatres or anything like that?"

"There are specific types of museums dedicated to the power of Kavylak. There are educational centres that teach about Kavylak's history and might. There are theatres with some plays in town. They're not too bad."

Oh boy! Kavylak can tell me how awesome Kavylak is! Sounds like a thrilling afternoon! Forget it. All bets are off. I'm okay with judging Kavylak.

"Oh, and bars," Amorette tacked on. "Lots of bars. If you want a beer, you'll find one." She laughed.

I laughed, too. "Yeah, I'm sure once I'm the legal drinking age, I'll love that."

"Legal drinking age?" Amorette looked at me like I'd grown ten heads.

"Yeah. To drink legally..." I mirrored her expression.

"Why would you need to be old enough to drink?" She was genuinely confused, which equally confused me.

"How old do you have to be to legally consume alcohol in Kavylak?"

That question seemed to confuse her even more. "I'm sorry, old enough? Everyone can drink what they want if they want it. Why would age have anything to do with that?"

Um, what?

"You mean...there's *no* age drinking law?"

"You mean...there *is* an age drinking law where you come from?" Her light-hearted impression of me made me chuckle, but I stuck my tongue out at her all the same, and she grinned.

"Yes, where I come from, you need to be nineteen ye—cycles to legally consume alcohol."

"That's silly. What does being nineteen have to do with what you drink?"

I took a breath ready to respond, but you know, that was a good question. "Dunno, really. I guess it's an age when you're considered to be a responsible adult." I shrugged. "It's just the law, and when you can legally buy it."

"Well, here, if you want a beer, drink a beer."

Good to know. My eighteen "ye—cycles" doesn't matter here.

We arrived at Mez' office door and Amorette knocked.

"Is that an attractive knocker or an ugly knocker?" Mez asked from behind the door. I shook my head in amusement. He never failed to have something weird to say to the person knocking on his office door.

I looked at Amorette like, "He's nuts!" and she looked back at me like, "Well? Are you pretty or not?"

Sighing I said, "Maybe somewhere in between. What does that get me?"

"Which side would you say you lean toward more?"

"Well, I did just discover that my cat has prettier jewelry than I do, so I guess that makes me the ugly one between us."

"Oh, good." Mez sounded relieved. "I wanted to be the pretty one in the office today. Come in."

Amorette giggled and kissed my cheek. "See you later. I'll be at home."

"Thanks! See you later."

She headed off down the hall, and I opened Mez' office door, shutting it behind me.

"Hello, Lieutenant Pretty. I hope I'm not disturbing you."

Mez looked like the most relaxed person in the world. He was sitting at his desk with his feet up, crossed at the ankles, and was reading something on a clipboard he was holding. I noticed he wasn't wearing his uniform jacket at the moment, and more importantly, he was dry.

"Hmm, Lieutenant Pretty. I don't know how comfortable I am with that." He looked up at me from the clipboard. "You're not disturbing me. I just got in. I was looking over some schedules."

I nodded, walking up to his desk and seating myself in one of the chairs that faced it.

"Guess what?" I said excitedly. "I wasn't kidding about my cat. I found Pounce, and she really does look pretty. Remms bought her from a scrounger, and she's been with him this whole time. He even got her this collar with all these gemstones on it."

Mez smiled broadly. "That's very good news! I knew Remms had a new cat. I didn't realize I'd bought it for him." He chuckled. "I'm glad she's alright."

I laughed. "Me, too."

Feeling ready to switch gears I asked, "So, did you find out anything? Do you think I can return to my apartment now?"

He took his feet down, depositing the clipboard on the desk. "I think it would be best if you didn't." He reached behind where he was sitting, picked up a leather duffle bag, and set it on his desk. "I brought you some essentials. If I missed anything, I'll have it fetched from your place. I think it would be best if you stayed with Aésha."

"Aésha?" I didn't hide my surprise.

Mez nodded. "Unless there is someone else in the building you feel would be better. I just know you two are close. I also know it's safest for you if you're staying right there on the Warriors' floor."

"I don't mind staying with Aésha, but why is it suddenly so dangerous in the compound? Did you find out who it was that attacked us like that?"

He shook his head. "No, and that's exactly why it's dangerous. She seemed to be looking specifically for you. I don't like that thought. Until we know more, it seems wisest to me to keep you in the building. You can start work, use the facilities open to civilian workers here, and move about freely as you always have, but staying inside is recommended for now."

I frowned, not liking the sound of that one bit. "Have you talked to Xandon?"

"Not yet, but I intend to."

I nodded and debated revealing to Mez that I had remembered something about "Elindria", the name the woman had called me before encasing us in ice. At that time, there was too much going on for me to recall that it was a name I'd heard in a dream involving Xandon.

Should I tell him? I've already told him that I genuinely believe I'm an alien from another planet, and he didn't laugh me out of his office then, so he likely won't now. He probably won't be shocked if he knows I experience weird Xandon dreams, too. Don't be stupid, Megan. Tell him.

"I don't think that ice woman was specifically targeting me, Mez. She used the name Elindria. I've remembered that Elindria is someone Xandon knows. I know because I've dreamed about them, and someone else called Enadria," I added, deciding to reveal the other name I'd remembered from the dreams. "When you talk to him, can you tell him you heard her use the name Elindria? Maybe he'll know more about all this."

Mez listened carefully and jotted down the names I'd mentioned on a piece of paper. "I'll bring them up. It sounds like too much of a coincidence to ignore," he agreed, and I nodded, glad that he was taking me seriously, even though the idea of bringing this up with Xandon left me feeling deeply uneasy for a reason I couldn't quite define.

Mez leaned forward on his desk, a lock of his long, smooth, silver hair falling across his arm. "Megan, how long have you been having dreams about Xandon? Have there been many?" His tone was calm, but there was an intensity to the question. Based on his posture and tone, I could tell the answer mattered to him very much.

"For some time now," I confessed, shifting a little in my seat. "The first one I can remember happened when I was in Syliza, and the last one occurred when we were on our way back from the People of the North. That's the one I remember the most, which is why I can recall the names," I leveled with him. "I didn't bring it up until now because, well, I thought that they were just bad dreams." Looking at him nervously, I decided to make my last dream confession: "I remember Irys being in some of the dreams, too."

He considered my words thoughtfully but hadn't been looking at me directly as I spoke. Instead, he had that "staring off into the distance" look people get when the wheels in their minds are turning, while they process information that they're taking seriously, but when they haven't yet figured out how all the pieces fit to complete the puzzle.

Finally, his gaze shifted to meet mine. "Did it happen when I was trying to help you remember with my skill, and you fainted?" It was more of a statement than a question. There was no doubt in his eyes. It didn't surprise me he'd figured that one out. Mez was clever and super-perceptive.

"Yes," I confirmed. "It happened then. That was the second time."

He nodded. "Do you remember what was happening to Irys or what she was doing?"

I shook my head. "I don't recall what was happening to Irys. The person I saw didn't even look like Irys. I just *knew* it was her. I know how silly that sounds, but with these dreams, it's not so much the visual that I remember, but the feelings." I paused, wrapping my arms around myself, feeling a chill creeping up into my bones as it did any time I thought about the dreams. "The feelings are very powerful, and they aren't usually good feelings. They're feelings of heart-wrenching sadness, longing, regret, betrayal, anger...hatred." My gaze met Mez'. "Extreme hatred toward Xandon."

I closed my eyes for a moment to let the intense emotions pass. Opening them, I refocused on Mez. "Before today, I just thought that maybe the dreams were because I was angry at Xandon for everything that's happened with Irys and me, you know?" I shrugged a little, trying to brush off the eerie, dark feelings. "Maybe that's all it is."

Mez nodded silently, looking thoughtful again, his brow furrowed slightly in concentration. "Perhaps," he said but didn't elaborate beyond that. I could tell there was still more processing going on in his mind and that he wasn't ready to share any hypotheses or conclusions he might have drawn. "Still," he added, "if it happens again, please try to remember as much as you can and tell me about it. The fact that you heard those names isn't something to be ignored."

I nodded and his expression softened.

"Are you alright, Megan?"

Realizing I was shaking, I took a couple of breaths to calm myself and relaxed my body-hugging posture. "Yes, I'm as alright as I've been and can be. Don't worry, Mez, I'll be staying with Aésha." I grinned. "Soon, I won't remember that there's anything I should be worried about," I joked to lighten the mood.

"I tell you what. I'll do everything I can to make this building as pleasant a luxury resort for you as possible. Of course, staying with Aésha will already have taken care of a lot of that," he said sharing my grin. "But I will make sure that you always have activities available to you, and if you let me, I would like to take you to dinner tomorrow night."

"You want to take me to dinner?" I blurted, shocked, instantly forgetting about the ice woman, Xandon, and the whole ugly Rebel business.

"You're surprised?" He looked at me with genuine curiosity filling his usually self-assured blue eyes.

"Yes. I was expecting coffee, not dinner." A smile tugged at my lips.

He chuckled. "I'd intended to take you to coffee, but if I'm trying to make this building seem appealing, coffee seems like a low target to aim for."

"I appreciate that, but I hope you don't feel that you have to go out of your way for me just 'cause some psycho ice queen wants to freeze me to death."

Oh my gosh! I think Mez actually *wants to have dinner with me!*

Mez smiled warmly at me. I loved that smile. Not only because it lit up his whole face, but because I felt like I was seeing the man beyond the Warrior. The one his late wife probably knew.

"Megan, I'd greatly enjoy having dinner with you tomorrow night if you'd be interested in joining me. I'd hoped to do this with you. Skipping 'boring coffee' gave me a good excuse."

Ahhhh! He does want to have dinner with me! Okay. Act cool, Megan.

"I'm interested."

That's a little too cool.

"What I mean is, I'd like that very much." I smiled.

Bingo!

"Wonderful! I'll meet you after work tomorrow." He sounded pleased, and I had to resist the urge to clap.

"Okay. Should I come here or meet you at your place?"

"I'll meet you. Just remain find-able."

"No problem. I'll wander around in a very obvious way. I'll flap my arms a lot, so you can easily spot me."

He laughed, no doubt at the mental image I'd just given him. "On the other hand..."

I grinned, liking that I'd made him laugh. Making Mez laugh like that felt like an incredible accomplishment.

Mez sighed. "I'd better get back to work. Let's see if Aésha is home."

I nodded. "I can check that myself if you want. I mean, I know you're busy, and I do know where she lives."

"I get it. Tired of me already. I knew I wasn't pretty enough today." He flashed me a goofy smile.

"Oh, we both know you're the prettier one between us." Standing, I reached for the bag on Mez' desk. "Thanks for grabbing some of my stuff for me."

Mez stood, reaching out at the same time as me and rested his hand over mine on the bag's handle. I looked at him, feeling my face flush from his gentle contact.

"I'm sure this will be over soon. If you need anything else, just say."

"Thanks, Mez. I will. I know you're here for me." I knew that he was, and I wanted him to know that I knew it and appreciated it.

He nodded and released my hand, walking to the door and opening it for me.

Knowing I should let the man get back to work, even though I secretly wished I could spend more time with him, I picked up the bag and headed for the door. "See you later, Mez."

He smiled. "Looking forward to it."

I could feel myself blushing again and decided to make a quick escape, not even glancing back as I made my way down the hall and then down the stairs to the fourth floor. I was certain that if I hadn't hightailed it out of there, I would have hugged him.

I knew it wasn't odd to hug him, I'd done it before. The problem was, this time, I was sure that if we'd embraced, I wouldn't be eager to let go. In fact, I couldn't lie to myself, I would want it to go further. There was no denying it. I liked Mez. My burning cheeks, rapid heartbeat, and the overall buzz I felt from my head to my toes as I thought about him was more than proof.

I really, really, *really* liked Mez.

I honestly didn't know if he felt the same way about me, but sometime between the People of the North and now, I'd forgotten what it was like to think of him as just a friend. To make things even more confusing, I would also have been lying to myself if I'd said I didn't still have feelings for Thayn. When I thought about him it hurt, and not in the way it hurt to miss Cole. My feelings for Thayn, like those for Mez, were something much different; they were not platonic or familial.

Was it possible to feel romantic feelings for two men – two very different men – at the same time?

I supposed it was possible, but I didn't like it, and I didn't want to think about it anymore. I'd have to ask Aésha her thoughts on it at some point and hopefully catch her in a mood that resulted in her honest opinion and not her typical innuendo-filled comments or advice.

Unable to stop the smile from spreading across my face, I felt a little more cheerful at the thought of spending some time with Aésha. I was looking forward to being her roomie for a while again and wondered what her apartment looked like compared to the quarters she had decorated on the ship.

There was no time like the present to find out. Reaching her door, I knocked eagerly, preparing myself to be smitten with my Charmer friend.

Chapter 9

Irys

I drifted in and out of consciousness as we rode, though I never fully fell asleep. It was hard to tell how long we'd been riding, but I imagined it had to have been a couple of hours at the very least. As the horses slowed, I blinked back into alertness once again.

"The bridge is flooded," Kaiwa said darkly, accusingly, as though the bridge would pay for its poor decision making.

Panic rose in my chest. I watched Rakej jump down from his horse and pick up a stick to poke at the bridge through the water, testing the depth of the flooding. He shook his head.

"We will have to wait it out," Kaiwa concluded.

"We can't wait it out. That could take days, depending on the weather," Acksil stated as though his vote counted within this group.

I looked up to the sky, watching light white clouds in the shape of a latholi flower drift nonchalantly until they became a skydasher bird in flight. How easily they moved across the world while we were trapped here behind a flooded bridge.

"The water isn't moving very fast. We could try to swim across," Lida said before casting me a dark look. "Do princesses float?"

"It's possible," Kaiwa replied. "The water isn't rapid at all."

Rakej's face betrayed his doubt in this plan.

"I don't like the idea," Mr. Dimog said. "It's too much of a risk. I'm all for taking chances, but not if it means one of us - or our horses - will be swept away."

"Is there no other bridge within reasonable reach? Perhaps the river is shallower at another place, and we can ford it?" I asked in desperation. Turning to see what Acksil might think, I couldn't seem to capture his attention. He appeared to be lost in thought.

"No. We cannot do that," Rrokth responded decidedly before any other member of his group could speak.

"We have to," Acksil suddenly spoke up. "The rest of you stay here to wait out the flooding. Irys and I will continue on to go across where it is passable."

Lida scoffed. "You're our prisoners. You're not doing anything unless we tell you to."

"Lida, I'm willingly your prisoner. We both know that. If we stay with you long enough for the trackers to find us, you will be in grave danger. Irys and I can't just sit here and wait for the Warriors to arrive."

Lida fixed him with a deadly glare. "Then you stay here with Rrokth and I, and the princess can go ahead with the rest of the group."

"Going across farther up is just as suicidal as attempting to swim across here," Mr. Dimog cut in, addressing Acksil. "You'll be within Sefaline's borders."

"I'll take my chances with the Sefaline," said Acksil. At first, I thought he was being defiant. Then I realized that this was not at all the case. As dangerous as it may have been to enter Sefaline's territory, being caught by the Warriors would be infinitely worse.

"They will kill you the moment you step into their territory," Rrokth said. I could see flashes of his fangs as he spoke. "You are not just foreigners. You are a Warrior."

Instead of replying to Rrokth, Acksil directed his next statement to me. "Irys, I need you to make this decision. I swore to you that I would keep you safe. I'm telling you that staying here to wait for the waters to recede is very dangerous. Still, I will stay here if you want to stay. I will help you to swim it if you want to swim. If you want to go through Sefaline, that's where we will go."

My eyes widened involuntarily. Opening my mouth to speak, I was immediately cut off by Lida.

"It's not her decision to make. It's not yours either, Nydo." She spat his name at him like a curse. "I am not releasing you for this."

Acksil continued to look at me. It was as though Lida had not spoken. He was waiting for my decision.

"How long would it take us to enter and exit Sefaline's territory?" I asked, trying to inform myself to make this impossible decision.

"Long enough for them to sniff you out and shred you both," Lida supplied.

"If we ride quickly, maybe an hour, more or less," Acksil responded.

I looked to Rrokth for my next question. "If we ride as quickly as I am able, would they catch us?"

"They will catch you if they want to catch you," Rrokth said. This was little comfort and certainly didn't make my choice any easier.

"Will they want to?" I continued.

"A Rrathss might."

The word was certainly something from the Sefaline language and seemed to begin on a snarl and end on a hiss. I wasn't sure what to make of it. I only knew that I hoped there were none of these Rrathss anywhere near the Sefaline border we would be crossing.

"Is there nothing we can trade for safe passage?" It was Acksil's turn to ask Rrokth a question.

"No," Kaiwa contributed. "Don't you think we would trade with them if it were possible?"

"Can you not come with us?" I asked Rrokth as he was, in fact, Sefaline and knew the most about the country and its people.

"No," he said firmly. "I cannot go back there."

"Thank you for these answers. I trust you," I told him, but then addressed the group, looking at Acksil. "But I also trust Acksil. I know you must stay here and wait for the waters to recede or find some other way across that does not involve travelling into Sefaline. However, I feel that my best chances are to ride as hard as I can with Acksil and cross where the river can be crossed. Between Sefaline's territory guards and Xandon's Warriors, I am safer in Sefaline. At least that way I know I have not brought dangers on the rest of you. I thank you all for your hospitality and look forward to seeing you on the other side. We are all headed to the same destination after all."

Rrokth was the first to react, giving me a small nod that clearly accepted my choice if not my reasoning for it.

"Then you're going alone," Lida spoke up. "This prisoner is mine," she said and appeared to look to Rrokth for his support in the matter.

"Let them go, Lida. If this woman believes that what hunts her is more dangerous than entering Sefaline, I believe her. This is the right choice. It gives us all our best chances," Rrokth said decisively.

Though I had expected Lida to object, she appeared to withdraw her complaints.

"We'll give you enough food to make it to Storr," Rakej said, already digging through the saddlebags on his horse. "Hopefully, we won't be far behind you."

Mr. Dimog nodded his approval. Kaiwa was stone-faced, making it impossible to tell what she thought on the matter.

"Thank you," Acksil and I said to Rakej in unison. The blue tattooed Lhador monk added a few wrapped packets to Acksil's saddlebags and untied the former Warrior. The two men exchanged a meaningful nod.

"If you feel you are in danger from the Sefaline, sing," Rrokth said, looking at me over his shoulder.

"Sing?" I asked quizzically, thoroughly confused by the instruction. "Sing what?"

"Sing your music. Your voice is very pretty. Sefaline, especially Rrathss, like song and pretty sounds."

I nodded and gave him a tight hug from behind. I appreciated this man more than I could possibly have expressed. "Thank you, Rrokth. They were just lullabies. I'll sing those if I have to."

Acksil rode up next to us as I released Rrokth. "We'll ride together, Irys. We won't go as fast, but it will make sure we're never separated."

I nodded, unsure as to whether it was best for us to risk a slower trip for something that may not happen, but I was glad not to need to ride astride on my own, particularly while I was this tired.

"One horse," I agreed, showing that the decision was mine as much as his.

Just as I was about to dismount Rrokth's horse, he stopped me, whispering near my ear. "If you are caught, and you want to save his life, tell them he is your mate. Never mention that this man was a Warrior. Never mention the Sefaline Warrior. Never mention me."

"My mate," I confirmed in my own whisper. "I won't mention anyone. Thank you." I leaned up and kissed his cheek before he helped me down to the ground. I was immediately lifted up onto Acksil's horse behind him. I settled in, adjusting my bag so it wouldn't be in the way.

Rrokth looked to me and nodded firmly. It was as though I had passed an important test. That said, it surprised me when he then looked to Acksil. "You're a fool," he said to him with disdain.

Acksil simply nodded to Rrokth in return, as though accepting his assessment.

Out of the corner of my eye, I could see Lida's expression crawl into a satisfied grin.

"May the Goddess protect you with her Light," Mr. Dimog said to us in kind parting words. I liked and respected this man. He was a fine leader for this group and a solid balance among the personality extremes.

My fingers flicked the sign of the Great Goddess through the air. "And may She walk with you," I replied.

"Thank you," Acksil said to Mr. Dimog. "See you at Storr's." At that, we rode off without looking back. For a while, we rode along the swollen riverbank, but eventually steered into the woods, a vast labyrinth of light and darkness, as the afternoon sun's rays strobed between the leaves of the canopy.

"We'll see them again, Irys," Acksil said after an extended silence. "We're strong. We both are. We can make it through anything. We escaped Xandon. We escaped the Raiders. This will be easy in comparison."

"I hope so," I replied, holding on a little more tightly. I wanted to believe him. I focused on ignoring the dread that filled my marrow. Very soon, we would enter Sefaline and know whether my decisions would be our deaths.

Chapter 10

Megan

There was no response after my first knock, so I tried again. When there was still nothing, I decided to try the knob. While I wasn't exactly a fan of breaking and entering, this was Aésha's place. She must have agreed to my staying with her. Besides, I was only going to drop my bag off. I tried to turn the knob, but it wouldn't budge. It was locked.

Oh well, guess I'll just go hang with Amorette for a while until Aésha returns home.

Taking the few short steps to Amorette's door, I raised my fist to knock but froze it mid-air before letting the first strike fall.

Wait. What if Amarogq's home from work?

I let my hand fall to my side and took a step back from the door. The thought of seeing Amarogq was even less appealing than the thought of seeing Xandon. I wasn't ready to face him knowing what I knew about his family from the People of the North.

I thought of my other options. Amorette did say I could explore the building, and I never did officially say I'd meet up with her again right after I spoke with Mez, so she wasn't exactly waiting for me to show up. Maybe I'd just wander around for a bit, come back to see if Aésha had returned, and then say a quick "good night" to Amorette to keep the awkward Amarogq encounters to a minimum.

Feeling that this was the best plan, I decided the first stop along my journey would be to find out where I worked. I made my way to the second floor because that's where Amorette had told me it would likely be, and also because the woman who had given Asimara and me our passes had been wearing a uniform identical to the one I'd been given.

I took my time wandering down the second-floor hallway, so I could read the signs on the closed doors. It was much busier than it had been a few hours ago.

Navigating the bustling, dingy grey hallway at my pace while holding a bag, turned out to be more challenging than I had anticipated. Although I did my best to stay to one side and held my bag in front of me, I was bumped several times by people hurrying along in both directions. One soldier who forced her way around me, because I was clearly moving too slowly for her pace, spared a moment to shoot me a dirty look. To my surprise, it had zero effect on me. I had officially encountered enough nasty looks and been in enough bad situations on Qarradune that I had way bigger fish to fry than to worry about somehow ruining that woman's day.

Finally, my eyes fell on a door that had the word "TRANSLATION" written across it in the same bold steel letters that identified most of the doors in this building.

Well, that was fun. At least I know where I'll be heading tomorrow morning at the crack of dawn.

Mission completed, I debated heading into the library, which was easily the nicest spot on this whole level, with its floor to ceiling glass windows and door. Amorette had told me that it was two stories and the second level connected to the third floor. I wondered how many people cut through the library to avoid walking these halls. In the end, I decided that using the library in my current frame of mind would do very little to distract me from my Xandon dream-worries and my romantic confusions about Thayn and Mez.

I made my way to the first floor, propelled by a new idea of what to do and where to go. I could totally go for a swim. The last time I'd been swimming had been at the start of the summer – well, my summer back home – and the thought of slipping into a pool and enjoying the peace and relaxation I got from sinking under the water's surface, was exactly what I needed to clear my head.

It occurred to me as I approached the room that I had no idea if a swimsuit was one of the essentials Mez had packed in my bag. Come to think of it, I didn't even know if a swimsuit had been a part of the items Aésha had given me. Either way, I was determined to find something in my bag that would allow me to swim. Worst case, I could always just sit on the edge, roll up my pants and dip my feet in.

The door marked "POOL" was shut. Hoping the pool wasn't closed – and kinda hoping I wouldn't run into Dendeon, that water Warrior I saw on my first tour of the building yesterday with Amorette – I turned the handle. It wasn't locked, so I pushed the heavy door open and entered. It promptly banged shut behind me, causing me to jump as the sound left a haunting echo in its wake.

Looking around the room in a state of disbelief, I felt like I'd walked into an old-fashioned insane asylum and not a public pool facility. The walls were a glossy, stark institutional white, a colour that was particularly hard on the eyes under the bright fluorescent-style lights that hung from the ceiling. Since I seemed to be alone in the room, the only sound I heard was the droning buzz of the lights, one of which has flickering, adding to the overall, windowless, asylum-feel of the room.

Yikes! This place is in dire need of a fun-makeover.

To make things even weirder, the scent of salt sea water filled the air, which I assumed had to be coming from the two equally sized, large rectangular pools in the room, and the one small square pool, which I guessed was *maybe* a hot tub.

Oh my gosh! Are these pools filled with ocean water? I never thought I'd long for the smell of chlorine.

From where I stood, just inside the door, the pools looked identical except that the water of the one to my left was clear and the one to my right was a pale green, like it had algae growing in it or something.

Ew. I knew which pool I was going to risk swimming in.

Not wanting the room to spook me further and wanting to take advantage of the fact that I seemed to be alone, I darted to one of the open metal changing stalls to my left, and latched the door once I was inside. Setting the bag down on the shelf jutting out from one of the stall walls, I opened it and rifled through the contents.

To my pleasant surprise, I found Rral's ring and Irys' handkerchief among the packed items. Mez had said he'd brought me some essentials from my apartment, and it warmed my heart that he would include these in my bag. He must have guessed that they were important to me. That said, the bone dagger Ash Dancer had given me was nowhere to be found. While it, too, meant something to me, I supposed Mez didn't think it "essential" for me to have the weapon in the building, and truth be told, I was glad it wasn't in the bag. Right now, it was hard enough living in the same building as Amarogq. The last thing I wanted to do was carry around a physical reminder of his ex-wife.

Not surprisingly, there was no bathing suit, bikini, or hint of clothing that suggested swim-friendly material. Deciding to improvise with what I had, I stepped out of my pumps, stripped out of Amorette's pants and blouse, and threw on one of my black T-shirts. It was long enough to dust the top of my thighs, and I was still wearing my underwear underneath it, which consisted of the standard Kavylak boyshort-style panties and a bralette.

I figured this would be decent enough. After all, the people of Kavylak seemed a little more chill with seeing skin than Syliza, from what I'd seen. I shuddered to think what sort of weird swim getup was considered appropriate in that country.

Putting Amorette's clothes and my shoes in the bag, I left the stall, grateful that I was still alone. I hastily raked my fingers through my dried, messy hair to secure it into a low ponytail. Wandering out toward the pool with my bag, I saw that there was a long metal bench in front of a wall of open metal storage shelves. Each shelf contained a folded white towel. I approached the shelves and figured that this was where you could store your bag while you swam, and the towel in your shelf was free to use. There was also a large woven basket at one of the bench ends, which contained some damp unfolded towels, so I assumed you'd deposit your used towel there to be laundered.

Hey! Not bad! This is still the freakiest indoor pool I'd been to, but I can't say the military isn't organized.

I shoved my bag into one of the shelves, and that's when I noticed there was another shelf in use.

That's odd. I don't see anyone in here. Maybe they just forgot their stuff.

Shrugging to myself, I made my way over to the clear saltwater pool. Stepping up to the edge, I dipped my toe in, but then pulled it out immediately with a gasp. I wasn't alone. Someone *was* here. They'd been sitting at the bottom of the pool the whole time.

The water Warrior, Dendeon.

As if he could detect the small disturbance in the water from my little toe dip, his eyes opened. He grinned as if he recognized me and rose with dolphin-like grace to the surface.

Oh, goodie.

"Amorette didn't warn you off me?" he asked with a mischievous smile, once his head was above the water.

I blinked at him in silence for a moment, taken aback by both his odd greeting and that, unlike other people, he wasn't wiping away the water that poured from his grackle-coloured hair into his intense orange eyes. He was completely unbothered by it. What was even more striking was that while his skin above water appeared a bland beige, the skin that was underwater was radiant and reflected different shades of green and blue when it caught the light.

"Um, no. Should she have?"

He chuckled in response, as if he were amused by his own joke.

I took a step back from the edge of the pool. "You're Dendeon, right?"

He nodded, remaining where he was, moving so smoothly that there was no indication that he was even treading water. His long hair, which shone like fish-scales in the fluorescent light, swirled around him, giving him a merman appearance.

"And you're Megan." He smirked. "Want to swim with me?" He arched a brow as if daring me to say "yes".

"Why?" I asked suspiciously.

He was unfazed by my cautious attitude toward him. "Because you're a civilian who has managed to befriend a number of my brothers. I want to know what this is all about."

Debating his invitation, I asked, "Do you mean, like, swim with you down there?" I indicated the bottom of the pool where he'd been sitting.

He looked down to the bottom of the pool and then back at me. "I meant for an actual swim, but if you'd be willing to head to the bottom of the pool for a while, I'd be more than happy to give you a view of the world you've never seen before," he practically purred at me.

What the heck does he mean by that?

"Well…" I trailed off considering the offer. On one hand, I didn't know this guy from a hole in the ground. On the other hand, accepting his offer would likely stop me from thinking about the stuff I didn't want to think about anymore.

Meh, why not?

"Alright. As long as you promise not to drown me, I'm game for trying something new."

He shook his head. "I won't drown you," he promised with a dashing smile. "When you run out of air, just let it out. I'll do the rest."

Um. What? Does he have an oxygen tank down there?

I hadn't a clue what he meant, but I guessed I'd find out. What was the worst that could happen?

You'd drown, Megan. That's what.

Before I could ask another question, Dendeon exhaled, sank to the bottom of the pool, and grinned up at me.

I threw caution to the wind, took a deep breath, plugged my nose, shut my eyes, and jumped into the pool. The water was cool but not uncomfortably so. Risking potential bacteria exposure and massive stinging, I dared to open my eyes. It didn't hurt.

As the fizz of bubbles that erupted from my jump dissipated around me, I slowly released air from my lungs, so I could sink to the bottom. When I drew closer to Dendeon, he held out his hand to me, which I took, glad for the anchor.

To my relief, his flirty, jokey nature was gone and was replaced by a peaceful calm. There was no question that he was in his natural element. While I floated and would have had to struggle to remain on the bottom if he hadn't been holding on to my hand, his feet were planted firmly on the floor as if we weren't under water.

"Welcome to my part of Capital City," he said, wearing a warm smile.

My eyes widened. I'd never heard someone speak so clearly underwater before. The sound was hard to describe, because what I was hearing wasn't exactly what would be classified as normal speech. It was more like vibrations that my brain somehow naturally understood were verbal communication and that it converted into a music-like language that I could understand.

"Uh...thanks." I attempted to say back, knowing that, in his case, what he likely heard was "glug, glug".

His brow raised at first and then he looked just as shocked as I had when he'd spoken. "You're from my people?" He was definitely confused. He wasn't the only one.

I shook my head, unable to say anything else because I needed air and had to save what was left to get back up to the surface. I attempted to release his hand, but to my alarm, he didn't let go.

"Do you need air?"

I nodded, figuring he'd release me now. He didn't. Instead, his hand clamped firmer on mine.

Panic exploded in my brain as I was now sure he was going to drown me.

"Push the last of your air from your mouth," he instructed. "Make sure you don't have water in your mouth."

I gave him the best "You're crazy! Let me go!" look that I could muster.

"Trust me," he replied to my expression.

I'm not sure if it was the confidence in his voice or the imploring look in his eyes, but I chose to trust him and released the last of my breath.

Immediately, he brought his face close, placed his mouth directly over mine, and breathed into me. Oxygen - the most amazing oxygen in the world - flooded into my lungs as I inhaled the air he gave me. Shutting my eyes with the phenomenal sensation, I felt lightheaded from the rich burst of oxygen I'd received.

Wowowowowow!

A dopey smile curved the corners of my lips upward. I lazily willed my eyes open to see that Dendeon, though still holding my hand, had placed distance between us again and was watching me with both interest and wonder. Nothing about what had just happened seemed out of the ordinary to him, giving me the distinct impression that I wasn't the first person he'd given an oxygen high.

So that's what he meant when he said he'd give me a view of the world I'd never seen before and that when I'd run out of air, he'd do the rest. He is the oxygen tank!

"How can you speak my language?" he asked.

"I don't know. I know lots of languages I've never heard before."

"Amazing! I haven't heard my mother tongue in a long time." He looked boyish with nostalgia.

I couldn't help but smile at his expression, especially because I was the cause of his positive feeling. "I didn't even know it was possible to speak or hear a language underwater."

'Cause, what?

"You do it very well." He chuckled and drew close to me again, without my having to tell him that I was running out of air.

Knowing his intentions, I accepted that if I wanted to continue having this possible once-in-a-lifetime underwater conversation, I'd need to let him breathe for me.

He arched a brow as if to ask "now?" In response, I released the last of my air and allowed him to refill my lungs with his incredibly refreshing oxygen.

He drew back again when he'd given me his air, and I opened my eyes. Now that I knew what the experience was like, and I was expecting it, I felt much calmer about the process, which was surprisingly comfortable.

When Dendeon gave me breath, it was nothing like a kiss. It was kinda like underwater CPR without the chest compressions and nose plugging. It was all about the transfer of air. He was also respectful of my space and never held on to any part of me while he breathed into me, other than my hand to keep me anchored.

"Have you ever been around other Water People before?" he asked.

"No. I didn't even know there were Water People until yesterday when Amorette told me they – you – existed."

"I can't understand how this happened, but I'm certainly not complaining."

I nodded in agreement, not bothering to waste the limited breath I had on explaining my freak-alien backstory.

He held both my hands between us. "I was a religious man when I lived with my people. Nearly a monk." He grinned, and if I wasn't fully submerged in water, I would have laughed at discovering this piece of news, since he'd given me a sleazy vibe upon our first meeting.

"There isn't an equivalent term in the land cultures I know for the type of religious man I was. I lived to pursue harmony through peace. Everything must be in balance for that. When you talk to me, it's like I can feel the way I used to be back then."

He leaned forward to give me air, which I eagerly accepted.

"How did you come to be a Warrior? Are your people still alive?"

He nodded, and I was momentarily distracted when a lock of his shiny hair tickled my skin as it meandered in slow-water-motion over my wrist.

"There is an entire country of us in the Great Southern Ocean. We were attacked from above by an island people. I was drafted to protect our people." He paused, giving me a wry look. "How could I fight? My existence was for peace. I meditated on it to try to find the answer. One day, I found myself with a spear in my hand, face-to-face with an Islander." He paused again to give me air. "I couldn't do it. I let my weapon go. The Islander thought I was attacking and speared me in the leg." He looked down, and I followed his gaze to a large scar on his thigh that was just below his black – *ahem* – fitted swim shorts.

Frowning, I nodded my understanding. Choosing not to speak my responses wasn't just because speaking depleted my air faster, but also because it produced bubbles, which was kinda annoying. When Dendeon talked, there were no bubbles. I figured he must have had some sort of gill-system built into his body somewhere, but so far, I hadn't seen any indication of gills on him.

"I ran away," he continued. "I ran away, shaming my family and abandoning who I was. I struggled and nearly died, trying to live a pathetic life on land, until the Warriors found me and made me what I am now." He leaned forward and gave me air. "I'm a bit different from who I once tried to be, but still good looking enough to get you to swim with me." He chuckled, in an obvious attempt to lighten the mood after his very sad story.

"I'm really sorry this happened to you," I said, hoping my sympathetic expression conveyed the empathy I felt for him. It must have been so difficult for him to go from being a peace-loving monk to a Warrior. "I was forced to leave my family, too," I told him. "They're very far away from here, and I don't know if I'll ever see them again," I confessed, never having voiced that fear aloud before.

He shared his air with me before smiling in a caring and compassionate way. "That's not an easy position for you. I understand that feeling of distance from those you love most. Of knowing you can't return, at least for now."

"It's a bad feeling, and it's a scary one."

"Yes. So, it's important to guide your life in a way that will give you good and hopeful feelings." He smiled warmly, adding, "I am not sorry for me. I have a family again. It was hard. Sacrifices were very big, of course. But I'm talking to you, hearing the language I grew up with. It's still possible to have a peaceful afternoon, even here." He moved forward to replenish my air.

"I do know that things can get better with time," I agreed. "It's just really hard to think like that when you're going through the bad parts, and the bad parts seem like they'll never end." He leaned forward, and I was grateful to take another Dendeon breath.

"They do, and it is. So, when you're in the bad parts, accept them. Understand them. You feel hurt because you've lost. You miss someone. You didn't get what you wanted. Feel that hurt. Then feel something else. Spend time with a friend...or sit underwater in your underwear with someone new." He grinned just a little, and my face flushed. I swatted his shoulder as best I could through the resistance of the water, and he laughed.

"When you spend time with someone else," he continued more soberly, "you may not feel happy, but you won't feel hurt anymore. It's a start and it makes you ready for the next feeling."

I nodded. What he said made sense. Every time I'd felt awful, I almost always felt better after talking to someone else. Nothing ever seemed so bad when I felt that I wasn't alone.

"Do you want to surface for a moment so that you can catch your breath?"

I nodded again. I did like receiving his oxygen, but I was reaching a point where I wanted to breathe on my own for a while.

Dendeon brought his arms around me and pushed off the pool floor, rocketing us upward and slowing before we hit the surface so that only our heads and shoulders popped out. He guided me to the side of the pool and released me once I had a hand on the ledge.

I was silent for a moment, while my breathing returned to normal. Dendeon just smiled, looking content. He didn't need to catch his breath.

"Well, this was not the swim I was expecting! How is it that you can breathe underwater? Do you have gills?" My curiosity was craving answers.

"Yes. They're like gills."

"Where are they?"

"Down my sides." He stretched out on his back like a starfish in the water. I saw nothing out of the ordinary at first, but then gill flaps opened all down his sides from just under his armpit to his hip.

"That is so cool!" I exclaimed, grinning hugely. He was truly fascinating.

He chuckled at my reaction and did a graceful backward somersault in the water, resurfacing to face me again.

"So, you can live both in the water and out of it?"

"Yes. Though I'm better in the water than out of it. I'm in a kind of training program to extend the amount of time I can stay out of the water, but it's a gradual process."

"That's incredible. I had no idea it was possible for people to live underwater. Where I'm from, your people don't exist."

He raised a brow and looked pleased. "You'll need to start teaching a class back where you used to live."

I chuckled, not having the heart to tell him that no one would believe me. "So, I guess your Warrior skill has something to do with water?"

He nodded. "I'm the underwater Charmer."

I cracked up at his joke. "With you underwater 'kisses' I can believe it."

He snorted and shook his head. "I can fight well underwater, but I can make the water fight for me, too."

Hmmm. Interesting.

"So, you mean that you can move the water how you want? Like, the currents or something like that?"

He shook his head. "Like this." He moved one of his hands in front of him, keeping it below the water. The palm of his hand faced me, fingers pointing toward the surface. Seconds later, I felt a stream of water nudge against my belly. I giggled at the odd sensation.

"But much, much bigger. People don't usually laugh when I do it."

"You mean, you don't giggle people to death?" I teased, knowing full well that getting hit by the much bigger water blast that he could probably make wouldn't be funny at all.

"Not recently…" His tone and the look on his face made me laugh more.

Now that my breathing had fully returned to normal, I felt like swimming again and pushed off the edge, slowly wading through the water in a lazy front stroke.

"Do you have someone special?" I asked. "Like an Amorette or a Fiffine?

He shook his head. "Are you offering?"

"No. I'm not really offering that to anyone. The last person I thought might be someone special, well, it turned out not to be a good idea." Because trying to be with Thayn was complicated to say the least, when you had Warriors chasing you down every five seconds.

"Not even Mez?" He looked playfully smug.

I rolled my eyes. "No. Why does everyone think I want to be with Mez? And why would you even guess that anyway?" I didn't mean to sound irritated, but I could hear it in my voice.

Oh, great! Now I'm starting to sound defensive when people talk about Mez and me.

His smug expression morphed into amusement with my reaction. "I may spend a lot of time underwater, but I talk to people." He fully submerged himself for a brief moment and then proceeded to glide through the water, keeping pace with me as I swam. "I heard you risked your life for him and Keavren. If you were with Keavren, he'd be telling the whole world about it." He chuckled. "I just figured you had to have a thing for one of them to risk yourself to save them."

"I don't need to have a 'thing' for anyone to save them," I protested. "I saved them because I could, and it was the right thing to do, especially since both of them have risked their necks for me before, too." I smiled at him sweetly. "Don't worry, I'd have saved you from the tree, too."

"Thanks. I feel safer around trees now."

Sighing, I shook my head at him and decided to change my style of swimming - opting for backstrokes - as well as the subject matter. I had come here not to think about how I felt about Mez, after all.

"You don't live in the pool room, do you?"

"Yes. This is my home," he replied straight faced. "Do you like what I've done with the place? I've left it open so all soldiers can do laps in it whenever they want."

Laughing, I stuck my tongue out at him. I knew it was stupid of me to ask, but I couldn't imagine him living in normal quarters with a couch, a bed, and a place that looked like Amorette's or Remms'.

Is his apartment a giant pool?

"I guess you have a small pool in your quarters? Somewhere to sleep?"

"It's more like a tank. A pond, if that gives you a better image."

It didn't actually give me a better image, but it sounded cool, and that was fine with me. "Sounds neat, even if it's not as big as this pool."

He shrugged. "This gives me a reason to get out and talk to women in their underclothes," he grinned in reference to his tease from earlier. "It's harder to ask them to do that in my quarters."

I swatted at him again, with greater success this time than when we were underwater. He smirked.

"I should probably get out soon," I said, noticing that my fingers were pruning. "I'm getting shrively. Guess you don't have that problem."

"No. I don't understand why that happens to you."

"We can't all be as good looking as you," I told him, swimming for the metal ladder to pull myself out of the pool.

"That's got to be it," he agreed, following me to the ladder.

Before climbing out, I turned to him and kissed his cheek. "Thanks for the company and for sharing your world with me. I feel a lot better now than when I first came to swim. I hope we can do this again sometime."

"I'd like that." He smiled warmly at me. "By the way, if we do ever meet in the pool again, just make sure you get into this one. Don't dive into the other one by mistake," he warned.

"The greenish one? Why? Is it off limits?"

"No, you're welcome to use it, though it's only slightly warmer than freezing. It's meant for my training alone, in case I'm ever deployed in the north. Someone like you wouldn't have long to try to escape it."

"Okay. Wow. Thanks for the warning."

Why in the world would they make such a dangerous pool so accessible? Shouldn't there be a giant warning sign or a fence around it? Leave it to Kavylak's military to offer you a complimentary towel and a pool that can kill you.

Climbing out of the water, I made my way over to the shelf I'd claimed and grabbed the towel to dry off.

Collecting my bag, I turned toward Dendeon who had remained in the water. "I'm gonna change. See you, Dendeon." I gave him a friendly wave that he returned.

"It's been nice talking to you, Megan. I hope we talk again soon."

"We will. Take care." We shared one last smile, before he disappeared under the water's surface.

In my tiny change-room stall, I quickly dried off and changed into fresh underwear, the black pants, and long black T-shirt that I'd sworn I wouldn't wear again for as long as I could help it. Apparently, I couldn't help it for no more than a handful of hours.

Sigh.

On the plus side, I was happy to slip my feet into the fresh socks and athletic shoes Mez had packed for me. Making sure my ID tags were displayed on the outside of my shirt, I released my damp hair from its ponytail, worked out most of the knots with my brush, and left it down to let it air dry.

Tucking Amorette's borrowed clothes under my arm, I carried my bag out of the stall and remembered to dump my towel into the basket before leaving the pool room. I didn't even want to guess at what might happen if I accidentally walked off with it.

My hopes that Amarogq would not yet be home were dashed as soon as I reached the fourth floor and heard the distinct sound of clicking paws on the hall's tiles. Although I couldn't see the wolf, I knew it was there. Seconds later a large grey wolf materialized in front of me as if walking out of some unseen dimension. I jumped, even though I knew it was coming. There was just no getting used to it.

"Hi Amarogq," I greeted the wolf, extending my free hand toward the spirit animal that I knew was named after its human pack leader.

The wolf bunted my hand for me to pet it, and I obliged, loving how its thick fur felt between my fingers. A second, lighter grey wolf appeared a moment later, wanting similar attention. I chuckled, because it was cute to see them looking all dopey as I stroked their fur.

"Come in, Megs," Amarogq, the man, called from inside his apartment, startling me.

"Coming," I called back, looking at the wolves. "Guess we should go in."

They observed me with their intelligent yellow eyes and didn't wait for me to open the door as I knew they wouldn't. Instead, they ran through the wall, disappearing.

Yup. Just like wolves do...oh boy.

Letting myself into the apartment, I shut the door behind me.

"Hey Megs." Amarogq looked up at me with a smile from where he sat on the couch, holding an open file folder. I'd become accustomed to seeing the deep scar that sliced diagonally across his face from his left eyebrow to his right cheek, but unlike the first time I'd seen it, I now found myself wondering how he had gotten it, and who might have given it to him.

Was he scarred before or after becoming a Warrior?

"Hey." I forced myself out my thoughts and managed to smile back. "Is Amorette here?"

He shook his head. "She's just run out to pick up a couple of things before she heads over to Remms' to make sure he's set for the evening."

"Oh, okay. I'm just here to return the clothes she lent me earlier. I'll just, uh, leave them here for her." I placed the folded pants and shirt on one of the chairs. "I'd stay, but I'm really tired and just want to go to Aésha's and relax because I'm staying with her for a while, and I've had a long day," I babbled, wanting to get out of there as fast as possible, knowing I wouldn't have the capacity to make small talk with him.

At first, Amarogq raised a bewildered brow, clearly wondering if I was alright, but his expression became more serious at the mention of Aésha.

"Aésha isn't home. She won't be home tonight," he informed me.

It was my turn to look bewildered. "Why not? Is everything alright?" This confused me, only because Mez had suggested I stay with her, and he wouldn't do that if he knew she was on a mission.

Amarogq shook his head, closed the file folder and stood, looking even more serious. "She's been taken."

Chapter 11

Irys

W e were in Sefaline. Nothing about our surroundings changed when we passed into the territory, but there was an awareness of something different. I held more tightly to Acksil as we rode, and he sped our pace. We would need to make our way through this country as quickly as we could if we were to survive.

Great Goddess, I honour all your peoples and the creatures on Qarradune. We mean no harm to the Sefaline to whom this land belongs. Please allow us safe passage through this territory, so we may peacefully continue our journey back into Dsumot.

I had not yet moved my fingers to complete my prayer with the sign of the Goddess, when Acksil slowed our horse.

"We're not alone," he said quietly.

Instinctively, I smelled the air for the scent to which I had become familiar after spending time with Lieutenant Fhurrk and Rrokth. At first, there was nothing, but soon I started detecting a spicy yet sweet scent that could only be Sefaline people nearby.

Stepping between two large, towering trees, we entered a clearing. On its other side was a Sefaline woman who stood confidently, facing us. If the fact that we were on a horse rattled her in any way, she did not show it.

Immediately, I started singing quietly. The first couple of notes shook with the pounding of my heart, but a fresh breath of air softened the song into one of the lullabies my Sefaline friends had both seemed to like.

Acksil gave me a quick look over his shoulder. My singing continued, and I nodded to him. He nodded in return. He understood.

We caught movement out of the corner of our eyes as a Sefaline male dropped from the large tree we had only just passed. I hadn't had any idea he was there, and my singing caught in my throat as he approached.

He had long, reddish brown hair and strode along next to us in a sleeveless leather shirt and pants. His feet were bare. His intense moss green-eyed stare, with pupils forming slits down the centres of his irises, was fixed on us the entire time. The markings on his arms showed sharp tangles that were both insect-like and reminiscent of a flower while being like neither of those things. His markings were nothing like Lieutenant Fhurrk's or Rrokth's, so I assumed that he could not be related to either of them.

"Why do you travel this way?" he asked in the Common Tongue. It was heavily accented with a growl in his throat as he spoke.

"Our bridge was flooded, and we could not cross the river," I answered quickly, urgently needing to speak before Acksil. I used a soft voice, trying to sound as soothing as possible. Without singing, I wanted to remind them of song. At the same time, I kept my arms around Acksil, hoping to imply that he was my mate, so I would not be forced to say it.

Acksil didn't seem to object to the fact that I was speaking for us. He brought the horse to a full stop to allow us to comfortably speak with the Sefaline man.

The man studied me as I spoke, and my hope bloomed as he lost some of the edge to his features. His expression relaxed.

"You should not have come this way," he informed us. "Return from where you came."

It seemed promising to me that we were not being threatened straight away. So far, things were progressing with far greater potential than I had anticipated.

"I am sorry for having trespassed on your territory," I spoke again in my softest voice. "May we proceed forward and exit by the most direct route possible?" I asked, indicating the direction in which we were travelling and that I hoped would take us back into Dsumot very soon. "We will not delay, only safely make our way across the river. We don't want to be on your land any more than you want us here."

"Do you make music with your voice?" he asked, ignoring my question.

"Yes. I can sing the entire time we are here on your territory if you'd like." Glancing over, I realized that the Sefaline woman who had been standing across the clearing from us had crossed the space and was now stepping up to the man. She had the same markings on her arms, and I wondered if they were mates. While he appeared calm and ready to talk, she looked suspicious and keen to be rid of us.

"You come with us," the man said. "Make your music as you follow."

"Where are we going?" I asked, knowing my voice revealed how fearful I felt. Something about the way this man was talking made me feel like we wouldn't be heading toward the Dsumot border. I would have been more than happy to sing all the way to Storr Dimog's home if I'd had to, but I didn't want to travel any farther into Sefaline than was needed.

"It is of great importance that we travel as quickly as we can. We do not wish to be in your territory for any longer than necessary, and we are expected at our destination," Acksil supplied, clearly having the same impression I did.

The man directed a stern gaze at Acksil, and the woman hissed at him. Rrokth was certainly right that the Sefaline would be far more willing to accept me than Acksil.

"You will come with us or you will not go any farther," said the man with a lip curl that revealed part of a fang.

"My mate is protective of me. He meant no insult," I said, speaking as softly and respectfully as I could. I felt the surprise in Acksil's body when I referred to him as my mate, but I refused to look at him in case I revealed something that I should not.

Both Sefaline nodded, seeming to accept my explanation of Acksil's behaviour.

"Where is it that you are taking us?" I repeated my question from earlier.

"We are going to see a Rrathss," said the man. "She will want to hear you sing."

"Will the honoured Rrathss allow us to leave after I sing for her?" I asked hopefully.

To that, he merely shrugged. "Maybe."

If I'd had any level of comfort in this situation at all, it fled. Desperation replaced it. I had to do something, to say something. I was starting to feel as though I had nothing left to lose.

"I ask only because others are pursuing me. It is why my mate and I could not wait for the river to recede at the bridge. We do not wish to bring our enemies into Sefaline," I said, hoping the idea of a mob of foreigners entering their country might make them more inclined to shorten our stay.

"What people?" the Sefaline man asked.

"Kavylak. Xandon's Warriors. Abominations," I said, trying to speak in their terms.

Neither Sefaline looked affected by my words. "Kavylak men come here sometimes. They regret it," said the man, looking uninterested.

"Forgive us," Acksil spoke up again. "We are afraid of the men who follow us. My mate is carrying our child. I need to keep them safe."

My face instantly flushed. I wasn't sure how I was supposed to react. Should I look demure? Ashamed? Proud? I decided to act upon the fear Acksil had expressed, looking to him with an anxious expression and holding onto him more tightly.

The Sefaline woman's eyes narrowed, and she approached us boldly, stopping short of actually touching us.

"Is this true?" she asked, looking at me as though she could detect a lie through her sense of smell.

"I believe it is," I replied. "All the signs say it is."

The woman continued staring at me. I felt that her gaze might cut right through me. Abruptly, she turned and said something to the man using the Sefaline language.

To that, the man nodded, looking resigned.

"Go." His voice was flat.

"Thank you," I replied, shocked that we were being released. Acksil clearly had his own strategy in mind, even without Rrokth's advice.

"Do not turn back and do not come this way again. Next time, there will be no words."

I had no doubt that the man meant what he'd said.

Acksil nodded to the Sefaline, and we rode past them. Neither one of us looked back.

Chapter 12

Megan

I stared at Amarogq blankly until my mind could process the meaning of what he'd just said.

"What? Taken? What do you mean Aésha's been taken?"

Oh my god! Was Aésha kidnapped by the Rebels? How is that even possible? She's a Warrior. Would they be that crazy?

"A number of people were taken in the disruption in the city today. She was one of them. Warriors have been dispatched. She'll be back."

"You mean, she's been taken by the Rebels?"

"No. Not the Rebels."

Not the Rebels? Who else is there? Syliza? No way. Couldn't be. Oh no! What if it was the freaky ice woman...?

"If not them, who?" I pressed.

Amarogq regarded me for a long moment, deciding what information to reveal to me. I was prepared to scream at him if he even dared to use the "it's classified" line on me.

"Vutol," he finally said.

Um, the who-tol what now?

"Vutol? Who or what's that? Another country? Some other group of fighters?"

Seriously, who hasn't Kavylak ticked off?

"No. Not another country." He shook his head, disgust crawling up his features. "Human traffickers."

"Human traffickers? You mean, the people who sell other people for your forced labour? You mean you have some freakish Department of Slavery?"

Amarogq clenched his jaw and gave a single brief shake of his head.

"No. It's not like the military labour slaves. We have laws for their use and for when they are freed. The Vutol is very different, and we have nothing to do with them. They are the worst of all underground groups, and they sometimes use strategies like the Rebel attack in the city to make their move. They're huge, international, and extremely organized. They're disgusting to say the least." He nearly spat. "They take people, even children, for any reason the buyer wants. For service, but more often for collections and...for far worse."

My body went numb with shock at his words. The colour drained from my face, my stomach twisted in revulsion, and I dropped the bag I'd been holding, barely feeling its weight as the leather hit my feet.

Oh god. There's really something more frightening than being a slave of the Kavylak Military?

Based on the expression on Amarogq's face, I knew there was.

"But...why would they take Aésha? She's a Warrior." That made absolutely no sense to me.

"Because she is perfect, and the rest is classified."

I frowned at Amarogq's words. His response didn't make sense, and it bothered me. Yes, Aésha was easily the most beautiful and desirable woman I'd ever met, but I still didn't get why the Vutol would target a Warrior or why it would be classified. I felt inclined to push him for more information, but I didn't know where to begin, and a large part of me didn't want to know.

"Is there anything that I can do, Amarogq?"

He shook his head. "You can do what you are meant to do. When she's home, if she wants anything from you, she'll take it." He smiled at me to reassure me, but I could see the effort behind his smile, and I didn't like it. He was worried.

"I'll go talk to Mez and find out where he wants me to stay, since she won't be home. Thanks for letting me know, Amarogq."

He nodded. "We've got a couch." He gestured back to the three-seater from which he'd risen. "You're always welcome to it. It's hard and uncomfortable, but it's all yours."

My eyes flicked from the couch to him. "Thanks. I'll keep that in mind." I gave him a weak smile, knowing my words were lacking the appreciation that would have been there if I hadn't been feeling so rattled.

"Amorette would make it nice for you," he assured me, his own smile growing in strength. "She has good taste. After all, she's engaged to me."

His cute humour should have helped to lighten the situation, but it only made it worse, because now all I could think about was a broken-hearted Ash Dancer, and what she wanted me to tell him.

"Thanks, Amarogq. I'll remember that. I should go." Not able to look at him or wait for him to reply, I picked up my bag and took off out of there, shutting the door behind me. I knew it was rude and that Amarogq would wonder what was wrong with me, but I was hoping he'd just think it was the news about Aésha that had frazzled me.

Hoping Mez would be home, I knocked on his door. A moment later, he opened it and looked glad to see me. I was so relieved to see him, I almost hugged him.

"Megan, I was just about to head over to Amarogq's to tell him to send you my way if he saw you."

"Oh. Well, surprise! Here I am." The light laughter that accompanied my words died quickly. "Were you going to tell me about Aésha?"

"Yes. She won't be home tonight. I was going to give you some alternative options if you don't mind. Would you like to come in while we discuss them?"

Nodding, I entered his apartment, and he shut the door behind me and wordlessly offered to take my bag. I handed it over, and he promptly took it and set it down inside the door.

"Would you like to sit?" He gestured toward the couch.

"Sure," I said, taking a seat.

"Would you like a glass of water? Can I get you anything?"

"Water would be good, thanks."

While Mez headed over to the kitchenette area to get me a glass of water, my eyes swept over his apartment as it was the first time I had ever been invited into his space. Though his couch, chairs, and coffee table were nothing special, in one corner of the room there was a cherrywood desk with a matching bookcase with shelves filled with expensive looking leatherbound books.

Beyond that, nothing else really stood out except for the large area rug beneath my feet. It was a striking shade of blue that was caught somewhere between electric and royal hues. The vibrant colour was beautifully accented with cream and gold patterns woven throughout the rug, giving it an overall regal appearance. It looked like the type of rug that you'd find in a palace or in the room of a prince. The desk, bookshelf, and rug aside, it surprised me that I found his office to have more character than his apartment.

Mez returned, and I took the glass of water from him, taking a generous sip. He sat beside me, keeping a cushion between us.

"Amarogq said, worst case, I can stay on their couch," I told him, resting the glass on my knee, my fingers laced firmly around it.

"There is that couch, or my bed...while I take the couch." He offered. "Or, if you're more comfortable, you could stay with Remms at Pounce's quarters."

My heart almost stopped beating when he offered me his bed, and my hands tightened around the glass. Thankfully, I managed to regain my composure when he mentioned Remms.

"Remms, wouldn't mind?" I asked a little too quickly. It was super-touching that Mez would be open to being roomies, but I was pretty sure I wouldn't get a wink of sleep in his bed when I was seriously starting to crush on him.

Mez grinned and shook his head. "No. I asked him. He said you could either have a sleepover with him or set up his cot for yourself." He chuckled.

Though I smiled a little at the idea of staying with Remms, it dawned on me that maybe I had another option. Maybe I could stay with Keavren. If he'd be willing to have a roommate, I was certain I would feel the most comfortable with him.

"Actually, what about Keavren? I haven't seen him since we got back to Capital City. Do you think he'd mind having me stay with him?"

Mez raised a brow. "He's on a mission until at least tomorrow."

"Oh! I didn't realize." I fixed a serious expression on Mez. "Has Keavren been sent to get Aésha back from the Vutol?"

He shook his head. "He's been sent to find someone else. We're hoping it won't be long."

Someone else? Seriously? How many people did this deplorable organization take?

"Was that ice woman from the Vutol?" I hoped that they didn't have people with super-human powers, too.

"No. Not that we can tell."

"Will Aésha be okay?"

Likely sensing how stressed I was, Mez reached out and gently rested his hand on my upper arm. I followed his hand to his face. "She'll be just fine," he assured me. "The Warrior we've sent is a skilled tracker, and when he takes his aim, he never misses."

"I hope she comes home soon. I didn't think anyone would kidnap a Warrior," I confessed, raising my hand to rest it over his fingers on my arm, hoping the gesture conveyed how much I appreciated the contact. I felt the desire to hug him returning, but I forced myself not to for fear that I would fall apart if I did. I felt like every time I was around Mez there was always some drama happening that resulted in me having an emotional breakdown. I wanted him to see that I could be calm and cool like he was.

To my pleasure, a small smile warmed his features when I touched his fingers. "She will. If you'd ever met Lieutenant Rakven Terredge, you'd know there is no need for your concern. She will be home soon."

I couldn't help but feel more reassured by Mez' confidence. If Mez had faith in this Rakven Terredge guy's ability, why shouldn't I? He certainly knew the Warriors and their talents far better than I did.

I nodded. "Should I be worried about the Vutol? Is this group here a lot?" I felt it was a fair question considering I had been nabbed by the Rebels easily enough, and I was in a country where slavery was legal.

He shook his head. "Not like that. The Vutol is, unfortunately, a little bit of everywhere. That is, even if they don't have a location in a specific place, they have their scouts, and they certainly have their customers." Mez' lip curled in revulsion, an expression I'd never seen him make, and he made no effort to conceal it from me.

I, on the other hand, couldn't control a violent shiver that raced down my spine at the word "customers". It was bad enough knowing that human trafficking existed at all, but it somehow seemed doubly worse when you realized it existed because there was a market for it.

"That's…" I grimaced, looking away from him, unable to finish my thought, wrapping my arms around myself in a tight hug. Shaking my head in an attempt to clear my mind of a zillion horrors that ran through it, I finally said, "I hope she's home soon."

Mez released my arm, and reaching behind me, draped a super-soft blanket over my shoulders. I looked into his caring eyes.

"She will be," he said softly. "She's very strong and Rakven is very skilled."

Nodding, I drew the blanket further around me, running my fingers over the velvety fur of the fabric that was the same striking blue as the one in the posh rug.

"Do you know where you'd like to stay?"

I want to stay with you.

"I think I'll stay with Remms," I said, because under the circumstances, I felt it was the logical decision. "I think we could both use the company, and he has Pounce, so it really makes the most sense."

"I agree. That's what I thought you would choose." Mez didn't look or sound the least bit surprised by my decision, and while I understood why he wasn't, a small part of me was a little hurt that he hadn't been at least a smidge hopeful that I would want to stay with him.

Don't be an idiot, Megan. Of course, he wouldn't want you to stay with him. You're lonely, and you miss Thayn. Don't let your silly crush on Mez fool you into believing that he might feel something more toward you than friendship.

"It was nice of you to offer to let me stay here, too," I tacked on. "If Remms hadn't been an option, I probably would have taken you up on it, because I can't stay at Amorette and Amarogq's. I just can't face him right now. I feel like I don't know how to talk to him anymore. Not with what I know."

Mez frowned. "He's the same man. You'll either become accustomed to talking to him or you'll tell him what you know. I imagine that it will be the former of the two, but you never fail to surprise me, so I'm keeping my mind open."

We shared a small smile at his comment and then I sighed. "I just feel like I'm the keeper of a secret I shouldn't know. Part of me feels that I should tell him, while the other part knows that if I do, it could rip his life apart. Neither option seems right."

"It's not a matter of shouldn't." Mez shook his head. "You'll know if the time comes to tell him. Otherwise, you'll adapt to how things are. This is still very new," he reminded me. "It's too early to know how you'll feel in time."

He had a point. I had literally known of Ash Dancer and her children's existence for just over two days. Maybe I should give myself a bit of a break.

"Do you ever find it hard to keep secrets?" I asked him, imagining that he probably had several of them, being part of a classified culture.

"Yes," he answered without hesitation. "Secrets are difficult. Some you can forget about. Some feel like they are tearing your soul away from the Goddess."

Frowning, I reached out and rested my hand gently on his knee. "I hope you don't have too many of the soul-tearing kind." I genuinely hoped that. I didn't like the thought of his soul tearing, particularly when I knew he'd already had a heartbreaking past.

"Thank you, Megan."

His small smile warmed me more than the soft blanket around my shoulders, and I had to resist the urge to hug him again.

"I guess I should probably get out of your hair. I know you're a busy guy."

His smile grew, and he ran his fingers through his hair. "Can't blame you for wanting to get in there for a while."

I stared at him blankly for a moment in surprise at his actions and words, and then burst out laughing. He chuckled, too, looking relieved to have broken the tension.

"You do have nice hair," I agreed. "You have a nice blanket, too. I think I might just steal it," I teased, sliding my fingers over the blanket's silky fuzz. "What is this made out of?"

His brow raised, and he smiled. "Take it. It can be your sleepover-at-Remms' blanket." There was no tease in his voice. "And it's made out of…" He paused to assess the fabric as if giving it careful thought. "Soft blanket stuff." He chuckled.

Laughing, I shook my head. "I'm not going to take your blanket. It looks expensive, and it's yours."

"Then borrow it," he suggested with a shrug.

Oh my gosh! He's serious. Could I really borrow his blanket? Yes. Yes, I can.

"Okay. Thanks."

He nodded looking pleased that he could offer me this comfort.

"Do you want me to go with you to Remms'?"

Standing and keeping the blanket around me like a giant fuzzy shawl, I shook my head. "No. That's alright, but thanks."

Mez stood, too, and fished a key out of his pocket, extending it to me. "You'll need this."

Accepting the key, I slipped it into my pocket and got an idea. Walking over to where Mez had rested my bag on the floor, I crouched, opening it, and rummaged through the contents until I found what I was looking for.

Returning to a confused looking Mez, I held out one of the black pumps Aésha had given me. "Here. In exchange for the blanket borrowing."

"Uh, I don't think it's my size," he said a little bewildered but accepted the shoe anyway to humour me. "But thank you for living up to your always-surprising-me tradition."

I grinned. "Look at its sole."

He flipped the shoe over, and I knew he understood the meaning of my offering the moment I saw his confident gaze falter, and he swallowed hard. He'd seen Aésha's pink kiss mark on the sole of my shoe. I had a hunch the kiss was her trademark, and Mez would know who the kiss belonged to. He looked at me, his confident expression restored, and he nodded with meaning. "Thank you. Good trade."

My hunch had been right.

"See you tomorrow, Mez. Thanks."

"See you tomorrow. If you need anything, just knock. I'm working from here tonight."

"I will," I promised, heading to the door and collecting my bag. He followed me and reached his arm around me. My heart immediately picked up speed at the anticipation that he might embrace me, but just as quickly returned to its normal pace when I realized that he was just reaching for the doorknob to open the door for me.

It's all in your head, Megan. He thinks of you as a friend. No matter how others might tease you about him, you're just friends. He cares and feels responsible for you. Be grateful for your friendship and go.

"Have a good night."

"You, too." I left his apartment, not daring to look at him as I did, too worried that he'd see right through me and know I had a crush on him.

A moment later, I knocked on Remms' door. When there was no reply, I used the key Mez had given me and let myself inside, quietly shutting the door.

"Remms? It's just Megan," I called.

"I'm in my room," he replied weakly.

Near Remms' couch, I set down my bag and the blanket Mez had let me borrow and walked to Remms' room. He was tucked into his giant bed, reclined on a sea of fluffy pillows. Pounce looked regal lying next to him.

With the way that Remms' hair was fanned on the pillows above his head, and the way that the light from the bedside lamp shone on it, I was able to observe its true colour for the first time. His long, shiny black hair was streaked with dark raspberry pink highlights. I wondered if the pink in his hair was natural, as I recalled that when I had seen Remms use his healing skill on Mez, the smoke he had exhaled had transformed in colour from grey to pink. Though at the time, there hadn't been enough daylight for me to make out the shade of pink, I was willing to bet it was the same hue as his hair highlights.

"Is it alright if I stay with you until I can head back to my place?"

He smiled softly and nodded. "I don't mind. I'm surprised that you picked me over Aésha. I guess she's still away? Mez mentioned that he was giving you options."

"Thanks. I appreciate this. I was going to stay with Aésha, but they haven't got her back from the Vutol yet. Mez said it shouldn't be too long before she's back, though."

Remms' deep cranberry-coloured eyes widened at the mention of "Vutol" and genuine fright flooded his face. "Oh no! I'm glad they'll get her back so fast. You're welcome here for as long as you like. You can take my couch or just climb in here with me."

"I'll probably take the couch so that you can have your space...or at least Pounce can have her space." I chuckled, watching as Pounce stretched out on her side to give Remms further access to her belly.

"It's your choice. I have more than enough space here. Arik got me this bed. I would have been fine with one of the smaller ones the quarters usually have, but he likes to spoil me," Remms said with a shy little shrug.

Hmmm...Arik likes to spoil Remms...Interesting.

"At least you're getting spoiled by the right person." I walked over to the bed and took a seat, reaching out to pet Pounce, who accepted my attention without complaint.

"He's a good brother to me." Remms giggled.

"I will be going to work tomorrow," I told him. "So, you don't have to worry about me being here too much, getting in the way, or anything."

"You're not intruding at all. It's nice to have someone here, especially since I'm all alone most of the time while I'm healing," he assured me. "You can make your breakfast and lunch with whatever you find in my kitchen or take any of the leftovers."

"Thanks, Remms." I smiled gratefully at him. "I'm glad to be here. I was actually really happy when Mez told me that you were one of my roommate options, when I knew I couldn't stay with Aésha as originally planned. You were my first choice."

He grinned, looking pleased. "We'll be sure to gossip a lot," he joked.

A knock at Remms' door stopped me from commenting.

"Remms? It's just me," Amorette announced herself, entering and shutting the door.

"We're in here," I called.

"Oh! Megan. I didn't know you were here," she replied. The sound of her placing something down on Remms' small kitchen table – I assumed the dinner she had brought for him – was followed by her footsteps approaching his room. "You alright?" she asked me when she entered. "Amarogq said you seemed a little jittery."

"Oh yeah, I'm alright. I'm definitely feeling on edge, but it's just been a long day." I had no idea if Amorette knew about the Aésha situation, and I certainly wasn't about to tell her the real reason I was so jittery around Amarogq.

"I understand," she empathized. "You were attacked, were homeless, and you're having a hard time accepting that Mez likes you." She then whispered, "He does." She shared a grin with Remms, who giggled. "It's a lot!"

I playfully rolled my eyes at them, shaking my head.

"I heard about Aésha," she added with greater seriousness. "You know you're welcome to stay with me and Amarogq."

"I do." I smiled. "Thanks for saying so, Amorette. You're a good friend. For now, though, I'm gonna stay with Remms. Pounce tells me this is a good place to crash."

She laughed. "She's right. There's lots of linens, too. Need help making up the cot with huge sheets?"

"Thanks. I think I'll manage," I said, joining in her laughter.

She nodded and looked to Remms. "I've brought you your dinner and dessert. There's enough for both of you."

"Thanks, Amorette. You always take such good care of me."

"I'm always happy to help a friend." She smiled sweetly at him. "Have a good night." Amorette turned to exit the room but then looked at me before leaving. "Good luck at work tomorrow."

I made an "eek" face at her. "Thanks. I have a feeling I'll need it."

She grinned knowingly, which made me feel even more nervous about tomorrow, and left.

Turning to Remms, I said, "Did you want any of the food that she brought?"

He shook his head. "Maybe later."

"Do you mind if I have some of it? I'm hungry and haven't really eaten much today," I confessed, because the little snack I'd had at Amorette's had long worn off.

"Not at all. Help yourself. Pounce and I will be waiting for you here when you're done."

"Thanks." I left the room and beelined for the kitchen table where Amorette's food was waiting. I took the glass container out of an insulated bag she'd brought it in and saw that it looked to be some kind of meat and potato stew. Finding a bowl and a spoon, I poured myself a glass of water and took a seat at the table to enjoy what tasted like the best warm meal I'd had in days.

When I was done, I cleaned my dishes and left them to air dry. I put the rest of the food Amorette had brought into Remms' fridge, which looked nothing like any of the traditional fridges I was accustomed to on Earth.

It consisted of a stack of deep drawers, each featuring a designated compartment for an ice block. Every drawer appeared to have a specific purpose. One was like a freezer, one was similar to what I'd call a crisper for fruits and veggies in my fridge back home, and one contained dishes with meals that I assumed Remms' friends had delivered to him but that he hadn't finished yet. I smiled to myself when I saw all the containers in it, because it was nice to see that the Warriors and their significant others really did take care of him, which was great since he was apparently bedridden any time he healed one of them.

Quietly returning to Remms' room, I peeked inside to make sure he wasn't asleep. He wasn't. He was stroking Pounce and talking to her in a low voice. She looked utterly content and was purring like a jet engine. It was such a cute scene.

"Hi," I announced my presence. "Dinner was good. How are you two doing?"

"Hi. I was just telling Pounce a story." He smiled.

I nodded. "I can see that she's very taken with it. Oh, and you don't have to worry about me eating your food all the time," I tacked on. "Tomorrow, I'll be going to dinner with Mez, so whatever your fan club brings you is all yours."

Remms suddenly looked very interested. "Is it a date?"

Uh...

"No. I mean, not really. It's just dinner. He's just being nice." I knew what I was saying was true, but even to my ears I sounded defensive. I wanted to kick myself for making this sound like some big deal. Honestly, Mez was just being a nice friend. I wasn't actually looking for a date, and he probably only felt sorry for me anyway.

"Alright. But is it a date?" Remms teased with a giggle.

"No," I protested and couldn't help but giggle in return. "At least, I don't think it is," I leveled with him. "I really don't think Mez thinks about me like that. I mean, he's nice, and he wants to make sure I'm feeling at ease after everything that's happened over the past couple of days, but it's nothing more."

"Would you be mad at him if it was a date?"

I blinked at Remms in surprise. "No. Of course not, but I'd be really, really surprised. I'm just, he's just..." I shook my head, frustrated at my inability to form a coherent thought. "There's no way he's interested in me. He's so out of my league. He's so together and established and smart, and every time he's around me something dangerous happens to him!" I declared, with a burst of uncontrolled laughter as I realized how often I'd said that today.

Remms' brow raised. "But if he likes you, he likes you," he said simply as if he couldn't understand my point. "The man never ever dates. He doesn't care about leagues or whatever. It's just that maybe he finally found someone he wants to go on a date with."

I supposed he had a point with his whole "if he likes you, he likes you" statement. I still didn't think that was the case, but Remms was right that it had nothing to do with leagues. A person's status or level of coolness was not how the heart made decisions. Sometimes you couldn't explain why you liked a person. You just did.

"Gosh!" Remms declared, startling me out my thoughts. "With both Charmers out of Capital City right now, that's just funny."

"I'm sorry. What? Funny?" I wasn't following.

"They would *love* to tease Mez about going on his first date as a Warrior, and then they'd probably be sending you all this stuff like clothes and things." He giggled.

I nodded with a smile, understanding what he'd meant. "You're right, Aésha would love that. She gave me a hard enough time when I went for a walk with Mez on board one of the military ships. I can only imagine what she'd..." I trailed off, realizing to my horror that I owned absolutely nothing that was "date-worthy", in my opinion.

If, on the craziest chance this is a date, what if he takes me somewhere nice? Will a simple casual skirt and blouse do? Not to mention, I lent one of the only pumps I owned to Mez. This was a disaster! I was a disaster!

"Are you alright, Megan?"

"Huh? Oh, uh, yeah. I was just thinking about the fact that if this is actually a date, and he takes me somewhere nice, I don't have any clothes that would be appropriate for that."

Remms smiled. "I'll make sure you have something that you can wear. When you come home from work, it'll be here."

I didn't hide my surprise or my gratitude. "Oh my gosh, Remms! Thank you! You're a lifesaver!"

He nodded cutely, looking pleased with himself. "I may not be able to leave, but all the girlfriends and wives love me for keeping the Warriors healed."

"That would definitely make you a favourite," I agreed, remembering all the food in his fridge.

Remms smiled and then yawned, and I yawned in return. "I think you read my mind," I told him. "I'm beat. I think I'm going to head to bed."

"Just make yourself at home. Sleep where you want. Use anything but my toothbrush in the bathroom." He giggled.

"Thanks. Don't worry, your toothbrush is safe from me."

'Cause, seriously, yuck!

"Once I'm all washed up, mind if I share with you?" I asked, indicating the other side of his giant bed. I wouldn't care about sleeping on the cot, but sleeping on it would mean I'd have to find it, set it up, add sheets and blankets to it, an effort I didn't feel like making at the moment. Plus, truth be told, for the past several nights, I'd slept next to someone and had grown accustomed to that arrangement. It was what I had expected to happen tonight with Aésha. The thought of sleeping on my own unnerved me. Ever since I was recaptured by Kavylak from the Godeleva Masque, there was a fear inside me at night that I couldn't shake when I was alone.

He smiled and nodded, and I could have sworn he looked almost as relieved as I felt. He pulled two pillows out from the nest of pillows behind him, setting them on the empty side of the bed for me.

Returning his smile, I left the room, collected my bag, and went into his bathroom to get cleaned up and ready for bed.

Remms' bathroom was exactly as I'd imagined it would be. It was perfectly organized, spotless, and everything matched from the robin's egg blue towels to the fancy-shaped soaps that lined a shelf on his shower wall. The entire room smelled of some type of fresh blossom, without being overpowering. It was comforting and pleasant, not nose-burning sickly sweet.

Deciding to take a fast shower to wash off the weirdness of the day, I made quick work of getting clean, knowing that when I actually felt like taking the time to have a nice long shower or bath, I would appreciate it.

Drying off, I slipped into a fresh black T-shirt and boyshorts, brushed my teeth (with my toothbrush), and ran a hairbrush through my seen-way-better-days red locks. Exiting the bathroom, I snagged Mez' blanket before returning to Remms' room, wrapping the soft fabric around me, and sliding into Remms' bed beside him.

Oh my gosh! Between this blanket and this bed, I don't think I could get any cozier if I tried! This is the ultimate in cozy!

"Wow! Remms, you have the best bed. I totally understand why Pounce never wants to leave. I'm going to live here now, too," I joked, as if I was telling Remms he was officially adopting me as well.

Remms giggled merrily and peeked over at me from behind the book he was holding. "It's really comfortable since I have to live here so much."

"It does suck that you have to stay here so much, but I am grateful you have it, and that you're willing to share. Thanks again for this, Remms."

He smiled and shut his book, resting it on his nightstand. "I hope you sleep really well tonight. Do you need me to put on my wake-up alarm?"

Although I scrunched my face at the thought of getting up to an early alarm, I nodded with a sigh. "Yeah. I suppose that's a good idea. Otherwise, I'll probably be late. That won't bother you?"

He shook his head. "It will wake me, but I have all day tomorrow to sleep. It's fine." Reaching over to his bedside table, he flicked a switch on some device I couldn't see from where I lay in bed.

"Thanks."

He nodded and yawned, settling into his nest of pillows. "Are you ready for sleep?"

"Yes. I'm always ready for sleep." I chuckled softly and curled on my side, cocooning into Mez' blanket under the covers and facing Remms.

There was still a huge space between us, but Pounce wasted no time claiming it as her own and stretching out. I gave her white belly a stroke, and she purred. I felt myself truly relax for the first time that day.

"Goodnight, Pounce. Goodnight, Remms."

"Goodnight, Megan," he whispered in reply.

Shutting my eyes, I continued to stroke Pounce a few more times, until I let the motion naturally come to an end, resting my hand on the bed. A moment later, I felt something warm and soft touch my hand, and I smiled. Curling my fingers gently around Remms', I felt happy and safe.

Choosing to hold on to only those feelings, I was able to drift off to sleep.

Chapter 13

Irys

"We're no longer in Sefaline," Acksil said, breaking our tense silence. He'd slowed the horse to a walk to take us across a narrow bridge spanning the river. "This is Dsumot."

"Thank the Goddess," I breathed, letting my fingers make the sign of the Goddess while still holding onto him as we rode.

"You were great back there, Irys. That male Sefaline respected you. I would almost have thought you were a Charmer," he teased.

"I started off well, but I nearly had us captured. It was your quick thinking that ensured our escape." For a moment, I thought about how terrifying the last day had been, and how things could have turned for the worse due to my choices in Sefaline.

Would Acksil have been able to save us if I'd made a fatal mistake?

"Acksil, if things had gone wrong, and the Sefaline had refused to release us, what would you have done? Do you have the magic skills some of the other Warriors have?"

"I do have a skill," he replied calmly. "All Warriors have those skills. My skill wouldn't have been much use to us unless the Sefaline had attacked. I can predict a person's physical actions moments before they make them. It gives me the advantage of working around an opponent's attacks and other movements so that I can act before they do."

"Can you read minds?" I asked, feeling increasingly nervous the more that concept sank in. I resisted the urge to let go of him.

"No," he replied, to my relief. "I cannot read minds. I can read body language."

"Do you know what I'll do next based on my body language?"

"For the most part, yes. It is more difficult because I'm not looking directly at you. But a moment ago, your arms around my waist told me that you debated releasing me when you asked me if I was able to read your mind."

I was glad he couldn't see my expression. I couldn't help but think over our interactions since we'd left Kavylak. My mind flashed to every little moment of hesitation. Every time I'd needed to correct my thoughts. Could he tell when I was daydreaming about Dynan? My cheeks flushed.

"It works only if you can see the person?" I hoped this was the case, and yet didn't at the same time. While I wanted to protect my own thoughts, I still hoped his skills would be as powerful as possible to keep us safe. "That's why Kaiwa surprised you when the Rebels first showed themselves?"

"Yes," he confirmed. "Usually, I need to know of the person's presence to be able to sense anything about their actions."

"I'm not sure how I feel about that," I chuckled a little. "Thank you for telling me. I've been wondering."

He laughed easily. "You're not the only one who isn't certain about how they feel about that. The Rebels know about my skill, too. That's one of the reasons Kaiwa knocked me out at first. She needed the chance to tie me up before questioning me. I've always had this ability. Xandon just made it stronger. It's what he does with all the Warriors. He takes our natural unique abilities and manipulates and enhances them."

"He's a monster," I muttered.

"He is," Acksil agreed, placing his hand over mine to give it a gentle squeeze before releasing it again.

"Will we still reach Storr Dimog's house today?"

"Yes. I think we're only about an hour away if we ride well. Let's stop and rest here for a little bit. There's a stream for the horse to get a drink. I know you're tired. You'll be safe to sleep comfortably when we reach Storr's."

I agreed with his decision to stop. All I wanted to do was ride as hard as we could for the next hour so we could stop travelling for a while. I wanted to feel safe again. I knew he was right that I needed some rest. That wasn't going to happen while we were out here. Still, we had only one horse, and we'd been riding it for too long. It would be silly to object. Instead, I let him help me down from the horse and walked with him as we stepped up to the edge of the stream.

All three of us - horse and humans - took the opportunity to drink the cold water rushing quickly through this lightly wooded part of Dsumot. The wind blew the trees above us and birds sailed across the sky overhead. It felt as though everything around us was in a hurry to make it through this place. I wasn't comforted by the sensation.

After having a drink and washing my face again, I felt a little better, taking the opportunity to stroll around the immediate area. Acksil took his time splashing water on his face as well. Dunking his hands into the water, he let out a startled hiss that caused me to turn sharply.

Withdrawing his hand from the water, I shrieked as I saw the source of his surprise. A small, brightly coloured snake had latched onto the side of Acksil's hand, its fangs embedded into the flesh.

"Acksil!" I cried uselessly, stepping closer to him.

He grabbed hold of the snake's body, causing it to release him, and he tossed it to the other side of the stream, looking at his hand with a shocked expression. "I didn't realize those little demons lived around here." His voice was calm, but his eyes belied his attempts to appear at ease.

"Are you poisoned?" I asked, dreading the answer.

"Yes."

"Great Goddess help us," I said as my fingers flung the sign of the Goddess through the air.

Acksil stood and stepped right up to me. The puncture marks in his hand were bleeding a little, but not as much as I would have expected. Not enough that he would risk losing too much. The poison was the true threat.

"Will they have medicine for you at Storr Dimog's house?" I asked hopefully.

"Yes," he replied and mounted the horse right away. This, alone, let me know that he didn't believe he would make it that far.

Grabbing onto his good arm and the saddle, I stuffed my foot on top of his in the stirrup, heaving myself miraculously onto the saddle behind him.

"Ride hard. The horse can rest when we do," I told him, relatively sure that was already the plan.

He nodded, and I held on as we took off at a pace much faster than was comfortable. I focused on remaining quiet and holding on so Acksil could send all his energy into staying upright and making it to our destination.

Shortly, it became more than clear that this wouldn't be the case. We'd only barely begun our final hour of riding when Acksil started to lose his posture. I could feel him sagging forward and tried desperately to keep him upright with my arms around him.

"Acksil, hold on," I begged.

"Isss alright Irysss," he slurred.

"No, it's not. What do I do? You're not going to make it to Mr. Dimog's, Acksil. We're too far away. You need to tell me what to do."

"Go east. Look for," he started to say but paused for a long moment. I'd assumed he'd lost consciousness until he started speaking again. "Look for big trees with white bark and orange...orange flowers."

"I will. I'll get us there. All you need to do is hold on, Acksil." One hand at a time, I released him and took the reins from him. I hooked my legs awkwardly around his to try to take full control of the horse without pulling his feet from the stirrups as they might have been helping to keep him in the saddle.

He nodded to my instructions, but I doubted he would be able to do much for long. It looked as though staying awake was already taking everything out of him.

To my surprise, he did hold himself up for quite a while, but eventually he started sagging again, and I found myself holding desperately to him. At first, I fooled myself into thinking I'd found a balance and would be able to hold him up and ride at the same time. However, it wasn't long before he started listing to one side.

"Acksil, wake up!" I shouted at him as I pulled back on the reins to slow the horse, holding onto him as tightly as I could. "Help!" I shouted into the woods in the hopes that there were Rebels about, perhaps secretly watching over the area approaching their leader's home.

He was too heavy for me, and his dead weight pulled us sideways. Desperate to protect him from the fall, I yanked at him, trying to keep him from falling head-first. His limp body dragged us both off the side of the horse, and I heard myself scream as my shoulder blades slammed into the ground under both my weight and Acksil's. I'd managed to turn us in the fall to protect his head. His foot had remained in a stirrup, keeping him above me.

My vision blurred as I blinked through the pain that sheared through what had to be a bruising point of impact.

"Help!" I called out again, turning away from the late afternoon sun, turning to the east. For the briefest moment, the sky looked ablaze. As my eyes cleared, I watched the flames turn into vibrant orange blossoms lining every branch of striking, white-barked trees.

Thank you, Great Goddess.

The thunder of rapid horses' hooves approached, and I shouted once more for help. They slowed as they saw me. A man and a woman dismounted, and the woman jogged over to where I was lying with Acksil unconscious on top of me.

"He was bitten by a little bright coloured snake in the stream," I said, only then discovering that I'd been crying as my voice hiccupped. "He was drinking water, and it bit his hand."

They gently pulled Acksil off me, unhooking his foot from the stirrup. The woman helped me to sit up. She was about my height and perhaps even my age, with dark brown hair fastened in a tight bun reminiscent of the military styles I'd seen back in Kavylak. Her skin was a rich golden shade as though the sun had kissed her without leaving a freckle behind. She was dressed in a brown jacket and pants that reminded me of the Rebels we'd left behind before we'd entered Sefaline.

"Was it dark brown with a bright yellow stripe and a red streak down its back?" the woman asked me.

"Yes," I nodded, rolling my shoulders through their building ache. I was nearly surprised that they weren't creaking as I moved them.

"A vink," she said, identifying the snake.

"Is he going to die?" I asked, preparing myself for the worst.

"No," the man said confidently before turning to the woman. "It's Nydo."

"Nydo?" Her eyes widened, and her mouth set into a tight line.

"Yes," I confirmed, trying to show that I had nothing to hide. "We left Rrokth, Lida, Sicer Dimog, Rakej, and Kaiwa a few hours ago. They're on the other side of the river, waiting to access the bridge that was flooded from the high water. We came through Sefaline, but they could not. Please help us. We're going to see Storr Dimog."

The woman gave me a single nod but appeared far less friendly. "Borte, take the traitor on your horse and bring him back to the house. Dyronin should still be there." Turning to me, she said, "Get back on your horse and follow me."

"Thank you. May the Goddess bless you both," I said gratefully, standing shakily, attempting to ignore the ache in virtually every part of my body. Stepping up to the horse, I stroked his muzzle and mane as I took up the reins. "Thank you for bringing us this far. It won't be long now," I whispered and placed my foot into the stirrup.

From up on my horse, I watched Borte unceremoniously pick up Acksil and walk toward his own horse. I would have continued watching to ensure Acksil was being treated well, but the woman started to ride, and I didn't want to draw any more of her ire by falling behind. I could only trust that Borte would take care of Acksil and bring him to Storr Dimog's house.

We didn't ride for long. It seemed that we weren't as far from the house as Acksil had guessed. After another few minutes of travelling through the gorgeous orange blossomed trees, we entered a stunning property with a sprawling bungalow that was carefully designed to suit the landscape. It looked as though whoever had built the structure had altered it to fit the hilly grounds, instead of altering the landscape to suit the building. It appeared natural and respectful, while still quite civilized.

"Leave your horse. It will be cared for," said the woman as we came to a stop near the house. She dismounted and walked over to me, taking my reins.

I slid ungracefully off my horse, giving it a final stroke in gratitude, and adjusted my bag on my shoulder. I could only imagine how rumpled I must have looked, but I tried to keep my chin up to preserve whatever dignity I might have had left.

"Who are you and why are you travelling with a Warrior?" she demanded, the moment I took my first step away from the horse.

"I am Irys, and he is no longer a Warrior. I had been a prisoner of the Warriors and Xandon, and he helped me escape," I replied.

She narrowed her eyes at me, studying me as though deciding whether I was being truthful. "Are you being hunted by the Warriors and Xandon?"

"I have every reason to believe so, but they don't know where we are or where we were headed. We also have a few days' head start."

"He was wise to bring you here. You're Sylizan?" Her question was worded as a statement, but she seemed to want me to confirm it.

"Yes. I'm a Godeleva."

She looked surprised. "You're related to Lord Imery Godeleva?"

"I was raised with him. His parents brought me up as their own daughter."

"My father will want to help you return home again. I am Skeltra."

"Thank you," I gushed. "It's an honour to make your acquaintance, Skeltra...Miss Dimog?" I guessed that the father to whom she'd referred might have been Storr Dimog.

To that, she nodded. "Come with me. Are you injured? Do you need medical assistance?"

"I don't think so," I replied. "Only bruised. Will Acksil...Nydo arrive soon? I want to make sure he's alright, and I cannot sleep without him there to guard me."

"Why is that?" Skeltra asked, looking unconcerned.

I didn't know what to say. I wished Acksil were there to explain the situation. He would know what she needed to hear. Indeed, he trusted these people, but did that mean I should tell them everything? Was there something I should keep to myself?

"I know this will sound strange," I prefaced my reply, making my decision. "Please do not think me a liar or mad, for that matter. We have reason to believe that Xandon is doing something to me in my sleep. We are afraid that he might somehow harm me in my sleep, and we don't know if he may somehow be able to use that time to discover my location. I don't understand it. I only know that it has changed the color of my hair. Even Rrokth has found that I am colder than I should be."

I hadn't meant to say quite that much, but I found that once I'd started talking, the details poured out of me. It was a relief to say them all out loud to another woman.

Miss Dimog listened to me with the same intensity she'd used before. Reaching out, she took my hand and examined it. I felt ashamed as I saw the dirt under my nails and in the ridges of my knuckles.

"You're freezing," she said and dropped the hand.

"I don't feel cold, but I believe everyone who says I am."

"You were never like this before you encountered Xandon? Do you think you have been infected with some sort of dark magics?"

"I don't know why this is happening. I know only that I wake up screaming and then I am worse. This never happened before I met him. Nydo firmly believes this is Xandon's magic. He knows more than I do, though I suspect that he doesn't have any meaningful understanding of it, either. It's why he helped me to escape."

"Do not call him Nydo. Nydo is dead," she said firmly.

"I meant only to call him by a name you know. His name is Acksil to me," I replied, unsure as to whether or not I should feel apologetic. I hadn't meant any offense.

"As it will be to us. He is not who he was before. That man died five cycles ago," she informed me.

"I understand."

We entered the house, which was bright and spacious. Fresh air moved through the large open windows, allowing the last of the day's sunlight to fill the space.

"Have a seat, and I will let my father know you are here," Miss Dimog instructed.

"I'm filthy. I don't want to soil your lovely furniture. May I wash before I meet your father?" I asked, realizing that my fingers weren't the only parts of me that were covered in dirt.

She rolled her eyes. "Stand if you don't want to sit. It won't be long. Do not leave this room."

"Thank you," I said meekly. I drew my cloak around myself, feeling the stiffness in my shoulder blade as I did so. Deciding to stand, I chose to embrace the feeling of discomfort. It would be a badge of my efforts to save Acksil's life. It was a reminder that I could be strong and that I needn't feel ashamed of everything I'd gone through to bring myself this far. I'd promised the Goddess that I would be strong and that's just what I had tried to do. Still, I would have preferred not to be wearing pants when meeting Mr. Storr Dimog for the first time.

A few minutes later, Miss Dimog returned with a middle-aged man. He was tall and stood to his full height, suggesting to me that he was solid and possibly proud as well. His long grey hair was tied in a low ponytail between his shoulders. He was dressed rather simply in what I assumed were Dsumot fashions. Despite the simplicity of the clothing, I could tell the fabrics were of fine quality. His face was weathered, but his expression was gentle. The gold colour of his skin was richer and deeper than that of his daughter, making me think that he'd either spent more time in the sun than she had or that her mother must have had a much fairer complexion than her father. Immediately, I was far more at ease in his presence than I had been in Miss Dimog's.

"I hear you have come to see me, Miss Godeleva. I am Storr Dimog. Tell me how I can help you." He spoke in Sylizan with an ease that showed perfect fluency in the language.

I curtsied to him, bowing my head in deep respect and obedience. "Thank you for your hospitality, Mr. Dimog," I replied in my mother tongue and set about telling him everything that had brought me to this point without holding anything back.

This man held my life – and Acksil's – in his hands.

Chapter 14

Megan

"*BING! BING! BING!*"
 Noooo...too early...more sleep....
 "BING! BING! Click."

"Megan?" Remms' groggy voice queried, after he turned off the alarm. "You up?"

"Yeah," I croaked and forced myself to unfurl from my cocoon of blankets, unable to silence the low grumble that escaped my lips, when I came in contact with the cool air.

It didn't matter if I was on Qarradune or Earth, there wasn't anything pleasant about waking up to an alarm before the crack of dawn. The only real benefit was that at least this alarm was far more normal sounding than the blaring wake-up siren that had gone off the day before. There was a definite advantage to living inside the building when compared to living in one of the apartments on the compound.

Dragging myself to the main room, I picked up my bag and stumbled to the bathroom. Sliding my hand blindly along the wall, I found the button that would light the space. Bracing myself, I pushed it, wincing as my eyes were assaulted by the harsh glare.

As quietly as I could, I washed my face at the sink, deciding to shower and wash my hair when I got off work, so I'd be fresh for what would possibly be my first date with Mez. Thinking about him, a smile spread across my face and made the process of dressing in my stiff, charcoal grey uniform far more pleasant.

Leaving on my black short-sleeved shirt, I pulled on thick dark stockings, then the shin-length A-line skirt, followed by the jacket. The hem of the jacket dusted my hips, and I was thankful that the cuffs reached my wrists, but I was less grateful that its high collar scratched midway up my neck. I'd never been a fan of fabrics and metals closely fitted to my neck, and unlike Aunt Vera who loved them, I'd always avoided mock necks, turtlenecks, choker necklaces, and tight-fitting scarves whenever possible. With a quiet sigh, I finished assembling myself, buttoning up the jacket and securing the matching belt at my waist.

Even though I felt that a bun would likely be better suited to the look, I didn't have the hairpins or the patience I needed to make that happen and wasn't about to wake up Remms for something so stupid, so I decided to tie my hair into a mid-level ponytail instead.

Scrutinizing my appearance in the mirror one final time, I grimaced at my stuffy reflection.

I look like I'm ready to join all the other grey drones. Yay...

Sighing again to myself, I shut off the bathroom light and quietly deposited my bag by the couch but out of the way, so Remms wouldn't trip over it if he were to get up. I ventured to the kitchen to down a glass of water, pretending in vain that it was coffee.

Breakfast done, I opened Remms' fridge and selected one of the food containers that didn't hold a liquid, deciding to make whatever it was my lunch. I put the container as well as a fork and a fancy cloth napkin - leave it to Remms to have only posh napkins - into the empty bag Amorette had brought last night.

"Lunch bag" in hand, I put on my flat black shoes and left Remms' apartment, remembering to lock the door behind me.

Walking down the hall toward the stairs, I was surprised at how everything in the building looked exactly the same as it always did. It didn't seem to matter what time of the day or night it was. The lights were always on, there were always people around, and it was business as usual.

When I arrived on the second floor, I headed to my destination. Pausing in front of the closed door, I took a few breaths, desperately trying to calm my rising nerves from the anticipation of what I might face.

You can do this, Megan. It's like the first day of high school. Nothing's worse than that...except pretty much everything you've had to face on Qarradune. AHHHH! Okay, breathe. Time to look on the bright side. You're no longer a slave. No one is trying to kill you at the moment, and you have a maybe-date later.

Using my positive Mez thoughts, I willed myself to open the door, ready to face what was on the other side.

Inside the windowless and metal clad room were a dozen personal-sized metal tables bolted to the floor, with matching metal chairs. At every table, save for one, sat a person wearing the exact same uniform as me. Every one of them had their heads down and was writing diligently. On each table was an inkwell, pens, and two thick stacks of papers. Not a single one of my peers looked up to see that I had entered the room.

Wow. How very anti-climactic.

Closing the door behind me, I walked over to the only empty chair, took a seat, and placed my bag under the table. I felt like I'd just entered a room where I'd be taking a final exam, except that the exam would decide whether I lived or died and not whether I would pass or fail.

Looking around briefly, I saw that there was nothing on the walls, except one of those weird clocks. Having no idea how to read that clock, I frowned a little, realizing that this was probably going to feel like one of the longest and most boring days of my life.

Beyond knowing time by cycles and seasons, I should probably make a concerted effort to find out how to read a Kavylak clock. Come to think of it, I don't recall seeing one of these or even a regular-looking clock in Irys' home. Maybe in Syliza they tell time differently? Or maybe they have fancier liquid-dripping clocks? The next time I get the...

"You need to start."

My eyes darted to the woman sitting across from me, who had spoken. She wasn't looking at me. Her eyes were focused on one sheet of paper in front of her while her hand rapidly wrote words across a second one. When the page she was writing was complete, she added it to the already done pile before taking another fresh sheet and starting the writing process all over again, without missing a beat.

Deciding it would be best not to continue watching Robot Girl work, I turned my focus to my own stacks of paper and took a fresh blank sheet and one sheet from the stack of paper that was already filled with words. I examined the words on the page for a moment. I had no trouble reading it, and based on the style of the writing, I guessed that what I was likely looking at was Sylizan. All I had to do was translate these words by writing them in the style of Kavylak. Since I was surrounded by Kavylak writing everywhere, I was confident this would be a piece of cake...until I remembered I'd have to write using a quill pen and inkwell.

Okay, this would be a piece of cake if I had a ballpoint pen. Seriously, Kavylak has Warriors with magical superpowers and ships with cloaking technology, but they're still using old-timey writing implements? I don't get it.

Warily eyeing the inkwell and quill pen, knowing I'd struggled to use them in the past, I took a quiet breath and picked up the wooden pen. Stealing a glance at Robot Girl, I watched how she put the ink on the pen and then worked it across the surface of the paper. The action was entirely flawless.

It was now or never. I dipped the tip of the pen into the well and wrote my first letter and gasped in horror. What should have been the letter "P" was a messy blob with a tail. I must have put too much ink on the pen.

"Can't you use a pen?" Robot Girl whispered in disbelief.

This time, when I looked her way, she was staring back at me.

"Not this kind," I whispered back, feeling both embarrassed and annoyed that it looked as though I couldn't write a simple letter. Meanwhile, if I'd had a normal pen, pencil, or even a keyboard, I could write just as fast as the rest of them. Even if I'd had access to the ink-filled pen I'd seen Mez use before, I likely would have had a better shot at forming legible letters. I guessed those pens must have been a luxury item, since no one in this room was using one.

Frustrated, I turned back to my page, accepting the fact that I would have to continue writing like a toddler, until I could figure this out. Before I could dip the pen into the inkwell, Robot Girl surprised me by placing a tiny pencil - no bigger than a golf pencil - on my table.

"You brought that yourself," she informed me, "and you won't get away with it after today, so you'd better learn tonight. Pull the string to sharpen it," she added.

I stared at her, stunned by her kindness. "Thanks," I whispered, setting the pen down and picking up the pencil. She didn't reply and was already back to work as if we'd never exchanged words.

Taking the hint, I discarded the messy paper, set up a fresh one, and started to translate the pages using the pencil. The pencil was nearly identical to the one Thayn had given me with the journal, when we had first met. I'd left both in my guest room at the Godeleva estate, and I assumed that they were long gone. It didn't matter anyhow. I couldn't think about that anymore. That was the past. I had decided to make Kavylak my future until I could find my way back home. Still, it hurt my heart to think about Thayn, even though I hoped that he was sailing far, far away from here. I had wanted to be his girlfriend. He was a good person. I missed him.

I continued writing, finding that focusing on the work was stopping my mind from taking too many emotional trips down memory lane. When I reached the point that I had to sharpen the pencil, I examined it for a moment, found the string my robot friend had mentioned, and pulled it. It was then that I realized the pencil was covered in layers of paper, which peeled back just like a wax pencil, instantly sharpening it.

Finally, when I was pretty sure I wouldn't be able to write one more letter and was convinced that my hand would be stuck in a permanent claw shape, I heard my robot friend set her pen down. I sneaked a sideways glance at her and saw her reach for a container under her table. She set it on the table surface and opened it to reveal other smaller containers, each holding food.

Yay! Lunch!

Placing my pencil down, I flexed my aching fingers before snatching up my own container of food and the fork. I was starving and my stomach grumbled in anticipation. The container held rice and mixed vegetables, which were coated in a sweet sauce. It probably would have tasted better if it was heated up, but I didn't mind it cold.

Eating contentedly, I glanced over at my robot friend to see her slowly drinking soup from a container as she stared off into space. Since everyone else was eating now and was quietly chatting, I figured talking wasn't against the rules.

"Have you been doing this job for a long time?" I asked.

"Yes," she replied, "Since I was no longer a child."

I paused mid-chew when she said that as my brain pieced together that she must have done this job for several years. She didn't look any younger than me, and I had no idea what age was considered "no longer a child" in Kavylak. With the overall vibe I'd been given from this country, or at least its capital city, I wouldn't have been shocked if once you hit the age of six you were considered an adult.

"Do you live on the base, too?" I asked.

"We all do."

Okay. Good to know. If you work for the military, you live here, too.

"I'm Megan, by the way," I introduced myself, hoping that she would tell me her name, though I wasn't holding my breath, since she wasn't the chattiest person in the universe.

"Nilaal."

Hoping that was her name and not some Kavylak colloquial slang for "whatever" or "shut-up" or something along those lines, I said, "Nice to meet you, Nilaal. I think you're the fastest writer I've ever met." That wasn't an empty compliment. I'd never seen anyone speed hand-write that quickly. I'd have loved to have seen what she could have done on a computer.

She nodded. "I'm fast. It's important. We are paid by the piece, and we don't go home until we are finished."

I mentally grimaced and subconsciously flexed my sore hand as I looked at the stack of papers I had left to translate, suddenly very glad that I had a pencil today and more motivated than ever to learn how to use the ancient quill pen.

"Thanks for the info. I didn't know that. I'm new here and was informed that this would be my job at sort of the last minute."

"You didn't know you would have this job?" she asked, not hiding that she found this odd.

"No. I knew I would be assigned a job, but I didn't know which one it would be."

"You are fortunate," Nilaal said, with an underlying speculation in her tone that made me feel like she was judging my character, and not in a good way.

"How so?" I asked, my brow furrowing a bit as I tried to sound curious and not offended.

My question didn't seem to sway her opinion of me in a positive direction. Her expression morphed from its general indifference to a mixture of resentment and disbelief at my utter stupidity.

"These jobs fill fast and there are nearly no openings. They pay well, and there is no physical labour. They are indoors and unsupervised until the end of the day." Although she didn't say it, the word "idiot" was definitely implied in her tone, silently punctuating the end of her statement.

"Oh," was my dimwitted reply. I genuinely had no idea that this was the case, and I suddenly realized how lucky I was that Mez had managed to secure me this job and not something else that – based on the impression Nilaal had given me – was far worse.

Thanks, Mez! You're awesome!

Nilaal didn't respond or continue the conversation. Instead, she finished the last sip of her lunch, put the container away, and immediately plunged into work with such intensity that you'd swear she'd never stopped for lunch and an awkward conversation.

Wow. Okay, don't count on being fast friends with Nilaal, Megan.

I decided that it would be best to return to work as well, even though I knew our break wasn't yet done, as everyone else in the room continued to eat and chatter. Jamming the last few bites of food into my mouth, I returned the container and fork to my bag, gave my hands a wipe on the napkin, and picked up my pencil to dive back in.

Determined to complete my stack of papers as quickly as possible, I worked without looking up or caring about the time. Hours passed until finally the door to the room opened and someone walked in. Glancing up, I saw that it was the pretty blond, scary-as-all-hell military woman, Major Relah Tovash.

Flicking my gaze back to my work, I forced myself to continue. I had only two pages to go, and I wanted to be done before she left.

Without a word, Major Tovash approached the area where Nilaal and I sat. Tension built in my body and remained, even as she breezed by me and stopped at Nilaal's desk. Out of the corner of my eye, I noticed that Nilaal had finished her work and had been sitting stone-faced, for who knows how long. The major picked up the thick stack of papers, flipped through a few pages to analyze them, and then placed a strip of paper around the entire bundle, using a ring she wore to place her seal on it.

Major Tovash nodded to Nilaal, who stood, bowed to her, and left the room without looking at anyone.

The major continued moving around the room, inspecting everyone's work, bundling it up, and giving them each her nod of approval. One by one they left, until there was only me. She stood close, hovering over me and watching as I completed the last page I was translating.

It's official. I'm living my worst school exam nightmare.

As soon as I deposited the final paper on top of the stack, she began checking my work. I held my breath, hoping I'd receive a nod, so I could get out of there.

To my surprise, she held her hand out in front of my face. "Give me the pencil," she demanded.

I handed it over, remembering that Nilaal had said something like this would happen.

The major took the pencil and tucked it into a pocket of her perfectly starched uniform. "You will work with a pen. If you are caught with another pencil, you will be terminated."

With how she said it, I genuinely wasn't sure if she meant I'd be fired or killed.

"Yes, Major Tovash."

She continued to check my work for what felt like an eternity and then finally bound and sealed it.

"Go home," she stated like she was instructing a dog. I stood, prepared to bow to her as Nilaal had done, but she turned and walked out of the room, leaving me standing there dumbfounded.

Snapping out of it, I grabbed my bag and left the room, glad that the worst of the day was now behind me.

"Hi Megs. Good first day?"

I jumped at the sound of Amarogq's voice.

"Oh! Amarogq. Uh, hey, uh, yeah. I mean, as good as it could be. It's work, right?" I babbled awkwardly.

Oh no! Not Amarogq. Not now.

Amarogq chuckled at my reaction, looking calm and casual, leaning against the wall just outside the room. The red and black feathers that were fastened to the single small braid he wore in his long black hair dusted the top of a garment bag that was draped over one of his arms. He was also carrying a paper shopping bag with a ribbon handle. Tissue paper was folded over the top of the bag's contents to keep it concealed.

"How could I have made you jump, Megs? This is my least startling face." He smiled warmly.

"Sorry. I'm a little on edge. It's been a very long day, and I just encountered one of the scariest women in the military, who threatened either my job or my life for using a pencil."

"That sounds about right for a translation job around here," he said amused, not sounding surprised at what I had told him. "Speaking of jobs, I've been assigned to you. Remms asked Amorette for a little wardrobe support on your behalf. She asked me to polish off the job by playing the role of courier." He gestured to the items he was carrying.

I looked at him blankly for a moment and then flushed when it sank in that Amarogq was holding my possible-date outfit.

"Oh! Um, right. Thanks, Amarogq."

He raised a brow. "Are you alright, Megs?"

"Yes." I faked a smile. "I didn't realize that the outfit would be delivered to me, and by you, no less. I thought it would just be waiting for me at Remms'. I hope she didn't go to too much trouble."

He shook his head. "It's no trouble." He pushed off the wall. "Shall I escort you to your quarters?"

I was glad it was no trouble, but I really didn't want to walk with Amarogq. "You don't have to. I imagine you have better things to do."

"Better things to do than walking you back to Remms' place?" He looked at me playfully like I was crazy for even thinking it. "Nah. I'm up for the stairs. Plus, I thought I'd use the brief time that you're stuck with me to make sure we're good," he added with a more meaningful gaze.

I mentally sighed and resigned myself to the fact that I'd have to walk with him and make up some story as to why I've been so weird around him lately. Nodding to him, I started walking, and he followed.

"You don't think we're good?"

"No. I remember when we were good once. You weren't all twitchy like this back then. Do I need a wolf to talk to you? They're fuzzy. People like fuzzy." I could hear his smile even though I resisted looking at him, and I couldn't help but smile, too. I missed my friend, but I felt that I had to lie because the truth would hurt him so much.

"Okay. You're right. Things are different now. It's just…" I trailed off, scrambling to come up with something that was remotely believable. "It's just really difficult to look at you without thinking about the People of the North," I blurted.

Wow, Megan. That's the best lie you can come up with? You find it hard to look at him without thinking about what happened with the People? Geeze, could I have made a more racist comment?

He rested his hand gently on my shoulder to stop me, before we made our way up the stairs. I looked at him, knowing it was what he wanted.

His expression was a mass of concern and confusion. "It's me, Megs. I'm not here to hurt you or anything. I'm just carrying your outfit for you. I'm the same guy who makes all the great dried meat you love so much."

I nodded and bit the inside of my cheek to keep my emotions in check and stop myself from telling him everything right then and there. I felt awful doing it, but I had to sell this lie. "Oh, I know that. I do. You're a good guy, Amarogq." Smiling a little I added, "I'll get over it. I know I will. It was just…a lot."

"Megs, what did they do to you?" he asked in a quieter voice, his dark brown eyes searching my face for answers. "Is it what happened to Mez and Keavren?"

"Yes." Sure, that works. Yup, that's why I feel all weird around him, it's because I see him and see what his people did to Mez and Keavren…it has nothing to do with Ash Dancer and his children…

He nodded with an understanding that gave me a sliver of hope that he believed me. "They're both healed. Keavren's even on a mission. You won't ever have to go back there." He assured me. "The People are actually good. I know I won't be able to convince you of that, but they are. They were reacting to the Warriors. It had nothing to do with you."

"I know they're not bad people, Amarogq." Okay, with the exception of Doom Breaker. It would take a lot of convincing for me to think that woman wasn't a bad person. "I do, really. The whole experience was just a lot, and it's not something I can forget in a day or two."

Frowning, he nodded. "I understand." He paused a moment before asking, "Would you rather I leave you alone for a while?"

It was my turn to frown. I felt terrible for making him think that I wasn't happy around him for reasons that weren't true, but the alternative would have been worse.

"Yes." I stated, adding quickly, "But not for long. Only until I can wrap my head around everything."

"Alright," he said without sounding like there were any hard feelings. "Come visit me whenever you're ready to see me again." He held out the garment bag and shopping bag to me. "I'll try to stay out of your path until then."

I took the bags from him, feeling more awkward and guilty than ever, and nodded. "Thanks for understanding, Amarogq. You really are a good friend."

He gave me a small nod. "Have a fun time with Mez, Megs. You deserve some time off," he stated genuinely.

And you deserve the truth. I only wish I felt I was the right person to tell you.

"Thank you, Amarogq." I hoped he could hear the genuine gratitude in my words.

"See ya, Megs."

"See ya."

Watching him turn and descend the stairs, I knew that even if his intended destination had been to return home, he was deliberately choosing to walk in the opposite direction from where I was headed, to respect my space as he had promised he would.

Amarogq was a true friend, and all I could think as I continued my journey to Remms' quarters, was that I was not.

Am I making the right choice by not telling him?

Glancing at the garment and shopping bags I carried, I knew that as hard as it was to keep this secret, it had to be the right choice. This secret wouldn't just hurt Amarogq, but Amorette, too.

Sighing wearily, I fished Remms' key out of my skirt pocket and unlocked the door. Right now, I couldn't think about the People of the North drama. I had to get ready for a potential date.

Chapter 15

Irys

"I've heard of you, Miss Godeleva," said Storr Dimog, after he had patiently listened to my tale. "Word that you have gone missing has reached my ear. Still, I'm surprised to see you in my home." He smiled warmly, the skin around his eyes crinkling in a way that made it look as though there were rays coming from their outer corners like little suns.

I was astonished to discover that he'd heard of me and that I'd gone missing. How could he have come across such news? I tried to push these thoughts aside to concentrate on the conversation before me.

"I'm glad to see you're here and that you look none the worse for wear despite an unkind journey," he continued.

"Thank you, Mr. Dimog. It wasn't my original intention to arrive here, but I thank the Goddess for having brought me to your door. Your home is beautiful, and I have been treated very kindly by your family and friends." I wasn't about to fault his daughter and some of the other Rebels for having been suspicious of me after I'd brought Acksil back to them.

He smiled again, and I felt as though I'd been rewarded for saying the right thing.

"Would you like to wash up and change into something clean and more to your taste? We can speak further once you are feeling refreshed and settled," he offered as though actively answering my prayers.

"I'd like that very much, Mr. Dimog. I can't thank you enough." I curtsied to him again, and he replied with a deep nod.

"I will ask Gebbie – the head of my household staff – to see to your needs. When you are ready, come see me in my study. I will have tea for you."

I felt like I had been hugged and told that everything would be fine from then on. "Thank you very much," I said, feeling silly for repeating the words, but no matter how many times I said them, they would never describe the depth of my gratitude.

As though she had been waiting for her cue just outside the door, a woman stepped into the room, and Mr. Dimog nodded to her. She was dressed in a loose tunic and a long skirt. The outfit was completed by a head scarf that hung loosely over her curling grey hair, which peeked out from under the decorative cloth. She was golden skinned like Mr. Dimog, and friendly upturned creases in her face suggested that she may have been around his age as well. She gave an overall congenial impression that I found quite appealing.

"Ah, just the person I was looking for. Gebbie, this is Miss Godeleva. Please help her with a bath and see that she has all the comforts she needs."

"Yes, Mr. Dimog," Gebbie said in a friendly, casual tone. "Come along, Miss Godeleva. Let's get you freshened up." Unlike Mr. Dimog, Gebbie spoke to me in mildly accented Sylizan.

"I look forward to speaking with you again, Mr. Dimog," I said as I followed Gebbie out of the room. "Thank you, Gebbie," I added.

"Aren't you a pretty little thing," Gebbie said as she stepped in beside me and brought her arm around my waist as a close aunt might have done. I was certainly surprised by the gesture but somehow wasn't upset by it. It was comforting. I felt protected and cared for. "It's not often we have such fine-looking ladies coming through our doors." She chuckled to herself as we travelled through a maze of hallways.

"I can't imagine that there is any part of me that looks pretty under all this filth, but you are kind to say so," I replied modestly.

"Oh hush!" Gebbie smilingly scolded. "You're lovely, and you know it. No amount of grime could hide that. And I can see by how fiercely you're holding that cloak around you that you're not so happy with your clothes, Miss Godeleva."

"Thank you, Gebbie," I replied quietly, feeling unbalanced by Gebbie's informal way of speaking to me. It was friendly, but I didn't know how to reply. "My clothes were selected for me for practicality, not appearance. They were meant to help me to make a swift escape, despite the impropriety," I added.

"I bet you look lovely in one of those grand Sylizan gowns," Gebbie concluded.

"I'm far more accustomed to that type of clothing, though I certainly don't have a gown in my bag with me." I chuckled a little.

To that, Gebbie just gave her hand a little wave like it didn't matter in the slightest. She brought me down yet another hall and slid open a door which revealed a large bathing room with a deep soaker tub.

Gebbie strode into the room and started the bath as I wondered whether I would ever be able to find my way back through the labyrinth of this house and its many hallways. My eyes fell on the water tumbling out of the polished faucet, and a smile crept onto my lips as I realized what was happening. I was going to have a bath! A clean, warm bath. It was nearly enough to distract me from my worry over Acksil's wellbeing. I imagined that he had already been cared for by the doctor and may even be soaking in his own tub.

"Oh, Gebbie, that must be the most beautiful bathing tub I've ever seen," I gushed with a chuckle, feeling slightly giddy.

She grinned, setting out everything I would need to scrub myself clean.

"It's all for you, Miss Godeleva. Will you require my assistance, or would you like to enjoy this time for yourself? Everything you need is here."

"I can manage on my own, thank you. A good soak is all I need," I replied, finding it hard to keep eye contact with her when all I wanted to do was look at the tub, which was filling with clear water.

"If you need anything, only ring for me, sweet lady. Now you get clean and feeling like yourself again. I'll go find you something to wear, hmm? Don't you worry, Miss Godeleva. I knew a lady like you once."

I nodded to her instructions and somehow knew that she would find me something far more appropriate than anything I'd worn in Kavylak while I was there. She would respect my modesty. I was certain of it.

"I'm in good hands. Thank you, Gebbie."

"The very best," she said cheerfully as she left the room, sliding the door shut behind her.

Once she was gone, I tried to move quickly to extract myself from the clothes Acksil had given me. They'd served me well, but I couldn't wait to be rid of them. My bruises complained loudly, but other than wincing on occasion, I did my best to ignore them. Instead, I slowly eased myself into the warm water, holding back a groan at the sensation.

Once my hair was thoroughly washed, I let myself soak for a while. I knew I should likely have moved faster so I could check on Acksil and talk to Mr. Dimog. It was true that taking time to luxuriate in the warm water was selfish of me. I did it anyway. Every minute that passed relaxed the parts of me that had suffered from sleeping on the ground, riding horses for far too long, and landing under Acksil when we'd fallen from our mount.

As the water started to cool, I took up the labour of thoroughly scrubbing myself clean. Just as I was finishing, there was a knock at the door.

"Miss Godeleva, it's Gebbie," said the woman's pleasant voice. It was as though she'd known precisely how much time I would need to bathe. "May I come in? I have your clothing."

"Yes, of course," I replied, feeling comforted with the thought of a friendly servant coming in to attend me with my bath. For a brief moment, it helped to suppress the feeling of homesickness I'd been suffering underneath the trauma of the last several days and that was increasingly making itself known to me with every new familiar thing.

My eyes widened as Gebbie entered carrying a tremendous garment bag. It was clear that I was not to be dressed in something similar to what the rest of the Rebels were wearing. My heart leapt at the thought that I might be about to dress in something closer to the gowns to which I was accustomed.

She hung the garment bag on a hook on the wall, unfastening it to release the lovely gown it had contained. It was Sylizan, I was certain of it. It was quite out of fashion, but it was made of a gorgeous deep navy-blue fabric with soft pink flowers growing up from its hem and into the bodice. As dated as it was, it was still lovely and would have been quite striking in its day.

"It's gorgeous," I gushed. "How is it that I have been blessed with a fine Sylizan gown to wear?"

"Mr. Dimog thought you'd like it," Gebbie said proudly. "It belonged to the late Mrs. Dimog. She was once a lady like you. She was Lady Laylia Anglemore before she married."

Mrs. Dimog had been an Anglemore!

"Goodness," I said stupidly.

The Anglemores were high nobility. The head of their family was currently Lady Galadzia Anglemore, who was powerful enough among Sylizan nobles that everyone was willing to turn a blind eye to her wild and eccentric choices.

"I see you know the Anglemore name, Miss Godeleva," Gebbie noted, looking amused at my expression.

"The Anglemores are quite the family," I responded noncommittally.

"Indeed, they are, and Lady Laylia was quite the lady." It was more than clear that Gebbie was very fond of the late Mrs. Dimog.

"She had wonderful taste in gowns." I stood, drawing my large, fluffy towel around me as I carefully stepped out of the tub.

Gebbie nodded, walked up behind me with a towel, and wrapped my hair. I felt as though I'd found a kind friend in this woman.

"You'll see many of Lady Laylia's influences in the decor through the house and the gardens as you see more of them. I think you'll appreciate them."

"I look forward to trying to spot them," I said with an eager smile.

As soon as I was dry, she worked efficiently to help me dress. It was more than evident that this wasn't the first time Gebbie had assisted a woman with a Sylizan gown.

I adjusted my necklace at my throat so my ring would fall under the modest neckline of the gown. "Do you style hair as well as you dress a lady?"

"I can." She nodded. "Would you prefer it styled up, or would you like some of it left down?"

"Up at the front and down at the back, please. I'd like to look neat and presentable without appearing stern or formal," I explained.

I was seated at the vanity and Gebbie went to work on my hair. I watched the iridescent streaks in the mirror the entire time as though I could somehow return them to normal with my eyes. No matter how hard I focused, they remained as prominent as ever. Despite their presence, Gebbie did a lovely job of creating a soft, intricate style that looked pleasant and in no way severe. It was quite different from what Desda would have done, but I enjoyed the soft design of it.

"This is just what I wanted. You've read my mind," I complimented, genuinely pleased.

"I'm glad. It's been several cycles, but I haven't lost my touch," she replied, then sounded mischievous as she continued. "Between you and me, I'm pleased that you've returned Nydo to us."

"Oh?" I asked curiously. "I was under the impression that he was not terribly welcome here anymore."

"You're not wrong. Most would rather see him dead and buried than here among us. But I always liked the boy. He's got a charm about him. I wouldn't say I agreed with his choice to leave, but I always believed in my heart that he'd find his way back to his true family."

It saddened me to hear confirmation of how badly Acksil had hurt his relationship with these people who were once so important to him. Equally, I was comforted to know that he had at least one ally here.

"He has become a good man. I understand why the others feel deeply betrayed. What he did was unkind, to say the least. But since I've known him, he has risked his life for mine more than once. He didn't have to do that. To bring me here, he has lost everything."

"That's the Nydo I know," Gebbie said as though speaking as a proud mother. "He's a good man who does what he thinks is right, even when he's wrong. You must be very special to him for him to have made such sacrifices for you and to risk coming back here."

"He's Acksil now, but his heart is the same," I confirmed, then blushed a little, feeling the heat rise in my cheeks. "I don't know if I'm very special to him. He was already helping me before he knew anything about me. He just seems to be inclined to do the right thing. He has goodness in him."

"He will always be Nydo, no matter what he calls himself. And I still say you are special to him," she teased.

"I certainly feel special now that you've dressed me properly, Gebbie," I complimented, hoping to steer the topic in a new direction that would allow my face to cool.

"Good. Are you feeling up to speaking with Mr. Dimog now?"

"Yes, if only to thank him for his hospitality. Still, I'm curious to talk to the man whose name is known across Qarradune as being the leader of the Dsumot Rebels, but who has been far from the man I'd expected him to be."

"Then come with me, child," she said, smiling. This was obviously not the first time Gebbie had spoken with someone who was surprised by Mr. Dimog.

I nodded obediently and picked up my bag, pushing my feet into the simple black satin slippers that were set on the floor for me. Gebbie brought her arm around me again and guided me back through the house, which was already appearing less labyrinthine as I made my way back through the same corridors.

"I'll take your bag to your room if you'd like," she offered.

"Thank you. Will my room be near Acksil's?"

"No. If you want to be near Nydo, you'll need to talk to Mr. Dimog about it."

"I will," I agreed.

We came to Mr. Dimog's study and Gebbie knocked on the open door.

"Mr. Dimog, Miss Godeleva is here to see you now," she said, causing Mr. Dimog to look up from a page he was reading while seated behind his desk.

He stood and stepped around the desk, indicating a seating area with a loveseat and two chairs and where tea had been laid out. "Please come in, Miss Godeleva. Have a seat."

"Thank you, Gebbie," I said quietly as I relinquished my bag to her and entered the room. The door slid closed behind me, and I curtsied to him before sitting in the loveseat to avoid crushing the gown. "Thank you for seeing me, Mr. Dimog."

"You look beautiful, Miss Godeleva. I'm glad the dress fits and is to your taste. I'm sure it's nothing like the latest fashion, but it was for its time."

"I feel like myself for the first time in many days," I replied, sharing my prettiest smile with him. "I'm grateful to you for lending it to me."

"It's good to see it worn again." He settled into the chair closest to me.

"I'm surprised your daughter does not wear her mother's gowns. They would suit her wonderfully."

"If you knew her better, you would not be surprised. My daughter is not fond of these gowns or anything else Sylizan."

He was right. It shouldn't have surprised me. From the small amount of time I'd spent with Miss Skeltra Dimog, she hadn't shown any love for what was beyond the Rebel cause.

"Please help yourself to anything you'd like." He gestured toward the tea, where there was also a plate of finger sandwiches and jam tarts.

I smiled, suddenly feeling very hungry indeed. "Shall I pour?" I offered.

When he nodded, I poured us each a cup of tea, noting that, like me, he did not add any lemon or sugar to his cup.

I sipped delicately at the tea, allowing the familiar flavour to embrace me.

"It's lovely." I could feel the tranquility it brought me sinking into my very bones.

He looked pleased and helped himself to the sandwiches. I eagerly joined him, laying a napkin on my lap before taking a small plate and eating with my fingertips. The familiarity of this simple moment restored me, making me feel inclined to dance. Mr. Dimog granted us a peaceful pause before beginning our conversation, and I was grateful for it.

"You've created a spot of paradise here in Dsumot, Mr. Dimog," I said, breaking our silence in case he was waiting for my cue to begin talking. "I couldn't have imagined that I would feel so comfortable and happy today."

"I'm pleased that you feel this way, Miss Godeleva. I must be honest with you. If I had not known who you were when you arrived, I can't say that you would have received quite this much hospitality."

I raised a brow, my curiosity piqued. "How is it that you know who I am, and why would knowing this change your treatment of me?"

"My Sylizan connections keep me informed about important news from that country. A Traveller visited me early this morning to tell me of your plight. A missing member of the Godeleva family doesn't go unnoticed. I was given a detailed description of you and was told that you were believed to be in Kavylak."

Of everything Mr. Dimog had to say, there was one part that sharply stood out to me. "A Traveller?"

"Yes. I believe you know him, though by which name you are acquainted with him, I could not say." He looked amused as he sipped his tea.

"Does he have long, pewter-grey hair?" I asked, hoping it might be Rimoth, who had the ability – and possibly the willingness – to bring me home again.

"He does indeed."

It has to be Rimoth! Great Goddess, how wise you are in your care of me and of those I love.

In that one moment, my home, which was more than half a world away, was brought within my reach once more.

"Will he be returning soon?"

"I don't know for certain. If he does, it shouldn't be in too many days."

"It is only that I believe he will be willing to bring me home. He was the reason I was abducted and taken to Kavylak. It was not intentional, but he was certainly to blame."

"He said as much. He feels he owes you a debt. I've never seen Lyir go out of his way for anyone as he has done on your behalf, Miss Godeleva."

My eyebrow raised again. "Lyir? I know him as Rimoth."

"Rimoth, Kaytar, Vitali," he listed with a nod. "He uses several names but from what I understand, Lyir is the name he considers to be his own. He enjoys his anonymity among everyone but those who are most important to him, which I can understand. He is hundreds of cycles old and lives all over Qarradune."

I pondered his words as I bit into one of the little tarts. It made sense that a man who lived for such a long time, and who had lives in many countries would create separate identities in case something should go awry. It struck me as a difficult and impersonal way to live.

"Lyir, Lord Godeleva, and I have a mutual friend who lives in Syliza. That's why I suspect your story was shared with me. Our friend wants to spread the word for Lord Godeleva's sake, in order to help bring you home."

Oh, the sound of his name! How it makes my heart ache. Lord Imery, I'm not far now!

I swallowed hard, pushing down the rush of homesickness that threatened to bring tears to my eyes. Determined, I chose to focus on the matter at hand. This was not the time for falling apart.

"Would I know this friend?" I asked, eager to learn the identity of this well-connected man.

"You would, but for the time being, I will not disclose her name," he replied.

A woman! How fascinating! Could it be Lady Brensforth? Perhaps Lady Anglemore?

I resisted the inclination to ask, choosing to respect the privacy upon which he was insisting.

"I understand. In that case, I'd like to talk about Acksil, if you would allow it. Has Miss Dimog had the chance to speak to you of my situation, to confirm why I feel it is necessary to remain near him?"

He nodded. "She told me some. The Warrior told me the rest."

"Acksil has been very good to me, and he isn't a Warrior anymore."

"I believe you when you say he has been good to you, Miss Godeleva, but forgive me if I do not share your belief that he is not one of *them* anymore."

"I can see why you have doubts about his intentions, but I know in my heart that he will convince you over time. He betrayed you, and I can't condone that. Still, I know that he will show you the better man he has become."

Mr. Dimog nodded, clearly respecting my perspective without agreeing with it. I chose not to insist upon the matter any further.

"Will his room be anywhere near mine?" I asked, getting to my point.

He shook his head. "No. You are welcome to visit him if you wish. You are my guest. But even after he has recovered from the venom, he will not be free to roam this building. He remains our prisoner."

It was clear from his tone that the issue was not up for debate. The last thing I wanted to do was upset Mr. Dimog and cause him to change his mind about me, too.

"I will not ask you to change your mind," I replied carefully. "I asked only because he has been taking care of me while I sleep. I can sleep for only short spans of time before I am placed at risk of Xandon's interference once more. Acksil has been waking me through the night to prevent such harm."

Flashes of moments appeared before my mind's eye. The more I permitted myself to think upon it, the more I realized how much Acksil truly had done for me. It wasn't just the rescues - which were tremendous, to say the least. He had kept me safe. He had done what he could to make me comfortable. Somewhere along the way, he had become a true friend. Even the resentment I'd once held against him for stealing my first kiss had lifted away.

Perhaps, one day, I may even smile at the thought of it.

"Any one of us could do that for you. I'm sure Gebbie would be happy to help you," Mr. Dimog said, pulling me from my brief disappearance into my own thoughts.

I nodded, hiding my disappointment that Acksil and I would be separated far more than I had expected. Mr. Dimog's decision made sense. "Thank you. I'm hoping that it is no longer necessary, but I'm not willing to take the risk. I'm afraid of Xandon and what he can do."

"As you should be, Miss Godeleva. I don't take your request lightly. This is a serious matter. No one understands the ancient magics used by that man. It's as though he was born from Chaos itself. You are safe from him as long as you're here. I also welcome you to visit anywhere in my house or its library and gardens."

"Will I be able to talk with you now and again?"

I was glad to have asked this question as he looked genuinely surprised and touched by the request. The corners of his eyes crinkled brightly as he smiled.

"I would like that very much, Miss Godeleva. You are always welcome to come see me. If I am available, I will be happy to share company with you."

I found myself feeling as touched by his words as he had looked by mine.

"As would I, Mr. Dimog. I will make use of your welcome."

I imagined that this must be how it would feel to have a favourite uncle or grandfather. I'd known this man for less than an hour but felt as though he was a family member I hadn't seen since childhood, the last time I'd had family other than Lord Imery. I liked the thought of such a familial relationship. It had been a very long time since Lord Imery and I had had anyone beyond each other.

Though I'd hoped to say more, a knock interrupted our conversation.

At Mr. Dimog's invitation, his daughter entered and opened her mouth to speak until her gaze landed on me. I watched her eyes skim over my gown before they narrowed into a glare. I was fortunate that her eyes could not light fires as I would have gone up in flames. I attempted to give her a friendly smile, hoping to sway her opinion of me.

"Why is *she* wearing Mother's dress?" she demanded of Mr. Dimog.

The smile rapidly faded from my lips. With Miss Skeltra Dimog in the room, the situation was about to become considerably more challenging.

Chapter 16

Megan

After about an hour of getting ready for what would possibly be my first date with Mez, I stood in front of the door to his quarters, feeling excited because I was going to do something fun with Mez. Not only that, but for once, I felt like I looked the best he'd ever seen me, and I was thrilled to take part in something new that wasn't related to the military or being kidnapped. The last time I'd felt this happy about something on Qarradune was when I had attended the Godeleva Masque. Although it had been only weeks ago, it felt like an eternity had passed since then.

Still, as thrilled as I was, I was equally apprehensive. I was nervous that something would go wrong tonight. Mez and I didn't exactly have the best track record in terms of positive encounters. Call me crazy, but having two near-death experiences had me feeling a little on edge. Plus, it wasn't like the Masque had ended well for me, either. On top of that, I continued to worry about Aésha. She still wasn't home.

Giving my head a little shake to clear my gloomy thoughts, I reminded myself that all I had to focus on right now was having a good time with Mez. Smoothing my hands over the dress Amorette had lent me, a smile crept up my face. The dress was easily the nicest piece of clothing I'd worn in Kavylak.

It was a black sleeveless dress. The skirt was flared with a pleated cream tulle overlay that swished when I moved and gave it a cool alternating black-to-cream coloured look. The shoes were black patent pumps with a slim ankle strap from which dangled cute little gold charms that matched the gold at the tip of their heels. Remms had tucked his key into a clutch that matched the cream part of the skirt. I was thankful it had a gold chain I could use as a strap so I wouldn't have to hold onto it the whole evening.

After washing my hair and using Remms' answer to a blow dryer to speed dry my hair, I had decided to leave it down for a change, instead of having it tied back as I usually did. Since my hair was blown dry, it was smooth, shiny, and more voluminous. This made me feel even dressier and different from how Mez usually saw me and gave my confidence a little boost. I only wished I had a bit of makeup to add to the look.

It's now or never, Megan.

Taking a deep breath, I raised my fist and knocked on Mez' door.

"It's open," he called from inside. "Unless you're Megan, in which case, I'll be right there!"

I laughed. I had been expecting him to make one of his usual quirky comments. Moments later, he opened the door. Mez was dressed in a black shirt and black pants and was wearing the black and white spat-style shoes I'd seen him wear before. What he wore wasn't extravagant by any means, but it still looked expensive, and it looked awesome on him, especially in contrast with his silver hair and the vibrant blue rose he held in his hand.

"Good evening. Won't you come in?" He extended the rose to me, and all the humour and confidence I had been feeling fled. I knew now that this had to be a one-hundred percent date. The gesture was simply too romantic. No one offers someone a rose like this for any other good reason.

Knowing I had been standing like a dunce, staring at the rose for way too long, I took it from him, hoping he hadn't seen the slight tremor of my hand that betrayed my nervousness.

"Thank you. This is really pretty. I've never seen a rose like this before." I wasn't lying. I'd seen blue roses on Earth at flower shops, but those roses were dyed blue. This one was a stunning shade of electric blue without any sign of dye in the vibrant green leaves or stem. I raised it to my nose to inhale its scent. It was beautiful.

"It's Dmevjekyan," Mez said with a hint of pride in his voice and a glint in his eye. "Would you like a drink before we head out or are you hungry?" He asked, shutting the door.

"I'm good." I smiled, shaking my head. "I had some water before I came here."

He looked at me oddly for a split second as if he were confused by what I had said. "I was thinking more in terms of a glass of wine or a cocktail before dinner."

"Oh! You mean a drink-drink...uh..." Mez' brow rose, and I felt my face turn scarlet as I realized how stupid I sounded.

"My apologies," he said with amusement, a playful but warm smile lit his face. "I must be out of practice with entertaining. What I meant to say is: 'Would you like a drink-drink before we head out or are you hungry?'"

I laughed at his rephrasing, so glad that he took my ditzy moments in stride. "No, thank you. I think I've made it more than clear that I'm not ready for a 'drink-drink'."

Chuckling with a nod, he took his black blazer off the back of a kitchen chair. Hooking it on his fingers over his shoulder, he stepped up to the door. "Let's head out to the city and see if you can have more fun than you did the last time."

"Yes." I agreed. "I'm ready for a different kind of excitement. The good kind."

"You look gorgeous by the way," he said as he opened the door for me, freezing me in my tracks. "I should have said that before I offered you the drink-drink."

So much for the redness in my cheeks cooling down.

"Thank you," I breathed out, getting a hold of my shaky nerves from his unexpected compliment. Glancing at him I said, "You look really nice, too, which surprised me. Um, I mean, not because I didn't think you'd look nice or anything, but because, um, you know, I've only really seen you in your uniform except for that one time when we went for a walk on the ship and..."

Oh my god, Megan, shut up!

I quickly stepped out the door in some lame attempt to escape my suckage as if the hallway would somehow cure me of my inability to form an intelligent sentence.

"I was aiming for cool, but I'll accept 'nice'."

I was too embarrassed to look at him but could hear the amused grin in his tone as he stepped out behind me, shutting and locking his door.

"Sure, 'cool' is definitely what I meant by 'nice'," I said, grateful he just rolled with my blabber, otherwise he'd be needing a lot of drink-drinks before this evening was over. "You are wearing your cool shoes after all," I tacked on to salvage whatever dignity I had left.

Mez extended a foot and turned it left then right as if to show off his shoes that I oh-so-admired, and chuckled. "Thank you."

His silly shoe demonstration instantly made me feel less awkward, and I smiled up at him as we walked together at a comfortable pace.

As we made our way to the building's exit, I noticed that the soldiers we passed looked surprised to see us. I wasn't sure if it was because they weren't used to seeing Mez, because maybe he chose to walk around invisible a lot; or if it was because he was out of uniform and with me; or because they knew what his skill was and were genuinely afraid of him. Whatever the reason, they were quick to give us ample room as we passed. Mez either didn't notice their surprise or didn't care. Considering what I knew of him, I felt it was more likely to be my latter guess.

"How was your first day?" he asked, once we were outside.

"It wasn't too bad. I met a very dedicated co-worker who gave me a few useful tips, including letting me know that I'd be able to get away with using a pencil today, which I did. My skills with an inkwell aren't the best, so at least tonight I'll be able to practice a bit before making a giant mess of my work tomorrow," I informed him wryly.

"You mean, you're not good with a pen?" He eyed me curiously.

"Well, I'm good with the pens I'm used to back on Earth, but the ones here that you have to dip into an inkwell? I'm terrible at using them. I drip the ink everywhere."

Mez nodded with understanding. "After dinner, I'll help you. I can show you how to use a pen. You can practice with mine," he said with easy confidence as if he was certain I'd have no problem using his pen. Unless he was referring to the fancy pen I'd seen him use before, he was going to be in for a shock.

"Thanks, I can use all the help I can get. My boss has me afraid for my life, and I'd rather die for a far worthier cause than messy ink writing."

"Major Tovash is frightening," Mez agreed, though sounded playful. It didn't surprise me that he knew who my boss was, since he was the one who got me the job.

"Quiet for a second?" he asked me politely as we approached the military compound gates.

Giving him a simple nod, I kept quiet, knowing that he was going to use his mind magic on the guards.

"Gentlemen," Mez said to the guards in a passing greeting as we walked past them. They nodded to him without appearing to notice that I was there. It occurred to me at that moment that I never thought I would need a pass to leave the compound. I had assumed that since I was with a Warrior, it didn't matter.

Guess not, and good to know.

Touching my hand to my chest, I breathed a silent sigh of relief, when I felt the metal of my ID tags press into my skin beneath my dress. It was strange and a little unsettling that something that I first thought was oppressive could become a security I was glad to have.

"Would you rather walk to the restaurant or get a ride?" Mez asked when we were out of guard range.

"I'd like to walk. I'm enjoying the fresh air, and it's kind of fun walking around all dressed up."

"I was hoping you'd say that." He grinned. "I like walking around with you 'all dressed up'."

Smiling at him, I reached out to take his hand. He slipped his warm fingers around mine and smiled back. It felt good to touch him, to be in the freedom of the open air, and to finally accept the truth of what Amorette, Dendeon, and Remms had said – and what I deep-down had known all along – that I was on a date with Mez Basarovka.

The sun was more than halfway below the horizon as we strolled along the sidewalk into the heart of the city and away from the smelly and pollution-filled harbour. All the shops and businesses we passed were closed for the day and the cafés, bars, and restaurants were coming to life. There were still plenty of people about, but it was nowhere near as crazy-busy as it had been the day before, when I'd gone to lunch with Asimara.

"You seem happier," Mez observed.

Laughing a little, I looked at him and nodded. "Yes. Once I finally realized that we're on a date, everything became a lot clearer." Secretly, I grinned inside in anticipation of his reaction to my revelation.

His left brow slowly rose as he said, "You didn't realize we were going on a date?"

And there it is!

Laughing more, I shook my head. "Nope. Although Amorette, Dendeon, and Remms were sure of it."

"Was I ambiguous about it when I asked you?" I could tell he was genuinely curious about whether he'd been too subtle.

"Likely not. Everyone else picked up on it. It's just been a crazy few days, and you're *you*, and well, I'm *me*." I said, because that really explained it all to me.

"I see." He nodded in slow playfulness. "In my defense, I thought that the fact that I'm *me* and you're *you* made it more appropriate for it to be a date. It seems I'm out of practice with that, too," he teased.

I laughed so hard I snorted. "You're really not. It's just...look, I'm going to be honest. I really, really didn't think you'd like me like that. I mean, Mez, you're really, really cool and every time you're around me, I'm either a disaster or you almost die!"

"I see," he said again with a nod as if he finally understood my point of view. "Allow me to make things clearer for this evening." He paused our walk, turned to face me, and looked me in the eyes, smiling warmly. "I really, really like you, Megan."

Time seemed to stop. Any laughter I had left in me at that moment died away, and heat instantly rushed to my face as I held his gaze. In any other situation I would have felt embarrassed for blushing, but this moment felt so unreal I had to resist pinching my skin to convince myself it was happening.

"I...I genuinely had no idea," I whispered. "I'm sorry I'm so dumb."

He shook his head. "You're not," he said softly and gave my hand an affectionate squeeze. "Is it alright with you if we continue this evening as a date?"

"Yes, I'd like that." I smiled, knowing it was true and officially not caring if I was dreaming or not. This moment was perfect.

He smiled back, and we continued our stroll. "I think I need a drink-drink," Mez said with a tension-easing chuckle.

Ha! I called it! I knew he'd be needing drink-drinks before this evening was over!

"Yeah, you're probably going to need a lot of drink-drinks to get through this date."

He laughed. "Come on, I have something I want you to see before we go to dinner."

He led us down a different street, and I was happy to go along, not in a rush to be anywhere and just happy to be with him.

"Are you warm enough?"

"Yup. I've been flustered pretty much since knocking on your door, so the heat of that is still very much with me." I wished I had been joking.

"When you stop feeling flustered, and if you get cold, just say something. I'm only carrying this jacket because I look cool this way. I'm not even planning to wear it." He was joking. Though I knew he would give me his jacket if I asked.

"Thanks, I'll let you know."

"It's easier for me to lend it to you than to keep flustering you," he teased.

"Don't worry." I chuckled. "I fluster myself all on my own. It's my Warrior skill, and it's a terrible one."

"Good to know." He grinned and turned us down another street that opened into a residential area.

The houses were not huge, but they weren't townhomes either. They were roughly about the size of the detached houses with two-car garages, where I'd grown up. That said, these homes didn't have garages, and they weren't built like Canada's typical cookie-cutter suburban houses. Most of these ones were two storeys and had their own unique designs. Some had wood paneling, some brick or stone, and others had a combination of materials. No matter the architecture however, I was impressed that each one had a large sized verdant yard. There was also a notable distance between the homes, something I was definitely not used to seeing in a city.

Wow! Nice homes in Kavylak. Who'da thought? I was expecting something more along the lines of rows and rows of square metal block houses or some large metal high-rises. I hope that the people who live in these homes have riding lawn mowers, though. I would not want to cut that grass with a push mower.

"These are really sweet homes," I told Mez. "I wouldn't have thought homes like these would exist in Kavylak."

"The towns have homes like these, but only the older part of the city has neighbourhoods like this. It wasn't until the last several cycles that the city started to look different," he explained calmly. "These are the places where people really want to live. Not right in the city, but just on its edge."

"That makes sense. We have neighbourhoods something like this back home. Some people do live in the heart of the big cities, but many like to live near them, not in them, for one reason or another. My house on Earth is located outside of my country's largest city. Not nearly as much on the edge as this one, but I get it."

He listened with interest as we turned down another street and nodded with a smile when I finished speaking. "I like it here. I walk here a lot."

I had no doubt in my mind that he did. The way he led us around, it was obvious he'd done this a hundred times. He could have been blindfolded, and his feet would have known the way.

He stopped us in front of a two-story house, nodding toward it. "That one used to be mine."

And just like that, the pins were kicked out from under my happy feelings. This was *the* house. The house Amorette had told me about, that she'd seen Mez visit. The house he'd owned with his late wife. The house he'd owned before he became a Warrior.

No, before he was forced *to become a Warrior.*

The home was a mixture of wood panelling and stone bricks in soft shades of light greys and browns. Tall trees surrounded the back of the house, and the front featured a garden of wildflowers that was ringed by a wooden fence and a trellis, both of which were covered by a climbing plant with large white blossoms.

This home had a rustic beauty and charm to it that was enchanting. Based on what I knew of Mez, it was the last place I would have thought he would have once called home. From his clothes to the rich decor in his office and apartment, right down to the way he carried himself, everything about him suggested that he came from a wealthy background. Even the gorgeous blue rose I was holding would have been out of place in this home. Don't get me wrong, the house was lovely, but it wasn't posh, it was quaint.

"Quaint" wasn't a word I would use to describe either the rose or Mez.

I dared a glance at him. He was gazing at the house as if he were looking at an old friend he hadn't seen in a long time.

"It's a really nice place," I said quietly.

"It's perfect," he responded wistfully, still gazing at the home as if lost in a dream.

"Do you miss living here?"

"I miss it. But there's a family there now. They have two boys."

Frowning, I squeezed his hand and said, "I'm sorry." I wished I could have said something more profound. I felt terrible for him, knowing what Amorette had told me and what he had lost.

"Sorry?" Mez queried, turning to look at me.

Shoot! Duh, Megan! He doesn't know you know what you know, remember?

"Yes, for whatever happened," I said quickly. "For whatever reason you had to leave this house and everything that mattered to you."

He nodded. "I became a Warrior."

"Yes..." I began carefully, holding his gaze, "but that's not all, is it?"

"It's not all," he agreed, "but it's why it happened. It's why I lost my old life, and why I'm a Warrior today." He indicated that we should walk, and we strolled along a path that took us through a park with trees, brightly coloured flowerbeds, and benches.

"Did you want to be a Warrior?" I knew the answer, but the question had to be officially asked.

"No. I was a psychiatrist. I had a practice in the city. Glenara and I..." He looked at me before continuing. "Glenara was my wife," he reminded me gently, and I nodded to assure him that I remembered.

When a guy sleeping next to you mistakenly calls you by the name of another woman, you don't forget it.

"We hadn't been married for a cycle," he continued. "We moved into the house because we were going to have our first child. I'd refused the military's invitation for an interview. I didn't want to be a Warrior," he stated again.

He was going to have a kid? Amorette didn't tell me that part!

A cold feeling of dread wormed its way through my body as it began to sink in that something really awful likely happened to Mez' wife and unborn child.

"They wouldn't take no for an answer," I said more to myself than to him.

He nodded. "An offer to become a Warrior isn't really an offer. I didn't realize that then. I grew up in privilege. I'd never heard of offers that weren't truly offers."

"What...what did they do?" I felt I had to know, even though I was terrified to find out.

Mez released my hand and took a seat on a nearby park bench, resting his jacket over one leg. I took a seat next to him, ready to wait for as long as he needed to tell me his story.

Staring at the flowerbed in front of us as if he were looking right through it, he slowly exhaled and said, "One day, I left my home to go to work, but I never arrived at the office. I didn't even see the person who knocked me unconscious. I awoke already having started the process of becoming a Warrior. I learned soon after, that everything else in my life was gone. Everything, except the house."

I had no idea what he'd meant about "the process of becoming a Warrior", but what disturbed me most was when he'd said, "everything in my life was gone".

"What do you mean 'gone'?" I knew his wife was dead, but now I was beginning to fear that she was taken from him on purpose. Nervously, I twirled the stem of the rose in my hand.

Blinking his gaze away from the flowerbed, he looked at me with immeasurable pain in his eyes. "They made sure I knew Glenara and our unborn child joined the Goddess in Her Paradise."

My hand froze and tears immediately welled up into my eyes. "Oh, Mez. I'm so very sorry."

I wouldn't dare ask him how they'd died, and I honestly didn't want to know because the haunted, pain-stricken look in his eyes told me that they were murdered, and that he'd either seen it happen or had witnessed the aftermath.

Dear sweet god....

Mez took my hand and squeezed it gently, giving a little nod of thanks for my condolences, he blinked a few times, and his expression returned to his usual calm nonchalance. That specific memory of Glenara obviously still gutted him, but overall, his past was an old hurt for him, and I got the feeling that he'd found a way to make peace with it some time ago. Still, the fact that he continued to return to look at his old house spoke volumes to me, and I wondered why he chose to bring me here.

"This wasn't the type of light-hearted discussion I'd thought we'd have before dinner," he said with a wry smile. "I should have shown you a different house."

"Why *did* you show me your old house, Mez?"

"I don't know. I've never shown anyone that house. I just wanted you to see it. I thought you'd understand what a perfect house it was. I thought you'd understand me better, and why I did ask you on a date, because I really do like you."

I nodded, but I couldn't say that I understood him better, even though I'd learned more about his past. That said, it meant a lot to me that he felt comfortable and safe enough with me that he would share this part of himself.

Acting on instinct, I hugged him tightly. I didn't know if he needed it, but I sure did.

"I'm glad you wanted to show me, and I'm glad that you felt that you could talk to me. I do really like you, too."

He returned my hug and gave my back a small rub. "I'm glad to hear that, and relieved."

Drawing away from the hug, I looked at him and admitted, "I've liked you since our adventure with the People of the North."

He smiled almost boyishly. "I've liked you since I requested not to be assigned to you in any counselling capacity," he confessed.

I blinked in surprise. "Really? I had no idea."

Wow. Very wow. When it comes to Mez, I'm terrible at picking up on signals. No kidding, Megan. You only realized like five minutes ago you were even on a date with him!

He chuckled. "I noticed. I'll start being more obvious. I've evidently been working against myself. I think I need to work on making this dinner very romantic, otherwise I won't be able to make up for this walk," he half teased, and I grinned.

Mez stood, casually tossing his jacket over his shoulder as he had when we'd left his apartment, and offered me his free hand. I took it, and we made our way out of the park, back through the residential area, and toward the city again.

The lamp posts along the streets were now lit by whatever power Capital City used. The cold white glow of their light mixed with the vibrant pinks, oranges, dark purples, and blues of twilight. It was beautiful and made the city seem a little magical; nothing like the

Kavylak I had come to know. I mentally crossed my fingers, hoping the rest of our date would be just as magical.

Chapter 17

Irys

"Miss Godeleva is our guest and as a lady of Syliza, this was the most appropriate clothing for her status and comfort," Mr. Dimog replied in a dismissal of his daughter's anger. "We have dresses, and I don't see any harm in lending one to her while she is here."

"You didn't see any harm? A stranger shows up at our door with one of the most hated men in Dsumot, and just because she's a Sylizan lady, you thought it was fine to let her wear one of Mother's dresses?" She spit each word with disgust.

Great Goddess, please help me to leave this room unnoticed to allow the Dimogs to argue privately...

Remaining silent, I prayed that Mr. Dimog and his daughter would set the argument aside until I'd had the opportunity to leave.

"Skeltra, calm yourself. I have made my decision. Miss Godeleva is our guest, the dress was not being used. You are overreacting and are being exceptionally rude." Turning his attention to me, he added, "Miss Godeleva, I apologize. Please excuse us."

Nothing he could have said would have brought me greater relief. I curtsied quickly. "Yes, of course," I replied and backed out the door. It was a relief to take my leave and allow father and daughter to argue this emotional subject without my presence. I could understand both sides and tried not to feel guilty as the luxurious fabrics of my skirt moved with me into the hallway.

Miss Dimog slid the door closed, and its soft sound was immediately followed by loud arguing in the Dsumot language. I stepped away from the noise and decided it was time to check on Acksil and spend as much time with him as I was permitted.

It didn't take me long to realize that I didn't know which direction to take, and I hoped to run into someone who could guide me. Slowly, I made my way down the hall but paused when I heard Mr. Dimog's door slide open again. Glancing back over my shoulder, I smiled as he stepped out into the hall. There was no sign of Miss Dimog, who must have chosen to remain in the study.

"I'll take you to see Fhir," he said calmly, without any indication that he had just finished arguing with his daughter.

"Thank you. That's just where I was headed," I replied gratefully.

He nodded, having known precisely where my next destination would be. I took his arm when he offered it to me, and we strolled down the hall together.

"Do you love him?" he asked without judgment.

It was an innocent-sounding question, though it nearly made me trip over my own feet. My breath caught in my throat as I glanced over at him.

How could he think I'm in love with Acksil? It's Sir Dynan Fhirell who makes my heart beat faster.

"No, of course not," I replied too quickly. "I barely know what he is like aside from his sense of justice. We have nothing in common."

He nodded, but his expression was noncommittal. It made me feel as though I needed to make things fully clear.

"I've always been in peril whenever I've met Acksil. It would have been impossible for me to think about such things at times like those. There is also a Knight who intends to speak with Lord Godeleva about his intentions. The Knight is a man I greatly admire."

Mr. Dimog nodded. "Do you think Fhir loves you?"

The question struck me hard enough to make me lose my breath. It was something that had never crossed my mind. "I can't imagine he would. I'm nothing like him."

Was I? No, of course not! I trust him. I respect him. But it is not love we share. There was once a kiss, of course...but love? That's impossible!

"Loving someone has nothing to do with how much you have in common with them, Dear One. The heart decides. My beautiful Laylia was nothing like me, but our hearts found each other, and I was lucky that she loved me as much as I loved her. Some are not as fortunate."

I found myself sinking into his description of his wife, despite my discomfort with the subject of Acksil's potential love for me. I liked neither thinking that Acksil would have such feelings for me, nor that Mr. Dimog thought it appropriate to ask about them.

"I am inexperienced with such things. He has never mentioned his feelings to me, and I have assumed that he does not have them," I told him earnestly. "It is something you would need to discuss with him."

"I have no intention of asking him about it," Mr. Dimog confessed. "The only reason I brought it up with you is that, in my experience, a man such as Fhir would protect you as he has for one of only two possible reasons. He is either in love with you, or this is a part of a larger scheme that could lead the Warriors directly to us."

"Or perhaps he could no longer watch as Xandon and the Warriors mistreated me. He could not be a part of such cruelty any longer," I suggested.

He smiled as though the thought that I could believe such a kind thing warmed him. "I do not believe that he would take those risks for just anyone. It isn't him."

We came to a stop outside a door guarded by Borte. The men nodded to each other and Borte stepped aside to allow access to the door.

"I will leave you alone to speak with him. Perhaps you might ask him for yourself," Mr. Dimog said, reaching forward to open the door for me.

"Yes, Mr. Dimog," I said obediently, though I hadn't yet decided whether or not I would pursue Acksil's motivations. "Thank you." I stood on my toes to kiss his cheek. I wasn't entirely sure why I'd done it, but it seemed like the thing a young woman would do for her favourite uncle or grandfather. "Thank you for everything."

"Borte will help you find your way to anywhere you'd like to go when you're done. Come and see me whenever you'd like," he said and turned to head away.

I entered the room where Acksil was being held prisoner. The former Warrior was lying on a bed with his eyes closed. His sheet and blanket were pulled up to his chest, with his bare shoulders and arms exposed. The hand that had been bitten by the snake was wrapped in several layers of bandages. Even in the dim light, he looked pale and feverish to me.

I didn't want to disturb him, but I wasn't ready to leave just because he was unconscious. Standing at his bedside, I checked him over and took his good hand. The room was pleasant enough. It had a large window, though I imagined it was locked and barred behind its closed curtains. There was a table and chair as well as a large potted plant on the floor with lush green leaves that calmed the space. The walls were bare, but their wood borders stopped the room from feeling stark. It was most certainly a space for healing and felt nothing like a jail cell.

When I looked back at Acksil, his caring hazel eyes were open, and his lips moved into a weak smile.

"I didn't mean to wake you." I spoke quietly.

"So, he let you see me after all," he replied.

I nodded and took a seat on the edge of his bed without making contact with him. It wasn't likely that he was receiving much friendly company, so I wanted him to feel more of my presence. He didn't deserve to be alone after all his kindnesses.

"He must really like you." He chuckled. "You must have learned a little charming from all that time you spent with Arik."

"He's a gentleman, that's all. I enjoy his company, and I believe he enjoys mine. He lent me a lovely gown to wear."

"You probably remind him of his late wife," he said with less playfulness but without fully losing his smile.

"I'm only glad that we are getting along so far," I said and rapidly diverted the topic. I disliked how often each of these men were talking about my relationships with the other. It made me uncomfortable for a reason I couldn't quite identify. "You must tell me how you're feeling."

"I feel about as good as I look," he said with a crooked grin. Even in this condition, he still managed to cling to enough playfulness that he would not complain to me. Always the protector. "But I'll live. Dyronin's got most of the venom out and treated the infection that was forming. I just have to keep drinking his disgusting tea, and I'll heal up. It's a matter of sweating it out."

"Have they been kind to you?"

"Kinder than I deserve. Not all of them hate me to the same degree. Those who don't didn't know me as well."

174

I nodded but felt a sting at the thought that he believed he did not deserve even the most basic kindnesses. Upon our arrival in Syliza, I would do everything I could to ensure his proper treatment for the rest of his life.

"Mr. Dimog said he'd spoken with you for a while. He doesn't trust you."

"He doesn't trust me," he confirmed. "There is likely very little I could ever do to change his mind." His expression turned very serious. "Irys, they may kill me. They'll imprison me for certain, but hanging or beheading aren't out of the question."

My eyes widened, and I nearly stood out of sheer repulsion of the thought. "No!" I said firmly as though I had some say in the matter. "I won't allow it. You won't be killed, Acksil."

"Not even your beauty and charm could prevent it if that's what they want, Dollface."

It is out of the question. Somehow, I will put a stop to it.

"I will talk to Mr. Dimog. I will stay here and guard you myself if I must. Once you're healed, we'll run if we have to." I held his hand more firmly in my own. The feeling of holding onto him comforted me, even though the gesture had been meant to reassure him.

His expression broke into a bit of a smile. He looked touched. "I'm honoured that you would do this, and I believe you would, but it isn't the right move. They will help you return home, Irys. That's what you need to do."

"I will insist that you go with me. You have been my protector until now. I'm not prepared to give up that privilege." I was not prepared to give up my friend, either.

"You won't have any say in the matter. You don't understand. I betrayed these people, Irys. They have every right to hate me, and I don't hold it against them. I knew what I would be facing by returning here." He squeezed my hand in return.

I studied him for a moment. Mr. Dimog's words flooded my mind.

"Mr. Dimog thinks there are two reasons that a man would rescue me as you have. One is that the man is in love. The other is that it is a part of a larger scheme, such as to lead the Warriors here. I trust you, Acksil. I don't think you are bringing the Warriors here." I took a breath and let it out. I would have to face the truth sooner or later. If I was going to convince Mr. Dimog to keep Acksil safe, then it was up to me to understand the situation in its entirety, not hide from it. "Why have you done all this for me, time and time again? Why have you lost everything for a woman you barely know?"

"You're right to trust me, Irys. I'm not plotting anything." His eyes held mine, imploring me to believe him. "I helped you the first time because I couldn't bring myself to kill you. Galnar's order was pointless after everything you'd been through, and because you were not a threat. You had a life to return to. The second time was happenstance. I saw you and acted on instinct. I knew if Galnar had found you, you'd have been killed, or worse. This time…" He paused and looked away as though arranging his thoughts. His gaze returned to mine as he spoke. "I just wanted to, Irys. I didn't know what Xandon had planned for you, but it wasn't going to be anything good. The thought of him being anywhere near you made me sick inside. I had to get you out of there. I didn't feel like I had a choice. It was the only thing I could do."

I brought my second hand over his. "I told Mr. Dimog just that. I knew you were a good man who had to do the right thing."

His expression turned to one of shame. "It wasn't just the right thing to do. I did it for you."

My brow furrowed in confusion. "I don't understand."

There was no hesitation to his reply.

"I love you, Irys. I don't know when it started, but I do."

Chapter 18

Megan

Mez and I arrived at a very modern and sleek-looking building with a lot of glass and angles. He opened the door for me, and I entered. It was a fancy restaurant with contemporary décor and warm lighting. There was nothing cold, metal, stark, or gloomy about this place. It was immediately my favourite spot in the city.

"I hope I haven't spoiled your appetite." Mez chuckled quietly as he stepped in beside me. "I had no intention of being this dramatic this evening."

Smiling at him, I shook my head. "I'm fine. It would take a lot more to spoil my appetite. Dramatic just seems to be what we do." He returned my smile, amused.

"Ah! Lieutenant Basarovka." A maître d' stepped up to us, his snooty look morphed into a smile as he greeted Mez. The man enthusiastically drew his arms up as if he were about to hug Mez, but only made a few sweeping motions with both of his raised hands from where he was, as though he were miming a hug that would have resulted in patting Mez on the back, before returning his arms to his sides.

Initially, I had thought Mez had used his mind powers to prevent the man from going through with the hug, until I saw him naturally return the brief mime-like hug-hug-hug gesture.

Um, that's a new one. I guess in Kavylak instead of kissing cheeks, hugging, handshaking, or fist-bumping non-military friends or acquaintances in greeting, you give...jazz hand hugs?

"Good evening, Islass. It's been a while."

"Yes," Islass responded and turned his smile on me, snapping me out of my bewilderment. "And you're with a beautiful woman tonight. I finally won my bet with the chef." He laughed and so did Mez. "Right this way," Islass said warmly, leading us through the busy restaurant.

Guess Islass and I weren't on "jazz hugging" terms yet.

All the tables in the restaurant were full, but it wasn't noisy by any means. There was only the hum of people talking in low voices, and the soft sounds of a string instrument. Islass took us to an area with heavy dark red drapes. He swept them aside to reveal a private alcove with an intimate dining table for two next to a window. After securing the drapes so they would remain open, Islass pulled out my chair, and I took a seat, resting my rose on the table beside my plate. Once Mez had taken his own seat, Islass placed a black leatherbound menu in front of each of us.

"Your server will be with you shortly. I'll start you off with an aperitif."

"Thank you," Mez said, while I looked around the restaurant in awe as though I was seeing in colour for the first time.

"Does this place seem 'okay'?" Mez asked with a glint in his eyes, knowing full well that this place was awesome.

"Are you kidding? This is way better than okay. This place is freaking incredible. It's so incredible that I can almost imagine I'm at a fine dining restaurant back home!" I was too thrilled about being here to give his glint a sarcastic reply.

"I'm glad." Mez didn't bother to hide the fact that he was proud of himself. I couldn't blame him. He did good. Really good.

The server arrived carrying a tray stand and a round tray on which there was a glass pitcher of what I assumed was water, two wine flutes, and a small ornate metal ice bucket that held a corked, dark grey, half-sized wine bottle. My heart fluttered in delight.

Oh my gosh! Am I about to be served Kavylak's answer to champagne?

"Good evening Lieutenant Basarovka and lovely guest," he greeted us, flashing me a pleasant smile as he unfolded the stand and set the tray on top of it. Returning his smile, I watched him place the flutes in front us and expertly pop the cork on the bottle. When he poured the bubbly contents into the wine flutes, my eyes widened in surprise at the fizzy liquid that filled the glasses. Instead of the light golden colour I was expecting, it was a robin's egg blue.

No way! Blue sparkling wine!

"The chef is delighted to know you're honouring us with your presence this evening," the server said genuinely, setting the bottle back into the fancy ice bucket and depositing the bucket onto a shelf that was built into the wall of our alcove. "He will be glad to make anything you'd like, of course, but would also be overjoyed to offer you something uniquely to your taste, if you'd prefer it," he added, filling our water glasses.

Wow! Now that's five-star service. I had no idea Mez was the type of celebrity customer a chef would do backflips for. They either go way back or Mez makes some seriously good money.

"That's very kind of the chef," Mez replied in a conversational tone. "My guest hasn't been here before. We would like a moment to look at the menus to see if there is anything she would particularly like before we decide if we'll accept his generous offer."

"Of course," the server replied as if what Mez had suggested was the most sensible choice. "I will return." He placed the water pitcher beside the ice bucket on the shelf and left us to our perusal of the menus.

Mez opened his menu and began glancing at the options. "If there is anything specific you would like, we can order from the menu. Otherwise, we can always ask the chef to choose for us."

Opening my own menu, I looked at the different appetizers and entrées. Naturally, beyond recognizing the basic names of certain meat and seafood, I wasn't even able to guess at what any of the foreign dishes were, but it didn't matter. I couldn't have cared less what we ended up eating. I was certain it was going to be fantastic. This place was simply too awesome for me to believe otherwise.

Then a thought struck me, and I had to grin.

"Think the chef will make 'laniania'?"

Mez laughed and so did I. The memory of him butchering the word lasagna when I had mentioned it to him when we had first met remained one my fondest memories of him.

"If you were able to describe it well enough, I'm absolutely certain that they would try their best to make it."

I believed him, but I didn't have any interest in trying to find the best words to describe how to make it. "That's good to know, but in all seriousness, I'm happy with whatever you choose for us. I'm sure everything tastes wonderful. Is there anything that's appealing to you?" I asked curiously.

Giving me the tiniest eye glint that made my heart skip a beat, Mez closed his menu. "I think we should see what the chef thinks we'll like."

While a part of me found his little glints to be unnerving because I knew they were full of mischief, at the same time, I adored them. They felt special as if he were letting me see a side of his personality he didn't share with many people. A side of himself that was completely unrelated to him being a Warrior.

"I like that option."

Mez turned his head toward where the server was waiting and gave him the tiniest hint of a nod. The server returned, and Mez collected our menus and held them out to the man. "We're placing our trust in the chef's capable hands."

"Wonderful choice. I know he was very hopeful you would." Wearing a pleased smile, the server took the menus and headed away.

With the server gone and our order placed, my entire focus returned to the blue sparkling wine that I was itching to try.

As if Mez could sense my anticipation, he picked up his glass and held it out toast-style. "To our first date and a chef worthy of our trust."

Grinning, I picked up my glass. He clinked it then took a sip of the wine.

I followed suit, letting the bubbles dance in my mouth a little before swallowing it. The taste was crisp and slightly sweet with a hint of a tart flavor that left my cheeks feeling pleasantly zingy. Not having had much experience with sparkling wine or any alcohol-based beverage, I didn't have much to compare it to, but I liked it, and the colour was so unique.

"This is really good." I beamed, enjoying the warm feeling the liquid left in its wake. "I've never seen blue bubbly wine before."

He smiled. "The restaurant keeps it for those of us from Dmevjekya. It's called 'golvibje', and it's from where I grew up."

"Is blue an important colour in Dmevjekya?" I asked, since I was beginning to notice a theme from the carpet in Mez' apartment to the fuzzy blanket he'd lent me to the blue rose, and now the wine.

"Not especially. The wine from there is blue because of the berries that are used. They grow only in Dmevjekya. Coincidentally, my family colours are also blue and silver. But for the country itself, blue is not necessarily important."

His family has designated colours? Isn't that a royalty or nobility thing?

The server returned, interrupting my thoughts by placing a tiny plate in front of each of us. On the plate were two matchbox-shaped pink rectangles with a green circle on top.

"Salted melon with pepper. Enjoy." He said and left us with what was most certainly the amuse bouche.

Watching which utensils Mez chose, I copied him – not wanting to look like I lacked proper etiquette – and politely ate the small portion of food, feeling like I had done Irys proud. The salted melon with pepper was a delight to my tastebuds. The melon tasted sweet, somewhere between a cantaloupe and watermelon, and the spicy pepper was tangy, reminding me of chili peppers like jalapeño. Combined, the sweetness, tanginess, and saltiness were an explosion of exotic flavour.

"Do a lot of families in Dmevjekya have a family colour?" I asked when we were done munching the melon. There was no way I could shake my curiosity, and I didn't want to start making assumptions. I mean, having a family colour could be a Dmevjekya thing, heck, it could be a Qarradune thing for all I knew. Seriously, I just discovered 'jazz-hands-hugs' a few minutes ago.

"Each family among the nobility has its own colours."

Ah-ha! I knew it. Okay, not really, but for once my assumptions weren't totally off base! Wait a minute...

"So, then, your family is nobility?" That would explain why he had such expensive-looking stuff and why he was a regular at posh restaurants, but it would not explain how he wound up in Kavylak in a cutesy cottage-house.

"Yes. The Basarovkas are an important family in Dmevjekya. Had I not left, I would have been in line to become Ranushdr. My cousin Kurpav has taken the title in my absence," Mez said as though he were aware that this was the first time I had heard this, but it was something everyone else knew. He took a casual sip of his blue bubbly, glinting at me as he did.

Mouth-dropped and wide-eyed, I stared at him.

Oh my god! He sounds like he's from big-time nobility!

There were so many thoughts swirling around in my head, but I knew what I wanted to ask first.

"What is a Ranushdr?"

He raised a brow in fake surprise at my question. "And here I thought you spoke my language," he teased.

Having overcome the initial Mez-is-nobility shock, I fixed him one of my best "I'm not amused" looks, to which he chuckled and gave a sober nod, losing the teasing expression.

"It is one of the highest titles in Dmevjekya," he explained. "And among the Ranushdr and Ranushdyria, the Basarovkas are one of the oldest and most respected noble families. I would have been Ranushdr of Stravjanya. Now, I am that member of the family nobody wants to talk about." He grinned a little, seeming completely unbothered by his last statement and took another sip of wine.

Taking a sip of my own blue fizzy, I let what he had told me sink in, enjoying the bubbles popping in my mouth and tickling my tongue.

Wondering how to best understand his nobility in comparison to what I knew of European nobilities on Earth I asked, "Is there any nobility higher than the Ranushdr of Stravjanya?"

"No, but there is someone who is equal to him. She is the Ranushdyria of Omuransk, Lady Lochka Ynna."

"Okay...so then the Ranushdr of Stravjanya is like the King of Dmevjekya, and the Ranushdyria of Omuransk is like the Queen?"

He laughed, but I could tell from his tone and the far-off look in his eyes that he wasn't laughing at my question. It seemed more like a reaction to the memory of an inside joke.

"Not exactly. There is no royalty in Dmevjekya, but our families are the most influential among the nobility. The Ranushdr and Ranushdyria of the most influential families are sometimes unofficially referred to as the Grand Ranushdr and Grand Ranushdyria out of respect for their positions." He smiled genuinely at me. "It struck me funny that you asked, because when we were growing up, Lady Ynna always called me the 'Spoiled Prince'."

Nodding, now understanding the reason for his laughter, I smiled because childhood nostalgia looked good on Mez. He appeared lighter somehow, untouched by the many harsh realities he'd faced since then.

"So, what happened? Why did you lose your mind and leave the 'Spoiled Prince' life behind?" It was my turn to tease him. I knew his reasons for leaving weren't any of my business, but I wanted to know, and it didn't seem to bother him to talk about his past.

"I didn't lose my mind. I'm just smarter than the rest of them," he joked back. "I wanted to study psychiatry and open a practice," he leveled with me. "I've never wanted to hold a position with that much power and responsibility. I'm not interested in politics, being a landowner, or deciding the lives of others. I wanted to live in Capital City and earn my own way."

That made sense. I could understand why he would want to walk away from it all. I'm sure it would be fun to be super-rich, but all the other stuff that comes along with it might outweigh the overall fun aspect of being wealthy and powerful for some people, especially someone who had no interest in it like Mez. Still, that's quite the life to give up.

"I guess you've always known what you wanted. Must have taken a lot of guts to leave, though."

Before Mez could respond, the server returned with a single plate of red fish on six mini crispy bread squares. A dot of thick white cream with a small curl of what looked like a green onion garnished the fish. He set the plate down between us and gave us each our own smaller plates so we could take what we wanted from the shared portion.

"Smoked lepsighe," he announced, topping up our wine glasses.

Nodding to the server, who promptly left with the ice bucket and empty bottle, Mez resumed our conversation. "I nearly always know what I want. I think it would have taken more from me to stay. Leaving wasn't easy, but it was easier than remaining and doing what my cousin Kurpav now does."

"Do you still talk to anyone in your family?"

"On rare occasions. I write to my cousin or Lady Ynna. My parents are with the Goddess now," he added, and I gave a nod of sympathy. "Lady Ynna is the only one who writes back. I don't hear from her often, but it is likely because the mail takes a long time to travel that far. She says as much as she can at once, knowing we'll likely not exchange many letters every cycle. Barely anything at all leaves Dmevjekya in the cold and snow seasons."

"I'm glad that your friend still likes to keep in touch with her 'Spoiled Prince'." Smiling, I tried the smoked lepsighe. The flavours were not unlike smoked salmon, cream cheese, and green onion, and the crispy cracker it was on added another bold flavour and a satisfying crunch.

"She just does it so that she can brag about everything wonderful in her life and tell me what I'm doing wrong with my life," he said with amusement and tried the food. "I like this one."

"Me, too. It tastes a bit like something I had back home, and only once at one of my Aunt Vera's friend's fancy parties." I clarified with a grin. "I wasn't a 'Spoiled Princess'."

He chuckled. "What else would you expect from dinner with a Spoiled Prince? I have to make sure your status changes."

I laughed, and we finished off our last portions of appetizer and the remaining bubbly blue wine.

As if he had been waiting for us to finish, a busboy swooped in with a tray and removed our dirty dishes and empty glasses. The server was hot on his heels and served us both what I assumed was the main course.

"Lamb, with new potatoes, carrots, beans, and a tart currant sauce."

I couldn't believe it. I had understood every food word he'd said. Recognizing the words felt so good I almost welled up, but I refused to reveal how emotional I felt about the meal. A quick explanation would be all Mez would need to get it, but there was no way the server would understand why I was suddenly bawling because he'd said "lamb", "potatoes", and "carrots".

On the plate were two lamb chops covered in a dark red sauce with the consistency of a mildly runny gravy, roasted golden potatoes that were dusted with green bits of herb, roasted purple carrots, and a neat bundle of identically cut steamed green beans that were fastened together with a green onion. Aside from the couple of meals I'd had as a guest at the Godeleva estate, this was easily the most impressive plate of food I'd seen on Qarradune.

I was so wrapped up with ogling my dinner and working on keeping my emotions in check that I hadn't noticed the server had given us two new wine glasses until I heard the liquid being poured. Like the bubbly, this wine was blue, but it was a deep shade of navy.

Once the server had left, Mez sipped some of the new wine and then tried the meat. "I hadn't expected lamb," he commented with pleasant surprise.

I smiled and tried the wine, glad he seemed happy with the chef's choice. The wine was light and dry with a taste that reminded me of blackberries, currants, and even elderberries. It was tasty, and I could see it complementing the meat, which looked to be on the rarer side, but if I had to pick, I liked the bubbly wine more.

Diving into my dinner, I noticed as I speared a potato that Mez' potatoes didn't have the sprinkling of the green herb that mine did.

"How come I have the green stuff and you don't?"

Mez glanced at my plate and then at his and smiled with a glint in his eye. "They know I don't eat 'green stuff'."

I raised a brow. "Allergy?"

He looked thoughtful before answering, "Psychological allergy."

I nodded. Made sense. I had a few of my own psychological allergies, either because I didn't like the taste or smell of something or some other bad association. I wouldn't judge.

"I think the chef has outdone himself," Mez commented after swallowing another bite of meat. "It's amusing because I always order a steak or a roast. Usually, if he surprises me with a meal, it's something similar. You must look like lamb to him." He chuckled.

"Baaaa."

Mez stopped mid-chew, and his eyes widened at my lamb impersonation. He then burst out laughing, and I laughed at his reaction. I loved how he wasn't afraid to show how much that amused him, in spite of being in a classy restaurant. I might not be a Spoiled Princess or be able to eye-glint, but I could "Baaaa" as good as the rest of them.

"I think I see what the chef saw in you."

"Yup. Just make sure you don't tell your Lady Ynna friend what the chef sees in me, or she might think you've lost your Spoiled Prince status and stop writing to you altogether," I joked.

He grinned. "On the contrary. She would write more. She would like you, she would spoil you, and then she would corrupt you because she is smarter than the rest of us."

"Really? She likes women who make silly farm noises at fine dining restaurants?"

He laughed. "I think she would be willing to overlook the farm noises."

"Lady Ynna and your family sound really nice. If they were closer, I'd love to meet them." It was true. It would be interesting to meet the people that Mez grew up with.

"They would love to meet you, too. You would entrance them," he said without any hint of play or sarcasm.

"Oh," I responded stupidly, flushing at his "entrance" comment. Immediately, I took a sip of wine hoping the maneuver would hide my reddening face, but the heat I felt from the wine only made the blush worse. There was just no way to save my dignity now, so I looked down at my plate and focused on finishing my food.

We finished what was left of our meal, and by the time I'd had my last bite, I was feeling calm, satisfied, and happy.

Our plates were taken away, and the server poured a clear liquid from a fancy-looking ruby coloured bottle into two long stem liqueur glasses and then gave us each a different dessert.

"Chocolate three ways," he said in reference to the three small portions on my plate. "Melted chocolate cake, chocolate ice cream, and a chocolate bombe."

Best. Dessert. Ever. I'm going to marry the chef!

"For you," the server turned to Mez, "poached pear in biloberry syrup."

Looking at the piece of pale golden fruit that was soaking in a deep magenta pool of syrup, personally I felt Mez got ripped off compared to the decadent dessert that had been prepared for me. A quick glance at his expression told me I couldn't have been more wrong. He looked very pleased with his plate.

"Thank you," he said to the server, and I nodded in agreement. The server smiled and left us to our sweets.

"I'm in love with the chef," I told Mez.

He laughed. "I was pleased when I saw what had been selected for you."

Grinning from ear to ear, I dug into my dessert and enjoyed every second of it. I couldn't decide what I liked more, the smooth dark chocolate ice cream, the rich chocolate lava-like cake, or the ganache-glazed bombe.

"Mmm. That was the best," I purred when I was finished.

Mez smiled with amusement and then dug his spoon into a piece of his half-eaten pear and held it out to me. "Would you like to try my pear?"

By the way he was holding it out to me, I could tell he was giving me the option of taking the spoon from him or inviting me to eat it directly from the spoon as he held it. Feeling giddy from the chocolate, I chose to eat it directly from the spoon and felt a thrill when he looked delighted that I had.

"That's actually quite nice," I said surprised. It wasn't too sweet and had a fresh flavour that was super pleasant.

"It's the perfect end to this meal for anyone but you. You need chocolate." He chuckled happily and finished his pear.

I picked up the glass of clear liquid to try it.

"Careful with that," Mez cautioned lightly with a nod to the glass. "It's strong."

"What is it?" I smelled it and my nose hairs were instantly overcome with a sharp burning sensation, and my eyes watered.

Woah! Whatever this is, it's strong stuff!

"Talischt," Mez responded, looking entertained by my smell-test reaction. "It is usually served in the evening in Dmevjekya while we relax with friends and family. This chef believes it is served with dessert, and I have never corrected him because everything he makes is wonderful."

I giggled. "That's very nice of you, especially since he knows about your psychological allergy."

"Exactly," he agreed and held up his glass by its fine little stem. "To Megan," he toasted me, looking deeply into my eyes before backing down the drink and setting the glass down on the table.

The blush returned to my cheeks quickly when he toasted me and looked at me as he did. I realized I was staring at him and snapped out of my stupor.

"To a second date that's just as much fun as the first and that I will actually know is a date," I toasted and backed down the drink as he had done.

Ahhhhhhhhhh! My throat is on fire! What is this? Battery acid?

"Wow," I croaked, when I felt I could speak. My face was scarlet, and my eyes were watering to the point of tears. "That is…" I coughed.

Mez grinned and pushed a glass of water close to me with his fingertips. I grabbed it and drained the glass, feeling much better.

"Thank you."

"It's everyone's first reaction to Talischt."

"Good to know. What's the second reaction?"

"I suppose you'll need to have that second date with me to find out." He laid one of his characteristic glints on me, and I laughed happily. I was really starting to like those glints.

The server returned. "Is there anything else that I can bring to perfect your evening?"

Mez smiled and shook his head. "Everything was wonderful. Please share our gratitude with the chef."

"Yes," I chimed in. "Everything was absolutely delicious!"

The server couldn't have looked more thrilled. "I look forward to telling him. Please stay as long as you would like and let me know if there is anything else that I can do for you."

"Thank you again," Mez said with a nod. "Have a pleasant evening."

"Thank you for this," I said, smiling warmly to Mez when the server had left. "This food was truly amazing. I wasn't expecting anything this fancy. It's been a lot of fun."

He looked pleased. "I'm glad you liked it. It made up for the start and showed you that this really is a date." He chuckled. "Are you ready to leave?"

"Yes."

He stood up, draping his jacket over an arm and offered his hand to help me rise. I took it and remembered to scoop up my blue rose from the table before we left. I didn't want to forget that.

Continuing to hold Mez' hand, we walked out of the restaurant into the cool night air, and I sighed contentedly, feeling all dreamy as I gazed at my rose. This *had* been a magical evening.

"Mez, this has…" I gasped, before I could finish my sentence as I was suddenly lurched backward by Mez when he abruptly came to a dead halt. I looked up at him in shock, but he didn't return my gaze. He was staring directly ahead of us with a dark and dangerous expression I'd never seen.

I followed his intense stare and saw that four men were blocking our path, but these didn't look like ordinary men. They were dressed identically and had the same cropped haircut. However, it wasn't their eerie identical quadruplet-like fashion sense that was unnerving, it was their faces.

At a second glance, I realized in horror what it was about them that was so upsetting. Their mouths had been crudely sewn shut with thick black thread.

Chapter 19

Irys

The colour drained from my face, and I had to force myself not to let go of Acksil's hand. I didn't want to insult him, but I was completely unprepared for his declaration.

He loves me. How could I not have known? Had he truly hidden it so well, or am I a fool? Great Goddess, am I taking advantage of this man's heart? How can I accept such affections when I do not return them? I care for him, of course. Deeply. But it's Sir Fhirell's love I desire...is it not?

"I had no idea," I replied stupidly. I felt lightheaded. The finger sandwiches and jam tart were flipping in my stomach. "I thought you were doing this out of a sense of justice."

"I wish I could tell you that's all it was. I don't want to disappoint you by being a lesser man, but you deserve honesty. A good man doesn't kill other people, Irys. Not for any reason, especially when they're unarmed."

An image of the dead Traveller flashed through my mind. My hands trembled in his, but I refused to let go.

"You did what you felt you had to do to help us to escape. She would have brought the Warriors upon us. You saved my life, and I can only be grateful."

His face betrayed his relief.

I could never condone the murder of another person, but I could not ignore the fact that it was an evil action done out of love and for our survival.

Great Goddess, I pray you understand. I beg you to forgive him, and please forgive me for accepting what he has done.

"I know your actions were sometimes dishonourable when you were a Warrior, but you chose to leave that life and rescue me in doing so. I pray for you Acksil." My hand no longer trembled, and I gave his a gentle, confident squeeze. "You are a decent person despite the deeds of your past."

He'd listened to every word. I'd thought he knew how I felt, but he took in my beliefs as though accepting the forgiveness of the Goddess herself. "Thank you, Irys. I don't deserve a friend like you."

I shook my head. "It is not for you to decide if you are deserving. It is for me to decide who deserves my friendship. You can only strive to live up to it through your actions. In return, I will do everything I can to make sure our friendship is a long one. They are not taking you from me."

The words came directly from my heart. Rarely had I meant anything more genuinely. This man loved me. He saved my life. I would do everything in my power to make myself worthy of a friendship between us that would last a lifetime.

"When you speak with such conviction, I can't help but believe you," he said, sounding quite convinced.

"I'm only ever honest with you," I said, hoping I was indeed being honest in this very statement. It wasn't until after I had spoken that it dawned on me that it was true. Since our escape, despite everything, I'd felt no inclination to lie to him. I trusted him.

A brief knock on the door gave us a quick warning before a man entered, carrying a leather bag with a flat bottom. I assumed that he must be the doctor. I automatically dropped Acksil's hand as though I didn't want to be caught with him.

The young man had long, glossy black hair and soft blue eyes in the same gentle shape as Kaiwa's.

"Good evening, Doctor Dyronin," I said, addressing him based on my assumption and using the name Acksil had mentioned earlier.

The man had a pleasant expression which formed a small but friendly smile. "Good evening, Miss Godeleva," he greeted in accented Sylizan. "Is the patient causing you any grief?"

I wasn't entirely sure whether the doctor was joking. He strode over to Acksil's side, opposite me, and began checking him over.

"None at all. He is nothing but the same gentleman who rescued me from Kavylak," I replied, making my position clear. It was likely unnecessary, but I wasn't interested in leaving any doubt behind.

"Ah yes, I've heard that he changed his line of work and recently became a hero." He grinned mischievously as he mixed powder into a cup of steaming water. "Drink," he said to Acksil, holding the cup out to him.

Acksil made a bit of a face but didn't object in any other way. He took the cup in his good hand and sipped at it.

"That must be your delightful-tasting tea." I nodded toward the cup in Acksil's hand.

The doctor laughed. "Yes. My teas are famous."

"It has motivated me to be especially careful to avoid injury," I joked in return, deciding to wait until my arrival home in Syliza before consulting with a medical professional as Rrokth had recommended.

At the same time that I liked Dr. Dyronin, I was also hoping to keep him feeling positive about Acksil's treatment. Even if the rest of the Rebels despised him, at least the doctor could wish him well.

"You learn quickly. Usually, my patients need to taste it before they realize how important it is to be careful." His expression was a merry one.

"I've always been a capable learner," I replied. *A Clever One.* I successfully blinked back the rapidly welling tears at the thought of Lord Imery's pet name for me.

"Honestly, Dyronin, how have you managed to make potions that work so well and taste so bad? Is there nothing you can do to improve them? I swear, these ones taste worse than they used to," said Acksil before he winced through another swallow of the tea.

"I made a special batch just for you, this time," Dr. Dyronin said, looking positively wicked.

Acksil laughed and nodded, accepting his punishment by taking his medicine. As he set the cup aside, he looked far sleepier than he had only moments before. I could only assume that the healing tea also made the patient drowsy.

"Enjoy your sleep. I'll be back to check on you later. Miss Godeleva, it was nice meeting you," said Dr. Dyronin as he packed up his bag and walked to the door.

"Thank you for your miracles, Dr. Dyronin," I replied, giving the sign of the Great Goddess with my fingers.

He smiled and headed out the door.

Acksil was rapidly slowing down. Even his blinking was taking longer. The tea must have offered powerful medicine.

"You sleep," I said, even though he didn't have much of a choice but to do just that. "Heal and be well again. Tomorrow, everything will be better," I leaned over and kissed his forehead.

He smiled with his eyes closed as I placed the kiss against his skin. "Thank you, Irys." He mumbled something incoherent before adding, "Lida will never forgive me. I hurt her most of all."

"Because you loved each other?" I ventured. Now seemed the easiest time to ask such things and receive an honest answer.

"Yes. But I still shattered her heart," he replied through a yawn.

"You may prove yourself once again. She may never love you again, but you could come to be friends. You can only try," I said in an attempt to comfort him. Even in his current state, he could likely see the weakness of my words. How could a woman forgive such a thing?

"Love you," he said unexpectedly and drifted off to sleep.

I stiffened, wondering whether the words were directed at me or at a dream-state version of Lida he may have been seeing. Neither thought brought me comfort. Waiting until I was certain that he was completely unconscious, I quietly left the room.

I slid the door closed and looked up at Borte. "I'm finished speaking with him for a while. Thank you. I'd like to speak with Mr. Dimog again."

Borte nodded just as Lida stepped up with a basket of various items.

"I'll watch him. You bring her back to Storr," she said, looking as though she was put out by the task.

"Just don't kill him," Borte said jokingly to her.

"I still plan to kill him, but I want him conscious and healthy first," she replied. I wasn't at all sure that she was joking, despite Borte's chuckle. This was the woman whose heart Acksil had broken. It bothered me that she would be the one caring for him in Borte's absence, and I wondered why she had accepted the burden in the first place. For reasons I could not explain, I felt defensive at the thought of Lida in Acksil's room with him.

As amused as Borte seemed, he didn't say a single word to me the entire time he walked me back to Mr. Dimog's study. When we arrived, he merely nodded and left without saying anything.

I could see Mr. Dimog writing something at his desk, and I knocked lightly on the door frame.

He looked up and smiled. "Come in and make yourself comfortable, Miss Godeleva."

I curtsied and entered, taking a seat in my former place on the loveseat. Pushing any uncertainty aside, I prepared to plead Acksil's case. I would nurture this friendship and make sure Acksil was no longer in danger even while imprisoned here. It was my turn to save his life again. I could not fail.

"Did you have a good talk with your friend?" Mr. Dimog asked, taking a seat on the chair next to me.

"I did," I said, arranging my skirts to display them at their best. "It was far more informative than I had expected."

"What did you learn?"

"I learned that I still trust Acksil absolutely," I said honestly, but then added, "He may indeed have feelings for me as you suspected. I also found that he does not have any plans to cause anyone harm here. In fact, he expects to die. He doesn't feel he has any chance of convincing anyone here that he can be trusted." I looked up at Mr. Dimog with tear-filled eyes. I'd tried to hold them back, but my heart pained at even the remotest thought that Acksil would not survive his time among the Rebels. "May I impose upon your generosity for just one more thing?"

He nodded with a look of concern.

"Would you either allow Acksil to come with me when the Traveller takes me home, or promise that you will spare his life? I know he has wronged you and everyone you care about. I'm not trying to trivialize his actions. His betrayals were wrong. But he is different now. He has saved my life and is my friend. He would prove himself to you if given the chance," I begged.

"He will not be killed," Mr. Dimog replied decidedly. "I will not promise that he will be freed from his imprisonment, but he will live."

"It's all I can ask," I said gratefully, feeling as though I was catching my breath for the first time in a long while.

His expression softened, and he smiled at me in a caring way. "You must be hungry and tired, Dear One."

"I am," I replied, feeling a smile crossing my own face. "But I'm in no hurry to retire quite yet. I'm overtired, I imagine. Would you be interested in inviting me to join you for a meal, perhaps?" After asking for a promise of Acksil's life, requesting an invitation to dinner didn't seem overly bold.

"I would if I did not already have other engagements," he said with a touch of regret.

"Of course. You're a busy man. I'm fortunate to have been granted this time to talk to you. I'll just have to look forward to the next occasion to sit down with you."

His eyes smiled at me, crinkling in their outer corners. "I'll look forward to that as well. Speak with Gebbie when you're ready to eat. She'll prepare something for you, and you can have it in the kitchen or in your room if that's what you prefer," he offered.

"I'm sure Gebbie will take good care of me. She certainly has until now," I said gratefully, rising and stepping up to him to kiss his cheek, giving his hand a gentle squeeze at the same time. "Thank you again, Mr. Dimog."

He stood after receiving my kiss, giving my hand a little squeeze in return. His fingertips and palms were tough and calloused but still smooth and cared for. As civilized as he was, this man was not handed anything in life. He'd fought for every comfort he had and for the protection he extended to those he cared about.

"You're very welcome. I wish you a good meal and a restful sleep," he replied, walking me to the door.

From there, he returned to his desk, and I set off to find the kitchen.

Chapter 20

Megan

"Go back inside the restaurant and lock the door behind you," Mez instructed me in an urgent no-nonsense tone, pulling me behind him.

"What? Why? What's happening?" Feeling frantic, I gripped onto Mez' arm, more frightened to leave him than to stay.

"Megan, do it!"

His sharp tone startled me into action. I released him and bolted toward the restaurant, but before I could reach the door, one of the frightening stitched-mouthed men grabbed hold of my arm and hauled me backward. Shrieking, I dropped my rose and immediately began to shove and hit the man in a desperate attempt to pull myself free from his iron grasp. The heels I wore made it impossible for me to secure solid footing, and I was quickly dragged away from the restaurant and Mez, who was dealing with the other three men.

Suddenly, a heavy *"PANG!"* sound erupted, and my attacker released me, dropping like a stone to the ground. My eyes quickly darted away from the unconscious man, and I stared in shock at our dinner server, who was lowering the cast iron pan he'd used to clobber the man in the head. Wasting no time, the server grabbed my arm, and I ran with him into the restaurant. He locked the door behind us.

"Thank you," I said breathlessly to him, noticing that the maître d', Islass, was also there at the ready with a cleaver.

"Are you hurt?" the server asked.

"No, I don't think so, but Mez..." I trailed off as the three of us turned to the scene unfolding outside the window.

I had been worried that we'd left Mez to fend for himself against the three remaining guys, but I soon found my worries were for nothing. As soon as Mez spied us through the glass, he focused an intense gaze on two of the men whose attacks he'd been deflecting. Abruptly, they stopped their attempts to strike him, looking dazed for a moment before turning their fists on each other, seeming to forget about Mez, entirely.

The third guy took this opportunity to rush Mez, who shoved him off. The man was gearing up for a second charge but then stopped dead in his tracks.

Gaping, flabbergasted, I watched in disbelief as a look of sheer horror crossed the man's face, and he dropped to his knees with utter and complete terror in his wild dark eyes. He began to yank at his short hair as if what he was seeing was driving him to the brink of madness. Although his stitches remained intact, blood appeared at the seams around his mouth as it failed to open into a scream. Just as his eyes were starting to roll back into his head, and I was positive he was about to lose consciousness or worse, he sprang into action, jumping up as if lit on fire, and tore down an alley out of sight.

The two fighting guys, who hadn't stopped beating on one another, followed him, not once pausing in their punching and kicking as they went.

Mez, looking physically none the worse for wear, picked up his abandoned jacket and stepped up to the unconscious man, who had been struck by the server. Mez went through his pockets, finding nothing but a switchblade-like knife, which he tucked away in his pants pocket. He then raised his hand in a waving motion, calling out to someone out of sight, and a few moments later, two Kavylak soldiers showed up and took away the unconscious man. When Mez finally approached the restaurant door, Islass unlocked it and opened it for him.

"Are you alright?" Mez asked me, looking concerned as he drew me out of the restaurant, nodding his thanks to Islass and the server.

"I dropped my flower," I answered stupidly and realized my teeth were chattering, and I was shaking.

Nodding gently at my response, he placed his jacket over my shivering shoulders. While he glanced around the ground in search of the flower, I slid my arms into his jacket sleeves, grateful for the extra layer. Finding the rose, Mez held it out to me, and I took it. The stem had broken in half, but the head of the flower was untouched.

"I'll need to get you another one." Taking my free hand, he tucked it into his arm.

"Are you okay?" I asked, seeing the telltale signs of the toll that using his skill had taken on him. He appeared as though he were suffering the start of a migraine.

"Yes." He spoke quietly, walking us toward the main street. "I'm going to get us a ride home. I don't think you want another romantic walk at the moment." A wry smile poked at his lips.

I shook my head, unable to make my lips do anything but frown. I was still distressed and hadn't fully shaken the upset of what had happened and what I'd seen him do to those men. If I was being honest, witnessing him hijacking the minds of those men wasn't what had disturbed me so badly. What scared me was knowing that they must have been truly vile with the worst intentions to have driven Mez to inflict such a vicious mind attack.

After popping one of those blue painkiller cubes I'd seen him take on more than one occasion, Mez held up his hand when he saw a rickshaw driver approaching. The man pulling the cart set it down so we could get in.

"Come on, I'll help you up."

Taking his hand, I stepped into the cart and took a seat on the little carriage-like bench. Mez sat next to me, spoke a few words to the man, who nodded and began to run us back toward the military compound. He then took my hand to hold it in his.

"It's over now," he assured me.

"What happened? Who were those men? Why did they look like that? Their mouths…" I trailed off, feeling as though I might gag if I finished the sentence.

"They are called 'He'." Mez explained. "The Hes serve the Vutol."

My breath hitched when he said the "V" word.

"You mean that horrible group that has Aésha?"

"Yes. *Them.* The Hes are not normally out like this. They usually stay closer to their camps or lairs or whatever they might call them," Mez explained, sounding more disgusted and on edge with every word he uttered. "I didn't find anything on them that would indicate why they would have been outside our restaurant, and they can't talk to tell us."

"What could they have been after?"

"I honestly don't know. If I had to guess, based on what just happened, I'd say they were after you. That's just a guess, though. Nothing about this makes any sense."

He squeezed my hand to comfort me, and I squeezed back, too numb for words. My gaze dropped to my broken flower. I was too terrified by Mez' speculation to ask him any more questions about the Vutol or their intentions, and he must have picked up on my uneasiness, because he didn't encourage conversation.

As we rode back to the compound in silence and as I thought about what had happened, I realized why Mez hadn't held back his anger when using his skill on those men. The Vutol wasn't just bad. It was pure evil. They had taken Aésha, and if I had been kidnapped, there was no telling what horrors I would have seen or been subjected to. Deciding not to dwell on the terrifying thought of what could have happened, I focused instead on being immensely grateful that Mez and the men at the restaurant had prevented me from being taken.

We reached our destination, and Mez moved to step down out of the rickshaw. After he gave the man a coin, I took Mez' offered hand and got out.

Remaining quiet, I walked with Mez into the compound where the guards let him through, likely still oblivious to my presence.

"Will you be alright at Remms' tonight?" Mez asked me once we were inside the building.

"Yes, but before I go there, would you mind showing me how to use a pen, if you're feeling up to it?" Scary Vutol experience aside, the most imminent threat I faced remained learning how to write with ink or facing the wrath of Major Tovash. That said, if Mez was suffering a migraine, I also didn't want to make it worse. I had no idea how fast that cubie painkiller medicine worked.

"Of course. I'd be happy to." He took me to his apartment, turned on the light, and indicated the dining table. "Have a seat."

Nodding to him, I took off his jacket and rested it on the back of one of the chairs at the table before taking a seat in it. Mez returned with some paper, an inkwell, and a silver pen that he held out for me. I took it and was instantly pleased with its weight and how it felt in my fingers. It immediately reminded me of the types of pens I was used to back home. That said, this was no ordinary two-dollar pen you'd buy at some office supplies store.

Engraved into the metal was a vine-wrapped stylized letter B that sprouted from an open book. The vine that wound its way around the B was covered in rose buds, save for one fully bloomed rose in which there was a sparkling vibrant blue stone in a shade nearly identical to the blue rose Mez had given me.

This was the type of pen you'd get if you got your PhD or for retiring from a company after 3,000 years of service, or if, you know, you're, like, a super-rich Spoiled Prince.

I wonder if it's some sort of Basarovka family crest.

"The pens you've worked with require you to dip the nib into the ink to write, correct?" he asked, taking a seat at the table.

"That's right."

"You'll find this pen easier if your struggle is with the inkwell. When you're ready, dip the nib into the ink." He smiled in a knowing way, clearly confident that I was going to like whatever resulted.

Following his instruction, I dipped the nib of the pen into the small jar of ink.

"See the lever on the side of the pen?"

I nodded.

"Draw that from the bottom all the way to the top."

My mouth quirked up into a smile at his words, because I was pretty sure I knew what was about to happen, and I was thrilled. After pulling the lever, the pen sucked up some of the ink from the jar, filling its interior chamber.

"Now, dab the excess from the nib on the side of the jar and write until the ink runs dry. Simply refill the pen whenever you need to."

I grinned at him and wrote a few words to test out the pen. It worked like a dream. Now all I'd have to remember was not to drag my hand through the wet ink and smudge the words.

"This is fantastic, Mez! Thank you so much! Would it be alright if I borrow a pen until I can find one to replace it? I don't mean this fancy one, of course, but maybe another one, if possible?"

"I'm happy to help." He smiled warmly at me and shook his head. "Keep it. You deserve to write with a fancy pen. You're a Spoiled Princess in training. Baaaa." He grinned.

I was taken off guard by his lamb noise, and I laughed so hard I snorted.

"Are you sure?" I asked once I'd sobered up. "This looks like an important pen."

"I'm sure."

"Thank you." I was genuinely touched that he would gift me something I truly needed, and to top it all off, it was cool, too!

I grinned as I wrote a quick note to Mez on a fresh sheet of paper:

Thanks for a great first date.

Baaaa! You're the coolest!

Love,

Your Spoiled Princess in training

I handed the note to Mez. He read it and smiled. "You're very welcome."

After holding his gaze for an extra long moment, allowing myself to get lost in the gravity of it, I reluctantly stood, holding my new pen and mangled flower.

"I should head to Remms' and turn in. I have to get up really early."

"I'll walk you as far as his door, so you don't need to worry about any new adventures popping up unexpectedly," he said, only half teasing as he headed to the door to leave with me.

I nodded, and we walked comfortably together down the hall. Although I was pretty sure I could walk the ten steps to Remms' door unscathed, considering how this night had gone, who knew what mysterious disaster could happen between here and there.

"I did enjoy tonight, Megan," Mez said, once we'd reached Remms' place.

Smiling and feeling all squishy inside, I took his hand and gave it an affectionate squeeze. "I did, too, Mez, it was a very special evening."

"Would you like to try for a very boring evening with me tomorrow?"

"I would like that very much. The blander the better." I giggled, and he chuckled.

"Have a good night, Megan."

"Have a good night, Mez." I raised up on my tippiest of toes and kissed his cheek. Drawing away, I saw that he'd momentarily shut his eyes, and I felt special that my little kiss had had such an effect.

He smiled softly at me, reaching out to gently stroke my hair before turning to walk back to his apartment. I watched him go for a brief moment and felt not only happy, but for the first time in a long time, hopeful.

Chapter 21

Irys

After a number of wrong turns, I arrived at the kitchen, using my nose to guide me around the final corner and to the correct door. I smiled to myself as I imagined that this must have been how the Sefaline felt when travelling just about anywhere.

My intention had been to peek in through the door to see if Gebbie was there, but I paused just outside as I heard her voice.

"Don't be afraid now," she said in a happy yet calm tone, speaking in Sylizan. "You go on and eat."

My curiosity was piqued. It sounded as though she was speaking to a child or a frightened animal, and she wasn't speaking in Dsumot or the Common Tongue. It felt wrong to eavesdrop, so I poked my head into the doorway, and when I spotted Gebbie, I whispered, "Might I come in?"

"Oh yes, dear," Gebbie said with a sigh to someone's sharp gasp. I looked farther into the room and heard some shuffling near the large kitchen table but saw no one.

The table was set with a meal for one, but it appeared untouched. The rest of the room was warm and inviting. If I hadn't known better, and if the space weren't slightly too large, I'd have thought I'd stepped into the kitchen of a country cottage.

"I'm sorry if I've disturbed someone's meal," I apologized, still uncertain as to what was happening.

"You didn't, I assure you," Gebbie said, sounding mildly exasperated. "She'll come on out when she's feeling brave enough. You have a seat, Miss Godeleva. Would you like me to fetch you some dinner?"

"Thank you, I'd like that very much," I said, taking a seat at the table across from the place that was already set.

"What would you like to eat, dear? Meat? Vegetables? Eggs? What appeals?"

"Perhaps some toast and eggs? I'm not entirely certain what's available or easiest. If there is something to be made into a salad, that would be just lovely," I replied uncertainly. What did people in Dsumot eat? Never having had to make my own meals, I didn't know what to request that would be quick and easy to prepare.

"I know just the thing. You leave it to me," she said, looking pleased with herself. I thanked her, and she bustled away and busied herself preparing something.

Glancing around the room, I decided that if the person whose dinner was across from me was still there, she had to be under the table. The last thing I wanted to do was to frighten this person any more than was already the case. Deciding to take a risk with my dignity, I reached a hand under the table and held it out as a kind of puppet, with my fingers making the top half of its mouth and my thumb comprising the lower half.

"Hello," said my puppet hand in Sylizan as I moved the "mouth" like a bird's beak.

Gebbie, who had started humming to herself, grinned in my direction.

My puppet hand looked around a little before speaking again. "I hope dinner is good here." I used a deep, whispered voice to try to imply that this little bird was a kind and gentle boy.

Glancing down, I spotted a child crawling over to sit next to my hand. She watched it intently without speaking.

Changing the position of my hand, I made this imaginary bird turn to look at the girl. Every motion was smooth and predictable. I didn't want to startle her.

"Nice to meet you," said my bird puppet.

"I like your dress," whispered the girl to my hand.

This made me grin. My little boy bird puppet didn't seem to have tickled her imagination. Instead, it appeared to provide her with a way to speak with me without fear. It hadn't been my intention, but I was glad it had worked, nonetheless.

"Thank you," replied the puppet. "I feel very pretty in it. You may touch it if you'd like."

The girl reached out her hand and carefully patted the fabric of my skirt. Soon after, she climbed out from under the table and slid into the chair next to mine.

Once I was able to see her better, I was surprised to discover that she was considerably older than I'd first assumed. I had thought I had been speaking to a girl of seven or eight cycles. This young lady had to be closer to twelve. She had a sweet appearance with long, full brown hair and large, innocent and yet inquisitive-looking dark eyes. Her lips were naturally set into the type of pout that was quite fashionable among Sylizan ladies. I'd seen many try to replicate the look using lip rouge. This girl came by it naturally.

I returned the puppet into a normal hand again and rested it neatly in my lap.

"Good evening," I addressed the girl. "Thank you very kindly for joining me for my meal. I do like to eat with other young ladies," I said, speaking to her as though she were another young woman of noble Sylizan birth.

The girl's precious gaze set upon me as she listened to every word I said.

"Are you a princess?" she inquired. Her voice tinkled delicately like a crystal bell.

"No, I'm a Godeleva," I replied with a smile.

She nodded, accepting my answer, and I wondered if she was just being polite or if she had heard of the Godeleva name.

I considered asking, but her face became alarmed, and she slid back under the table again. A moment afterward, I had my explanation in the form of the sound of footsteps approaching. I held my hand out for the girl in case she could find comfort in holding it. Her fingers slid into mine and held on tightly. I held her back, glad to be there for her.

A young man of around my age, or perhaps slightly younger, stepped into the room. He had a pleasant smile on his tan-coloured face as his bright blue eyes glanced about the room from behind a mop of glossy black hair. Just as they fixed on me, they darted back to Gebbie, who scolded sharply.

"Alee! You know the kitchen's off limits to men at this hour. Get!" she said in the Common Tongue before letting out a stream of scolding in the Dsumot language, swatting her large wooden spoon in his direction.

Alee grinned widely, holding up his hands in mock surrender throughout the tirade. He responded in Dsumot with a baby-faced frown and a darling tone, to which Gebbie rolled her eyes and tossed a dinner roll at him. He caught it with a chuckle and bit it, backing out of the room with a final wink to me, before Gebbie swatted the air with her spoon, and he darted away.

I couldn't help but giggle at the scene and at whatever Gebbie was muttering under her breath as she turned her attention back to the meal she was preparing.

"It's alright, little lamb," she spoke in Sylizan, this time. "He's one of the good ones. You come on out now."

I leaned back to look under the table at the girl, nodding in agreement to Gebbie's words. The girl looked at me in return, holding my hand as though clinging to a lifeline.

"Come have dinner with me. You can hold my hand as long as you'd like. It's important for us to eat our dinners to be polite to our hosts. Ladies must do these things even when it is difficult for us," I informed her.

When I was her age, Lord Imery's mother, Lady Godeleva, would tell me about all the things ladies must do to be proper, and I loved to learn them. I could only hope this girl would feel the same way.

After a moment of debate, the girl slid back into the chair next to me, keeping my hand in hers.

"My name is Miss Irys Godeleva. What may I call you?" I continued under the same theme, which she appeared to enjoy.

"I'm Lesoué," she replied quietly, tentatively.

"It's good to meet you, Miss Lesoué. I'm very glad to share your company."

Though Lesoué didn't smile outright, calling her "Miss Lesoué" caused her to light up a little, and she sat slightly taller in her chair.

Gebbie chose that moment to approach and set a plate down in front of me. It contained two poached eggs on thick toast with fresh fruit and a mixed green salad. It was perfect, of course, as I'd been certain it would be when Gebbie had looked as confident as she did when starting to prepare it.

To my amusement, Gebbie then set a smaller version of my meal in front of Lesoué, taking away the meal from the setting opposite me. I smiled warmly to Gebbie for her generosity and genius.

"This is perfect, Gebbie. Thank you. I wouldn't have known just what appealed to me until you set it down in front of me. I'm delighted," I told her honestly.

The head of Mr. Dimog's household staff grinned at me, looking proud of herself indeed.

"You deserve it, Miss Godeleva, even more so now that you've got this little one here to speak to you and tell you her name, no less."

"I think Miss Lesoué will be the perfect dinner company for such a lovely meal. I couldn't be more pleased," I replied, giving the girl's hand a secret squeeze.

"Well then, it looks like you're both fine here. If you'll excuse me, I'm going to go check on the other one. I'll be back shortly." She walked to the doorway before turning to Lesoué. "You stay here with Miss Godeleva."

"We'll be just fine," I assured Gebbie.

Lesoué nodded obediently to Gebbie's instruction.

It was time to become the perfect example for Lesoué. I felt strongly that this would not only help to keep the girl entertained and calm until Gebbie's return, but it would also help her to learn some important skills should she ever return to Syliza, which I could only assume was her home.

Holding Lesoué's hand but placing my other hand over my heart, I shut my eyes to give thanks for the meal Gebbie had prepared for me.

"Thank you, Great Goddess, for the nourishing meal you have laid before me and for the new friends you have shared with me. Thank you for granting me Miss Lesoué's company, which is a true blessing on my heart." After making the sign of the Goddess with my fingers, I opened my eyes. As I did, I caught the last flicker of the sign on Lesoué's fingers as well.

With her arm raised as it was, her sleeve slid up her forearm enough to expose what looked like a dark but healing bruise. As soon as she lowered her arm, it was covered once again. I took a brief moment to take a closer look at her. She wore a plain dress that was clean but slightly too big for her.

I turned to focus on my dinner, noticing that Lesoué was mirroring virtually everything I did.

"Miss Lesoué, I will need both my hands to eat properly. Would you allow us to push our chairs together so we will still be close even if we don't hold hands while we eat?" I asked her calmly and reasonably, allowing her to make the choice. I was willing to accept whatever reply she gave.

At first, she appeared distressed, biting her lip, but she seemed to calm a little and nodded. Still, the look of distress had upset me. I rose and pushed our chairs together, sitting down immediately next to her. Then, I smiled.

"I have an idea. I promise you will like it," I assured her. Instead of taking her hand, I drew my closest arm through hers, linking them together. This freed our hands to use our cutlery, yet still allowed us to remain connected.

I watched Lesoué to be sure I had not broken my promise to her. To my great joy, she sighed relief and without smiling looked very pleased with my decision.

I smiled at her, then turned my attention to my meal, determined to show her how to eat like a fine young lady. I cut into my poached egg, allowing the yolk to run over the toast – something I always found greatly satisfying – and proceeded to neatly and politely eat my meal. Throughout it, I made small talk with Lesoué, to which she participated minimally but seemed quite content in doing so. She mirrored every move I made throughout my entire meal, eating her smaller version of what I had been served, just as I ate my own.

"Have you lived here a long time, Miss Lesoué?" I asked her finally, once I felt we'd discussed enough things to know she was comfortable saying as much or as little as she wanted.

"No, Miss Irys," she replied with a small shake to her head.

"I'm glad you're here now. I'm very happy to have a new friend."

Lesoué pressed her lips together as though trying to prevent herself from smiling. After a moment, she failed, and a smile broke through her resistance. I was elated. It was gone as quickly as it had appeared, but I'd seen it, and it meant the world to me. I smiled in return, without any hesitation.

Footsteps halted our moment, and I feared that Lesoué would hide under the table again. Fortunately, Gebbie spoke just in time. "It's just me, ladies."

Keeping her arm linked in mine, Lesoué relaxed.

Gebbie entered the room. Her apron was wet and stained, and she took it off and tossed it into a laundry hamper that appeared to be half full of other aprons, towels, and table linens.

"Is everything quite alright, Gebbie?" I asked, knowing that her apron had been spotless when she'd left the kitchen earlier.

Before Gebbie could answer, Lesoué replied. "Kaziki is sick."

Gebbie nodded in agreement and washed her hands at the sink.

"Kaziki? Is she a friend of yours, Miss Lesoué?" I asked.

Lesoué nodded. "We got out together. I helped her. She's still not feeling good."

"Out?" I inquired, though I wondered if I should. Considering the state of this girl, I hesitated to think on what her former situation might have been.

Again, Lesoué nodded, but this time, she said nothing. To a degree, I was relieved, though not at all comforted.

In a voice without expression Gebbie supplied the missing detail. "They're Vutol children, Miss Godeleva."

Chapter 22

Megan

Thanks to the amazing pen Mez had given me, writing with ink was a breeze. That said, I was the only one who appreciated it. I had shown the pen to Nilaal, when I'd first arrived at work – to let her know I was grateful for her help yesterday – and had hoped that she'd be as pleased as I was that I'd be using ink today. I couldn't have been more wrong about her reaction. All I had received in response was intense silence and a very judgy look that more than suggested she'd thought I'd done some salacious act to get the pen. Then and there, I knew we'd probably never be friends, but I was okay with that.

Like the day before, the hours of my shift dragged on. Since I no longer struggled to write, and what I was translating was of no interest to me, my thoughts drifted to the events from the night before as I scratched words across page after page on autopilot.

I had told Remms about my date and our scary encounter with the Vutol. While I hadn't been surprised that Remms was shocked that we'd been attacked, I *was* surprised when he'd revealed some information about Aésha's past. After he'd told me that he'd found it strange for the Vutol to attack Mez and me, he added that it made more sense to him that Aésha would be taken. When I asked why, he explained in confidence that it wasn't only because she was a Charmer but that Aésha had long been enslaved by the Vutol before she had become a Warrior.

After greater insistence on my part, I managed to convince Remms to tell me more of the Vutol and what they did. While I'd had a rather strong idea, Remms confirmed my worst fears, including everything Amarogq had told me earlier, and that anyone captured and sold by the Vutol could be used for any purpose from caged human collections to forced prostitution.

Even now, hours after our conversation, the hair on the back of my neck stood up, and my stomach twisted in knots. It was madness to know that such an organization could be real, that it could have clientele, that Aésha was in their clutches, that she'd known that hell before she was a Warrior, and that I could have just as easily been subjected to that hell if Mez and the men at the restaurant hadn't acted so swiftly.

I paused my writing momentarily, because I couldn't control the shiver that shot up and down my spine like lightning. Taking a few short breaths to steady myself, I forced my mind back to the task at hand and continued my work, occasionally allowing myself to think about the nice time I would have with Mez this evening.

I managed to finish the last page just before Major Tovash arrived to check our work. She flipped through Nilaal's work first and dismissed her, then turned to me.

"It seems you can be taught after all," she said in a condescending tone that was purposely meant to be heard as she examined my work. She glanced up from the pages and looked like she was either going to dismiss me or roll her eyes, but then her gaze fell to the pen on my desk, and her jaw set with such intensity that I was certain she was going to ream me out for not using the type of pen everyone else was using.

Oh my gosh! Did Mez give me some kind of illegal writing tool?

Without warning, she suddenly slammed the pages down on my desk, and I jumped.

"Get out. Be on time tomorrow. You'll need to finish more than this amount every day to be worth your while." She spat out the words with disdain and turned sharply on her heel and stormed out of the room.

Um, what just happened?

Not wanting to contemplate whether the Major had a split personality, a serious hate for ink-filled pens, or some other hang-up, I gathered my things and high-tailed it out of there. The more time I had to get ready before my second date with Mez, the better.

I hadn't taken three steps out of the room, when to my delight, I saw Mez heading in my direction.

"Hi!" I greeted him brightly.

He stopped when he saw me and smiled. "Hi. Good day?"

"Yes. Your pen is amazing, and Major Tovash didn't kill me, even though I thought she might when she saw the pen I was using."

He looked slightly guilty. "Always a good sign when she doesn't kill you."

"What was that look for?" I asked him.

"What?" He raised a brow.

"You just had this look when I told you that she looked murderous when she saw your pen. A look like you're not really surprised about her reaction, like you kinda anticipated it."

He nodded with an eye glint. "But she didn't kill you, so it's a good day."

Oh my gosh. Did something happen between him and Major Tovash? Was she...jealous?

"What are you not telling me?"

"I'm not telling you that we need to delay our evening a little," he said regretfully.

"What?" That wasn't the response I had been expecting or wanted to hear. "We do? Why?"

"Xandon has summoned you."

The blood drained from my face, and my hands instantly became clammy with the mention of Xandon's name. "He..." I tried to swallow but failed. "He summoned me?"

Mez' brow furrowed in concern and confusion when he observed my expression. "Yes. I thought you wanted that. To talk to him about going home," he stated carefully. "I kept my promise. I asked him to speak with you."

Duh! Megan. He's right, and he kept his word. Give the guy a break and stop being so dramatic.

"Yes. You're right. I mean, of course I do." I smiled a little. "Thank you for keeping your promise."

He nodded. "I'll walk you up there."

Walking with him toward the stairs, I couldn't shake the cold and clammies. Yes, I did want to talk to Xandon about going home, but for some reason I didn't think it would be this soon. Although I should have been feeling grateful at how swiftly Mez had acted and Xandon had complied, an unsettling feeling was growing in my gut with each step I took. Every fiber in my being was warning me that seeing Xandon was a bad idea.

Eerie feeling aside, I knew I was being a bit of a drama queen. I was just feeling anxious to see and talk to Xandon, because the last time I'd talked to him, I'd been naive and thought he was my friend, and the last time I'd seen him, he hadn't uttered a word to help me or Irys with Galnar. Since then, I'd found out that he was more powerful than I'd realized, the leader of the Warriors, a man feared by many, and someone about whom I'd had strange dreams more than once.

I have to do this. I want to do this.

"He knows why you want to talk to him," Mez reassured me as we climbed to the fifth floor. "There will likely be other people there, too. They're there to help him."

Xandon needs other people to help him? Help him do what? I don't remember him needing other people to help him the last time I'd talked to him.

"Okay."

I didn't ask Mez about the other people. I didn't want to overthink things more than I already was. Since he didn't sound concerned, I decided that I didn't need to be concerned, either. I mean, I was pretty sure he'd have warned me if Galnar was going to be there, for instance. That said, I didn't get the impression that Mez was going to be one of the people, either.

"Are you going to stay?"

"Do you want me to stay?"

Well, that mystery was solved. I debated my response for a second before shaking my head.

"No, that's alright. I was only curious. I mean, I'm sure you've got other things to do, and it's not like I haven't talked to Xandon before." I did my best to sound as casual as possible.

"Sure. I'll just wait outside, wondering if I should be getting jealous," he teased with a grin.

A small, amused snort erupted from my nose at his attempt to keep things light. "Thanks for this, Mez. I hope I get some answers."

"I hope you learn something important."

When we reached Xandon's door, Mez rested a supportive hand on my shoulder. "I'll be just down the hall in my office when you're done."

"See you soon."

He smiled and headed down the hall toward his own office. Turning, I raised my fist and knocked on the metal door.

"Enter."

I started at the sound of Xandon's voice. For some reason, I hadn't expected Xandon to respond. Before I could lose my nerve, I grasped the handle and opened the door, stepping in, and shutting it behind me.

The room was nothing like I thought it would be. Unlike Mez' office, which had plenty of character, warm woods, and personality, this room looked nearly identical to the Translation room. The walls and floors were bare. With the exception of the especially tall black wing chair in which Xandon sat, and a very out-of-place ostentatious wooden floor mirror, everything else was metal, including a long rectangular table in front of him and four chairs opposite him.

Xandon looked just as otherworldly as I remembered. In the light, his long, smooth opal white hair had nearly the same iridescent luster as the precious stone it resembled. His celestial eyes shone like aquamarine gemstones. These features, coupled with his flawless marble complexion and the sharp angles of his face, gave him a somewhat sculpted appearance, making him look more like a statue than a man. The only characteristic that jarred with his near seraphic form was his metal arm, which was currently resting in full view atop the table in front of him. The unnatural silver appendage was perfectly polished yet crudely designed, extending into long fingers with sharp tips.

"Have a seat, Megan." The timbre of Xandon's voice when he spoke my name was deep, soothing, and compelling, exactly as it had been when we'd first met. I immediately felt more at ease and nearly sighed when some of the tension I'd been carrying left my body.

Xandon's arresting gaze never left me as I took a seat in one of the four unoccupied chairs, setting my bag down on the floor. It was only then that I realized there was no one else in the room but us.

Didn't Mez say there would be other people here?

"I have learned from Mez that you wished to see me to help you find your way back to your home."

"Yes. Is it something that you can do?"

"It is something that I can try to help you to do."

I stared at him for a long moment, wondering what that meant and if he was telling the truth.

"I know why you are hesitant to trust me, Megan. You would be a fool to trust me based on the experiences you have had upon arriving on Qarradune, what you have likely heard about me, and what you have seen for yourself. However, I know that you believe me to be the only one who can help you to return to your home. This is why you chose to stay in Kavylak, and why you have decided to face me after all this time."

I nodded slowly, wondering how much he knew on his own, and how much Mez had told him.

Did he know I had initially intended to escape with Thayn?

"You were wise to stay. No one in Syliza, or in all of Qarradune for that matter, has my particular abilities, and you are not the first person from your Earth whom I have met."

"What?" I gasped. "I'm not?" I slid to the edge of my seat, leaning toward him. "You mean, there are other people from Earth, here?"

"No." He shook his head. "It was cycles ago. The person appeared suddenly, just as you did, and was as confused about how they found themselves here as you are. I did my best to return this person to their home, just as you are requesting of me now, but my efforts failed. They were too weak and died in the process."

My mouth dropped open in shock. "Y—you mean, you killed them when you were trying to get them back home?"

"Yes."

"How?"

"I know of only one logical explanation for how you could be here. It would take a skill that would allow you to travel across great distances in the blink of an eye. In our world, we refer to those who possess this skill as Travellers."

I stared at him blankly. My mind reeled, having no idea how to process this information. "So... you think that I'm one of these Travellers?"

"It is what I have hypothesized, yes."

"And there are other Travellers on Qarradune?"

"Yes, but with the possible exception of the one other like you whom I have met, none were from your Earth. Travellers, who can instantly cross any distance at will, must be aware of the existence of a place in order to be able to Travel to it. Your ability to Travel here and Travel unscathed, without knowing of Qarradune, is an anomaly."

"So, what do I have to do?" I asked with a modicum of hope.

"To help you return home, I would need to activate the skill you must possess. For me to bring this skill to your surface, you would need to undergo a series of therapies that would try your mental and physical well-being. If these therapies are successful, you would be changed, but would possess the ability to access and use your Traveller skill. If not, undergoing the therapies will kill you. I will be candid, there is a greater chance of death than there is of success."

"Why...why are you telling me this only now? Why didn't you tell me this when we first met?"

"Because what you ask of me, to help you find a way home, is no small request and is as draining for me as it will be for you. More to the point, you would not have believed me," he stated plainly. "Based on what you and the other person told me of your Earth, you come from a world where skills of the extraordinary, such as those you have now witnessed among my Warriors, are either not widely known or simply do not exist. Had this been our first conversation after you had awoken confused and alone, stranded in a foreign land, would you have believed me?"

Okay. He has a bit of a point, but still...

"Are you saying the reason that you didn't help me when I traded places with Irys to become Galnar's slave was that you wanted to help me understand your world better?" I didn't mask the incredulity in my tone.

"I would not have planned it that way, but when the opportunity presented itself, it was the most logical path for you at the time. If I had intervened, you would not have been thrown into the confusion and chaos that has led you to this point. It was not a kindness, but if you are seeking an apology, I have none to give."

Wow! So, I was his unapologetic social experiment. Nice...

"The woman who sits before me now has proven that she is a strong survivor of this harsh world and could thrive here," he continued. "She has a greater understanding of Qarradune and can live with the consequences of her choices."

"My choices?" I almost snorted from the derision I felt. "What choices? I've barely had any choices since being here."

"You have always had choices," Xandon said dismissively. "Everyone does, no matter their station or predicament or how impossible a choice may seem. You have a choice now Megan Wynters: you can risk your life trying to return to Earth or you can make a new life on Qarradune."

Gee! What a choice: likely die trying to get home or stay forever trapped on a foreign planet.

As blunt as Xandon was being, I still didn't entirely trust him, but I had to try to get home, even if it meant risking my life.

"I want to go home."

He nodded. "Then let us begin."

Without another word, he rapped his metal knuckles on the table, causing me to jump. Seconds later, an interior door I hadn't previously noticed in the room, opened. Two people entered and took a seat.

"This is Lieutenant Awndore Fynx and Ms. Theather Cryx. They will be assisting me."

Lieutenant Awndore Fynx had a stereotypical Halloween Goth look, only without the makeup. His pale skin stood out in sharp contrast against his black Warrior's uniform, dark eyes, and obsidian coloured hair that was cut in various jagged lengths and fell haphazardly to the tops of his shoulders.

Although she wasn't wearing a uniform, Ms. Theather Cryx was also clad in black from neck to toe. However, unlike Lieutenant Fynx – who looked like darkness incarnate – Ms. Cryx looked like a fallen angel with soft and friendly Polynesian-like features, glittering bright blue eyes, and raven tresses with glistening platinum silver streaks.

I inclined my head in a wordless "hello" to them, to which Ms. Cryx smiled and cutely wiggle-waved her pointer finger at me in greeting.

"Take this." Xandon said, resting a paper-wrapped cube onto his desk.

"What is it?" I asked, eyeing the cube as if it were poison.

"It is a sedative. It will relax your body and your mind, placing you in a state between asleep and awake so that I can access your subconscious."

Whaaaat?

"You don't have to do this." Xandon reminded me, sensing my obvious discomfort and uncertainty. "You still have a choice and will continue to have this choice, even after this first session. We can stop if ever you should decide that you would prefer to explore your second option."

A strong part of me wanted to call it off and leave, but I knew it was my fear talking. When someone tells you that you would either be forever changed or possibly die to get what you want, that's not easy to swallow, but I didn't just *want* to get back home, I *needed* to get back home.

Before losing my nerve, I reached forward, took the cube, unwrapped it, and put the contents into my mouth. It dissolved fast, and its effects took hold instantly. All the tension in my body melted away, and I slumped into the chair. The last thing I recalled before losing consciousness was Xandon's pleased smile.

Chapter 23

Irys

My beautiful comforting dinner felt like a brick in my stomach. I had no doubt that all colour had drained from my face.

"At least, they were Vutol children until this morning," Gebbie amended.

It was important to me that I not make the girl feel that I was rejecting her after what I'd just learned. Lesoué had been a slave of the most deplorable, heartbreaking, and devastating kind. Even as icy water flowed through my veins, I would never cause her to feel shame in my presence.

"I'm very glad you're here now, Miss Lesoué. I do hope Kaziki feels better soon," I said to her, with the same tone of voice I'd been using all along.

Lesoué nodded to me, returning to her efforts to sit just as I was sitting.

"Is Kaziki permitted visitors?" I asked Gebbie, who looked over her shoulder at me.

"You can visit her if you'd like, Miss Godeleva, but she's in a bad way right now. The drugs aren't all out of her system."

I couldn't bring myself to inquire as to what drugs Gebbie meant. My imagination was supplying all the answers I could need, and I only prayed that the truth of it couldn't be worse than that.

"I thought it might be nice for Miss Lesoué and I to take a little walk to find some flowers or some petals as a gift for Kaziki," I said conversationally. It was the best idea I could think of that would take me outside for some fresh air.

"Would you like that, Lesoué?" Gebbie asked the girl.

Lesoué needed very little time before nodding decidedly to Gebbie. To me, she said "I'm happy to stay with you, Miss Irys."

"Thank you, Miss Lesoué," I smiled at her, pleased. "It's late, so we won't stray far from the house," I added to Gebbie.

I rose from my seat, taking my arm from Lesoué before offering her my hand, which she took, standing next to me.

"Great Goddess!" Gebbie exclaimed as she turned to look at us. "Lesoué, you finished your meal! Miss Godeleva, you perform miracles!" The woman looked as pleased as any person could, and pride brimmed within me.

"Thank you, Gebbie. We enjoyed our meals very much, didn't we, Lesoué? Particularly the eggs," I replied.

Lesoué nodded in agreement but remained quiet.

I thanked Gebbie again on behalf of both Lesoué and myself, before we headed out of the kitchen, taking Lesoué to the first exit door I could find. I was glad that we didn't become lost in the house even before we could take our walk.

"We may pass people as we walk," I reminded Lesoué. "We'll hold hands the whole time and you'll be fine. I'll do all the talking. You mustn't mind anyone when you're with me."

"Alright," she agreed. We strolled through far more gardens than I had noticed when I had first arrived.

There were paths that meandered up and down the slope of the hills, with carefully positioned rocks, trees, and flowers to guide us along the way. Beyond the more manicured gardens, I could see rows upon rows of the brightly blossomed trees that I'd spotted when Miss Dimog had first found Acksil and me. It was a gorgeous place, and I enjoyed the gift of being able to stop here safely along my journey home.

Lesoué and I chatted quietly as we walked along. I did most of the talking, but she occasionally agreed that this was a pretty place and that flowers were a lovely gift to give an ailing friend. I didn't pursue the topic of her time with the Vutol – for both our sakes – but did my best to make sure she knew she could talk to me about anything she wanted.

As it was not my intention to destroy Mr. Dimog's beautiful gardens, I decided that instead of plucking the flowers, it might be nicer to collect some of the petals that had fallen off the trees that grew all around us.

"Shall we gather some of those lovely orange petals and float them in a dish of water for Kaziki? I think it would look very pretty and will smell nice, too. Do you agree, Lesoué?" I asked. I knew she would want anything I suggested, but it also felt important to encourage her to make the choice.

"Yes, I think she'll like that. She said she came from a place with these trees," Lesoué informed me. It interested me that she was willing to say this much while we were out here walking, though she'd said very little in the house.

"In that case, if we get enough of them, perhaps their perfume will help her have good dreams," I suggested.

Lesoué looked peaceful at that thought and turned her attention toward the trees and all the blossoms that covered them. We took care to keep away from others by politely directing our path away from them, and my companion remained calm the entire time.

Once we were among the trees, I crouched and started collecting some of the petals in my hand. Lesoué did the same, looking perfectly content – though always on watch – as she did so. We chatted about many more simple topics including whether the bright orange or pale orange petals would be prettier in the dish we would create for Kaziki.

When we'd collected enough, I took a final glance at the darkening sky and drew in a few more breaths of fresh air before standing up.

"Let's get a bowl from the kitchen and put a bit of water into it so these petals will float," I said.

The girl nodded, and we headed inside once more. I retraced our steps and managed not to become lost in the house.

Stepping into the kitchen, I'd imagined that Gebbie would be there alone as we'd left her, but Miss Dimog was standing and speaking with her. Hearing us, she turned and fixed her gaze on me, with only the slightest glance to Lesoué. I imagined that the only reason Miss Dimog was not glaring at me was that Lesoué was there.

"Ah, they're back," Gebbie said brightly.

"We are. We've collected quite a few lovely petals that fell from the trees. We thought it might be nice to place them in a bowl of water for Kaziki. Is there a bowl we might use for that?" I tried to avoid meeting Miss Dimog's stare.

"That was very nice of you," said Miss Dimog in a soft voice I'd never heard her use, and in Sylizan, which surprised me to say the very least. When I turned toward her, I saw that she was speaking to Lesoué. My respect rose for this intense woman. I knew how she felt about me, particularly while I was wearing this gown. It was good of her to pretend that it wasn't an issue as she addressed this vulnerable girl.

"Thank you, Skeltra. Miss Irys was really good at finding the petals," Lesoué informed Miss Dimog. A touch of enthusiasm slid into her voice.

"Miss Godeleva helped Lesoué to eat her entire dinner, too," Gebbie added.

I hoped my cheeks weren't turning pink. The last thing I'd wanted to do was to become the centre of attention in front of Miss Dimog. I smiled a little as I did not want to appear ungrateful.

To my surprise, Miss Dimog looked impressed. "It's good that you've found a nice friend in Miss Irys," she praised Lesoué.

"I'm fortunate to have a new friend, too," I said, taking a risk by participating in the conversation.

Still, Miss Dimog looked at me civilly and gave me a nod. "I have my tea, so I'll see you ladies later," she excused herself. "Good evening to you all, especially you, Lesoué."

"Pleasant evening, Miss Dimog," I replied.

Lesoué nodded, and Miss Dimog left without ceremony.

For her part, Gebbie looked through a cupboard until she produced a pretty cut-glass bowl. She filled it just above halfway, setting it out so Lesoué and I could add our flower petals. I sprinkled mine into the bowl, then Lesoué added her own. I couldn't help but smile with approval. It looked very pretty indeed.

"Would you like to carry it to Kaziki's room, Miss Lesoué?" I asked, hoping to give her an important task.

"Yes, please," she replied, picking up the bowl.

"Thank you, Gebbie," I said to the woman, who looked delighted with us.

We walked out of the kitchen, and I placed a hand gently on Lesoué's shoulder as we were no longer able to hold hands. I was glad I had as the girl became visibly less tense as soon as she could tell I wasn't letting go.

She seemed to know where she was going as she walked directly down a hall and around a corner to a room with a closed door.

"It's me, Kaziki," she said in the Common Tongue as she opened the door.

The other girl gave no reply, but Lesoué entered regardless, so I followed her in. The room had a nice-sized bed and a chest of drawers. The nightstand had a pitcher and basin with a neatly folded washcloth resting on its edge. The window's curtains were drawn. On the bed, Kaziki had her eyes closed. She looked about Lesoué's age and had the general appearance of the Rebels who were born in Dsumot. She was feverish with perspiration glistening on her brow. Her expression was troubled, and I wondered if she was caught in a nightmare.

Lesoué set the bowl down next to the pitcher and basin before crawling onto the bed next to Kaziki. She moved in directly next to her, bringing her arms protectively around her. Kaziki mumbled a little but appeared to be comforted by the presence of the other girl.

Without anything else to do, I poured a bit of water into the basin and wet the cloth, wringing it out. Very gently, I dabbed at Kaziki's hot forehead and gently wiped down her cheeks and neck before starting again at the forehead. I folded the cloth and laid it there, across her brow.

Slowly, Kaziki's eyes opened. Her pupils were fully dilated, and she muttered something in Dsumot.

"Shh," Lesoué whispered to her in the Common Tongue. "This is Miss Irys. She's a very nice lady. We're safe now, Kaziki. Safe."

Kaziki muttered something again and drifted back to sleep. I imagined that it was likely best that she remained sleeping.

"Poor sweet soul," I said quietly to Lesoué.

"She will be alright, Miss Irys. It's hard to feel better again, but it happens," Lesoué reassured me.

I was struck by this girl's strength. Only a short while ago, she was too afraid to come out from under a table to eat. Now, she was soothing this girl and comforting me at the same time.

"Did you have to go through this?" I asked.

"Yes, but before. Not when I was here," she answered without looking bothered by it.

"Why does it happen?"

"From the drugs that make sure we don't run. There's a sleeping one we have to take. Then the waking one that stops us from getting sick from the sleeping one."

"If you don't take medicine upon waking, then the sleeping drug will make you sick in the morning?" I inquired, quite certain that I didn't want to know the answer.

She nodded. "Kaziki is sick because the sleeping drug is coming out of her body now."

"I understand. I've had medicine make me very sick. I know how difficult that can be," I told her. It seemed only fair to be honest with her after she had shared so much with me.

"The Vutol had you, too?"

I fought the inclination to recoil. Instead, I shook my head, making the sign of the Goddess with my fingers.

"I did it to myself. I made mistakes taking medicine," I replied.

"I'm glad you're better now, Miss Irys."

"Thank you, Miss Lesoué. Now we can both turn our prayers to heal Miss Kaziki, too."

"I'm going to stay here with her, Miss Irys. You can stay with us, too, if you want."

"That's very kind of you, Miss Lesoué," I told her, meaning every word. I could see the comfort these girls brought each other simply by being together. That she would extend this invitation to me told me that she wanted me to feel safe with them and help them to feel safe in return. It was a sizeable compliment. "I will be returning to a room of my own tonight. I'm glad to know that I may return if I should like to, though. Is this your room, too?"

"Yes. We share it."

"I'm glad you have each other."

She nodded and held Kaziki a little tighter.

"I'm going to return to Gebbie so she can show me my own room. It has been a very long day for me, too. I look forward to seeing you tomorrow, Miss Lesoué."

"I look forward to seeing you, too, Miss Irys."

Leaning down, I kissed her forehead. "Goodnight, Miss Lesoué."

She shut her eyes as she was kissed and smiled a little to herself. "Goodnight."

I stepped into the doorway and turned back to look at the sweet girls who, like me, had found safety in this place. Shutting the door behind me, I headed back to the kitchen.

"Good evening again," I said as a greeting to Gebbie, who had been humming to herself as she wiped down the countertops.

"Are our girls all tucked in?" she asked, wringing out the dishcloth and hanging it over the faucet. "You must be ready for your own bed."

"The girls are all settled together," I nodded. "I'm more than ready for my own."

"Come along, dear," Gebbie said comfortingly and guided me out of the kitchen. She took me past the room where the girls were resting and down another hall. We stepped up two stairs to another hall with only two doors. She opened the one on the left and smiled. "There you go."

I walked into the room and took in the space that was to be my own for the night. Like the girls' room, it had a nice bed with a nightstand and a chest of drawers. My room also contained a number of features that made it quite different from Lesoué and Kaziki's. These included several Sylizan items, such as a chaise near the window, a vanity, a wardrobe, and a very pretty lamp on the bedside table. A rug of soft blues, greens, pinks, and purples drew all the room's colours tastefully together.

"Thank you," I said to Gebbie as I spotted my bag. "I will feel quite at home here."

"Mr. Dimog thought you might. There are clothes for you in the wardrobe. You may wear whatever you like," she said without entering.

I stepped up to the wardrobe and opened it, seeing nightgowns and a robe, two day dresses, and an evening dress, all in Sylizan styles.

"I have everything I could possibly need," I said. "I'll need to thank Mr. Dimog tomorrow."

"I'm sure he'll like the chance to talk to you again. Your presence has brightened his day."

"I'm glad," I told her, and I was. "He's a kind man. I've felt comfortable with him since we first met. I feel like he's family."

Gebbie grinned to herself. "I just know he feels the same."

"Thank you for everything, Gebbie. Goodnight."

"You're very welcome, Miss Godeleva. Have a good night's rest. If you need anything, ask anyone here," she said and quietly shut the door.

Once the latch clicked, it was as though my last reserves of energy drained away. I felt like there was something else I should have said to Gebbie, but I couldn't call to mind what it was.

I selected a nightgown and worked to extract myself from the gown I was wearing, setting it gently aside on the chaise. I washed up, slipped into the nightie, and then under the sheets. I hadn't realized how exhausted I was until I sank into the featherbeds, feeling my body relax right down to its bruises.

Shutting my eyes, I tried to remind myself of all the things I wanted to tell Mr. Dimog the next day, but I couldn't focus. Instead, in my mind's eye, all I could see was Acksil. Acksil, who loved me.

Chapter 24

Elindria

"Wake up, Elindria."

Elindria's eyes opened wide at the sound of his voice. She sat up abruptly from the hard table where she lay, scanning the stark metal space for Xandon. He sat smugly in a tall black chair, like some omniscient God of Chaos.

"Where is my sister?" she seethed.

"That is precisely what I want to know." Xandon replied.

Elindria scrutinized the man in front of her, wondering what game he was playing. "You know where she is. I have seen you with her more than once. You have kept her from me. Stop playing games. I want to see Enadria now."

Xandon stood. "She has escaped me, not by her own choosing. I need you to find her."

Elindria smirked and pushed herself off the table, landing on her feet. "What makes you think I would help you?"

"Because you love your sister, and you want to see her again. Once I have managed to separate her spirit from her host, I can help you do the same with yours."

"Ha! I do not believe you," Elindria scoffed. "After thousands of cycles you are still the same man, dedicated to creating Chaos, manipulating nature, and bending my sister to suit your will. I can still feel the cold metal of your fingers squeezing my neck. You would leave me to rot so that you could further poison Enadria's mind to please your whims."

"Think what you will of me, Elindria. We have not been friends since before the war, but I have always loved your sister, and she loves you. I am willing to put our differences aside for her sake." Xandon paused briefly before adding, "Help me, and I will help you reunite with Freyss."

She froze at the mention of her beloved Freyss' name. It had been thousands of cycles since she had last seen him. Since she had last held him.

"You lie."

"No. You have known me to be many things, Elindria, but a liar is not one of them. I grow tired of our ageless war. I am tired of being alone. I want my beloved back, and you want yours. The time is right. Our people are returning."

"Returning? What do you mean? What poor spirit have you tried to resurrect through your twisted science?" Elindria stared intently at Xandon. Unflinching, he held her intense gaze in return. There was no smugness, no pride, no anger behind his brilliant eyes. She saw only weariness and a glimmer of hope.

Xandon walked around the table, stopping before her. "Rin was here," he confessed soberly. "She discovered your host somehow and nearly killed her and one of my Warriors."

"Rin!" Elindria could not hide her surprise at the mention of her best friend's name. If she had returned, then Xandon must have been closer than ever to drawing Enadria's sleeping spirit to the surface of her host, and Elindria's to hers. She had made Rin swear never to let that happen. After thousands of cycles, she had found a way to keep her promise.

"Where is she now?"

"I do not know." Xandon shrugged. "Waiting for another chance to finish her mission, I presume," he added, a touch of annoyance detectable in his tone.

"Is Rin the only one?"

"No. Beyond Rin, as far as I know, only Zevren and Shevutol have returned."

"How fitting that it is your allies who are clawing their way back to a corporeal existence."

"Shevutol is no longer my ally. She has had a taste of this new world for too long, and she uses her gift for her own...agenda."

"She always did."

"Not like this."

Elindria's brow rose at Xandon's words and the disgust she could detect in his voice, but whatever chaos Shevutol was brewing was not her primary concern.

"How can you bring Freyss back to me?"

"I do not entirely know," Xandon admitted, "but I know that it can be done," he continued quickly, seeing the distrust flood her eyes. "I believe the answer lies in your descendants."

She gasped, clasping her hands together. "They live?"

"They do." He confirmed, not masking the rancour in his tone. "The People of the North - your people - are just as stubborn and troublesome as you and your man from Earth."

She smiled in the knowledge that those descended from her and Freyss had survived over millennia. Her smile then grew wider as a sharp realization struck her.

"So, you have finally figured it out."

"Yes." Xandon nodded. "I cannot have what I want, without giving you what you want. Let us end this conflict between us and start anew. We share a common enemy. Help me free you both."

Turning from him, Elindria walked up to the large ornate floor mirror in the room. She did not believe the conflict between them would end, but she understood his meaning. At the moment, they did share common enemies. Pausing in front of the glass, she looked to see the face of one of those enemies staring back at her, the young red-haired, green-eyed Earth woman who held Elindria prisoner. Her gaze flicked to Xandon.

"I will help you," Elindria said.

She watched Xandon's reflection in the mirror growing closer as he moved to stand behind her. When she felt Xandon's natural hand rest on her shoulder, and his energies flow through her body, she shut her eyes, lifting her hand and resting it on the center of her chest.

Xandon's powers gained Elindria a faint reach with her Traveller senses – only a whisper of the strength she held when she was alive. Still, it wasn't long before she could feel the gentle and familiar pull toward the purple Earth crystal she had gifted her sister millennia ago. A gift so she could always be found.

"Sister, hear me."

Elindria opened her eyes to see the reflection of her twin sister staring back at her. Enadria's sage green eyes and silvery iridescent hair, a mirror image of her own.

Chapter 25

Enadria

"Sister, hear me." *Elindria's words echoed in Enadria's ears.*

Enadria opened her eyes. She had seen this room before. It was the bedroom where the girl was sleeping. Her gaze shifted to the large floor mirror with its intricately carved frame, completely out of place in this space.

Stepping up to it, her eyes widened, seeing Elindria and Xandon through its glass: her sister and her love, both alive, and possibly more surprisingly, not in battle with each other.

"Sister," repeated Elindria, pressing a hand to her side of the glass.

"Sister," Enadria replied in her identical voice. It had been millennia since they had last seen one another.

"I will be brief. Time is short," said Elindria in a kind and gentle voice that still suggested urgency, watching as Enadria placed her own hand on the glass opposite hers.

Enadria nodded, breath held, awaiting what her twin would have to say.

"Xandon and I have reached a truce. I have agreed to help him in his effort to free us from our hosts," Elindria explained. As she did, her image began to waver and blur, until it reappeared, looking nothing like she previously had; tall with flowing iridescent silver hair and sage-green eyes. Her hair was apple red, and her eyes had turned green. Her skin had darkened, and she had diminished in height. "This is the appearance of the woman who traps me."

"Her name is Megan Wynters, My Love," added Xandon, his eyes never leaving Enadria. "Remember her face."

Enadria winced at the loss of her sister's image but studied the face, just as she was instructed.

"Is she aware of you, Elindria?" she asked.

"I do not believe she is aware of Elindria," Xandon answered on behalf of the woman next to him. "She has heard the name, and she has heard your name, but she shows no indication that she knows to whom they belong."

"Good," replied Enadria, looking lovingly at Xandon. "The less they know, the easier it will be to remove them."

To this, both Xandon and Elindria nodded their agreement.

"Enadria, can you show me the face of your host?" asked Elindria, returning her form to her own.

Enadria released a long breath. She knew it was in her abilities to comply, but she didn't want to. She had been confined in that girl for cycles and bearing her appearance for even a moment longer than necessary was far from appealing. Looking at the two people she loved most in the world, she knew it was best to obey. She shut her eyes and opened them again. Her hair and eyes had turned purple. Her frame smaller and more delicate.

Elindria studied her with methodical attention.

"Irys Godeleva," Xandon informed Elindria, to which Enadria nodded confirmation. "Do you remember, Zevren, My Love?"

"Of course," Enadria replied, calling to mind the image of her old friend. "We were in university together before The War. I was with him when he discovered his elemental union."

"He has returned to us. He remains our ally," said Xandon.

Enadria was as delighted as if she had been given a precious gift. "Was it you, My Love? Did you bring him back?"

"No. He is not like my Warriors. I did not manipulate him into existence. He has returned as was prophesied by the Oracle Cingatt, just as she prophesied that you would one day return to me."

"Has Cingatt also returned?" she asked with a smile. "Does she know more of how we will all return?"

Elindria, whose face had remained impassive all this time, looked to Xandon with interest, clearly wanting to know the answer as well.

"No, not to my knowledge," replied Xandon. "I do not know anything beyond what she wrote on the walls of her sanctuary."

"What do you need me to do? Is Zevren searching for my host?" Enadria asked.

"Yes. He has been tasked with finding Irys Godeleva. He is in Syliza, and he is disguised as a BlackRobe, one of their religious representatives."

"I am not in Syliza, but it is her goal. I will watch for him when I arrive there, should I have any control or awareness," she asserted.

"Trust him, and he will bring you to Elindria and me. She is with me now," he assured her.

"I will, My Love," she said with an adoring look before placing her hand on the glass once again, her appearance returning to her own.

Elindria smiled at her sister, placing her hand on the glass opposite. "Soon, we will all be together. You have my crystal with you. I have always been with you."

Enadria's heart ached. She returned to the form of the girl and looked down at the ring on the necklace she always wore. There within its setting was Elindria's crystal. She returned to herself again.

"Yes. She wears it always. You are always with me."

Elindria nodded but visibly weakened. Without warning, her eyes rolled back in her head, and she collapsed into Xandon's arms. The mirror faded to black.

Enadria gasped as she faded away.

Chapter 26

Megan

I awoke with a splitting headache. Slowly squinting my eyes open, I felt utterly disoriented as I tried to figure out what was happening. The last thing I remembered was being in Xandon's office. I'd taken that cube drug he'd offered me, but I couldn't remember anything after that point.

I guess not being dead is a good sign, but where the hell am I?

I was lying on a comfortable bed in a dimly lit room, and I was alone. I was still in my work uniform, but my jacket and shoes had been removed, and a soft throw blanket covered me. Turning my head to the side, away from the curtained window, I spotted a cherrywood chest of drawers. On top of its surface was a brilliant blue rose in a glass bud vase.

Was I in Mez' bedroom? Shouldn't I be in Xandon's office? What am I doing here?

I was about to rise from the bed to find Mez when I heard: "Are Arik and Asimara back, too?"

My gaze flicked to the door that had been left ajar. Mez was talking to someone in the sitting room.

"Yes, with the Eransian boy, and now they're a family," Aésha replied in the teasing voice I knew so well.

My heart leapt with joy at the sound of her voice.

She's back!

Ready to make a second attempt at rising, I froze when she spoke again.

"The boy had been one of She's slaves," she said, the tease in her voice dying away. "I can't imagine he's older than five or six cycles. He'll be good for them while Asimara recovers. He'll answer some of Arik's questions when I'm not there to help them. Asimara's strong, and she's through the drugs, but it's going to take her a long time." Aésha's voice wobbled slightly at the end of her statement.

What does she mean Asimara is recovering? Recovering from what? Oh no...

"And what about you?" Mez asked with gentle caring. "How often will you see me? This one session is hardly going to be enough. You're one of the strongest of us, Aésha, but like you said, it's not just a matter of being strong."

"I'll get through it," she teased, although her tease didn't sound as convincing as the last time. "I always do." There was a short silence followed by the sound of shifting fabric. "You're saving us, Mez. All of us who will go. We can't keep going on like this. We can't. We'll lose ourselves," she stated adamantly.

He's going to save them from what? Where are they going?

"I'm with you and Rakven and Arik. I'll talk to some of the others, but it'll be up to you to ask the ones we're not sure about. You can convince them the discussion never happened. Whereas nobody wants to forget a talk with me." Her natural teasing tone had returned full force.

Mez chuckled lightly yet affectionately at her comment. "Very true. You go talk to Dendeon. I need to check on Megan."

Without a verbal response, although I'm sure she blew him a kiss or flashed him some other flirty gesture, I heard a door open and shut, signalling Aésha's departure. Between my headache and confusion from their discussion, I didn't have it in me to jump off the bed and tear after her to tell her how glad I was that she was safe.

Hearing Mez' footsteps approach, I slowly rose to a sitting position, wincing and resting my hand against my forehead as the world spun with the movement.

"You're awake," Mez greeted me softly. "How are you feeling? Would you like some water?"

"I'm okay, I think," I spoke quietly. "Thanks." I took an offered glass of water from him. "I have a pretty bad headache though. Do you by any chance happen to have something for that?"

He nodded with a sympathetic expression. I knew I was talking to the right person when it came to headaches. He went to his nightstand and returned with one of the blue cubes I'd seen him take before. Taking it from him, I popped it into my mouth and was surprised to find it had a bit of a gingery flavour. It dissolved fairly quickly, and within ten seconds, I could feel the throbbing pain in my head easing.

"Oh my gosh! Thank you! That feels so much better."

He nodded and took a seat on the bed beside me as I sipped at the water.

"Were you just talking to Aésha?"

"Yes. She's back. She came to see you, but you were still asleep. We had a good talk."

"Is she okay?"

"She's unharmed. We'll work through the rest together."

"And Asimara? What happened to her? Is she okay?"

Mez looked at me for a moment, a debate about what to tell me was clearly going on in his head. "The Vutol took her," he said finally, confirming my worst fear. "I don't know a lot of the details yet, but I have a session scheduled with her first thing tomorrow."

"Thanks for being honest." My voice was barely above a whisper.

My god! They'd had Asimara. Why had she been drugged? What had she been through...?

My god...It could just as easily have been me!

"Megan, things have happened." Mez said, blessedly pulling me from my downward horror-thought spiral. "I'm going to need to talk to you about them when you're ready. Everything is about to change."

Woah! What's happening? Why is everything changing? Weren't we just going to be having some boring dinner?

"Oh, um, of course. If you don't mind, I just want to use your bathroom to freshen up and then maybe you can tell me over our boring dinner?" I asked hopefully.

"Dinner won't be for a while Megan," Mez answered carefully. "You slept through the evening, the night, and the morning. It's just after lunch," he informed me gently.

"I...what? How long was I with Xandon?"

"Longer than expected."

Feeling more than slightly disturbed by that response, and even more disoriented, I rose from the bed.

"Okay. I'm just going to use the bathroom. I'll be ready to talk after I wake up a little and splash my face with some water." I moved to leave the room, but Mez stopped me by taking my hand.

"Before you go, there's something you should know."

I raised a brow.

"Your hair...it's changed."

"What?"

He released my hand, and I bolted to the bathroom, switching on the light. After squinting at the sudden assault of illumination, I gasped, staring dumbstruck at my reflection. My once full head of red hair now had a garish two-inch-wide silvery-white streak, from root to tip, on the upper left side of my head.

What the hell did Xandon do to me?

Chapter 27

Irys

Birds were chirping. Their songs were lively and cheerful. Even with my eyes closed, I could see the bright yellow sunlight filling the room. I could smell its warmth. The sheets were soft against my arms and feet. Stretching, I blinked my eyes open and gasped, sitting straight up.

It's morning! I slept through the night. I didn't have a nightmare. I didn't scream myself awake...or...no...there was something. It wasn't the same as before. Xandon was there, but not with me.

Crawling off the bed, I stumbled to the vanity and peered into the glass. I looked just the same as I had the night before.

Had Xandon found me? Great Goddess, have I travelled too far for him to reach? He wasn't with me. He was with other women. Twins. Elindria and Enadria...and Megan. Why Megan?

Looking at my reflection again, I sighed relief despite my profound confusion. It had to have been only a dream. A strange but typical dream. My hair was the same. I hadn't screamed. Megan was fine. She was in Kavylak, but not with Xandon.

Thank you, Great Goddess, for this place of safety where I can sleep. I feel like myself again. Please, grant Megan such a place as well.

I took my time washing up and chose the day dress I thought Mr. Dimog would like the most. The dress was a flawless powder blue with a wide V-neck and short puffed sleeves that tied with a ribbon halfway between my shoulders and elbows. The wide matching skirt sat over the late Mrs. Dimog's gorgeous petticoats. From the skirt's hem,

238

skillfully embroidered orange blossomed branches reached their graceful arms up toward the sun. The flowers were the same kind as those on the trees surrounding Mr. Dimog's property. Wearing this dress felt like a way to honour the great man whose home had been made temporarily my own.

Once I was dressed, I took a seat at the vanity and neatly fixed my hair. It was a simple look, but it felt like a pretty one. It was clean, groomed, and respectful. I was ready to face the day.

I left my room and walked in the direction that I was fairly certain would bring me to Acksil's room. Before visiting Mr. Dimog, Lesoué, Gebbie, or even having breakfast, I wanted to see Acksil and check on his healing. That was what I told myself. I was ignoring the idea that I wanted to see him for very selfish reasons, too; to be in his company and feel the sense of security that came with being in the same room as him.

I passed a few people along the way and nodded politely to them, receiving courteous smiles in return. After taking only one wrong turn and realizing it nearly right away, I knew I'd successfully arrived at Acksil's door. It wasn't difficult to spot as Borte was still standing as its guard.

"Good morning," I greeted him pleasantly. "May I visit your prisoner, please?" I wasn't entirely certain if I had permission to be here, and as it seemed that he was friends with Miss Dimog, I couldn't imagine that he liked me very much. Equally, I hoped that there wouldn't be any objections to my intentions to visit Acksil quite frequently.

"Yes," he replied flatly, confirming my suspicion that he didn't think very highly of me. He opened the door, and I nodded my gratitude to him.

I knocked lightly on the frame to announce my presence as I stepped into the room.

Acksil looked like a man remade. He was sitting up in bed, reading a book while appearing refreshed and greatly healed. He wore a loose linen shirt buttoned most of the way up his chest and seemed to be quite comfortable. His lower half was covered by a soft-looking sheet and blanket.

"Good morning," I said as a bright smile lit up my face with the relief I felt from his improvement. "You look like you've come a long way since I last saw you." I approached his bed.

"Hey there, Dollface. Thank you, I feel much better. You look rather well-rested yourself. Is it safe to assume there weren't any nightmares last night?"

"None at all. I slept the entire night through." It wasn't entirely true, but as last night's dream hadn't had any of the telltale signs of Xandon's affects on me, I wasn't about to concern him over what was more than likely a typical dream caused by nothing more than my exhaustion from the events of the day before.

He smiled. "Join me for some tea?" He gestured to a serving tray on his bedside table with a teapot and cups, as well as a stack of toast, a little dish of jam, some fruit, and what looked to be what was left of a boiled egg.

I smiled to myself as I imagined Gebbie putting together Acksil's first meal since his return. In my mind, she was humming to herself and adding extra touches to make especially sure that he'd like it, despite his prisoner status here.

"Thank you, I'd like that very much," I accepted, "as long as it's not Dr. Dyronin's terrible-tasting tea." I chuckled.

He laughed lightheartedly. "No, I'm free of that stuff for now, thank goodness. It's tea you'll like. I promise. Help yourself."

"I'm relieved for you," I grinned, stepping up to the tea tray to pour a cup for myself and to warm his half-empty one.

Holding my cup, I took a seat on the edge of his bed to sip at it.

"Have you spoken with anyone else today," I inquired lightly, wondering if I was to be his first visitor aside from whoever had delivered his meal.

"Only Gebbie," he replied, and I couldn't help but smile.

"Your day started in good company."

"It did," he agreed, looking pleased. "Lida visited me after you left, yesterday."

I nodded. "I saw her arrive as I was leaving. I'm surprised you remember anything after I left. That tea is powerful medicine!" I said, hoping he might not remember some of the things he'd said to me, such as professing his love. "You were falling asleep and spouting a bit of nonsense by the time I stepped out the door." I tittered awkwardly and despised myself for doing it.

"Oh, I can imagine that I was saying some pretty interesting things with both that venom and Dyronin's tea in my system," he said with amusement.

"Bad taste or not, Dr. Dyronin's tea clearly worked. You seem just like yourself again, Acksil."

"I feel like myself again. Although, I should probably pretend that I'm not healing as fast as I am. I don't think they're likely to keep me in this comfortable room once I'm healed." Even at the suggestion that he would be headed to an unknown prison cell, he still punctuated it with a half grin.

I wasn't sure if this was for my benefit, his, or if he was truly unconcerned.

Reaching out and lightly taking his hand, I decided to strike into some of the more important topics of the day before. "I spoke with Mr. Dimog as I promised I would. I don't know if you remember, but I gave my word to discuss your situation with him. He has assured me that, no matter what, your life will be spared. It's not my belief that you're being held prisoner as a punishment for your betrayals. They are holding you here to keep themselves safe from you because they do not trust you," I said, speaking frankly.

"Thank you, Irys," he said, looking touched by my words. "It means a lot that you'd do that for me."

"I had to do what I could for you, Acksil. You're my friend. We escaped together. Mr. Dimog is a reasonable and pleasant man. It was not difficult to convince him. In truth, I'm not certain that it took any convincing at all. You may not have been correct in assuming they meant to kill you in the first place." I glanced at our held hands before looking back into his eyes. "How was your talk with Lida?" Heat rose to my cheeks, and I could feel tension's claws sinking into my shoulders.

I'm not jealous. I'm concerned because she hates him.

"Difficult. There was a lot between us once, and as I mentioned to you before, she's got a lot of hate for me. I put an ugly wound into the relationship we had, and I don't think I helped to heal it by talking to her. I kept getting the feeling that she wanted me to say things to her that I didn't say." His response was far more honest and detailed than I had expected it to be.

"Perhaps she didn't know what she wanted you to say," I speculated. "Perhaps there isn't anything to say, but she was still hoping that you might come up with something even so."

He nodded. "It's one of the worst situations I've ever experienced. It's terrible to have to face people again after you've hurt them and when you still care about them."

"I wish you could travel home with me," I confessed. It hurt me to think that I would likely be leaving him behind as a prisoner of the Rebels when Rimoth was to bring me home.

"Why?" he asked. It was clear that this genuinely surprised him, and his reaction hurt me quite unintentionally. After everything he had been through, he didn't know why I would want to continue to travel with him. It wasn't clear to him why I wouldn't want to part ways with him as I returned home to comfort and family, and he remained here with people who hated him.

"You're my friend, Acksil. I feel like Lord Godeleva might extend his protection to you for having rescued me. And," I hesitated but continued, "I will miss you. I don't want to just leave you here, Acksil."

He smiled. It was a gentle expression. "I understand that, Irys, but they will never let me go with you. You've already saved me, even without Lord Godeleva's help. You heard it from Storr, himself. They'll spare my life."

"What if the Warriors hunt you down and find you here?" I asked. I couldn't help but voice my concern. "Everything you've done can't come to an end in a prison cell."

"My fate isn't to die in a prison cell, Irys," he said with a calm confidence. "They're angry with me, and they hate me right now. After enough time, I'll either become a burden or an asset. If they feel threatened by the Warriors, they'll release me, so they don't bring Kavylak to their doorstep. If they think they can trust me enough to use me and my skill, they'll do that. I talked to Lida about it. The threat against their cause has never been stronger. They would be foolish not to try to use me to help them."

"Did Lida appear to support you, despite her anger?" I asked, relieved to know that even if Mr. Dimog was determined not to trust

Acksil, there were some who believed it would be helpful to allow him the opportunity to prove himself useful to them.

"She doesn't support me," he said with certainty. "She supports the rebellion, and she knows that I can be of use to it. I think she believes that I have left the Warriors."

"I hope that Mr. Dimog will come to see things this way, too, over time. It's a start."

"He will. He won't like it, but he will. Kavylak is coming for them. Even if we weren't here, they'd be coming for the Rebels eventually. Dsumot will fall. It's only a matter of when. I need to convince them to leave."

"Where will you go if...when Dsumot falls? Will you come to Syliza?" I could feel hope glimmering in the centre of my chest.

"That's what I'll likely recommend to them. It makes the most sense."

"If you do, you must reach out to me. All of you. My position is limited, but Lord Godeleva is a powerful man. He has influence." I swallowed hard. "If I must, I will speak to Emperor Gevalen, myself. He is taken with me. That was why I was travelling on the mission to Gbat Rher in the first place – to escape his attentions – but I would use his willingness to give me an audience to speak on your behalf." At that moment, I felt determined enough that even accepting the emperor's invitation to the Imperial Palace did not shake me.

A look of disgust crossed his face as he heard me describe the emperor's inappropriate interest in me, but he seemed to push it away before he replied.

"Thank you, Irys. I will tell them. I'm sure Storr will consider it seriously if you tell him, too," he said. I could hear the genuine appreciation in his voice. It made me feel proud, strong, and determined.

"I'll do that," I said, and on a whim that made more sense to me the more it swirled around in my head, I added, "I'm also thinking of asking if he will let me bring two girls with me. There are two girls here who were rescued from the Vutol..." I paused in my description as Acksil started nodding knowingly.

"Yes, Gebbie told me about them and how great you are with them." He smiled.

"I didn't do anything special. I just held Lesoué's hand. But she is from Syliza, and it seems only right to return her there. Still, it would be wrong to separate her from Kaziki. They need each other," I reasoned.

"Dollface, it's very special when a Vutol rescue trusts you. They don't respond well to most people. Trust usually takes ages to build. Whatever you did, it was huge."

I wasn't sure what I could have possibly done that was special, but I nodded in gratitude at the compliment.

"I'm just happy that, provided Mr. Dimog approves, I will be bringing them to a place where the Vutol doesn't exist and could never frighten them again," I said, feeling relieved that I would be doing something meaningful for these girls.

"No. It's in Syliza, Irys. The Vutol is everywhere. It's in the nice cities, the poor ones, everywhere," he said to me as though breaking devastating news.

I furrowed my brow. "How could it be in Lorammel? The Knights are headquartered there. The Imperial Palace is there. The nobility there would never allow it. Anyone else could not afford such atrocities," I explained. I was certain that if the Vutol had managed to sink its disgusting claws into any part of Syliza, it would have had to be a newly adopted borderland or outer area affected by social unrest.

"For the most part," Acksil seemed to agree. "Most people don't accept it. But Irys, you know your life in Lorammel has been sheltered. Do you really think you know the nobility beyond what you've seen on the surface or read in a book?"

I could tell that he wasn't trying to be cruel, but his words still managed to wound me. It was likely the truth of them that caused the pain. Setting down my teacup, I wrung my hands in my lap.

"No," I confessed in a tiny voice. It turned my stomach to think that such horrors could be happening under the surface of my own home city.

Acksil rested his good hand on top of my fidgeting ones, and I stilled them.

Turning one of my hands around to hold his, I frowned. "If the girls come with me, I will give them a world as hidden from the Vutol as mine had been until now. Then, I will reach out to some of the ladies in Lorammel to see if we might work together to make sure that the city is swept clean of those terrible people. There are powerful women who might speak with me and whose names are great enough that a mention of the Vutol will not tarnish them. Lady Sarriun Pammel and Lady Galadzia Anglemore, for instance. They're known for their unique strength and stances and yet society still adores them."

"You're a good woman, Irys. The best I've ever met," a gentle smile touched his lips. "You see the decency and beauty in people and in the world. I love that about you. The world isn't a beautiful place most of the time. I could see that in the way I grew up and in the people I've known until now. Somehow, it hasn't corrupted you."

I gave his hand a squeeze. "That's one of the finest compliments I've ever received, Acksil. Thank you. It means a lot, particularly from a man I respect as much as you."

He squeezed my hand in return. We spent a moment in comfortable silence, taking the time simply to be in each other's company, an opportunity we both knew was becoming increasingly rare.

"If you get the chance while you're here, talk to Skeltra. She might be able to provide you with some information to share with those Sylizan ladies," he said after a moment of thought. "Gebbie tells me that Skeltra was one of the women who rescued those girls."

"Miss Dimog can't stand me," I replied with a shake of my head.

"In my experience, people usually put their differences aside to fight a common enemy."

"I'll try, but if she hurts me, I'm blaming you." I grinned.

"I will accept full responsibility." He grinned in return.

I chuckled but was halted from my intention to respond by a knock at the door.

"Miss Godeleva?" asked Mr. Dimog's voice.

I straightened my posture and released Acksil's hand. "Yes, Mr. Dimog?" I asked, turning toward the door.

The door opened, and Mr. Dimog greeted me with a smile that I returned.

"Would you please join me in my study?" he requested pleasantly. "There is something I'd like to discuss with you."

"Yes, of course. I was just here appreciating Dr. Dyronin's impressive skills," I said with a giggle, but then turned to Acksil. "I'll come to visit again when I can. Continue your healing so you can avoid that dreadful tea."

Acksil grinned at me and nodded. "See you soon, Dollface."

Rising, I joined Mr. Dimog. Just before stepping out the door, I turned and gave Acksil another smile. I hadn't been ready to leave quite yet, but this was my promise to return soon.

Mr. Dimog and I walked comfortably down the hall toward his study. The short distance we travelled together came with the feeling of being a regular habit despite the fact that we had no such traditions between us.

"You're looking refreshed. May I assume you had a restful night?" he asked, offering his arm, which I took.

"I slept very well. Better than I have in many days," I agreed. "My room is just lovely. I couldn't help but feel comfortable there."

"I'm glad to hear it," he said, with the look of a man proud of having taken good care of his family. "I was also pleased to discover that you have been befriended by our two young guests. Gebbie is very impressed, as am I, for that matter."

"We shared lovely company last evening," I agreed. "Though I can only truly say that I have a budding friendship with Lesoué. Kaziki was resting during my brief visit with her. Still, I feel a closeness to the girls that I cannot deny. In fact, this morning I had an idea involving them that I wished to discuss with you. Were the girls the reason you were hoping to talk to me as well?"

"We may discuss them, of course, but there is someone here to see you first." He paused to allow me to enter his study ahead of him.

As I entered and saw who it was, I thought my knees would give out from beneath me.

Chapter 28

Megan

I was still gawking at my hair when Mez stepped into the doorway. "It's white," I said in disbelief to his reflection.

"Yes."

"Why?'

"It's part of what I want to talk to you about."

"Okay. I just...I just need a minute."

Nodding, he stepped out of the bathroom, shutting the door behind him.

I made quick use of the facilities before splashing cold water on my face, hoping it would help sober my swirling thoughts and fears. It didn't. Looking at myself again in the mirror as I patted my face dry, I half expected the streak to be gone. It was still there, like a nightmare from which I couldn't wake. Picking up the lock of white hair, I pulled it in front of me, so I could examine it close up. When it caught the light, I gasped as it shimmered with an iridescence that reminded me of Xandon's hair. Dropping it as if it had bitten me, I left the bathroom, wanting answers.

Mez was seated on the couch and gestured for me to join him. I was a bundle of nerves, and the last thing I felt like doing was being still. I resisted the urge to pace around the room and opted to sit beside him instead.

"Xandon has a mission that some of us among the Warriors have been tasked with completing," he began once I was settled. "None of us knows what it's for. We know only our own little pieces of a larger puzzle. I have been blindly working on my own piece," he confessed, "but I'm choosing not to do this anymore. I don't like where my piece fits into the completed picture." He inhaled a long deep breath and released it slowly.

I looked at him, and a pit of dread blossomed in my gut. I braced myself for what his next words would be.

"My next assignment was to convince you that you'd gone home after work and had a nap before getting ready to go to dinner with me as we'd planned. You wouldn't remember that Xandon saw you or anything that happened after work until that point, and you would think the change in your hair was brought on by stress. I'm not going to do it, Megan, but I'll need you to pretend as though you had no idea that you saw Xandon yesterday evening. Will you do that?"

"I...I've been a mission for you?"

Had it all been a lie? Did he actually care for me or had I just been some project, some assignment to him, all along?

"You were supposed to become a mission for me, but I'm refusing." He wasn't apologetic but was fully respectful in his tone. "Making you forget that you'd talked to Xandon was my little piece to that larger puzzle. I can't do that to you, Megan. I won't. That piece needs to stay empty, but Xandon needs to think I've done my job."

Not wanting to face what he was telling me, I let my head fall forward and roughly dragged my fingers through my hair, pulling at it once I'd reached its ends.

"The white piece in your hair," Mez spoke gently, "is the same thing that happened to Miss Godeleva. It's something Xandon is doing to both of you."

Shocked, I snapped my head up to look at him. "This is happening to Irys, too? She's here? Is she safe?"

"I don't know if she is safe. I learned that she was here while we were with the People of the North, but she escaped. Acksil deserted and has taken her with him." Mez levelled with me, furthering my surprise. "I think Acksil found out more than I know about Xandon's plans and had discovered that he was causing her harm. I believe that's why he ran off with her."

Irys was here? Acksil is gone? What's happening..?

"What does Xandon want with Irys? With me? I thought he was..." I trailed off as a harsh reality slapped me in the face. Looking at Mez,

I felt my shoulders slump, and a frown pull down my mouth as I asked, "He's not trying to help me find my way home, is he?"

He shook his head, looking deeply saddened. "No. I don't believe he is. I hadn't known he'd made these changes to Miss Godeleva before he saw you," he added apologetically. "I don't know what his goal is."

The truth stung, and it filled me with shame, misery, and anger. Once again, I'd been a fool to think that Xandon would help me. Of course he hadn't had any intention to try to help me find my way home. I didn't know why Irys had been in Kavylak, but she certainly wasn't trying to get back to Earth. If he had given the same "therapies" to her as he'd given to me, it had never been his intention to help me. Not to mention, why would he have ordered Mez to alter my memories, especially when I had volunteered to undergo Xandon's therapies of my own free will? When would I learn that everything that came out of that man's mouth was a lie? I was so desperate to get home that I was willing to believe him when he'd said I wasn't the first person from Earth he'd met. I believed his bogus theories about people who could cross any distance in the blink of an eye.

Ha! Travellers. What a joke.

"Megan," Mez said, drawing my thoughts and eyes back to him. "I'm not going to do this anymore. It's wrong. Xandon is working on some secret project, and he won't tell any of us what it is. He's obsessed with it, and it has something to do with you and Miss Godeleva. It's consuming all his time. He's stopped caring that the Rebels are becoming more disruptive here. He doesn't care that the Vutol has taken people – including one of his own Warriors – right off the streets in broad daylight."

His Warriors...

"Do you think he's attempting to turn us into Warriors?" Once upon a time, asking that question would have sounded ridiculous to my ears. Now, I genuinely worried about the answer.

"No," Mez said with certainty. "This isn't how Warriors are made."

I nodded, my gaze dropping to my hands as I curled them into fists in my lap. I knew I should have felt somewhat grateful that Xandon wasn't trying to turn me or Irys into Warriors, but I only felt less at ease.

If he's not trying to make us Warriors, then what is he doing to us? Has Irys been dreaming of him, too? Has she seen those other women in her dreams? I wish you were here, Irys.

Mez tentatively reached out a hand and rested it on top of my right fist. It was more than evident that he wasn't sure if his touch was welcome, and he was half expecting me to pull away. I didn't, but I didn't take his hand in return, either. Slowly, I lifted my head to face him.

"Megan, I've had people I care about taken from me before. I'm not letting Xandon do this again. There are a few Warriors who feel the same way." After taking a steadying breath, he spoke even more quietly. "We're leaving. We're defecting. I want you to come with us."

"Come with you where?" I asked, not masking how bowled over I was by his news. "Won't he come after you?"

"He might. We're going to go to Syliza and seek asylum there."

I stared at Mez as if he'd gone crazy. "Syliza! But they hate you. What will you do there?"

"I'm not entirely sure what we will do. We won't be Warriors anymore, but we won't be regular people, either. We may hire ourselves out to Syliza. We may try to establish normal lives there if we think we can hide there safely. We'll need to see what opportunities are open to us once we reach their shores. We'll come up with some ideas to propose while we're on the ship. This is all very new. We just know we need to get out."

"Will you fight Xandon if he pursues?"

"I'm hoping it won't come to that, but if we must, yes. Xandon *won't* take any more away from me. He *won't* let the Vutol simply walk in and take Aésha. He's getting darker than we ever dreamed. We can't go that way." He looked at me and a flash of genuine fear entered his ice blue eyes. "I'm terrified of what I would become if I were to stay." I'd never heard Mez speak with such vulnerability in his tone.

Uncurling my fist, I turned my hand and held his. "I get why you want to leave, and you should. It's a brave thing to do, and you deserve a better life."

Nodding, he observed me thoughtfully. "I will respect whatever decision you choose to make, Megan, but I need to tell you that if you decide not to come, as a precaution, I will convince you that this conversation about the defection did not happen. It's safer for everyone – including you – if you don't know anything if you choose not to go."

"I understand." And I did. He had to protect the people he loved.

"I also want you to know that whatever decision you make, you won't be alone. If you choose to stay, I will help the others to escape, but I won't leave you."

"You won't?" I was both surprised and confused. "Why? You don't owe me anything, Mez."

He shook his head. "It's not a matter of owing, Megan. I care about you. More than I've cared about anyone in a long time." He gently stroked the side of my hair with his free hand. "I couldn't abandon you here alone, without me, without Aésha, or likely everyone you're close to as you watch your hair slowly turn white while he does whatever he does to your mind." Mez rested his hand on my cheek. "I know you want to go back to your world, Megan, and if I could take you back, I would. I would leave my world if it meant I could return you to yours."

Deeply touched by his words and feeling overwhelmed with gratitude, tears welled into my eyes, and I hugged him tightly. He returned the embrace just as tightly and kissed the side of my head.

"This will become easier. Things will be okay. We're in this together," he assured me.

We're in this together.

Nothing he could have said in that moment could have mattered more than those four words. No one had ever made me feel so important, so valued, so accepted, so loved.

"Thank you, Mez." I whispered.

He slowly drew back from me and took my hands. "Megan, I'm trusting you to tell me your honest choice. If you say you're coming with us, I'll believe you."

Although everything Xandon had said to me was likely a lie, one thing he'd said was true. "You've always had choices," he'd told me. At the time, I didn't believe him and though the intentions behind his statement hadn't been honest, it turned out, he was right. I did have choices, and one of them was to choose never to be one of his victims again.

Maybe I would find my way back home one day, but dreams or not, I knew now that Xandon wasn't the answer. Maybe I'd been brought to Qarradune for a reason, a purpose I didn't yet understand.

Maybe once it was fulfilled, I'd return home or maybe Qarradune was my home now. Whatever the future held, I had to stop existing in the limbo in which I'd imprisoned myself, desperately waiting, wishing, and hoping someone would rescue me or that I'd wake from a nightmare. I had to face reality. I had to start living my life again. Even if that meant building my life here.

Leaving with the Warriors, with Mez, was my chance to start living, and I wasn't going to miss it. My life mattered, *our* lives mattered. I wanted something to live for, and I wanted to belong.

"I want to leave with you. What can I do to help?" I squeezed Mez' hands, and he smiled in relief. "We're in this together."

Chapter 29

Irys

It was Rimoth. He had been perusing the books on Mr. Dimog's shelves and turned to see us when we entered. He looked nearly as relieved as I felt.

"Miss Godeleva, you're safe," he said, stepping closer to me without breaching a proximity that could be considered inappropriate. He was dressed finely in the type of clothes a nobleman from home might wear. They suited him, though I imagined that throughout his long and unique life, he had developed a skill for wearing clothes from many places.

"Mr. Rimoth, thank the Goddess!" I said in a rush, releasing Mr. Dimog's arm as my hands flew to my face, my eyes filling with happy tears.

"Call me Lyir. It's my true name," he replied in a familiar way that was very pleasant to hear.

"I will, thank you! Mr. Lyir, it is very good to see you here and healed. Did you find Sir Fhirell? Is he home now? And Desda? Does anyone know just where I am right now?" I gushed. It hadn't been my intention to say quite that much, but as I started speaking, it all came out at once.

"Sir Fhirell is well. He and Desda are home again. The rest of the group that was headed to Gbat Rher continued the mission and is working with the Paladins there. No one knows you are here as I only just learned it myself. I can return you home now so you can tell them everything, if you'd like," he said, extending a hand to me.

I froze, overwhelmed. I wanted to go home, of course. There were few things I had ever wanted more. At the same time, I wasn't finished with everything here. What of Lesoué and Kaziki? What of thanking Gebbie and saying goodbye to her?

What of Acksil?

"I'm nearly ready. I'm very eager to go home and more than grateful to you for offering to take me, Mr. Lyir. I must ask Mr. Dimog a question first, and I must say goodbye to someone very important to me." I could feel myself filling with a flurry. For all the calm and comfort the morning had brought me until now, a whirlwind was taking over. "Do I have enough time to sort those things, dear, Mr. Lyir?"

"You have whatever time you need. I owe you a great debt, Miss Godeleva," Lyir replied without any hint of strain.

"Thank you, Mr. Lyir. You're a blessing. I should be ready by mid-day. Is that too much time? Do you plan to stay?"

"I will return in the early afternoon," he replied, clearly having no intention to remain.

"Thank you again," I smiled. "If you happen to see Lord Godeleva or Sir Fhirell along your visits this morning, please tell them I am well and will be home."

"Do you want me to visit them both and give them your message?"

"If you are in Syliza, yes, that would mean a lot to me. If you do see Lord Godeleva, please let him know that I may need the guest suite prepared," I added. "But only if that's where you'll be, of course. It's not my intention to consume your entire morning. If it is too great a bother, I will understand and will be home soon enough regardless," I babbled, tripping over my words.

"I'll let him know," Lyir responded, looking greatly amused.

"Thank you, Mr. Lyir." I smiled brightly as it all started to become real to me. I was going home today and would be safe again.

"You're welcome, Miss Godeleva," he said with a nod of his head as a symbolic bow. "I'm glad to see that you are indeed safe and well."

"As I'm glad to see you are, too," I replied with an involuntary bob of a curtsy. He had, after all, been in rough condition indeed when I had last seen him.

"See you this afternoon," he said and was gone.

I gasped as my intention to reply was cut off by his sudden disappearance. I couldn't imagine ever becoming comfortable with a Traveller's unexpected comings and goings.

"No matter how many times I've seen it, I've never become used to it," Mr. Dimog said, smiling and perfectly reading my expression.

I could only laugh. Then, filled with a burst of mirth, I threw my arms around his neck and hugged him. There was no other way to express the sheer joy, relief, and gratitude that brimmed within me.

He chuckled and gave my back a gentle pat in return.

"Thank you," I said as I drew away, collecting myself and giving my skirt a little pat to make sure it was falling properly.

"You're welcome, Dear One."

"Oh, but now I'm running out of time with you, Mr. Dimog. May I speak with you of the girls now? I'd expected to have another day with you at the very least. I'm not complaining, of course, but it seems I must be quite the rude guest and rush things a little."

He merely gestured toward the sitting area, and I quickly settled on the loveseat where I'd sat the day before.

"I'd like to propose to take Lesoué and Kaziki back to Syliza with me. I feel that I can find a good home for them. I know that Lesoué was originally Sylizan and though Kaziki is not, it doesn't seem right to separate them unless she has any family here." I poured it all out without preamble. There simply wasn't time for formalities, though it irked me to speak with Mr. Dimog in such a businesslike way.

"If they want to go with you, I have no objections," Mr. Dimog replied. "Do you know where they will live?"

I shook my head. "I will provide for them until I can find the right home for them. I plan to look to some of the ladies I know to begin an effort to push the Vutol out of Lorammel. It is my hope that through such an effort, we will also find a family or other similarly warm circumstance for them. Until then, I will simply insist upon keeping them in my own home."

Great Goddess, I was a foundling once and the Godeleva home provided for me. I pray you will give me the strength and wisdom to do the same for these precious girls for as long as I am needed.

"That is honourable of you, Miss Godeleva," he said approvingly.

"It feels like the right thing to do."

He nodded, and I couldn't help feeling that he was proud of me. It made me feel proud of myself, too.

There was a knock on the open study door. Two dusty Rebels who must have been returning from a long ride were standing and looking keen to speak with Mr. Dimog.

"I should say my goodbyes and fetch my bag. I will return in good time to see you before Mr. Lyir takes me home."

He nodded both in an acknowledgement to what I'd said and in appreciation that I was not making his Rebels wait any longer than necessary to report to him.

I rose, as did he, and I bobbed a curtsy before stepping quietly from the room. Though I'd intended to go see Acksil first, I decided to visit the kitchen instead. I wasn't yet prepared for what I would have to face upon visiting Acksil. I wanted to delay that meeting for as long as possible.

Gebbie was just where I'd expected her to be, cooking and humming to herself.

"Good morning, Gebbie. Might I quickly speak with you?" I asked politely, hoping she would not be bothered by the interruption.

"Good morning! Of course. What is it, dear?" She set her wooden spoon down on a rest and turned her attention to me.

Taking a breath to steady myself, I prepared for my first goodbye. I wondered at how I had become this attached to the people in Mr. Dimog's house in such a short time.

"It seems I will be returning home this afternoon," I began. "Aside from thanking you for everything and telling you that I hope to see you again should you ever be in Lorammel for any reason, I would also like to speak to you regarding Lesoué and Kaziki." The words plummeted out of me without grace or the tenderness I'd hoped they would carry. I was trying to say far too many things at once and was only managing to trivialize all these points that were so dear to me.

In a rush to correct my rudeness, I stepped up to Gebbie and took her hand. "Thank you, Gebbie. The Goddess blessed me by putting me under your care during my stay here. I'm very grateful," I said. "And I must apologize that I have far too little time to be truly gracious as you deserve, but I must also ask for your assistance. Will you help me find out if Lesoué and Kaziki would like to come with me and to prepare them if they choose to travel to Syliza? Mr. Dimog has given his approval. May I have your help and your blessing, too?"

Gebbie's smile embraced me as warmly as arms could have done. Squeezing my hands in hers, she leaned forward and kissed my cheek. "Of course, you may, dear. The girls are in their room. Kaziki is better this morning. She's got her mind back, thank the Goddess. Aren't they lucky to have such a nice, caring lady to want to help them find their way?"

"I'm relieved to hear that they are both well today. Hopefully they are well enough to make such a large decision and to do it quickly."

"Now those girls aren't in any state to make such decisions for themselves, Miss Godeleva. You know it, Mr. Dimog knows it, and I know that the best thing for those girls is to go with you and return to being normal young ladies again. Neither of them has a soul in the world other than us, so it's settled. They're going and now we'll go and tell them," Gebbie said decidedly, without a hint of hesitation.

I nodded obediently. "I'll tell them now. We don't have much time, and there are other things I must do before we leave as well." It was my turn to kiss Gebbie's cheek. "Thank you for everything. Every little thing, Gebbie."

"Glad to serve a fine lady again. I hope to see you soon, dear. I'll make you a good dinner. Nobody makes those poached eggs better than I do." She laughed.

"I couldn't agree more," I chuckled, wishing I could bring Gebbie with me.

"You take care of yourself, Miss Godeleva."

"You, too, Gebbie. May the Goddess walk with you." My fingers flicked through the Sylizan version of the Great Goddess sign as hers did the Dsumot version just as naturally.

She quickly turned to the stove again, picking up the spoon and vigorously stirring a pot before using her wrist to dab one of her eyes as casually as she could.

I turned quickly to leave to stop myself from facing that same struggle. Walking briskly down the hall, I paused outside the girls' door, making sure I was collected and strong before I would have to face them and change their lives.

When I was ready, I knocked lightly using my fingertips. I didn't want to frighten them with an aggressive sound on the door.

"Good morning," I said brightly so they would know who was knocking.

Lesoué opened the door and shyly looked up at me. "Good morning," she said quietly but using the same tones I did.

"Good morning, Miss Lesoué. I'd like to speak with you and Miss Kaziki, if you wouldn't mind," I said pleasantly to let her know that there wasn't anything to be concerned about. "I've heard that Miss Kaziki is feeling much better. That's wonderful news."

"Kaziki is better," Lesoué confirmed, stepping out of the way to allow me entry into the room. She climbed up onto the bed to join Kaziki, who was sitting up and looking much improved. She still appeared tired and run down, but she looked sober and conscious."

"Good morning, Miss Kaziki," I greeted the second girl, having no reason to believe she remembered me from the evening before. "I'm Miss Irys Godeleva."

"Miss Irys is the nice lady I told you about, Kaziki," Lesoué assured the second girl.

"I've been talking to Mr. Dimog and Gebbie. We have decided that it would be lovely if you would join me when I return home to Lorammel in Syliza today. I'd like you both to stay with me. You'll share a comfortable suite in my house, so you can be safe until we find a nice family for you, who will give you everything you need and keep you safe, if that's what you want."

Both girls listened, looking entirely fixated on me.

"You want us to live with you, Miss Irys?" Lesoué asked after an extended silence.

"Yes. It would be a temporary stay with me. It would be until we find a family to raise you both. You won't be separated. I will help to find parents for you, who will love you and care for you," I replied.

At first, neither girl responded. Not with words or even a change in expression. Then, Lesoué burst into tears. Kaziki brought her arms around her friend, holding her to comfort her.

"You are a very nice lady, Miss Irys," Kaziki said. Her voice was soft, but her words were very clear.

I focused on my posture so I wouldn't suddenly join Lesoué in tears as joyous as they may have been.

"I want you ladies to be safe and happy. It's your turn to feel this way as all young women should," I replied to Kaziki.

"We will go with you," Kaziki said, speaking for both girls.

Lesoué nodded, her breathing returning to normal.

"I'm very happy to hear that," I said to them both with a genuine smile. "I'd like you to start getting ready and to pack anything that is yours so you can bring it with you. If you can, please have a little something to eat. I know Gebbie will be glad to prepare something for you. I'm not sure how long it will be before mealtime upon our arrival, so I don't want you to be too hungry. Please don't forget to take the time to say goodbye to the good people you've met here, if you can. We will be going with a Traveller and will be at our new home this afternoon."

Both girls nodded, and I trusted that they would do as I had requested.

"I must speak to a few people before we go. May I trust that you will both speak with Gebbie and get yourselves ready?" I asked them.

They nodded solemnly.

"We will be ready, and we'll talk to Gebbie," Kaziki promised.

"I'm very proud of you both," I said, looking them in the eye and smiling. I knew how much it meant when Mr. Dimog looked proud of me. Now it was time for these girls to feel the same way.

Lesoué looked just as I felt when Mr. Dimog showed his pride. Kaziki looked collected.

I stepped up to the girls, giving them each a kiss on the forehead before turning to leave.

"I will see you both before we depart," I said pleasantly and stepped out of the room.

My feet were feeling increasingly heavy as they realized where I was asking them to take me. It was time to face Acksil. I didn't want to say goodbye.

Biting into my lip, I forced myself forward. Turning the corner, I nearly came to a stop as I saw who was standing in front of Acksil's door. Borte was there, as usual, but Skeltra Dimog was talking to him. Her very presence rattled me at a time when I was already feeling vulnerable. I squared my shoulders, hoping I looked stronger than I felt.

"Good morning, Miss Dimog, Mr. Borte. I'm not sure if you've heard, but I will be leaving this afternoon," I greeted them and then turned my attention to Miss Dimog. "I will be bringing Lesoué and Kaziki home with me. I want to take care of them until I can find them a family who will love and protect them. Acksil told me that you were one of the people who helped to rescue these girls and that you would know the most about how to care for them. Is there any advice you can give me to make sure I do this properly? Is there anything I should know to make sure I don't fail them?"

At first, Miss Dimog looked as though she was preparing to roll her eyes, but she listened. As I continued to speak, she looked surprised instead, and she lost her expression of doubt.

"They are going to be very nervous around new people, especially men," she informed me. "It's good that you're taking them both. They need each other. When you get back to Syliza, speak with my great aunt, Lady Galadzia Anglemore. She should be able to help you find a good home for them."

"Thank you, Miss Dimog. I was already planning to contact her and Lady Sarriun Pammel to begin an effort to stop the Vutol in Lorammel. I will take your advice and discuss Lesoué and Kaziki's future with her as well."

She gave me a single nod of approval. "If your efforts against the Vutol are successful, find a way to reach me. I want to be a part of that kind of effort."

Now, it was my turn to be surprised. "Of course. I would be honoured to include you, Miss Dimog," I said, meaning every word.

"My cousin Jhingen, Lady Anglemore's son, may also be able to help you. He and his friend Mirla Framhail run a large home in the city that acts as a rehabilitation residence for people rescued from the Vutol, and who need to adapt to normal life."

"I will remember that as well. It sounds like they may be able to provide me with the guidance I need to make sure my own girls have everything they require."

I swallowed hard. How could I have been so blind to everything that was going on just outside the gates of my own home? How could I have imagined that Lorammel would be different from all the other places in this Vutol-infested world? I could no longer excuse my ignorance with my position in high society.

The Anglemores were nearly as powerful as the Godelevas, and they were not only aware of the problem but were fighting to rescue its victims. While I fretted about wearing the perfect gown, people around me were suffering, and it was only within the last season that I had opened my eyes to see them.

Thank you, Great Goddess, for giving me this opportunity. I will make a difference. I will make up for lost time.

"That's a good idea. Hopefully their recovery will be a manageable one. The right care will make all the difference for them," Miss Dimog advised and warned at the same time.

"I understand," I assured her. "I will do everything I can to provide for them. I will seek out help from others when I know they can advise and support us. I'm not pretending that I know what I'm doing, Miss Dimog. However, I have what is needed to safely house them until a permanent home is found."

"You're doing a good thing for those girls. It's a lot more than many others would do. Safe journey home." It was easily the kindest thing she had ever said to me.

"Thank you, Miss Dimog. It means a lot to me, as does your advice. I will use it wisely. May the Goddess walk with you." I made the sign of the Great Goddess, which she did not return.

"May I say goodbye to the prisoner?" I asked Borte.

He nodded and stepped aside.

I gave a little knock on the door and entered.

Acksil was lying down again but was awake. "Missed me too much, huh?" he said with a playful smile.

Without wasting any time, I walked up to him and sat on the edge of his bed.

"I'm going home, Acksil," I blurted, unwilling to delay the news any further. I felt as though I were making a confession.

He looked at me and though he smiled, there was sadness in his tender hazel eyes. "That's good news, Dollface. I'm glad it won't be long before you're home where you should be."

"I don't want to leave you here, Acksil," I whispered to him sadly. I didn't want Miss Dimog or Borte to hear. "I want to bring you, too."

"I know, but you're going home, and I need to stay here. We both have things to do," he said, taking my hand in his.

I held his hand firmly in return. My eyes filled, but I refused to blink. I would not let any tears fall.

"Promise me that I'll see you again," I said as though I had any right at all to make demands of him.

He brought his bandaged hand up to my face and stroked my cheek with his warm and gentle fingertips. I could smell the soap they had used to bathe him. "You'll see me again, Doll." He sounded so confident that I couldn't help but be convinced.

I nodded and when I blinked, the tears spilled over, dropping onto his hand. "I believe you. Don't make a fool of me, Acksil. I'm trusting you."

"I won't make a fool of you, Irys. I've only ever done that once, and it was completely accidental. You can trust me," he assured me.

My heart picked up speed as the image of my first kiss appeared in my mind's eye. Indeed, I'd felt fooled at the time. He had pretended to be someone else, and I had fallen for it. Under the stars and next to the fountain, he had held me in his arms as we danced at the Masquerade that started so magically and ended so tragically. Somehow, the memory had changed. I didn't feel foolish from it anymore. My temperature rose as I looked at him now, just as he truly was: a man who loved me and who had given up everything for me.

"Be good here, Acksil. Let them see the man I see. Charm them. You don't need a Warrior skill for that. Just show them who you truly are. Show them that you're on their side."

"I won't let you down," he said with a grin.

I could only believe him.

"I want to say so many things to you before I go, and I can't think of what they are, other than 'thank you'," I said, a stupid and empty thing to say when all I wanted to do was share with him everything I was feeling about him, about us. I had so many thoughts in my head, but none of them were defined enough to put into words.

"Will you write to me?" he asked, giving me hope.

Writing him a letter hadn't even occurred to me. The only letters I'd ever sent across a border - those from Kavylak to Sir Fhirell - never made it to the recipient. It had all been a lie. In fact, Acksil had played a role in perpetuating that lie and was the one who told me it had happened in the first place. I hadn't become accustomed to the idea of having a Traveller's services available to me.

"Will that be something we can continue?" I asked.

Would Lyir truly deliver mail over time, and would Acksil be willing to keep up our letters even if he were to be permitted to become a Rebel once again? The idea of being able to exchange letters with him made this goodbye feel just slightly less painful than it had a few moments ago.

Just slightly.

"Only one way to find out," he replied.

I nodded and leaned forward to kiss his cheek, holding his hand as though I would lose him right away if I were to accidentally let go. Though it had been my intention to sit up again after my lips had touched his cheek, it wasn't what I did. Turning toward him, I rested my head down on his shoulder. I watched him, and he watched me in return.

My heart filled but at the same time it ached. I was awed at how much he had come to mean to me in only a handful of days. The thought of leaving him - likely forever - stung to the point that it seemed hard to breathe.

Finally, I sat up again and couldn't help the sad expression I knew was on my face. He shut his eyes, and I felt as though I'd hurt him.

"No sad eyes, Dollface," he said with a smile and opened his eyes again. It was a statement, but somehow he was pleading at the same time.

"I'm afraid I can't help it," I said apologetically. I couldn't imagine looking anything but saddened - at the very least - at such a time. He was a part of me. Leaving him felt like abandoning a portion of my soul.

"You're going home, Irys. You'll see me again. Those are two things to smile about. Come on. Let me see it. Don't let my last memory of you be your sad eyes."

I tried to force myself to break the sadness on my face, but it was as though I didn't have any control over a single muscle.

"I'm trying," I said as my eyes filled again. "I'm afraid I'll have to save that smile to be something for you to look forward to when you see me next."

He nodded with understanding and gave my hand another squeeze before he released it. I felt as though I'd lost him even while he was still in front of me. His eyes closed and remained that way. He was giving me the opportunity to leave without having to say another word.

I knew I was supposed to go. I knew I should stay silent.

This can't be it. I cannot leave him like this.

Leaning down, I wrapped my arms around him as much as I could, wedging my hands between his back and the bed and pressing my cheek to his chest. I could hear his heart rate picking up and that alone made me feel I'd made the right move.

After only the briefest surprised instant, his arms came around me, holding me tightly. It was a secure feeling, though the gesture had nothing to do with protecting me. Tears ran sideways, leaving a damp patch against his linen shirt.

When I finally drew away, I looked at him and smiled. It was a happy smile. At least, it was happy enough. To my great relief, the smile he gave me in reply was soft, but happy, too.

"Until then," I said, surprised at the stability of my voice.

"Until then," he replied.

We said nothing else, only held each others' gaze. I rose and took two steps backward before turning to walk to the door. I glanced back over my shoulder, then faced forward and headed out into the hallway.

Miss Dimog was no longer there, but Borte nodded to me as I passed him. I nodded in return but was now too shaken to speak. I looked both ways down the hall and squared my shoulders.

Thank you for my strength, Great Goddess. I can feel your gift. I can do this. Please, take care of him.

I walked with confidence and found my way to my room without making a single wrong turn. Once there, I looked around the lovely space that had been my own for such a short time. I'd spent one night in the room, but to me, it was indeed *my* room. Within these walls, I was safe and comfortable. Mr. Dimog had made certain of it. It felt right to show my gratitude to my room by taking some time to appreciate it.

As I did, I shut the door, and layer by layer, removed the pieces that comprised my beautiful gown. As I laid them out on the bed, I gave thanks to the Goddess, to Mr. Dimog, and to his late wife for lending me this armor that held me together on this bittersweet gift of a day.

The clothes in which I had arrived - the tunic and leggings, small clothes, and my cloak - had been washed and folded next to my bag. Setting aside any sense of regret for having to put them back on, I dressed and walked up to the vanity, peering at my reflection. I was just as much myself in this outfit as I was in the beautiful gown. These were the clothes given to me to help me escape from Kavylak and take me home. Now, they would complete that journey with me.

At the same time, I was still a decent, modest Sylizan woman, so I drew the cloak around myself, and taking my bag with me, I walked out of the room in the direction of Mr. Dimog's study. It was time to meet with my new girls, say goodbye to Mr. Dimog, and go home.

Home.

Thank you, Great Goddess.

Mr. Dimog's study door wasn't fully closed, but I paused before knocking as I heard voices on the other side. Through the slightly open door, I could see that Mr. Dimog was still talking to the two Rebels who had arrived at the end of my last discussion with him.

Taking half a step back, I intended to wait my turn but found myself listening to the conversation, instead.

It couldn't be too private if he didn't take care to fully close the door.

"Azori didn't return with you?" asked Mr. Dimog in the Common Tongue. He sounded both surprised and concerned.

"She chose to stay with a man she met in Dmevjekya. He's a Ranushdr. Fyotor Grusha. He's a good one and a connected one. His family is close to both the Basarovkas and the Ynnas. I believe he intends to marry her, and she intends to give him the time to convince her." The speaker was a young woman with features reminiscent of people from both Sorcheena and Dmevjekya, a formerly independent country, which was now one of Kavylak's northern states. I wondered if she may have had a parent from each place. She was a proud and confident speaker with golden auburn hair and dark brown eyes.

Mr. Dimog didn't hide the fact that this news was unexpected. "I see. I trust your judgment, Katyalina. There is no one I would trust more when it comes to Dmevjekya and her people."

"Thank you, Storr," she said proudly. "I think it's important to tell you that several of the noble families are more sympathetic to our cause than we'd initially believed. They have pledged their resources to us should we need them. That includes wealth, possessions, and several large cruising boats. They would be very useful if we should ever need to travel in numbers by sea."

I was surprised to hear that the Dmevjekyan nobility was supporting these Dsumot Rebels and wondered if they had intentions to try to regain their independence. It seemed a dangerous gamble. Kavylak's military and Warriors were a threat only Syliza could withstand.

"I can confirm what she's saying," said Lyir's voice. I hadn't seen him when I'd glanced into the room, and he continued to be hidden by the partially closed door. I wondered why he would be included in that conversation.

"They have already discussed who among them would leave if they should need to escape Kavylak's influence. I know they have made arrangements for the management of their lands while they are away. They've taken this seriously, Storr," said Katyalina.

Silence followed. Everyone was either exchanging looks or nodding. Whatever their responses, I couldn't hear anything for a thoughtful moment.

"Does Pammel know, Lyir?" Mr. Dimog asked.

Lyir either nodded or shook his head because he didn't give an audible response.

"Your mission was more than successful. Thank you for all you've done, Katyalina, Kadsyr," said Mr. Dimog. "Will your family be among those who leave?"

"Likely not," replied Katyalina. "There are too many of them and most don't want to go. They have agreed to help keep things running as usual, as much as possible, while the others are away. The families who will be leaving include the Grushas, the Ynnas, the Basarovkas, the Karovnas, the Bishenkas, and the Kandaras. They're also bringing a number of skilled people with them - people who are close to them and who aren't nobility, but who will be useful. These are very powerful families and very skilled people, Storr. Every one of the Basarovkas will be with us. Lady Ynna is a Ranushdyria. Those two families are like Dmevjekyan royalty."

"It's true," Lyir confirmed. "And when Lochka Ynna is in any group, you know it's a serious cause."

"She's a unique lady." I could hear the smirk in Katyalina's voice. "Always keep her on your side, because she's smarter than all of us combined." She chuckled.

"I look forward to meeting her one day. I have a great respect for strong, intelligent, and independent women," Mr. Dimog replied.

"I think she'll like you, too, Storr. She likes strong, intelligent, and independent men," said Katyalina, sounding amused.

Mr. Dimog chuckled. "Did Azori give you instructions for Vinusyr?"

The other Rebel, who had been silent until now, spoke. He had the distinct look of someone from Sorcheena with long glossy black hair and dark eyes. What I found interesting about his appearance was that he was dressed virtually identically to Kaiwa. They both wore well-made fitted black clothing as though always ready to slip into shadows.

"She did," said the man Mr. Dimog had referred to as Kadsyr. "She said that as long as we remain in Dsumot, Vinusyr should remain with the Robes. If we leave, we are to bring him with us. She asked Skeltra to see to it personally."

"I'll inform Skeltra," Mr. Dimog said.

Footfalls approached from down the hall around the corner, and I stepped away from the door to make it look as though I was respectfully waiting my turn outside Mr. Dimog's study. It was Sicer Dimog. He was jogging by the time he reached this part of the house and didn't even seem to notice me. Throwing open the door, he burst into the room without bothering to slide the door closed behind him. I retook my position just out of sight.

"Sicer?" his father asked, sounding alarmed.

The men spoke rapidly in Dsumot. I couldn't understand the words, but it was clear that there was a great deal of urgency.

"What happened?" asked Katyalina, making me think that she didn't speak the Dsumot language, either.

"Sicer says that Galnar is burning Hatinaad to the ground," Kadsyr answered her.

She gasped as did I. Hatinaad was the country next to Dsumot sharing the same border with Kavylak. If it was falling, it would allow Kavylak to attack Dsumot from two sides. This country wouldn't have a chance, particularly without Hatinaad's support.

"Byuka, a woman from Hatinaad, saw it with her own eyes," Sicer Dimog said in the Common Tongue. "She barely escaped. We found her on the edge of the main road. Dyronin is seeing to her now."

"Are we sending people to help Hatinaad? That's practically at our doorstep." Katyalina was understandably upset.

"Hatinaad is lost," Sicer Dimog said firmly.

"If Hatinaad is lost, it's only a matter of time before Dsumot follows." Lyir said. The voices in the room halted. None of them wanted to believe it, but there was nothing to be done. It was true. Lyir was right.

"We must be able to mount some kind of defense. How could they have moved this quickly?" Katyalina protested.

"They have Travellers, and that pyromaniac Warrior can burn entire towns at a time, especially considering all the forests that surround the towns in Hatinaad. I once saw him destroy a whole Sylizan fort in a matter of hours," Lyir said, sounding grim.

Fort Picogeal. It was terrifying. Those poor people in Hatinaad! Galnar is heartless and merciless. Destroying and causing pain are what bring him his only joy. Hatinaad will be burned from the map...and Dsumot may be next.

"We couldn't have gained Dmevjekyan support at a better time. We have the ships. Where will we take them?" Katyalina asked the Dimogs.

"Lorammel." *Great Goddess, that was my voice!*

I was standing in the open doorway with no recollection of having stepped into it. Every face in the room was directed toward me.

"Take everyone you can to the boats and sail them to Lorammel. During the time that you are travelling, I will do everything I can to make sure you are welcome there. If you speak to anyone in Syliza before you reach Lorammel, tell them you are a friend of the Godeleva family. If Lyir is willing to share messages between us, I will keep you up to date." My hands were trembling, but my voice was steady.

Lyir crossed the room and stood next to me as though ready to protect me from the Rebels. That said, when looking at all the other faces in the room, I saw confusion, interest, and doubt, but no aggression.

"We cannot just leave our home and the people of Dsumot. We need to fight for them," argued Sicer Dimog.

"Fight for them by spreading the word that they should run to Edilnir. Keep fighting for them by travelling to Syliza where you might find support strong enough to stand up to Kavylak. Syliza will not want Kavylak to continue taking the countries along the Sylizan border. You may find the help you need, as we share a common enemy." The ideas were forming faster than I could set them straight, but I was determined to try to help as much as I could.

"I will tell Lady Pammel of what has happened, and I agree with Miss Godeleva. She will find you the support you need in Lorammel," Lyir said. I nodded to him in appreciation.

"Will the Anglemores also come to your aid?" I asked Mr. Dimog. Since they shared a family connection, I wondered if the Dimogs might be able to obtain more support than they had realized.

"I don't know," replied Mr. Dimog who had been silently and objectively absorbing each detail of the conversation. He was visibly weighing every statement in his mind. Without saying a word, he was the most active participant in this discussion. Still, it was clear that allying with Syliza had never been an option he had considered.

"They will," Lyir said. I looked at him, and he nodded to me with certainty. This man was far better connected than I could have imagined. I wondered if Lord Imery was also friends with him without even knowing he was a Traveller.

"I will speak with anyone who could potentially lend their support to the cause," I said, determined. "I will find out who else should join this conversation. You've already mentioned some powerful Sylizan names. The Imperial Couple may be swayed if enough of those families agree that we should help you." I hoped that the confidence I felt at this moment would carry me through to keep my promise. This would be a daunting task. I could only pray that I would be worthy of it, and that I could somehow reach the Couple without having to meet with the emperor.

Mr. Dimog gave a slow nod.

"Father," Sicer Dimog objected. "We can't do this. We can't just abandon Dsumot. This is our home and our people."

"You can. Tell everyone. Use everyone you can. Mobilize. Use Acksil," I encouraged Sicer Dimog.

He turned a sharp look on me. His single eye cut straight through my confidence. "This is easy for you to say, Miss Godeleva. Your home is not under attack. You are not telling your entire country that they must flee everything they have and that they've ever known."

"You're right. This is not my country being threatened," I said in a voice much softer than I had been using. The boldness was gone. "I have faced Galnar in person. I was at Fort Picogeal on the same day as

Lyir. I saw it burn. I ran from the flames and breathed the smoke. All the port's docks and every building along the shoreline were ablaze. It happened in hours. I might not be alive today, if it hadn't been for Acksil. A few minutes is all Galnar needs, Mr. Dimog. If he is moving around with a Traveller's help, he could be here – right here – whenever he wants. This isn't easy for me to say, but it is what I believe."

"Miss Godeleva is right, Sicer," Lyir said. "If you stay here, you'll lose. You'll lose your home and possibly your life. So will anyone else who stays here. If you leave, you still have a chance to live and to fight and will have another day to rebuild. This isn't your home anymore. Not until you're able to return one day."

I was more than grateful to have Lyir at my side.

"What you're saying is that those of us who have pledged our lives to defending Dsumot will run and abandon the people we promised to protect." Katyalina spat the words with distaste. "We're just supposed to run from one enemy toward another and hope for the best because you think you can change everybody's mind?" She looked at me as though I were a foolish child who should be sent away from the room.

"If Kavylak is coming here, you will lose whether you stay or you leave. Everything will burn," I said and found myself shaking at the thought of this gorgeous home in flames. "If you run, you'll give yourself the chance to come back and fight with the power you need. It may feel brave to stay and fight, but it won't let you keep that promise to protect the people who need you. Instead, give everyone as much time as possible to find somewhere safe to wait until you can come back and take your country."

How can I convince Sicer Dimog and Katyalina that a virtual stranger from an enemy nation is the voice of reason they need? How can I possibly convince them that I will be able to bring them the military might they require to overcome Kavylak's threat to everything they hold dear? Am I right? Great Goddess, who am I to try to guide an entire nation – one I know virtually nothing about? Can I feel so strongly about this and be wrong?

Katyalina appeared entirely unconvinced. I was prepared to be put in my place and for the rest of the Rebels in the room to side with her.

"I must agree with Miss Godeleva," said Kadsyr. His voice was calm and quiet. It was as though he had chosen the specific volume that would allow us all to hear him without straining, but not any louder than that. "As much as I do not want to leave Dsumot, it is the only path that makes sense. Look at what has been happening over the last few cycles and over the last season. Look at what happened to Sabear, she barely recovered. These Warriors are not like normal men. They have abilities we cannot beat with our small numbers. I was there when Sorcheena fell. I know what will happen when Kavylak arrives. If Hatinaad has fallen, we must do everything we can to bring our people to safety. We must save ourselves so that we can strengthen our forces and stand a chance when it comes time to fight. Homes and structures can be rebuilt after destruction, but people and their culture cannot."

Thank you, Great Goddess. Kadsyr's words were everything I needed to hear. I have something to contribute, after all. I can be a part of saving Dsumot and my friends, Rebels who didn't hesitate to help a Sylizan stranger who travelled with their worst betrayer. I can be a part of saving Mr. Dimog, a man who has treated me like family and for whom I feel the same.

Katyalina looked frustrated with Kadsyr but didn't say anything to him.

Mr. Dimog raised a hand as he began to speak. I could feel my muscles tense as I knew that whatever he would decide would be accepted by everyone in the room, including myself.

"Thank you, Miss Godeleva and Lyir. We accept your invitation and welcome your assistance," he said. It was respectful and simply spoken, but I could tell that this had been a difficult decision for him to make and that the words weren't easy for him to say.

"You have friends in Syliza," I said softly. "We will make sure we are ready for you when you arrive."

Mr. Dimog nodded deeply at me.

"I will do what I can to help you move your people to safety," Lyir added to Mr. Dimog, who looked genuinely surprised.

"Thank you," he said to Lyir.

"Are you ready to leave, Miss Godeleva?" Lyir asked me.

I couldn't blame him for the brusque way in which he asked the question. His day – and many to follow – had just become much busier.

"I am," I replied. "Only the two girls who will be coming with me are missing. May I fetch them?"

Lyir nodded, and I dashed out of the room. Once again, I noted how easy it was to move in the clothing Acksil had provided. After having worn Sylizan gowns again, the difference was difficult to ignore. I paused outside the girls' room and caught my breath before knocking.

"Ladies?" I said, so they would know who was on my side of the door.

To my surprise, Gebbie opened the door.

"We're ready in here, Miss Godeleva," she said, sounding pleasant.

"That's good. It's time," I replied.

"Alright girls. You be good for Miss Godeleva and listen to her. She's going to take you to a safe home now."

Lesoué and Kaziki were standing, holding hands. Each had a bag on her back. They nodded to Gebbie, and Lesoué held a hand out to me. I took it, holding it securely in mine.

"They will be safe and happy," I told Gebbie.

"I know they will, dear. You'll all be safe now," she said, smiling happily. Blowing each of us a kiss, she made the sign of the Goddess, and I knew it was time for us to go.

I returned the sign to Gebbie and guided the girls down the hall. I spent the time on the way to Mr. Dimog's study by preparing the girls for the fact that there would be people in the room and some of them would be men. I found out that Gebbie had already readied them for the Traveller. I was grateful to the woman once again.

"I'm very proud of you both, ladies," I said, sharing a smile with each of them before stepping across the threshold into Mr. Dimog's study. There, everyone had left except Mr. Dimog and Lyir.

Stepping closer to Mr. Dimog, I released Lesoué's hand. "Thank you for everything, Mr. Dimog. I will see you again soon. I will make you proud. We will save Dsumot," I said, determined to live up to my promise. I would not let this man down. Too much was at stake.

"I know you will," he replied, sounding like the gentle family member I'd always wanted, not the leader of the Dsumot Rebels who had been in this study only a few minutes earlier. He raised my hand and kissed it.

Even through all my fear and tension, I couldn't help but smile. The gesture was sweet and pure. I would spend many prayers begging the Great Goddess to let me see him again. Rising onto my toes, I kissed his cheek.

"Be well and be safe, Mr. Dimog," I said quietly. "Please don't leave Acksil behind." I couldn't help but make that final request. I needed to put my heart at ease, and I knew only Mr. Dimog could do it.

He smiled. The expression was warm and understanding. "We won't leave him behind. I have had time to listen and time to think. He will have the chance to prove himself to us if this is what he wants."

"You're a good man, Mr. Dimog. I'm blessed to know you. I'm blessed that I will be able to return the safety you provided me when I needed it. Safe journey."

If only there were more words. Better words.

Great Goddess, I feel as though I've just met my father for the first time, only to have to let him go. Please bless him and his loved ones. Keep him safe.

"Safe journey, Dear One." The cadence of his voice was proof that he felt the same for me as I felt for him.

Lyir approached. "I can Travel the girls together. Do you want to go before them?"

I was equally disappointed and relieved that the Traveller had stepped in. If only there had been something else to express how much this had all meant to me. There was nothing else to be said. There was nothing else I could do. I nodded to Lyir.

"Yes. That way, I'll be there when you arrive with them," I replied and looked to Lesoué and Kaziki. "I'm about to disappear because this Traveller is bringing me home. Then, he'll be back, and he'll bring you both to stay with me. It takes only a blink and doesn't hurt at all. Are you ready?"

Both girls looked uncertain but nodded.

"Good," I smiled at them, hoping my confidence would be catching. "I'll see you both in a moment."

Giving a final glance to Mr. Dimog, I held out a hand to Lyir. "I'm ready."

Lyir took my hand and immediately, I found myself in the gardens of the Godeleva estate. I squinted against the bright sunlight shining down on us. Lyir released my hand, and I used it to shade my eyes.

Great Goddess, I am home. Thank you. You are truly merciful. Thank you!

"Thank you," I said to Lyir, who also deserved my gratitude.

"Welcome home," he replied, looking proud of himself.

"I'll wait right here for the girls," I said, so he'd know where I would be upon his return.

He nodded and disappeared. I jumped and rolled my eyes at myself for having done so.

All I wanted was to turn and take advantage of my final moments in this outfit Acksil had given me so that I could run inside and tell Lord Imery I was home. Then I would embrace him and hold on until Mr. Dimog arrived with the Dmevjekyan boats.

I didn't run inside. I stayed just where I said I would, and after an instant that lasted an eon, Lyir and the girls appeared not far from me. Lesoué and Kaziki were hugging each other tightly, their eyes squinted shut. The Traveller stepped back from them.

Rushing to the girls, I resisted the urge to touch them to bring them comfort, for fear that I would startle them instead.

"You're here. You're safe. It's over." I smiled as I spoke so they would hear the expression in my voice.

At the same time, they opened their eyes. Though both girls had known they would be travelling here, I couldn't blame them for looking awed by their surroundings. What did surprise me was that they simultaneously released each other and threw their arms around me, instead. Wrapping an arm around each, I leaned down and kissed the top of Lesoué's head and then Kaziki's.

"If you no longer need me, Miss Godeleva, I'll be on my way," Lyir said, looking increasingly bored. I'd expected him to find this scene to be a moving one. Somehow, it was more touching to me that he had helped the girls when he felt this way about it than it would have been if he'd had a tear in his eye.

"Thank you. Whenever you have the slightest opportunity, please visit and let me know how Mr. Dimog and his people are progressing. You are always welcome here as my guest," I said without hesitation.

Reaching behind his head, Lyir untied the ribbon holding back his hair. He proffered the black ribbon, and I took it.

"If you ever need to speak with me, hang this in your window. I'll check for it, and when it's there, I'll come see you," he explained.

Tying the ribbon around my wrist, I brought my arms back around the girls again. They hadn't made any move to let me go.

"Thank you, Lyir. You've made everything right again. I only hope we can do enough to provide a safe place for Mr. Dimog and his group."

"We will do what we can. Mr. Dimog and his Rebels have powerful allies in many countries, including Syliza. That will be important when the war comes. It won't be long," he said as though he could see the future. "Until we meet again, Miss Godeleva." He bowed and vanished.

Across the pristine garden was the gorgeous home I'd called my own for thirteen cycles. I'd come here with nothing and gained everything I'd had since then. I'd been surrounded by beauty and sheltered from the world's ugliness. Within those walls, I had come to know Qarradune as it appears through carefully curated words and images. Now that I'd seen it with my own eyes, I'd discovered a complexity that terrified me, but that made me feel and love as I could never have done before.

I could not unlearn these lessons. Upon entering my home, the walls could no longer stop me from knowing what was outside and likely approaching. They would serve a new purpose. They would protect a new people. They would shelter these girls who had already experienced far more of the world than anyone should. They would remind me that there were many other people who deserved this same sense of safety, and who were relying on me to provide it to them.

I was home. It was time to stop running and start fighting.

Mr. Dimog, you have a Rebel here, too.

Note from the Authors
& Acknowledgements

We've done it! We've finally released the fourth book in the Perspective series! Not only does this mean that Megan and Irys' adventures continue, but we can finally prove that the Perspective series is 100% *not* a trilogy (LOL)!

The journey to complete *So On and So Fourth* was a long one (far longer than we anticipated or intended, but, you know, life happens…). While the process was certainly a struggle at times, we did it, and we couldn't be happier with the result. We're delighted with how well the series is unfolding.

Of course, this journey wouldn't have been as smooth or polished without our team of incredible editors, Donna Campbell and John Campbell. Thank you both so much for your patience and for being the editors we needed to help us make *So On and So Fourth* everything that it is.

We also want to give a huge thank you to our team of alpha readers, Sean Evans, Laura Campbell, Linda Evans, Bill Evans, Pat Giasson, and Jason Giasson. We appreciate you all so much for taking the time to provide us with your invaluable feedback. Your sharp eyes, thoughts, opinions, and knowledge of the first three Perspective books, helped us to avoid plot holes that we might not have otherwise noticed.

And last, but certainly not least, we'd like to thank you, Reader! Thank you for travelling with us to Qarradune over the years and for your continued support. We hope you enjoy *So On and So Fourth* as much as we loved creating it. Megan and Irys look forward to sharing the next part of their stories with you in Book 5. :)

Until then, stay Crisp!

About the Authors

The Perspective book series was written by two authors: Amanda Giasson and Julie B. Campbell. After having met by chance in the lineup at their university bookstore on their first day of classes, Amanda and Julie became fast friends. They credit their survival of many of their 3-hour long lectures to their ability to escape to the world of Qarradune. The truth is that Megan and Irys were born of note-passing in the form of creative writing. While neither author condones this behavior in-class, as it likely does nothing for a student's grades, it did happen to work out, in their case. It also helped to define the unique writing style shared by the authors in the creation of the story. The two authors have been steadily working on the Perspective book series, ever since.